Riverside Edition

THE WRITINGS OF

HARRIET BEECHER STOWE

*WITH BIOGRAPHICAL INTRODUCTIONS
PORTRAITS, AND OTHER
ILLUSTRATIONS*

IN SIXTEEN VOLUMES
VOLUME III

The Writings of Harriet Beecher Stowe

Riverside Edition

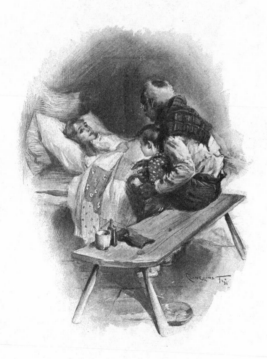

HOUGHTON, MIFFLIN & CO

DRED
A Tale of the Great Dismal Swamp

TOGETHER WITH

ANTI-SLAVERY TALES AND PAPERS, AND LIFE IN FLORIDA AFTER THE WAR

BY

HARRIET BEECHER STOWE

IN TWO VOLUMES

VOLUME I

"Away to the Dismal Swamp he speeds:
  His path was rugged and sore, —
Through tangled juniper, beds of reeds,
Through many a fen, where the serpent feeds,
  And man never trod before.

And when on earth he sunk to sleep,
  If slumber his eyelids knew,
He lay where the deadly vine doth weep
Its venomous tears, that nightly steep
  The flesh with blistering dew."

AMS Press, Inc.

New York

1967

AMS Press, Inc.
New York, N.Y. 10003
1967

Manufactured in the United States of America

CONTENTS OF VOLUME I

PAGE

INTRODUCTORY NOTE vii

     AUTHOR'S PREFACE xiii

DRED: A TALE OF THE GREAT DISMAL SWAMP.

CHAPTER

    I. THE MISTRESS OF CANEMA 1

   II. CLAYTON 13

  III. THE CLAYTON FAMILY AND SISTER ANNE . . 26

  IV. THE GORDON FAMILY 37

   V. HARRY AND HIS WIFE 59

  VI. THE DILEMMA 78

 VII. CONSULTATION 91

VIII. OLD TIFF 97

  IX. THE DEATH 120

   X. THE PREPARATION 126

  XI. THE LOVERS 138

 XII. EXPLANATIONS 153

XIII. TOM GORDON 172

XIV. AUNT NESBIT'S LOSS 193

 XV. MR. JEKYL'S OPINIONS 204

XVI. MILLY'S STORY 211

XVII. UNCLE JOHN 230

XVIII. DRED 245

XIX. THE CONSPIRATORS 254

XX. SUMMER TALK AT CANEMA 267

XXI. TIFF'S PREPARATIONS 281

XXII. THE WORSHIPERS 289

XXIII. THE CAMP-MEETING 304

XXIV. LIFE IN THE SWAMPS 340

XXV. MORE SUMMER TALK 349

XXVI. MILLY'S RETURN 366

XXVII. THE TRIAL 373

XXVIII. MAGNOLIA GROVE 382

XXIX. THE TROUBADOUR 401

XXX. TIFF'S GARDEN 416

XXXI. THE WARNING 426

XXXII. THE MORNING STAR 432

CONTENTS

XXXIII. THE LEGAL DECISION 439
XXXIV. THE CLOUD BURSTS 452
XXXV. THE VOICE IN THE WILDERNESS 466
XXXVI. THE EVENING STAR 471

The frontispiece (Dred, page 248) and the vignette (" Now, Tiff, can you say anything ? " page 118), are from drawings by B. West Clinedinst.

INTRODUCTORY NOTE

THE preparation of *A Key to Uncle Tom's Cabin* was also directly a preparation for Mrs. Stowe's second great novel based on the moral and social conditions induced by African slavery in the United States. Out of the familiarity which she acquired with the history and the laws of the slave States both through her own investigation and through that of her friends, especially her legal friends, sprang almost as a matter of necessity the tale of *Dred*. She has herself in her Preface spoken of the use she made of Judge Ruffin's decision which she had already included in *A Key*. The basis of the entire story, as is well known, is the insurrection led by Nat Turner in eastern Virginia in 1831. One of the principal participators in that affair was named Dred. Years afterward when bringing out a new edition of the novel Mrs. Stowe changed the title to *Nina Gordon*, the name of the principal heroine; but it bore this title for a few years only, the old title being restored finally.

The story was written in 1855 and the spring of 1856, and in his Life of his mother Mr. Stowe gives an interesting incident illustrative of her artistic care in her work. On a sultry summer night, he says in effect, there was a terrific thunderstorm, which threw the young daughters of the house into a panic, and they crept trembling to their mother's room, to find her lying quietly in bed, with the window-shades drawn, watching with intense interest the action of the storm. " I have been writing a description of a thunderstorm for my book," she said, "and I am watching to see if I need to correct it in any particular." The description occurs in the chapter entitled *Life in the Swamps*.

It was important for her own interests that Mrs. Stowe should secure a copyright for the book in England, where a great audience awaited her, and she made a journey abroad in the early summer of 1856 with this end particularly in view. She had already arranged with Messrs. Sampson Low & Co. for its republication, and she wrote for the English edition a special preface which states concisely the aim she had in view in writing *Dred*.

"The author's object in this book is to show the general effect of slavery on society; the various social disadvantages which it brings, even to its most favored advocates; the shiftlessness and misery and backward tendency of all the economical arrangements of slave States; the retrograding of good families into poverty; the deterioration of land; the worse demoralization of all classes, from the aristocratic, tyrannical planter to the oppressed and poor white, which is the result of the introduction of slave labor. It is also an object to display the corruption of Christianity which arises from the same source, — a corruption that has gradually lowered the standard of the church, North and South, and been productive of more infidelity than the works of all the encyclopædists put together."

The success of the book was immediate and great both in the United States and in England. In the latter country a hundred thousand copies were sold in a month. It was not received with unanimous favor by the critics. The great vogue of *Uncle Tom's Cabin* naturally led to a challenge of the author when she appeared a second time, and Mrs. Stowe sums up in one of her letters the reception *Dred* had from various organs. "It is very bitterly attacked," she writes to her husband, "both from a literary and a religious point of view. The *Record* is down upon it with a cartload of solemnity; the *Athenæum* with waspish spite; the *Edinburgh* goes out of its way to say that the author knows nothing of the society she describes; but yet it goes everywhere, is read everywhere, and Mr. Low says that he puts the hundred and twenty-fifth thousand to press confidently." One of the most thorough-going appreciations of the book was from Harriet Martineau, who writes : "The genius carries all before it, and drowns everything in glorious pleasure. So marked a work of genius claims exemption from every sort of comparison ; but, as you ask for my opinion of the book, you may like to know that I think it far superior to *Uncle Tom*. I have no doubt that a multitude of people will say it is a falling off, because they made up their minds that any new book of yours must be inferior to that, and because it is so rare a thing for a prodigious fame to be sustained by a second book ; but in my own mind I am entirely convinced that the second book is by far the best. Such faults as you have are in the artistic department, and there is less defect in *Dred* than in *Uncle Tom*, and the whole material and treatment seem to me richer and more substantial. . . . I see no limit to the good it may do by suddenly splitting open Southern life, for everybody to look into. It is precisely the thing that is most wanted, — just as *Uncle Tom* was wanted, three years since, to show what negro slavery in your republic was like. It is plantation life particularly, in the present case, that I mean."

The two books *Uncle Tom's Cabin* and *Dred* were the great contributions which Mrs. Stowe made toward the illumination of the Christian world on the subject of slavery. They stood side by side in a momentous period, buttressed by the storehouse of facts contained in *A Key*. Her interest in the subject went far back into her childhood, as has been shown in the Introduction to *Uncle Tom's Cabin*, and it was of course impossible that she should become so great a figure in the anti-slavery movement without pushing her labors in many directions beyond the accomplishment of her notable books. She threw herself into the agitation of the subject, and especially aimed by her correspondence with people of distinction in Great Britain to bring to bear upon public opinion in America the weighty influence of literary and social forces abroad. *The Two Altars* is an early contribution to the subject in fiction and was included in *The Mayflower*. In the dark days of the war Mrs. Stowe availed herself of her acknowledged position and fortified the great cause for which the armies of the country were consciously or unconsciously fighting by her *Reply* to the English women's address made eight years before. In natural company with these papers are placed the tribute to the Duchess of Sutherland and the narrative of Sojourner Truth.

Mrs. Stowe had spent her early womanhood on the borders of slave territory. In her mature life, after the abolition of slavery, she made her home for many years, in the winter months, in the extreme southern portion of what was once slave territory. Naturally her interest was both contemporary and retrospective. She contributed a paper, *Our Florida Plantation*, to *The Atlantic Monthly*, but she had before that written a series of familiar letters from Florida, in 1872, which were gathered into a volume the following year under the title *Palmetto Leaves*.

" Many were the pleasant descriptions of her home," writes Mrs. Fields in her *Days with Mrs. Stowe*, " sent forth to tempt her friends away from the busy North. ' Here is where we read books,' she said in one of her letters written in the month of March. ' Up North nobody does, — they don't have time; so if —— will mail his book to Mandarin, I will " read, mark, learn, and inwardly digest." We are having a carnival of flowers. I hope you read my

Palmetto Leaves, for then you will see all about us. . . .
Our home is like a martin box. . . . I cannot tell you the
quaint odd peace we have here in living under the oak.
" Behold she dwelleth under the oak at Mamre." All that
we want is friends, to whom we may say that solitude is
sweet. We have some neighbors, however, who have made
pretty places near us. Mr. Stowe keeps up a German class
of three young ladies, with whom he is reading Faust for
the nine hundred and ninety-ninth time, and in the evening I read aloud to a small party of neighbors. We have
made up our home as we went along, throwing out a chamber here and there, like twigs out of the old oak. . . .
The orange blossoms have come like showers of pearl, and
the yellow jessamine like golden fleeces, and the violets and
the lilies, and azaleas. This glorious, budding, blossoming
spring, and we have days when merely to breathe and be is
to be blessed. I love to have a day of mere existence.
Life itself is a pleasure when the sun shines warm, and the
lizards dart from all the shingles of the roof, and the birds
sing in so many notes and tones the yard reverberates; and
I sit and dream and am happy, and never want to go back
North, nor do anything with the toiling, snarling world
again. I do wish I could gather you both in my little
nest.' "

AUTHOR'S PREFACE

THE writer of this book has chosen, once more, a subject from the scenes and incidents of the slave-holding States.

The reason for such a choice is two-fold. First, in a merely artistic point of view, there is no ground, ancient or modern, whose vivid lights, gloomy shadows, and grotesque groupings, afford to the novelist so wide a scope for the exercise of his powers. In the near vicinity of modern civilization of the most matter-of-fact kind exist institutions which carry us back to the twilight of the feudal ages, with all their exciting possibilities of incident. Two nations, the types of two exactly opposite styles of existence, are here struggling; and from the intermingling of these two a third race has arisen, and the three are interlocked in wild and singular relations, that evolve every possible combination of romance. Hence, if the writer's only object had been the production of a work of art, she would have felt justified in not turning aside from that mine whose inexhaustible stores have but begun to be developed.

But this object, however legitimate, was not the only nor the highest one. It is the moral bearings of the subject involved which have had the chief influence in its selection. The issues presented by the great conflict between liberty and slavery do not grow less important from year to year. On the contrary, their interest increases with every step in the development of the national career. Never has there been a crisis in the history of this nation so momentous as the present. If ever a nation was raised up by Divine Providence, and led forth upon a conspicuous stage, as if for the express purpose of solving a great moral problem in the sight of all mankind, it is this nation. God in his providence is now asking the American people, Is the system of slavery, as set forth in the American slave code, *right?* Is it so desirable, that you will directly establish it over broad regions, where, till now, you have solemnly forbidden it to enter? And this question the American people are about to answer. Under such circumstances the writer felt that no apology was needed for once more endeavoring to do something towards revealing to the people the true character of that system. If the people are to establish such a system, let them do it with their eyes open, with all the dreadful realities before them.

One liberty has been taken which demands acknowledgment in the outset. The writer has placed in the mouth of one of her leading characters a judicial decision of Judge Ruffin, of North Carolina, the boldness, clearness, and solemn eloquence of which have excited admiration both in the Old World and the New. The author having no personal acquaintance with that gentleman, the character to whom she attributes it is to be considered as created merely on a principle of artistic fitness.

To maintain the unity of the story, some anachronisms with regard to the time of the session of courts have been allowed; for works of fiction must sometimes use some liberties in the grouping of incidents. But as mere cold art, unquickened by sympathy with the spirit of the age, is nothing, the author hopes that those who now are called to struggle for all that is noble in our laws and institutions may find in this book the response of a sympathizing heart.

DRED

A TALE OF THE GREAT DISMAL SWAMP

CHAPTER I

THE MISTRESS OF CANEMA

"BILLS, Harry? — Yes. — Dear me, where are they? — There! — No. Here? — Oh, look! — What do you think of this scarf? Is n't it lovely?"

"Yes, Miss Nina, beautiful — but" —

"Oh, those bills! — Yes — well, here goes — here — perhaps in this box. No — that's my opera-hat. By the bye, what do you think of that? Is n't that bunch of silver wheat lovely? Stop a bit — you shall see it on me."

And, with these words, the slight little figure sprang up as if it had wings, and, humming a waltzing-tune, skimmed across the room to a looking-glass, and placed the jaunty little cap on the gay little head, and then, turning a pirouette on one toe, said, "There, now!"

"There, now!" Ah, Harry! ah, mankind generally! the wisest of you have been made fools of by just such dancing, glittering, fluttering little assortments of curls, pendants, streamers, eyes, cheeks, and dimples! The little figure, scarce the height of the Venus, rounded as that of an infant, was shown to advantage by a coquettish morning-dress of buff muslin, which fluttered open in front to display the embroidered skirt, and trim little mouse of a slipper. The face was one of those provoking ones which set criticism at defiance. The hair, waving, curling, dancing hither and thither, seemed to have a wild, laughing grace of its own; the brown eyes twinkled like the pendants of a chandelier; the little, wicked nose, which bore the forbidden upward curve, seemed to assert its right to do so with a saucy freedom; and the pendants of multiplied brilliants that twinkled in her ears, and the nodding wreath of silver wheat that set off her opera-hat, seemed alive with mischief and motion.

"Well, what do you think?" said a lively, imperative voice, — just the kind of voice that you might have expected from the figure.

The young man to whom this question was addressed was a well-dressed, gentlemanly person of about thirty-five, with dark complexion and hair, and deep blue eyes. There was something marked and peculiar in the square, high forehead, and the finely formed features, which indicated talent and ability; and the blue eyes had a depth and strength of color that might cause them at first glance to appear black. The face, with its strongly marked expression of honesty and sense, had about it many careworn and thoughtful lines. He looked at the little, defiant fay for a moment with an air of the most entire deference and admiration; then a heavy shadow crossed his face, and he answered abstractedly, "Yes, Miss Nina, everything you wear becomes pretty — and that is perfectly charming."

"Isn't it, now, Harry? I thought you would think so. You see, it's my own idea. You ought to have seen what a thing it was when I first saw it in Mme. La Blanche's window. There was a great hot-looking feather on it, and two or three horrid bows. I had them out in a twinkling, and got this wheat in — which shakes so, you know. It's perfectly lovely! — Well, do you believe, the very night I wore it to the opera, I got engaged?"

"Engaged, Miss Nina?"

"Engaged! — Yes, to be sure! Why not?"

"It seems to me that's a very serious thing, Miss Nina."

"Serious! — ha! ha! ha!" said the little beauty, seating herself on one arm of the sofa, and shaking the glittering hat back from her eyes. "Well, I fancy it was — to him, at least. I made him serious, I can tell you!"

"But is this true, Miss Nina? *Are* you really engaged?"

"Yes, to be sure I am — to three gentlemen; and going to stay so till I find which I like best. Maybe, you know, I sha'n't like any of them."

"Engaged to three gentlemen, Miss Nina?"

"To be sure! — Can't you understand English, Harry? I am now — fact."

"Miss Nina, is that right?"

"Right? — why not? I don't know which to take — I positively don't; so I took them all on trial, you know."

"Pray, Miss Nina, tell us who they are."

"Well, there's Mr. Carson; he's a rich old bachelor — horridly polite — one of those little, bobbing men, that always have such shiny dickies and collars, and such bright boots, and such tight straps. And he's rich — and perfectly wild about me. He wouldn't take no for an answer, you know; so I just said yes, to have a little quiet. Besides, he is very convenient about the opera and concerts, and such things."

"Well, and the next?"

"Well, the next is George Emmons. He's one of your pink-and-white men, you know, who look like cream-candy, as if they were good to eat. He's a lawyer, of a good family, — thought a good deal of, and all that. Well, really, they say he has talents — I'm no judge. I know he always bores me to death; asking me if I have read this or that

— marking places in books that I never read. He's your
sentimental sort — writes the most romantic notes on pink
paper, and all that sort of thing."

"And the third?"

"Well, you see, I don't like *him* a bit — I'm sure I
don't. He's a hateful creature! He isn't handsome;
he's proud as Lucifer; and I'm sure I don't know how he
got me to be engaged. It was a kind of an accident.
He's real good, though — too good for me, that's a fact.
But, then, I'm afraid of him a little."

"And his name?"

"Well, his name is Clayton, — Mr. Edward Clayton, at
your service. He's one of your high-and-mighty people —
with such deep-set eyes — eyes that look as if they were in
a cave — and such black hair! And his eyes have a desperate
sort of sad look, sometimes — quite Byronic. He's tall, and
rather loose-jointed — has beautiful teeth; his mouth, too,
is — well, when he smiles, sometimes it really is quite
fascinating; and then he's so different from other gentlemen! He's kind — but he don't care how he dresses; and
wears the most horrid shoes. And, then, he isn't polite —
he won't jump, you know, to pick up your thread or scis-
sors; and sometimes he'll get into a brown study, and let
you stand ten minutes before he thinks to give you a
chair, and all such provoking things. He isn't a bit of
a lady's man. Well, consequence is, as my lord won't
court the girls, the girls all court my lord — that's the
way, you know; and they seem to think it's such a
feather in their cap to get attention from him, — because,
you know, he's horrid sensible. So, you see, that just
set me out to see what I could do with him. Well, you
see, I wouldn't court him; — and I plagued him, and
laughed at him, and spited him, and got him gloriously
wroth; and he said some spiteful things about me, and
then I said some more about him, and we had a real up-

and-down quarrel; — and then I took a penitent turn, you know, and just went gracefully down into the valley of humiliation — as we witches can; and it took wonderfully — brought my lord on to his knees before he knew what he was doing. Well, really, I don't know what was the matter, just then, but he spoke so earnest and strong that actually he got me to crying — hateful creature! — and I promised all sorts of things, you know — said altogether more than will bear thinking of."

"And are you corresponding with all these lovers, Miss Nina?"

"Yes — is n't it fun? Their letters, you know, can't speak. If they could, when they come rustling together in the bag, would n't there be a muss?"

"Miss Nina, I think you have given your heart to this last one."

"Oh, nonsense, Harry! Have n't got any heart! — don't care two pins for any of them! All I want is to have a good time. As to love, and all that, I don't believe I could love any of them; I should be tired to death of any of them in six weeks. I never liked anything that long."

"Miss Nina, you must excuse me, but I want to ask again, is it right to trifle with the feelings of gentlemen in this way?"

"Why not? — Is n't all fair in war? Don't they trifle with us girls, every chance they get — and sit up so pompous in their rooms, and smoke cigars, and talk us over, as if they only had to put out their finger and say, 'Come here,' to get any of us? I tell you, it's fun to bring them down! — Now, there's that horrid George Emmons — I tell you, if he did n't flirt all winter with Mary Stephens, and got everybody to laughing about her! — it was so evident, you see, that she liked him — she could n't help showing it, poor little thing! — and then my lord would

settle his collar, and say he had n't quite made up his mind
to take her, and all that. Well, I have n't made up my
mind to take him, either — and so poor Mary is avenged.
As to the old bach — that smooth-dicky man — you see,
he can't be hurt; for his heart is rubbed as smooth and
hard as his dicky, with falling in love and out again.
He 's been turned off by three girls, now; and his shoes
squeak as brisk as ever, and he 's just as jolly. You see,
he did n't use to be so rich. Lately, he 's come into a
splendid property; so, if I don't take him, poor man, there
are enough that would be glad of him."

"Well, then, but as to that other one ? "

"What! my lord Lofty ? Oh, he wants humbling! — it
would n't hurt him, in the least, to be put down a little.
He 's good, too, and afflictions always improve good people.
I believe I was made for a means of grace to 'em all."

"Miss Nina, what if all three of them should come at
once — or even two of them ? "

"What a droll idea! Would n't it be funny ? Just to
think of it! What a commotion! What a scene! It
would really be vastly entertaining."

"Now, Miss Nina, I want to speak as a friend."

"No, you sha'n't! it is just what people say when they
are going to say something disagreeable. I told Clayton,
once for all, that I would n't have him speak as a friend to
me."

"Pray, how does he take all this ? "

"Take it! Why, just as he must. He cares a great
deal more for me than I do for him." Here a slight little
sigh escaped the fair speaker. "And I think it fun to
shock him. You know he is one of the fatherly sort, who
is always advising young girls. Let it be understood that
his standard of female character is wonderfully high, and
all that. And then, to think of his being tripped up before me! — it 's *too* funny ! " The little sprite here took off

her opera-hat, and commenced waltzing a few steps, and stopping midwhirl, exclaimed: "Oh, do you know, we girls have been trying to learn the cachucha, and I've got some castanets! Let me see — where are they?" And with this she proceeded to upset the trunk, from which flew a meteoric shower of bracelets, billets-doux, French Grammars, drawing-pencils, interspersed with confectionery of various descriptions, and all the etceteras of a schoolgirl's depository. "There, upon my word, there are the bills you were asking for. There, take them!" throwing a package of papers at the young man. "Take them! Can you catch?"

"Miss Nina, these do not appear to be bills."

"Oh, bless me! those are love-letters, then. The bills are somewhere." And the little hands went pawing among the heap making the fanciful collection fly in every direction over the carpet. "Ah! I believe now in this bonbon-box I did put them. Take care of your head, Harry!" And, with the word, the gilded missile flew from the little hand, and opening on the way, showered Harry with a profusion of crumpled papers. "Now you have got them all, except one, that I used for curl-papers the other night. Oh, don't look so sober about it! Indeed, I kept the pieces — here they are. And now don't you say, Harry, don't you tell me that I never save my bills. You don't know how particular I have been, and what trouble I have taken. But, there — there's a letter Clayton wrote to me, one time when we had a quarrel. Just a specimen of that creature!"

"Pray tell us about it, Miss Nina," said the young man, with his eyes fixed admiringly on the little person, while he was smoothing and arranging the crumpled documents.

"Why, you see, it was just this way. You know, these men — how provoking they are! They'll go and read all sorts of books — no matter what *they* read! — and then they are so dreadfully particular about us girls. Do you know, Harry, this always made me angry?

"Well, so, you see, one evening Sophy Elliot quoted some poetry from 'Don Juan,' — I never read it, but it seems folks call it a bad book, — and my lord Clayton immediately fixed his eyes upon her in such an appalling way, and says, 'Have you read "Don Juan," Miss Elliot?' Then, you know, as girls always do in such cases, she blushed and stammered, and said her brother had read some extracts from it to her. I was vexed, and said, 'And, pray, what's the harm if she did read it? *I* mean to read it, the very first chance I get!'

"Oh! everybody looked so shocked. Why, dear me! if I had said I was going to commit murder, Clayton could not have looked more concerned. So he put on that very edifying air of his, and said, 'Miss Nina, I *trust*, as your friend, that you will not read that book. I should lose all respect for a lady friend who had read that.'

"'Have you read it, Mr. Clayton?' said I.

"'Yes, Miss Nina,' said he, quite piously.

"'What makes you read such bad books?' said I, very innocently.

"Then there followed a general fuss and talk; and the gentlemen, you know, would not have their wives or their sisters read anything naughty, for the world. They wanted us all to be like snowflakes, and all that. And they were quite high, telling they wouldn't marry this, and they wouldn't marry that, till at last I made them a curtsy, and said, 'Gentlemen, we ladies are infinitely obliged to you, but *we* don't intend to marry people that read naughty books, either. Of course you know snowflakes don't like smut!'

"Now, I really didn't mean anything by it, except to put down these men, and stand up for my sex. But Clay-

ton took it in real earnest. He grew red and grew pale,
and was just as angry as he could be. Well, the quarrel
raged about three days. Then, do you know, I made him
give up, and own that he was in the wrong. There, I
think he was, too, — don't you? Don't you think men
ought to be *as* good as we are, anyway?"

"Miss Nina, I should think you would be afraid to
express yourself so positively."

"Oh, if I cared a sou for any of them, perhaps I should.
But there isn't one of the train that I would give *that*
for!" said she, flirting a shower of peanut-shells into the
air.

"Yes, but Miss Nina, some time or other you must
marry somebody. You need somebody to take care of the
property and place."

"Oh, that's it, is it? You are tired of keeping accounts, are you, with me to spend the money? Well, I
don't wonder. How I pity anybody that keeps accounts!
Isn't it horrid, Harry? Those awful books! Do you
know that Mme. Ardaine set out that ' we girls ' should keep
account of our expenses? I just tried it two weeks. I
had a headache and weak eyes, and actually it nearly ruined
my constitution. Somehow or other, they gave it up, it
gave them so much trouble. And what's the use?
When money's spent, it's *spent;* and keeping accounts
ever so strict won't get it back. I am very careful about
my expenses. I never get anything that I can do without."

"For instance," said Harry, rather roguishly, "this bill
of one hundred dollars for confectionery."

"Well, you know just how it is, Harry. It's so horrid
to have to study! Girls must have something. And you
know I didn't get it all for myself; I gave it round to all
the girls. Then they used to ask me for it, and I couldn't
refuse — and so it went."

"I did n't presume to comment, Miss Nina. What have we here? —Mme. Les Cartes, $450?"

"Oh, Harry, that horrid Mme. Les Cartes! You never saw anything like her! Positively, it is not my fault. She puts down things I never got: I know she does. Nothing in the world but because she is from Paris. Everybody is complaining of her. But, then, nobody gets anything anywhere else. So what can one do, you know? I assure you, Harry, I am economical."

The young man, who had been summing up the accounts, now burst out into such a hearty laugh as somewhat disconcerted the fair rhetorician.

She colored to her temples.

"Harry, now, for shame! Positively, you are n't respectful!"

"Oh, Miss Nina, on my knees I beg pardon!" still continuing to laugh; "but, indeed, you must excuse me. I am positively delighted to hear of your economy, Miss Nina."

"Well, now, Harry, you may look at the bills and see. Have n't I ripped up all my silk dresses and had them colored over, just to economize? You can see the dyer's bill, there; and Mme. Carteau told me she always expected to turn my dresses twice, at least. Oh, yes, I have been very economical."

"I have heard of old dresses turned costing more than new ones, Miss Nina."

"Oh, nonsense, Harry! What should you know of girls' things? But I 'll tell you one thing I 've got, Harry, and that is a gold watch for you. There it is," throwing a case carelessly towards him; "and there 's a silk dress for your wife," throwing him a little parcel. "I have sense enough to know what a good fellow you are, at any rate. I could n't go on as I do, if you did n't rack your poor head fifty ways to keep things going straight here at home for me."

A host of conflicting emotions seemed to cross the young man's face, like a shadow of clouds over a field, as he silently undid the packages. His hands trembled, his lips quivered, but he said nothing.

"Come, Harry, don't this suit you? I thought it would."

"Miss Nina, you are too kind."

"No, I'm not, Harry; I am a selfish little concern, that's a fact," said she, turning away, and pretending not to see the feeling which agitated him.

"But, Harry, wasn't it droll, this morning, when all our people came up to get their presents! There was Aunt Sue, and Aunt Tike, and Aunt Katy, each one got a new sack pattern, in which they are going to make up the prints I brought them. In about two days our place will be flaming with aprons and sacks. And did you see Aunt Rose in that pink bonnet, with the flowers? You could see every tooth in her head! Of course, now they'll be taken with a very pious streak, to go to some camp-meeting or other, to show their finery. Why don't you laugh, Harry?"

"I do, don't I, Miss Nina?"

"You only laugh on your face. You don't laugh deep down. What's the matter? I don't believe it's good for you to read and study so much. Papa used to say that he didn't think it was good for" —

She stopped, checked by the expression on the face of her listener.

"For servants, Miss Nina, your papa said, I suppose."

With the quick tact of her sex, Nina perceived that she had struck some disagreeable chord in the mind of her faithful attendant, and she hastened to change the subject in her careless, rattling way.

"Why, yes, Harry, study is horrid for you, or me either, or anybody else, except musty old people, who don't know

how to do anything else. Did ever anybody look out of
doors, such a pleasant day as this, and want to study?
Think of a bird's studying, now, or a bee! They don't
study — they live. Now, I don't want to study — I want
to live. So now, Harry, if you 'll just get the ponies and
go in the woods, I want to get some jessamines, and spring
beauties, and wild honeysuckles, and all the rest of the
flowers that I used to get before I went to school."

CHAPTER II

THE curtain rises on our next scene, and discovers a tranquil library, illuminated by the slant rays of the afternoon's sun. On one side the room opened by long glass windows on to a garden, from whence the air came in perfumed with the breath of roses and honeysuckles. The floor covered with white matting, the couches and sofas robed in smooth glazed linen, gave an air of freshness and coolness to the apartment. The walls were hung with prints of the great masterpieces of European art, while bronzes and plaster-casts, distributed with taste and skill, gave evidence of artistic culture in the general arrangement. Two young men were sitting together near the opened window at a small table, which displayed an antique coffee-set of silver, and a silver tray of ices and fruits. One of these has already been introduced to the notice of our readers, in the description of our heroine in the last chapter.

Edward Clayton, the only son of Judge Clayton, and representative of one of the oldest and most distinguished families of North Carolina, was in personal appearance much what our lively young friend had sketched — tall, slender, with a sort of loose-jointedness and carelessness of dress, which might have produced an impression of clownishness, had it not been relieved by a refined and intellectual expression on the head and face. The upper part of the face gave the impression of thoughtfulness and strength, with a shadowing of melancholy earnestness, and there was about the eye, in conversation, that occasional

gleam of troubled wildness which betrays the hypochondriac temperament. The mouth was even feminine in the
delicacy and beauty of its lines, and the smile which sometimes played around it had a peculiar fascination. It
seemed to be a smile of but half the man's nature; for it
never rose as high as the eyes, or seemed to disturb the
dark stillness of their thoughtfulness.

The other speaker was in many respects a contrast; and
we will introduce him to our readers by the name of Frank
Russel. Furthermore, for their benefit, we will premise
that he was the only son of a once distinguished and
wealthy, but now almost decayed family of Virginia.

It is supposed by many that friendship is best founded
upon similarity of nature; but observation teaches that it
is more common by a union of opposites, in which each
party is attracted by something wanting in itself. In Clayton, the great preponderance of those faculties which draw
a man inward, and impair the efficiency of the outward
life, inclined him to overvalue the active and practical faculties, because he saw them constantly attended with a kind
of success which he fully appreciated, but was unable to
attain. Perfect ease of manner, ready presence of mind
under all social exigencies, adroitness in making the most
of passing occurrences, are qualities which are seldom the
gift of sensitive and deeply thoughtful natures, and which
for this very reason they are often disposed to overvalue.
Russel was one of those men who have just enough of all
the higher faculties to appreciate their existence in others,
and not enough of any one to disturb the perfect avail-
ability of his own mind. Everything in his mental fur-
nishing was always completely under his own control, and
on hand for use at a moment's notice. From infancy
he was noted for quick tact and ready reply. At school
he was the universal factotum, the "good fellow" of the
ring, heading all the mischief among the boys, and yet

walking with exemplary gravity on the blind side of the
master.   Many a scrape had he rescued Clayton from, into
which he had fallen from a more fastidious moral sense, a
more scrupulous honor, than is for worldly profit either in
the boy's or man's sphere; and Clayton, superior as he
was, could not help loving and depending on him.

The diviner part of man is often shamefaced and self-
distrustful, ill at home in this world, and standing in awe
of nothing so much as what is called common sense; and
yet common sense very often, by its own keenness, is able
to see that these unavailable currencies of another's mind
are of more worth, if the world only knew it, than the
ready coin of its own; and so the practical and the ideal
nature are drawn together.

So Clayton and Russel had been friends from boyhood;
had roomed together their four years in college; and
although instruments of a vastly different quality, had
hitherto played the concerts of life with scarce a discord.

In person, Russel was of about the medium size, with a
well-knit, elastic frame, all whose movements were characterized by sprightliness and energy.   He had a frank, open
countenance, clear blue eyes, a high forehead shaded by
clusters of curling brown hair; his flexible lips wore a good-
natured yet half-sarcastic smile.   His feelings, though not
inconveniently deep, were easily touched; he could be
moved to tears or to smiles, with the varying humor of a
friend; but never so far as to lose his equipoise — or, as he
phrased it, forget what he was about.

But we linger too long in description.   We had better
let the reader hear the *dramatis personæ* and judge for
himself.

"Well, now, Clayton," said Russel, as he leaned back in
a stuffed leather chair, with a cigar between his fingers,
"how considerate of them to go off on that marooning
party, and leave us to ourselves, here!   I say, old boy,

how goes the world now? — Reading law, hey? — booked
to be Judge Clayton the second! Now, my dear fellow, if
I had the opportunities that you have — only to step into
my father's shoes — I should be a lucky fellow."

"Well, you are welcome to all my chances," said Clayton, throwing himself on one of the lounges; "for I begin
to see that I shall make very little of them."

"Why, what's the matter? — Don't you like the
study?"

"The study, perhaps, well enough — but not the practice. Reading the theory is always magnificent and grand.
'Law hath her seat in the bosom of God; her voice is the
harmony of the world.' You remember we used to de-
claim that. But, then, come to the practice of it, and what
do you find? Are legal examinations anything like search-
ing after truth? Does not an advocate commit himself to
one-sided views of his subject, and habitually ignore all the
truth on the other side? Why, if I practiced law according to my conscience, I should be chased out of court in a
week."

"There you are again, Clayton, with your everlasting
conscience, which has been my plague ever since you were
a boy, and I have never been able to convince you what a
humbug it is! It's what I call a *crotchety* conscience —
always in the way of your doing anything like anybody
else. I suppose, then, of course, you won't go into political life. — Great pity, too. You'd make a very imposing
figure as senator. You have exactly the cut for a conscript
father — one of the old Viri Romæ."

"And what do you think the old Viri Romæ would do
in Washington? What sort of a figure do you think
Regulus, or Quintus Curtius, or Mucius Scævola, would
make there?"

"Well, to be sure, the style of political action has altered somewhat since those days. If political duties were

what they were then, — if a gulf would open in Washington, for example, — you would be the fellow to plunge in, horse and all, for the good of the republic; or, if anything was to be done by putting your right hand in the fire and burning it off — or, if there were any Carthaginians who would cut off your eyelids, or roll you down hill in a barrel of nails, for truth and your country's sake, — you would be on hand for any such matter. That's the sort of foreign embassy that you would be after. All these old-fashioned goings on would suit you to a T; but as to figuring in purple and fine linen, in Paris or London, as American minister, you would make a dismal business of it. But still, I thought you might practice law in a wholesome, sensible way, — take fees, make pleas with abundance of classical allusions, show off your scholarship, marry a rich wife, and make your children princes in the gates — all without treading on the toes of your too sensitive moral what-d'-ye-call-'ems. But you've done one thing like other folks, at least, if all's true that I've heard."

"And what is that, pray?"

"What's that? Hear the fellow, now! How innocent we are! I suppose you think I haven't heard of your campaign in New York — carrying off that princess of little flirts, Miss Gordon."

Clayton responded to the charge only with a slight shrug and a smile, in which not only his lips but his eyes took part, while the color mounted to his forehead.

"Now, do you know, Clayton," continued Russel, "I *like* that. Do you know, I always thought I should detest the woman that you should fall in love with? It seemed to me that such a portentous combination of all the virtues as you were planning for would be something like a comet — an alarming spectacle. Do you remember (I should like to know if you do) just what that woman was to be? — was to have all the learning of a man, all the graces of a woman (I think I have it by heart); she was to be practical, poetical, pious, and everything else that begins with a *p;* she was to be elegant and earnest; take deep and extensive views of life; and there was to be a certain air about her, half Madonna, half Venus, made of every creature's best. Ah, bless us! what poor creatures we are! Here comes along our little coquette, flirting, tossing her fan; picks you up like a great solid chip, as you are, and throws you into her chip-basket of beaux, and goes on dancing and flirting as before. Are n't you ashamed of it, now?"

"No. I am really much like the minister in our town, where we fitted for college, who married a pretty Polly Peters in his sixtieth year, and, when the elders came to inquire if she had the requisite qualifications for a pastor's lady, he told them that he did n't think she had. 'But the fact is, brethren,' said he, 'though I don't pretend she is a saint, she is a very pretty little sinner, and I love her.' That's just my case."

"Very sensibly said; and, do you know, as I told you before, I 'm perfectly delighted with it, because it is acting like other folks. But then, my dear fellow, do you think you have come to anything really solid with this little Venus of the sea-foam? Is n't it much the same as being engaged to a cloud, or a butterfly? One wants a little streak of reality about a person that one must take for better or for worse. You have a deep nature, Clayton. You really want a wife who will have some glimmering perception of the difference between you and the other things that walk and wear coats, and are called men."

"Well, then, really," said Clayton, rousing himself, and speaking with energy, "I 'll tell you just what it is: Nina Gordon is a flirt and a coquette — a spoiled child, if you will. She is not at all the person I ever expected would obtain any power over me. She has no culture, no read-

ing, no habits of reflection; but she has, after all, a certain
tone and quality to her, a certain *timbre*, as the French
say of voices, which suits me. There is about her a
mixture of energy, individuality, and shrewdness, which
makes her, all uninformed as she is, more piquant and
attractive than any woman I ever fell in with. She never
reads; it is almost impossible to get her to read; but, if
you can catch her ear for five minutes, her literary judg-
ments have a peculiar freshness and truth. And so with
her judgment on all other subjects, if you can stop her
long enough to give you an opinion. As to heart, I think
she has yet a wholly unawakened nature. She has lived
only in the world of sensation, and that is so abundant and
so buoyant in her that the deeper part still sleeps. It is
only two or three times that I have seen a flash of this
under nature look from her eyes, and color her voice and
intonation. And I believe — I 'm quite sure — that I am
the only person in the world that ever touched it at all.
I 'm not at all sure that she loves me *now;* but I 'm almost
equally sure that she will."

"They say," said Russel carelessly, "that she is generally engaged to two or three at a time."

"That may be also," said Clayton indolently. "I
rather suspect it to be the case now, but it gives me no
concern. I 've seen all the men by whom she is surrounded, and I know perfectly well there 's not one of them
that she cares a rush for."

"Well, but, my dear fellow, how can your extra fastidious moral notions stand the idea of her practicing this
system of deception ? "

"Why, of course, it is n't a thing to my taste; but then,
like the old parson, if I love the 'little sinner,' what am
I to do ? I suppose you think it a lover's paradox; yet
I assure you, though she deceives, she is not deceitful;
though she acts selfishly, she is not selfish. The fact is,

the child has grown up, motherless and an heiress, among servants. She has, I believe, a sort of an aunt, or some such relative, who nominally represents the head of the family to the eye of the world. But I fancy little madam has had full sway. Then she has been to a fashionable New York boarding-school, and that has developed the talent of shirking lessons, and evading rules, with a taste for sidewalk flirtation. These are all the attainments that I ever heard of being got at a fashionable boarding-school, unless it be a hatred of books, and a general dread of literary culture."

"And her estates are " —

"Nothing very considerable. Managed nominally by an old uncle of hers; really by a very clever quadroon servant, who was left her by her father, and who has received an education, and has talents very superior to what are common to those in his class. He is, in fact, the overseer of her plantation, and I believe the most loyal, devoted creature breathing."

"Clayton," said his companion, "this affair might not be much to one who takes the world as I do, but for you it may be a little too serious. Don't get in beyond your depth."

"You are too late, Russel, for that — I am in."

"Well, then, good luck to you, my dear fellow! And now, as we are about it, I may as well tell you that I'm *in* for it, too. I suppose you have heard of Miss Benoir, of Baltimore. Well, she is my fate."

"And are you really engaged ? "

"All signed and sealed, and to be delivered next Christmas."

"Let 's hear about her."

"Well, she is of a good height (I always said I should n't marry a short woman), — not handsome, but reasonably well looking — very fine manners — knows the world — plays and sings handsomely — has a snug little fortune.

Now, you know I never held to marrying for money and
nothing else; but then, as I 'm situated, I could not have
fallen in love without that requisite. Some people call
this heartless. I don't think it is. If I had met Mary
Benoir, and had known that she had n't anything, why, I
should have known that it would n't do for me at all to
cultivate any particular intimacy; but, knowing she had
fortune, I looked a little further, and found she had other
things too. Now, if that 's marrying for money, so be it.
Yours, Clayton, is a genuine case of falling in love. But,
as for me, I walked in with my eyes wide open."

"And what are you going to do with yourself in the
world, Russel?"

"I must get into practice, and get some foothold there,
you know; and then, hey for Washington! — I 'm to be
President, like every other adventurer in these United
States. Why not I as well as another man?"

"I don't know, certainly," said Clayton, "if you want
it, and are willing to work hard enough and long enough,
and pay all the price. I would as soon spend my life
walking the drawn sword which they say is the bridge to
Mahomet's paradise."

"Ah! ah! I fancy I see you doing it! What a figure
you 'd make, my dear fellow, balancing and posturing on
the sword-blade, and making horrid wry faces! Yet I
know you 'd be as comfortable there as you would in political life. And yet, after all, you are greatly superior to
me in every respect. It would be a thousand pities if such
a man as you could n't have the management of things.
But our national ship has to be navigated by second-rate
fellows, Jerry-go-nimbles, like me, simply because we are
good in dodging and turning. But that 's the way.
Sharp 's the word, and the sharpest wins."

"For my part," said Clayton, "I shall never be what the
world calls a successful man. There seems to be one in-

scription written over every passage of success in life, as far as I've seen, — ' What shall it profit a man if he gain the whole world, and lose his own soul?' "

"I don't understand you, Clayton."

"Why, it seems to me just this. As matters are going on now in our country, I must either lower my standard of right and honor, and sear my soul in all its nobler sensibilities, or I must be what the world calls an unsuccessful man. There is no path in life, that I know of, where humbuggery and fraud and deceit are not essential to success, — none where a man can make the purity of his moral nature the first object. I see Satan standing in every avenue, saying, 'All these things will I give thee, if thou wilt fall down and worship me.' "

"Why don't you take to the ministry, then, Clayton, at once, and put up a pulpit-cushion and big Bible between you and the fiery darts of the devil?"

"I'm afraid I should meet him there, too. I could not gain a right to speak in any pulpit without some profession or pledge to speak this or that, that would be a snare to my conscience by and by. At the door of every pulpit I must swear always to find truth in a certain formula; and living, prosperity, success, reputation, will all be pledged on my finding it there. I tell you I should, if I followed my own conscience, preach myself out of pulpits quicker than I should plead out at the bar."

"Lord help you, Clayton! What *will* you do? Will you settle down on your plantation, and raise cotton and sell niggers? I'm expecting to hear, every minute, that you've subscribed for the ' Liberator,' and are going to turn Abolitionist."

"I do mean to settle down on my plantation, but not to *raise* cotton or negroes as a chief end of man. I do take the ' Liberator,' because I'm a free man, and have a right to take what I have a mind to. I don't agree with Garri-

son, because I think I know more about the matter, where
I stand, than he does, or can, where he stands.   But it's
his *right*, as an honest man, to say what he thinks; and
I should use it in his place.   If I saw things as he does,
I should be an Abolitionist.   But I don't."

"That's a mercy, at least," said Russel, "to a man with
your taste for martyrdom.   But what are you going to
do?"

"What any Christian man should do who finds four
hundred odd of his fellow men and women placed in a state
of absolute dependence on him.   I'm going to educate
and fit them for freedom.   There isn't a sublimer power
on earth than God has given to us, masters.   The law
gives us absolute and unlimited control.   A plantation
such as a plantation might be would be 'a light to lighten
the Gentiles.'   There is a wonderful and beautiful development locked up in this Ethiopian race, and it is worth
being a life-object to unlock it.   The raising of cotton is
to be the least of the thing.   I regard my plantation as a
sphere for raising men and women, and demonstrating the
capabilities of a race."

"Selah!" said Russel.

Clayton looked angry.

"I beg your pardon, Clayton.   This is all superb, sublime!   There is just one objection to it — it is wholly
impossible."

"Every good and great thing has been called impossible
before it is done."

"Well, let me tell you, Clayton, just how it will be.
You will be a mark for arrows, both sides.   You will
offend all your neighbors by doing better than they do.
You will bring your negroes up to a point in which they
will meet the current of the whole community against
them, and meanwhile you will get no credit with the
Abolitionists.   They will call you a cut-throat, pirate,

sheep-stealer, and all the rest of their elegant little list of
embellishments, all the same. You 'll get a state of things
that nobody can manage but yourself, and you by the
hardest; and then you 'll die, and it 'll all run to the devil
faster than you run it up. Now, if you would do the
thing by halves, it would n't be so bad; but I know you
of old. You won't be satisfied with teaching a catechism
and a few hymns, parrot-wise, which I think is a respectable religious amusement for our women. You 'll teach 'em
all to read and write and think and speak. I should n't
wonder to hear of an importation of black-boards and spelling-books. You 'll want a lyceum and debating society.
Pray, what does sister Anne say to all this? Anne is a
sensible girl now, but I 'll warrant you 've got her to go in
for it."

"Anne is as much interested as I, but her practical tact
is greater than mine, and she is of use in detecting difficulties that I do not see. I have an excellent man, who
enters fully into my views, who takes charge of the business interests of the plantation, instead of one of these
scoundrel overseers. There is to be a graduated system of
work and wages introduced — a system that shall teach the
nature and rights of property and train to habits of industry and frugality, by making every man's acquirements
equal to his industry and good conduct."

"And what sort of a support do *you* expect to make out
of all this? Are you going to live for them, or they for
you?"

"I shall set them the example of living for *them*, and
trust to awaken the good that is in them, in return. The
strong ought to live for the weak — the cultivated for the
ignorant."

"Well, Clayton, the Lord help you! I 'm in earnest
now — fact! Though I know you won't do it, yet I wish
you could. It 's a pity, Clayton, you were born in this

world. It is n't you, but our planet and planetary ways that are in fault. Your mind is a splendid storehouse — gold and gems of Ophir — but they are all up in the fifth story, and no staircase to get 'em down into common life. Now I've just enough appreciation of the sort of thing that's in you, not to laugh at you. Nine out of ten would. To tell you the truth, if I were already set up in life, and had as definite a position as you have, — family, friends, influence, and means, — why, perhaps I might afford to cultivate this style of thing. But I tell you what it is, Clayton, such a conscience as yours is cursedly expensive to keep. It's like a carriage — a fellow must n't set it up unless he can afford it. It's one of the luxuries."

"It's a necessary of life with me," said Clayton dryly.

"Well, that's your nature. I can't afford it. I've got my way to make. I must succeed, and with your ultra notions I could n't succeed. So there it is. After all, I can be as religious as dozens of your most respectable men, who have taken their seats in the night train for Paradise and keep the daylight for their own business."

"I dare say you can."

"Yes, and I shall get all I aim at; and you, Clayton, will be always an unhappy, dissatisfied aspirant after something too high for mortality. There's just the difference between us."

The conversation was here interrupted by the return of the family party.

CHAPTER III

THE family party, which was now ushered in, consisted of Clayton's father, mother, and sister. Judge Clayton was a tall, dignified, elderly personage, in whom one recognized, at a glance, the gentleman of the old school. His hair, snowy white, formed a singular contrast with the brightness of his blue eyes, whose peculiar acuteness of glance might remind one of a falcon. There was something stately in the position of the head and the carriage of the figure, and a punctilious exactness in the whole air and manner, that gave one a slight impression of sternness. The clear, sharp blue of his eye seemed to be that of a calm and decided intellect, of a logical severity of thought; and contrasted with the silvery hair with that same expression of cold beauty that is given by the contrast of snow mountains cutting into the keen, metallic blue of an Alpine sky. One should apprehend much to fear from such a man's reason — little to hope from any outburst of his emotional nature. Yet, as a man, perhaps injustice was done to Judge Clayton by this first impression; for there was, deep beneath this external coldness, a severely repressed nature, of the most fiery and passionate vehemence. His family affections were strong and tender, seldom manifested in words, but always by the most exact appreciation and consideration for all who came within his sphere. He was strictly and impartially just in all the little minutiæ of social and domestic life, never hesitating to speak a truth or acknowledge an error.

Mrs. Clayton was a high-bred, elderly lady, whose well-preserved delicacy of complexion, brilliant dark eyes, and fine figure spoke of a youth of beauty. Of a nature imaginative, impulsive, and ardent, inclining constantly to generous extremes, she had thrown herself with passionate devotion round her clear-judging husband, as the Alpine rose girdles with beauty the breast of the bright, pure glacier.

Between Clayton and his father there existed an affection deep and entire; yet as the son developed to manhood, it became increasingly evident that they could never move harmoniously in the same practical orbit. The nature of the son was so veined and crossed with that of the mother, that the father, in attempting the age-long and often-tried experiment of making his child an exact copy of himself, found himself extremely puzzled and confused in the operation. Clayton was ideal to an excess; ideality colored every faculty of his mind, and swayed all his reasonings, as an unseen magnet will swerve the needle. Ideality pervaded his conscientiousness, urging him always to rise above the commonly received and so-called practical in morals. Hence, while he worshiped the theory of law, the practice filled him with disgust; and his father was obliged constantly to point out deficiencies in reasonings, founded more on a keen appreciation of what things ought to be, than on a practical regard to what they are. Nevertheless, Clayton partook enough of his father's strong and steady nature to be his mother's idol, who, perhaps, loved this second rendering of the parental nature with even more doting tenderness than the first.

Anne Clayton was the eldest of three sisters, and the special companion and confidante of the brother; and as she stands there untying her bonnet-strings, we must also present her to the reader. She is a little above the medium height, with that breadth and full development of

chest which one admires in English women. She carries
her well-formed head on her graceful shoulders with a positive, decided air, only a little on this side of haughtiness.
Her clear brown complexion reddens into a fine glow in
the cheek, giving one the impression of sound, perfect
health. The positive outline of the small aquiline nose;
the large, frank, well-formed mouth, with its clear rows of
shining teeth; the brown eyes, which have caught something of the falcon keenness of the father, are points in the
picture by no means to be overlooked. Taking her air
altogether, there was an honest frankness about her which
encouraged conversation, and put one instantly at ease.
Yet no man in his senses could ever venture to take the
slightest liberty with Anne Clayton. With all her frankness, there was ever in her manner a perfectly defined
"thus far shalt thou come, and no further." Beaux, suit-
ors, lovers in abundance, had stood, knelt, and sighed protesting, at her shrine. Yet Anne Clayton was twenty-
seven, and unmarried. Everybody wondered why; and as
to that, we can only wonder with the rest. Her own account of the matter was simple and positive. She did not
wish to marry — was happy enough without.

The intimacy between the brother and sister had been
more than usually strong, notwithstanding marked differences of character; for Anne had not a particle of ideality.
Sense she had, shrewdness, and a pleasant dash of humor
withal; but she was eminently what people call a practical
girl. She admired highly the contrary of all this in her
brother; she delighted in the poetic-heroic element in him,
for much the same reason that young ladies used to admire
Thaddeus of Warsaw and William Wallace — because it
was something quite out of her line. In the whole world
of ideas she had an almost idolatrous veneration for her
brother; in the sphere of practical operations she felt free
to assert, with a certain good-natured positiveness, her

own superiority. There was no one in the world, perhaps, of whose judgment in this respect Clayton stood more in awe.

At the present juncture of affairs Clayton felt himself rather awkwardly embarrassed in communicating to her an event which she would immediately feel she had a right to know before. A sister of Anne Clayton's positive character does not usually live twenty-seven years in constant intimacy with a brother like Clayton, without such an attachment as renders the first announcement of a contemplated marriage somewhat painful. Why, then, had Clayton, who always unreservedly corresponded with his sister, not kept her apprised of his gradual attachment to Nina? The secret of the matter was, that he had had an instinctive consciousness that he could not present Nina to the practical, clear-judging mind of his sister as she appeared through the mist and spray of his imaginative nature. The hard facts of her case would be sure to tell against her in any communication he might make; and sensitive people never like the fatigue of justifying their instincts. Nothing, in fact, is less capable of being justified by technical reasons than those fine insights into character whereupon affection is built. We have all had experience of preferences which would not follow the most exactly ascertained catalogue of virtues, and would be made captive where there was very little to be said in justification of the captivity.

But, meanwhile, rumor, always busy, had not failed to convey to Anne Clayton some suspicions of what was passing; and though her delicacy and pride forbade any allusion to it, she keenly felt the want of confidence, and of course was not any more charitably disposed towards the little rival for this reason. But now the matter had attained such a shape in Clayton's mind that he felt the necessity of apprising his family and friends. With his

mother the task was made easier by the abundant hopeful-
ness of her nature, which enabled her in a moment to throw
herself into the sympathies of those she loved.   To her
had been deputed the office of first breaking the tidings to
Anne, and she had accomplished it during the pleasure-
party of the morning.

The first glance that passed between Clayton and his
sister, as she entered the room, on her return from the
party, showed him that she was discomposed and unhappy.
She did not remain long in the apartment, or seem disposed to join in conversation; and after a few abstracted
moments, she passed through the open door into the garden, and began to busy herself apparently among her
plants.   Clayton followed her.   He came and stood
silently beside her for some time, watching her as she
picked the dead leaves off her geranium.

"Mother has told you," he said, at length.

"Yes," said Anne.

There was a long pause, and Anne picked off dry leaves
and green promiscuously, threatening to demolish the
bush.

"Anne," said Clayton, "how I wish you could see
her!"

"I 've *heard* of her," replied Anne dryly, "through the
Livingstons."

"And what have you heard?" said Clayton eagerly.

"Not such things as I could wish, Edward; not such as
I expected to hear of the lady that you would choose."

"And, pray, what *have* you heard?   Out with it," said
Clayton, — "let 's know what the world says of her."

"Well, the world says," said Anne, "that she is a coquette, a flirt, a jilt.   From all I 've heard, I should think
she must be an unprincipled girl."

"That is hard language, Anne."

"Truth is generally hard," replied Anne.

"My dear sister," said Clayton, taking her hand, and seating her on the seat in the garden, "have you lost all faith in me?"

"I think it would be nearer truth," replied Anne, "to say that you had lost all faith in me. Why am I the last one to know all this? Why am I to hear it first from reports, and every way but from you? Would I have treated you so? Did I ever have anything that I did not tell you? Down to my very soul I've always told you everything!"

"This is true, I own, dear Anne; but what if you had loved some man that you felt sure I should not like? Now, you are a positive person, Anne, and this might happen. Would you want to tell me at once? Would you not, perhaps, wait, and hesitate, and put off, for one reason or another, from day to day, and find it grow more and more difficult the longer you waited?"

"I can't tell," said Anne bitterly. "I never did love any one better than you, — that's the trouble."

"Neither do I love anybody better than you, Anne. The love I have for you is a whole, perfect thing, just as it was. See if you do not find me every way as devoted. My heart was only opened to take in another love, another wholly different; and which, because it is so wholly different, never can infringe on the love I bear to you. And, Anne, my dear sister, if you could love her as a part of me" —

"I wish I could," said Anne, somewhat softened; "but what I've heard has been so unfavorable! She is not, in the least, the person I should have expected you to fancy, Edward. Of all things I despise a woman who trifles with the affections of gentlemen."

"Well, but, my dear, Nina isn't a woman; she is a child — a gay, beautiful, unformed child; and I'm sure you may apply to her what Pope says: —

'If to her share some female errors fall,
Look in her face, and you forget them all.'"

"Yes, indeed," said Anne, "I believe all you men are alike — a pretty face bewitches any of you. I thought you were an exception, Edward; but there you are."

"But, Anne, is this the way to encourage my confidence? Suppose I am bewitched and enchanted, you cannot disentangle me without indulgence. Say what you will about it, the fact is just this — it is my fate to love this child. I've tried to love many women before. I have seen many whom I knew no sort of reason why I should n't love, — handsomer far, more cultivated, more accomplished, — and yet I've seen them without a movement or a flutter of the pulse. But this girl has awakened all there is to me. I do not see in her what the world sees. I see the ideal image of what she can be, what I'm sure she *will* be, when her nature is fully awakened and developed."

"Just there, Edward — just that," said Anne. "You never see anything; that is, you see a glorified image — a something that might, could, would, or should be — that is your difficulty. You glorify an ordinary boarding-school coquette into something symbolic, sublime; you clothe her with all your own ideas, and then fall down to worship her."

"Well, my dear Anne, suppose it were so, what then? I am, as you say, ideal, — you, real. Well, be it so; I must act according to what is in me. I have a right to my nature, you to yours. But it is not every person whom I *can* idealize; and I suspect this is the great reason why I never could love some very fine women with whom I have associated on intimate terms; they had no capacity of being idealized; they could receive no color from my fancy; they wanted, in short, just what Nina has. She is just like one of those little whisking, chattering cascades in the White Mountains, and the atmosphere round her is favorable to rainbows."

"And you always see her through them."

"Even so, sister; but some people I cannot. Why should you find fault with me? It's a pleasant thing to look through a rainbow. Why should you seek to disenchant, if I *can* be enchanted?"

"Why," replied Anne, "you remember the man who took his pay of the fairies in gold and diamonds, and, after he had passed a certain brook, found it all turned to slate-stones. Now, marriage is like that brook; many a poor fellow finds his diamonds turned to slate on the other side; and this is why I put in my plain, hard common sense against your visions. I see the plain facts about this young girl; that she is an acknowledged flirt, a noted coquette and jilt; and a woman who is so is necessarily heartless; and you are too good, Edward, too noble, I have loved you too long, to be willing to give you up to *such* a woman."

"There, my dear Anne, there are at least a dozen points in that sentence to which I don't agree. In the first place, as to coquetry, it isn't the unpardonable sin in my eyes — that is, under some circumstances."

"That is, you mean, when Nina Gordon is the coquette?"

"No, I don't mean that. But the fact is, Anne, there is so little of true sincerity, so little real benevolence and charity, in the common intercourse of young gentlemen and ladies in society, and our sex, who ought to set the example, are so selfish and unprincipled in their ways of treating women, that I do not wonder that, now and then, a lively girl, who has the power, avenges her sex by playing off our weak points. Now, I don't think Nina capable of trifling with a real, deep, unselfish attachment — a love which sought her good, and was willing to sacrifice itself for her; but I don't believe any such has ever been put at her disposal. There's a great difference between a man's

wanting a woman to *love him* and loving her. Wanting
to appropriate a woman as a wife does not, of course, im-
ply that a man loves her, or that he is capable of loving
anything. All these things girls feel, because their instincts are quick; and they are often accused of trifling
with a man's heart when they only see through him, and
know he has n't any. Besides, love of power has always
been considered a respectable sin in us men; and why
should we denounce a woman for loving her kind of
power ? "

"Oh, well, Edward, there is n't anything in the world
that you cannot theorize into beauty. But I don't like
coquettes, for all that; and then, I 'm told Nina Gordon
is so very odd, and says and does such very extraordinary
things sometimes."

"Well, perhaps that charms me the more. In this conventional world, where women are all rubbed into one uniform surface, like coins in one's pocket, it 's a pleasure
now and then to find one who can't be made to do and
think like all the rest. You have a little dash of this
merit yourself, Anne; but you must consider that you have
been brought up with mamma, under her influence, trained
and guided every hour, even more than you knew. Nina
has grown up an heiress among servants, a boarding-school
girl in New York; and, furthermore, you are twenty-seven
and she is eighteen, and a great deal may be learned between eighteen and twenty-seven."

"But, brother, you remember Miss Hannah More says,
— or some of those good women, I forget who: at any
rate it 's a sensible saying, — ' that a man who chooses his
wife as he would a picture in a public exhibition-room
should remember that there is this difference, that the picture cannot go back to the exhibition, but the woman may.'
You have chosen her from seeing her brilliancy in society; but, after all, can you make her happy in the dull

routine of a commonplace life? Is she not one of the sort
that must have a constant round of company and excitement to keep her in spirits?"

"I think not," said Clayton. "I think she is one of
those whose vitality is in herself, and one whose freshness
and originality will keep life anywhere from being commonplace; and that, living with us, she will sympathize,
naturally, in all our pursuits."

"Well, now, don't flatter yourself, brother, that you can
make this girl over, and bring her to any of your stan-
dards."

"Who — I? Did you think I meditated such an impertinence? The last thing I should try, to marry a wife to
educate her! It's generally one of the most selfish tricks
of our sex. Besides, I don't want a wife who will be a
mere mirror of my opinions and sentiments. I don't want
an innocent sheet of blotting-paper, meekly sucking up all
I say, and giving a little fainter impression of my ideas.
I want a wife for an alterative; all the vivacities of life
lie in differences."

"Why, surely," said Anne, "one wants one's friends
to be congenial, I should think."

"So we do; and there is nothing in the world so congenial as differences. To be sure, the differences must be
harmonious. In music, now, for instance, one does n't
want a repetition of the same notes, but differing notes that
chord. Nay, even discords are indispensable to complete
harmony. Now, Nina has just that difference from me
which chords with me; and all our little quarrels — for
we have had a good many, and I dare say shall have more
— are only a sort of chromatic passages, — discords of the
seventh, leading into harmony. My life is inward, theo-
rizing, self-absorbed. I am hypochondriac — often mor-
bid. The vivacity and acuteness of her outer life make
her just what I need. She wakens, she rouses, and keeps

me in play; and her quick instincts are often more than a match for my reason. I reverence the child, then, in spite of her faults. She has taught me many things."

"Well," said Anne, laughing, "I give you up, if it comes to that. If you come to talk about reverencing Nina Gordon, I see it's all over with you, Edward, and I'll be good natured, and make the best of it. I hope it may all be true that you think, and a great deal more. At all events, no effort of mine shall be wanting to make you as happy in your new relation as you ought to be."

"There, now, that's Anne Clayton! It's just like *you*, sister, and I could n't say anything better than that. You have unburdened your conscience, you have done all you can for me, and now very properly yield to the inevitable. Nina, I know, will love you; and if you never try to advise her and influence her, you will influence her very much. Good people are a long while learning that, Anne. They think to do good to others by interfering and advising. They don't know that all they have to do is to live. When I first knew Nina, I was silly enough to try my hand that way myself; but I've learned better. Now, when Nina comes to us, all that you and mamma have got to do is just to be kind to her, and *live* as you always have lived; and whatever needs to be altered in her, she will alter herself."

"Well," said Anne, "I wish, as it is so, that I could see her."

"Suppose you write a few lines to her in this letter that I am going to write; and then that will lead in due time to a visit."

"Anything in the world, Edward, that you say."

CHAPTER IV

THE GORDON FAMILY

A WEEK or two had passed over the head of Nina Gordon since she was first introduced to our readers, and during this time she had become familiar with the details of her home life. Nominally she stood at the head of her plantation, as mistress and queen in her own right of all, both in doors and out; but, really, she found herself, by her own youth and inexperience, her ignorance of practical details, very much in the hands of those she professed to govern.

The duties of a southern housekeeper, on a plantation, are onerous beyond any amount of northern conception. Every article wanted for daily consumption must be kept under lock and key, and doled out as need arises. For the most part, the servants are only grown-up children, without consideration, forethought, or self-control, quarreling with each other, and divided into parties and factions, hopeless of any reasonable control. Every article of wear, for some hundreds of people, must be thought of, purchased, cut and made, under the direction of the mistress; and add to this the care of young children, whose childish mothers are totally unfit to govern or care for them, and we have some slight idea of what devolves on southern housekeepers.

Our reader has seen what Nina was on her return from New York, and can easily imagine that she had no idea of embracing, in good earnest, the hard duties of such a life.

In fact, since the death of Nina's mother, the situation

of the mistress of the family had been only nominally filled
by her aunt, Mrs. Nesbit. The real housekeeper, in fact,
was an old mulatto woman, named Katy, who had been
trained by Nina's mother. Notwithstanding the general
inefficiency and childishness of negro servants, there often
are to be found among them those of great practical ability.
Whenever owners, through necessity or from tact, select
such servants, and subject them to the kind of training and
responsibility which belong to a state of freedom, the same
qualities are developed which exist in free society. Nina's
mother, being always in delicate health, had, from necessity, been obliged to commit much responsibility to "Aunt
Katy," as she was called; and she had grown up under
the discipline into a very efficient housekeeper. With her
tall red turban, her jingling bunch of keys, and an abundant sense of the importance of her office, she was a digni-
tary not lightly to be disregarded.

It is true that she professed the utmost deference for her
young mistress, and very generally passed the compliment
of inquiring what she would have done; but it was pretty
generally understood that her assent to Aunt Katy's pro-
positions was considered as much a matter of course as the
queen's to a ministerial recommendation. Indeed, had
Nina chosen to demur, her prime minister had the power,
without departing in the slightest degree from a respectful
bearing, to involve her in labyrinths of perplexity without
end. And as Nina hated trouble, and wanted, above all
things, to have her time to herself for her own amusement,
she wisely concluded not to interfere with Aunt Katy's
reign, and to get by persuasion and coaxing what the old
body would have been far too consequential and opinion-
ated to give to authority.

In like manner, at the head of all outdoor affairs was
the young quadroon, Harry, whom we introduced in the
first chapter. In order to come fully at the relation in

which he stood to the estate, we must, after the fashion of historians generally, go back a hundred years or so, in order to give our readers a fair start. Behold us, therefore, assuming historic dignity, as follows.

Among the first emigrants to Virginia, in its colonial days, was one Thomas Gordon, Knight, a distant offshoot of the noble Gordon family, renowned in Scottish history. Being a gentleman of some considerable energy, and impatient of the narrow limits of the Old World, where he found little opportunity to obtain that wealth which was necessary to meet the demands of his family pride, he struck off for himself into Virginia. Naturally of an adventurous turn, he was one of the first to propose the enterprise which afterwards resulted in a settlement on the banks of the Chowan River, in North Carolina. Here he took up for himself a large tract of the finest alluvial land, and set himself to the business of planting, with the energy and skill characteristic of his nation; and as the soil was new and fertile, he soon received a very munificent return for his enterprise. Inspired with remembrances of old ancestral renown, the Gordon family transmitted in their descent all the traditions, feelings, and habits which were the growth of the aristocratic caste from which they sprung. The name of Canema, given to the estate, came from an Indian guide and interpreter, who accompanied the first Colonel Gordon as confidential servant. The estate, being entailed, passed down through the colonial times unbroken in the family, whose wealth, for some years, seemed to increase with every generation.

The family mansion was one of those fond reproductions of the architectural style of the landed gentry in England, in which, as far as their means could compass it, the planters were fond of indulging. Carpenters and carvers had been brought over, at great expense, from the old country, to give the fruits of their skill in its erection; and it was a fancy of the ancestor who built it to display, in its wood-work, that exuberance of new and rare woods with which the American continent was supposed to abound. He had made an adventurous voyage into South America, and brought from thence specimens of those materials more brilliant than rosewood, and hard as ebony, which grow so profusely on the banks of the Amazon that the natives use them for timber. The floor of the central hall of the house was a curiously inlaid parquet of these brilliant ma-terials, arranged in fine block-work, highly polished.

The outside of the house was built in the old Virginian fashion, with two tiers of balconies running completely round, as being much better suited to the American climate than any of European mode. The inside, however, was decorated with sculpture and carvings, copied, many of them, from ancestral residences in Scotland, giving to the mansion an air of premature antiquity.

Here, for two or three generations, the Gordon family had lived in opulence. During the time, however, of Nina's father, and still more after his death, there appeared evi-dently on the place signs of that gradual decay which has conducted many an old Virginian family to poverty and ruin. Slave labor, of all others the most worthless and profitless, had exhausted the first vigor of the soil, and the proprietors gradually degenerated from those habits of energy which were called forth by the necessities of the first settlers, and everything proceeded with that free-and-easy abandon, in which both master and slave appeared to have one common object, — that of proving who should waste with most freedom.

At Colonel Gordon's death, he had bequeathed, as we have already shown, the whole family estate to his daugh-ter, under the care of a servant, of whose uncommon intel-ligence and thorough devotion of heart he had the most ample proof. When it is reflected that the overseers are

generally taken from a class of whites who are often lower in
ignorance and barbarism than even the slaves, and that their
wastefulness and rapacity are a byword among the planters,
it is no wonder that Colonel Gordon thought that, in leaving his plantation under the care of one so energetic, competent, and faithful as Harry, he had made the best possible provision for his daughter.

Harry was the son of his master, and inherited much of
the temper and constitution of his father, tempered by the
soft and genial temperament of the beautiful Eboe mulat-
tress, who was his mother. From this circumstance Harry
had received advantages of education very superior to what
commonly fell to the lot of his class. He had also accompanied his master as valet during the tour of Europe, and
thus his opportunities of general observation had been still
further enlarged, and that tact, by which those of the
mixed blood seem so peculiarly fitted to appreciate all the
finer aspects of conventional life, had been called out and
exercised; so that it would be difficult in any circle to
meet with a more agreeable and gentlemanly person. In
leaving a man of this character, and his own son, still in
the bonds of slavery, Colonel Gordon was influenced by
that passionate devotion to his daughter which with him
overpowered every consideration. A man so cultivated, he
argued to himself, might find many avenues opened to him
in freedom; might be tempted to leave the estate to other
hands, and seek his own fortune. He therefore resolved
to leave him bound by an indissoluble tie for a term of
years, trusting to his attachment to Nina to make this service tolerable.

Possessed of very uncommon judgment, firmness, and
knowledge of human nature, Harry had found means to acquire great ascendency over the hands of the plantation,
and, either through fear or through friendship, there was
a universal subordination to him. The executors of the

estate scarcely made even a feint of overseeing him; and he proceeded, to all intents and purposes, with the perfect ease of a free man. Everybody, for miles around, knew and respected him; and had he not been possessed of a good share of the thoughtful, forecasting temperament derived from his Scottish parentage, he might have been completely happy, and forgotten even the existence of the chains whose weight he never felt.

It was only in the presence of Tom Gordon — Colonel Gordon's lawful son — that he ever realized that he was a slave. From childhood there had been a rooted enmity between the brothers, which deepened as years passed on; and as he found himself, on every return of the young man to the place, subjected to taunts and ill usage, to which his defenseless position left him no power to reply, he had resolved never to marry, and lay the foundation for a family, until such time as he should be able to have the command of his own destiny and that of his household. But the charms of a pretty French quadroon overcame the dictates of prudence.

The history of Tom Gordon is the history of many a young man grown up under the institutions and in the state of society which formed him. Nature had endowed him with no mean share of talent, and with that perilous quickness of nervous organization which, like fire, is a good servant, but a bad master. Out of those elements, with due training, might have been formed an efficient and eloquent public man; but brought up from childhood among servants to whom his infant will was law, indulged during the period of infantile beauty and grace in the full expression of every whim, growing into boyhood among slaves with but the average amount of plantation morality, his passions developed at a fearfully early time of life; and before his father thought of seizing the reins of authority, they had gone out of his hands forever. Tutor after tutor was employed on the plantation to instruct him, and left, terrified by his temper. The secluded nature of the plantation left him without that healthful stimulus of society which is often a help in enabling a boy to come to the knowledge and control of himself. His associates were either the slaves, or the overseers, who are generally unprincipled and artful, or the surrounding whites, who lay in a yet lower deep of degradation. For one reason or another, it was for the interest of all these to flatter his vices and covertly to assist him in opposing and deceiving his parents. Thus an early age saw him an adept in every low form of vice. In despair, he was at length sent to an academy at the North, where he commenced his career on the first day by striking the teacher in the face, and was consequently expelled. Thence he went to another, where, learning caution from experience, he was enabled to maintain his foothold. There he was a successful colporteur and missionary in the way of introducing a knowledge of bowie-knives, revolvers, and vicious literature. Artful, bold, and daring, his residence for a year at a school was sufficient to initiate in the way of ruin perhaps one fourth of the boys. He was handsome, and, when not provoked, good natured, and had that off-hand way of spending money which passes among boys for generosity. The simple sons of hard-working farmers, bred in habits of industry and frugality, were dazzled and astonished by the freedom with which he talked and drank and spit and swore. He was a hero in their eye, and they began to wonder at the number of things, to them unknown before, which went to make up the necessaries of life. From school he was transferred to college, and there placed under the care of a professor, who was paid an exorbitant sum for overlooking his affairs. The consequence was, that while many a northern boy, whose father could not afford to pay for similar patronage, was disciplined, rusticated, or expelled, as the case might be, Tom Gordon exploited gloriously through college, getting drunk every week or two, breaking windows, smoking freshmen, heading various sprees in different parts of the country, and at last graduating nobody knew how, except the patron professor, who received an extra sum for the extra difficulties of the case. Returned home, he went into a lawyer's office in Raleigh, where, by a pleasant fiction, he was said to be reading law, because he was occasionally seen at the office during the intervals of his more serious avocations of gambling and horse-racing and drinking. His father, an affectionate but passionate man, was wholly unable to control him, and the conflicts between them often shook the whole domestic fabric. Nevertheless, to the last Colonel Gordon indulged the old hope for such cases made and provided, that Tom would get through sowing his wild oats some time, and settle down and be a respectable man; in which hope he left him the half of his property. Since that time, Tom seemed to have studied on no subject except how to accelerate the growth of those wings which riches are said to be inclined to take, under the most favorable circumstances.

As often happens in such cases of utter ruin, Tom Gordon was a much worse character for all the elements of good which he possessed. He had sufficient perception of right, and sufficient conscience remaining, to make him bitter and uncomfortable. In proportion as he knew himself unworthy of his father's affection and trust, he became jealous and angry at any indications of the want of it. He had contracted a settled ill will to his sister, for no other apparent reason except that the father took a comfort in her which he did not in him. From childhood it was his habit to vex and annoy her in every possible way; and it was for this reason, among many others, that Harry had persuaded Mr. John Gordon, Nina's uncle and guardian, to place her at the New York boarding-school, where she

acquired what is termed an education.   After finishing her
school career, she had been spending a few months in a
family of a cousin of her mother's, and running with loose
rein the career of fashionable gayety.

Luckily, she brought home with her unspoiled a genuine
love of nature, which made the rural habits of plantation
life agreeable to her.   Neighbors there were few.   Her
uncle's plantation, five miles distant, was the nearest.
Other families with whom the Gordons were in the habit
of exchanging occasional visits were some ten or fifteen
miles distant.   It was Nina's delight, however, in her muslin wrapper and straw hat, to patter about over the plantation, to chat with the negroes among their cabins, amusing
herself with the various drolleries and peculiarities to
which long absence had given the zest of novelty.   Then
she would call for her pony, and, attended by Harry or
some of her servants, would career through the woods,
gathering the wild-flowers with which they abound; perhaps stop for a day at her uncle's, have a chat and a romp
with him, and return the next morning.

In the comparative solitude of her present life her mind
began to clear itself of some former follies, as water when
at rest deposits the sediment which clouded it.   Apart
from the crowd, and the world of gayeties which had diz-
zied her, she could not help admitting to herself the folly
of much she had been doing.   Something, doubtless, was
added to this by the letters of Clayton.   The tone of them,
so manly and sincere, so respectful and kind, so removed
either from adulation or sentimentalism, had an effect upon
her greater than she was herself aware of.   So Nina, in
her positive and off-hand way, sat down, one day, and
wrote farewell letters to both her other lovers, and felt
herself quite relieved by the process.

A young person could scarce stand more entirely alone,
as to sympathetic intercourse with relations, than Nina.   It

is true that the presence of her mother's sister in the family caused it to be said that she was residing under the care of an aunt. Mrs. Nesbit, however, was simply one of those well-bred, well-dressed lay-figures, whose only office in life seems to be to occupy a certain room in a house, to sit in certain chairs at proper hours, to make certain remarks at suitable intervals of conversation. In her youth this lady had run quite a career as a belle and beauty. Nature had endowed her with a handsome face and figure, and youth and the pleasure of admiration for some years supplied a sufficient flow of animal spirits to make the beauty effective. Early married, she became the mother of several children, who were one by one swept into the grave. The death of her husband, last of all, left her with a very small fortune alone in the world; and like many in similar circumstances, she was content to sink into an appendage to another's family.

Mrs. Nesbit considered herself very religious; and as there is a great deal that passes for religion, ordinarily, of which she may be fairly considered a representative, we will present our readers with a philosophical analysis of the article. When young, she had thought only of self in the form of admiration and the indulgence of her animal spirits. When married, she had thought of self only in her husband and children, whom she loved because they were hers, and for no other reason.

When death swept away her domestic circle, and time stole the beauty and freshness of animal spirits, her self-love took another form; and perceiving that this world was becoming to her somewhat *passé*, she determined to make the best of her chance for another. Religion she looked upon in the light of a ticket, which, being once purchased, and snugly laid away in a pocketbook, is to be produced at the celestial gate, and thus secure admission to heaven.

At a certain period of her life, while she deemed this ticket unpurchased, she was extremely low spirited and gloomy, and went through a quantity of theological reading enough to have astonished herself, had she foreseen it in the days of her belleship. As the result of all, she at last presented herself as a candidate for admission to a Presbyterian church in the vicinity, there professing her determination to run the Christian race. By the Christian race, she understood going at certain stated times to religious meetings, reading the Bible and hymn-book at certain hours in the day, giving at regular intervals stipulated sums to religious charities, and preserving a general state of leaden indifference to everybody and everything in the world.

She thus fondly imagined that she had renounced the world, because she looked back with disgust on gayeties for which she had no longer strength or spirits. Nor did she dream that the intensity with which her mind traveled the narrow world of self, dwelling on the plaits of her caps, the cut of her stone-colored satin gowns, the making of her tea and her bed, and the saving of her narrow income, was exactly the same in kind, though far less agreeable in development, as that which once expended itself in dressing and dancing. Like many other apparently negative characters, she had a pertinacious intensity of an extremely narrow and aimless self-will. Her plans of life, small as they were, had a thousand crimps and plaits, to every one of which she adhered with invincible pertinacity. The poor lady little imagined, when she sat, with such punctilious satisfaction, while the Rev. Mr. Orthodoxy demonstrated that selfishness is the essence of all moral evil, that the sentiment had the slightest application to her; nor dreamed that the little, quiet, muddy current of self-will, which ran without noise or indecorum under the whole structure of her being, might be found, in a future day, to

have undermined all her hopes of heaven. Of course,
Mrs. Nesbit regarded Nina and all other lively young
people with a kind of melancholy endurance — as shocking
spectacles of worldliness. There was but little sympathy,
to be sure, between the dashing and outspoken and almost
defiant little Nina and the sombre, silver-gray apparition
which glided quietly about the wide halls of Nina's paternal mansion. In fact, it seemed to afford the latter a
mischievous pleasure to shock her respectable relative on all
convenient occasions. Mrs. Nesbit felt it occasionally her
duty, as she remarked, to call her lively niece into her
apartment, and endeavor to persuade her to read some such
volume as Law's Serious Call, or Owen on the One Hundred and Nineteenth Psalm; and to give her a general and
solemn warning against all the vanities of the world, in
which were generally included dressing in any color but
black and drab, dancing, flirting, writing love-letters, and
all other enormities, down to the eating of peanut candy.
One of these scenes is just now enacting in this good lady's
apartment, upon which we will raise the curtain.

Mrs. Nesbit, a diminutive, blue-eyed, fair-complexioned
little woman, of some five feet high, sat gently swaying in
that respectable asylum for American old age, commonly
called a rocking-chair. Every rustle of her silvery silk
gown, every fold of the snowy kerchief on her neck, every
plait of her immaculate cap, spoke a soul long retired from
this world and its cares. The bed, arranged with extrem-
est precision, however, was covered with a *mélange* of
French finery, flounces, laces, among which Nina kept up
a continual agitation like that produced by a breeze in a
flower-bed, as she unfolded, turned, and fluttered them,
before the eyes of her relative.

"I have been through all this, Nina," said the latter,
with a melancholy shake of her head, "and I know the
vanity of it."

"Well, aunty, I have n't been through it, so *I* don't know."

"Yes, my dear, when I was of your age, I used to go to balls and parties, and could think of nothing but of dress and admiration. I have been through it all, and seen the vanity of it."

"Well, aunt, I want to go through it, and see the vanity of it, too. That 's just what I 'm after. I 'm on the way to be as sombre and solemn as you are, but I 'm bound to have a good time first. Now, look at this pink brocade!"

Had the brocade been a pall, it could scarcely have been regarded with a more lugubrious aspect.

"Ah, child! such a dying world as this! To spend so much time and thought on dress!"

"Why, Aunt Nesbit, yesterday you spent just two whole hours in thinking whether you should turn the breadths of your black silk dress upside down, or down side up; and this was a dying world all the time. Now, I don't see that it is any better to think of black silk than it is of pink."

This was a view of the subject which seemed never to have occurred to the good lady.

"But now, aunt, do cheer up, and look at this box of artificial flowers. You know I thought I 'd bring a stock on from New York. Now, are n't these perfectly lovely? I like flowers that mean something. Now, these are all imitations of natural flowers, so perfect that you 'd scarcely know them from the real. See — there, that 's a moss-rose; and now look at these sweet peas, you 'd think they had just been picked; and there — that heliotrope, and these jessamines, and those orange-blossoms, and that wax camellia " —

"Turn off my eyes from beholding vanity!" said Mrs. Nesbit, shutting her eyes, and shaking her head: —

> " ' What if we wear the richest vest, —
> Peacocks and flies are better drest;
> This flesh, with all its glorious forms,
> Must drop to earth, and feed the worms.' "

"Aunt, I do think you have the most horrid, disgusting set of hymns, all about worms, and dust, and such things!"

"It's my duty, child, when I see you so much taken up with such sinful finery."

"Why, aunt, do you think artificial flowers are sinful?"

"Yes, dear; they are a sinful waste of time and money, and take off our mind from more important things."

"Well, aunt, then what did the Lord make sweet peas and roses and orange-blossoms for? I'm sure it's only doing as he does, to make flowers. He don't make everything gray, or stone-color. Now, if you only would come out in the garden, this morning, and see the oleanders, and the crape myrtle, and the pinks, the roses, and the tulips, and the hyacinths, I'm sure it would do you good."

"Oh, I should certainly catch cold, child, if I went out doors. Milly left a crack opened in the window, last night, and I've sneezed three or four times since. It will never do for me to go out in the garden; the feeling of the ground striking up through my shoes is very unhealthy."

"Well, at any rate, aunt, I should think if the Lord didn't wish us to wear roses and jessamines, he would not have made them. And it is the most natural thing in the world to want to wear flowers."

"It only feeds vanity and a love of display, my dear."

"I don't think it's vanity or a love of display. I should want to dress prettily if I were the only person in the world. I love pretty things because they are pretty. I like to wear them because they make me look pretty."

"There it is, child; you want to dress up your poor perishing body to look pretty — that's the thing!"

"To be sure I do. Why shouldn't I? I mean to look as pretty as I can, as long as I live."

"You seem to have quite a conceit of your beauty!" said Aunt Nesbit.

"Well, I know I am pretty. I 'm not going to pretend I don't. I like my own looks, now, that 's a fact. I 'm not like one of your Greek statues, I know. I 'm not wonderfully handsome, nor likely to set the world on fire with my beauty. I 'm just a pretty little thing; and I like flowers and laces, and all of those things; and I mean to like them, and I don't think there 'll be a bit of religion in my not liking them; and as for all that disagreeable stuff about the worms, that you are always telling me, I don't think it does me a particle of good. And if religion is going to make me so *poky*, I shall put it off as long as I can."

"I used to feel just as you do, dear, but I 've seen the folly of it!"

"If I 've got to lose my love for everything that is bright, everything that is lively, and everything that is pretty, and like to read such horrid stupid books, why, I 'd rather be buried, and done with it!"

"That 's the opposition of the natural heart, my dear."

The conversation was here interrupted by the entrance of a bright, curly-headed mulatto boy, bearing Mrs. Nesbit's daily luncheon.

"Oh, here comes Tomtit," said Nina; "now for a scene. Let 's see what he has forgotten, now."

Tomtit was, in his way, a great character in the mansion. He and his grandmother were the property of Mrs. Nesbit. His true name was no less respectable and methodical than that of Thomas; but as he was one of those restless and effervescent sprites who seem to be born for the confusion of quiet people, Nina had rechristened him Tomtit, which sobriquet was immediately recognized by the whole household as being eminently descriptive and appropriate. A constant ripple and eddy of drollery seemed to pervade his whole being; his large, saucy black eyes had always a laughing fire in them, that it was impossible to meet without a smile in return. Slave and property though he was, yet the first sentiment of reverence for any created thing seemed yet wholly unawakened in his curly pate. Breezy, idle, careless, flighty, as his woodland namesake, life to him seemed only a repressed and pent-up ebullition of animal enjoyment; and almost the only excitement of Mrs. Nesbit's quiet life was her chronic controversy with Tomtit. Forty or fifty times a day did the old body assure him "that she was astonished at his conduct;" and as many times would he reply by showing the whole set of his handsome teeth, on the broad grin, wholly inconsiderate of the state of despair into which he thus reduced her.

On the present occasion, as he entered the room, his eye was caught by the great display of finery on the bed; and hastily dumping the waiter on the first chair that occurred, with a flirt and a spring as lithe as that of a squirrel, he was seated in a moment astride the foot-board, indulging in a burst of merriment.

"Good law, Miss Nina, whar on earth dese yer come from? Good law, some on 'em for me, is n't 'er?"

"You see that child!" now said Mrs. Nesbit, rocking back in her chair with the air of a martyr. "After all my talkings to him! Nina, you ought not to allow that; it just encourages him!"

"Tom, get down, you naughty creature, you, and get the stand and put the waiter on it. Mind yourself, now!" said Nina, laughing.

Tomtit cut a somerset from the foot-board to the floor, and striking up, on a very high key, "I'll bet my money on a bobtail nag," he danced out a small table, as if it had been a partner, and deposited it, with a jerk, at the side of Mrs. Nesbit, who aimed a cuff at his ears; but as he adroitly ducked his head, the intended blow came down upon the table with more force than was comfortable to the inflictor.

"I believe that child is made of air! — I never can hit him!" said the good lady, waxing red in the face. "He is enough to provoke a saint!"

"So he is, aunt; enough to provoke two saints like you and me. Tomtit, you rogue," said she, giving a gentle pull to a handful of his curly hair, "be good, now, and I'll show you the pretty things by and by. Come, put the waiter on the table, now; see if you can't walk, for once!"

Casting down his eyes with an irresistible look of mock solemnity, Tomtit marched with the waiter, and placed it by his mistress.

The good lady, after drawing off her gloves and making sundry little decorous preparations, said a short grace over her meal, during which time Tomtit seemed to be holding his sides with repressed merriment; then gravely laying hold of the handle of the teapot, she stopped short, gave an exclamation, and flirted her fingers, as she felt it almost scalding hot.

"Tomtit, I do believe you intend to burn me to death, some day!"

"Laws, missus, dat are hot? Oh, sure I was 'tickler to set the nose round to the fire."

"No, you didn't! You stuck the handle right into the fire, as you're always doing!"

"Laws, now, wonder if I did," said Tomtit, assuming an abstracted appearance. "'Pears as if never can 'member which dem dare is nose, and which handle. Now, I's a-studdin' on dat dare most all de morning — was so," said he, gathering confidence, as he saw, by Nina's dancing eyes, how greatly she was amused.

"You need a sound whipping, sir — that's what you need!" said Mrs. Nesbit, kindling up in sudden wrath.

"Oh, I knows it," said Tomtit. "We's unprofitable servants, all on us. Lord's marcy that we ain't 'sumed, all on us!"

Nina was so completely overcome by this novel application of the text which she had heard her aunt laboriously drumming into Tomtit, the Sabbath before, that she laughed aloud, with rather uproarious merriment.

"Oh, aunt, there's no use! He don't know anything! He's nothing but an incarnate joke, a walking hoax!"

"No, I doesn't know nothing, Miss Nina," said Tomtit, at the same time looking out from under his long eyelashes. "Don't know nothing at all — never can."

"Well, now, Tomtit," said Mrs. Nesbit, drawing out a little blue cowhide from under her chair, and looking at him resolutely, "you see, if this teapot handle is hot again, I'll give it to you! Do you hear?"

"Yes, missis," said Tomtit, with that indescribable sing-song of indifference which is so common and so provoking in his class.

"And now, Tomtit, you go downstairs and clean the knives for dinner."

"Yes, missis," said he, pirouetting towards the door. And once in the passage, he struck up a vigorous "Oh, I'm going to glory, won't you go along with me;" accompanying himself, by slapping his own sides, as he went down two stairs at a time.

"Going to glory!" said Mrs. Nesbit, rather shortly; "he looks like it, I think! It's the third or fourth time that that child has blistered my fingers with this teapot, and I know he does it on purpose! So ungrateful, when I spend my time, teaching him, hour after hour, laboring with him so! I declare, I don't believe these children have got any souls!"

"Well, aunt, I declare, I should think you'd get out of all patience with him; yet he's so funny, I cannot, for the life of me, help laughing."

Here a distant whoop on the staircase, and a tempestuous chorus to a Methodist hymn, with the words, "Oh come, my loving brethren," announced that Tomtit was on the return; and very soon, throwing open the door, he marched in, with an air of the greatest importance.

"Tomtit, did n't I tell you to go and clean the knives?"

"Law, missis, come up here to bring Miss Nina's love-letters," said he, producing two or three letters. "Good law, though," said he, checking himself, "forgot to put them on a waity!" and before a word could be said, he was out of the room and downstairs, and at the height of furious contest with the girl who was cleaning the silver, for a waiter to put Miss Nina's letters on.

"Dar, Miss Nina," appealing to her when she appeared, "Rosa won't let me have no waity!"

"I could pull your hair for you, you little image!" said Nina, seizing the letters from his hands, and laughing while she cuffed his ears.

"Well," said Tomtit, looking after her with great solemnity, "missis in de right on 't. Ain't no kind of order in this here house, 'pite of all I can do. One says put letters on waity. Another one won't let you have waity to put letters on. And, finally, Miss Nina, she pull them all away. Just the way things going on in dis yer house, all the time! I can't help it; done all I can. Just the way missus says!"

There was one member of Nina's establishment of a character so marked that we cannot refrain from giving her a separate place in our picture of her surroundings, — and this was Milly, the waiting-woman of Aunt Nesbit.

Aunt Milly, as she was commonly called, was a tall, broad-shouldered, deep-chested African woman, with a fullness of figure approaching to corpulence. Her habit of standing and of motion was peculiar and majestic, reminding one of the Scripture expression "upright as the palm-tree." Her skin was of a peculiar blackness and softness, not unlike black velvet. Her eyes were large, full, and dark, and had about them that expression of wishfulness and longing which one may sometimes have remarked in dark eyes. Her mouth was large, and the lips, though partaking of the African fullness, had, nevertheless, something decided and energetic in their outline, which was still further seconded by the heavy moulding of the chin. A frank smile, which was common with her, disclosed a row of most splendid and perfect teeth. Her hair, without approaching to the character of the Anglo-Saxon, was still different from the ordinary woolly coat of the negro, and seemed more like an infinite number of close-knotted curls, of brilliant, glossy blackness.

The parents of Milly were prisoners taken in African wars; and she was a fine specimen of one of those warlike and splendid races, of whom, as they have seldom been reduced to slavery, there are but few and rare specimens among the slaves of the South. Her usual head-dress was a high turban, of those brilliant colored Madras handkerchiefs in which the instinctive taste of the dark races leads them to delight. Milly's was always put on and worn with a regal air, as if it were the coronet of the queen. For the rest, her dress consisted of a well-fitted gown of dark stuff, of a quality somewhat finer than the usual household apparel. A neatly starched white muslin handkerchief folded across her bosom, and a clean white apron, completed her usual costume. No one could regard her, as a whole, and not feel their prejudice in favor of the exclusive comeliness of white races somewhat shaken. Placed among the gorgeous surroundings of African landscape and scenery, it might be doubted whether any one's taste could have desired, as a completion to her appearance, to have blanched the glossy skin whose depth of coloring harmonizes so well with the intense and fiery glories of a tropical landscape.

In character Milly was worthy of her remarkable external appearance. Heaven had endowed her with a soul as broad and generous as her ample frame. Her passions rolled and burned in her bosom with a tropical fervor; a shrewd and abundant mother wit, united with a vein of occasional drollery, gave to her habits of speech a quaint vivacity.

A native adroitness gave an unwonted command over all the functions of her fine body, so that she was endowed with that much-coveted property which the New Englander denominates "faculty," which means the intuitive ability to seize at once on the right and best way of doing everything which is to be done. At the same time, she was possessed of that high degree of self-respect which led her to be incorruptibly faithful and thorough in all she undertook; less, as it often seemed, from any fealty or deference to those whom she served, than from a kind of native pride in well-doing, which led her to deem it beneath herself to slight or pass over the least thing which she had undertaken. Her promises were inviolable. Her owners always knew that what she once said would be done, if it were within the bounds of possibility.

The value of an individual thus endowed in person and character may be easily conceived by those who understand how rare, either among slaves or freemen, is such a combination. Milly was, therefore, always considered in the family as a most valuable piece of property, and treated with more than common consideration.

As a mind, even when uncultivated, will ever find its level, it often happened that Milly's amount of being and force of character gave her ascendency even over those who were nominally her superiors. As her ways were commonly found to be the best ways, she was left, in most cases, to pursue them without opposition or control. But favorite as she was, her life had been one of deep sorrows.

She had been suffered, it is true, to contract a marriage with a very finely endowed mulatto man, on a plantation adjoining her owner's, by whom she had a numerous family of children, who inherited all her fine physical and mental endowments. With more than usual sensibility and power of reflection, the idea that the children so dear to her were from their birth not her own — that they were, from the first hour of their existence, merchantable articles, having a fixed market value in proportion to every excellence, and liable to all the reverses of merchantable goods — sank with deep weight into her mind. Unfortunately, the family to which she belonged being reduced to poverty, there remained, often, no other means of making up the deficiency of income than the annual sale of one or two negroes. Milly's children, from their fine developments, were much-coveted articles. Their owner was often tempted by extravagant offers for them; and therefore, to meet one crisis or another of family difficulties, they had been successively sold from her. At first, she had met this doom with almost the ferocity of a lioness; but the blow, oftentimes repeated, had brought with it a dull endurance, and Christianity had entered, as it often does with the slave, through the rents and fissures of a broken heart. Those instances of piety which are sometimes, though rarely, found among slaves, and which transcend the ordinary development of the best instructed, are generally the results of calamities and afflictions so utterly desolating as to force the soul to depend on God alone. But where one soul is thus raised to higher piety, thousands are crushed in hopeless imbecility.

CHAPTER V

HARRY AND HIS WIFE

SEVERAL miles from the Gordon estate, on an old and somewhat decayed plantation, stood a neat log cabin, whose external aspect showed both taste and care. It was almost enveloped in luxuriant wreaths of yellow jessamine, and garlanded with a magnificent lamarque rose, whose cream-colored buds and flowers contrasted beautifully with the dark, polished green of the finely cut leaves. The house stood in an inclosure formed by a high hedge of the American holly, whose evergreen foliage and scarlet berries made it, at all times of the year, a beautiful object. Within the inclosure was a garden, carefully tended, and devoted to the finest fruits and flowers.

This little dwelling, so different in its air of fanciful neatness from ordinary southern cabins, was the abode of Harry's little wife. Lisette, which was her name, was the slave of a French creole woman, to whom a plantation had recently fallen by inheritance. She was a delicate, airy little creature, formed by a mixture of the African and French blood, producing one of those fanciful, exotic combinations that give one the same impression of brilliancy and richness that one receives from tropical insects and flowers. From both parent races she was endowed with a sensuous being exquisitely quick and fine, — a nature of everlasting childhood, with all its freshness of present life, all its thoughtless, unreasoning fearlessness of the future.

She stands there at her ironing-table, just outside her

cottage door, singing gayly at her work. Her round, plump, childish form is shown to advantage by the trim blue basque, laced in front, over a chemisette of white linen. Her head is wreathed with a gay turban, from which escapes, now and then, a wandering curl of her silky black hair. Her eyes, as she raises them, have the hazy, dreamy languor which is so characteristic of the mixed races. Her little, childish hands are busy, with nimble fingers adroitly plaiting and arranging various articles of feminine toilet, too delicate and expensive to have belonged to those in humble circumstances. She ironed, plaited, and sung, with busy care. Occasionally, however, she would suspend her work, and running between the flower borders to the hedge, look wistfully along the road, shading her eyes with her hand. At last, as she saw a man on horseback approaching, she flew lightly out, and ran to meet him.

"Harry, Harry! You've come, at last. I'm so glad! And what have you got in that paper? Is it anything for me?"

He held it up, and shook it at her, while she leaped after it.

"No, no, little curiosity!" he said gayly.

"I know it's something for me," said she, with a pretty, half-pouting air.

"And why do you know it's for you? Is everything to be for you in the world, you little good-for-nothing?"

"Good-for-nothing!" with a toss of the gayly turbaned little head. "You may well say that, sir! Just look at the two dozen shirts I've ironed, since morning! Come, now, take me up; I want to ride."

Harry put out the toe of his boot and his hand, and with an adroit spring, she was in a moment before him, on his horse's neck, and with a quick turn, snatched the paper parcel from his hand.

"Woman's curiosity!" said he.

"Well, I want to see what it is. Dear me, what a tight string! Oh, I can't break it! Well, here it goes; I'll tear a hole in it, anyhow. Oh, silk, as I live! Aha! tell me now this isn't for me, you bad thing, you!"

"Why, how do you know it isn't to make me a summer coat?"

"Summer coat!—likely story! Aha! I've found you out, mister! But, come, do make the horse canter! I want to go fast. Make him canter, do!"

Harry gave a sudden jerk to the reins, and in a minute the two were flying off as if on the wings of the wind. On and on they went, through a small coppice of pines, while the light-hearted laugh rang on the breeze behind them. Now they are lost to view. In a few minutes, emerging from the pine woods in another direction, they come sweeping, gay and laughing, up to the gate. To fasten the horse, to snatch the little wife on his shoulder, and run into the cottage with her, seemed the work only of a moment; and as he set her down, still laughing, he exclaimed, —

"There, go, now, for a pretty little picture, as you are! I have helped them get up *les tableaux vivans*, at their great houses; but you are my tableau. You aren't good for much. You are nothing but a humming-bird, made to live on honey!"

"That's what I am!" said the little one. "It takes a great deal of honey to keep me. I want to be praised, flattered, and loved, all the time. It isn't enough to have you love me. I want to hear you tell me so every day, and hour, and minute. And I want you always to admire me, and praise everything that I do. Now"—

"Particularly when you tear holes in packages!" said Harry.

"Oh, my silk — my new silk dress!" said Lisette, thus reminded of the package which she held in her hand.

"This hateful string! How it cuts my fingers! I *will* break it! I'll bite it in two. Harry, Harry, don't you see how it hurts my fingers? Why don't you cut it?"

And the little sprite danced about the cottage floor, tearing the paper, and tugging at the string, like an enraged humming-bird. Harry came laughing behind her, and taking hold of her two hands, held them quite still, while he cut the string of the parcel, and unfolded a gorgeous plaid silk, crimson, green, and orange.

"There, now, what do you think of that? Miss Nina brought it, when she came home, last week."

"Oh, how lovely! Isn't she a beauty? Isn't she good? How beautiful it is! Dear me, dear me! how happy I am! How happy we are! — ain't we, Harry?"

A shadow came over Harry's forehead as he answered, with a half-sigh, —

"Yes."

"I was up at three o'clock this morning, on purpose to get all my ironing done to-day, because I thought you were to come home to-night. Ah! ah! you don't know what a supper I've got ready! You'll see, by and by. I'm going to do something uncommon. You mustn't look in that other room, Harry — you mustn't!"

"Mustn't I?" said Harry, getting up, and going to the door.

"There, now! who's curiosity now, I wonder!" said she, springing nimbly between him and the door. "No, you sha'n't go in, though. There, now; don't, don't! Be good now, Harry!"

"Well, I may as well give up first as last. This is your house, not mine, I suppose," said Harry.

"Mr. Submission, how meek we are, all of a sudden. Well, while the fit lasts, you go to the spring and get me some water to fill this teakettle. Off with you now, this minute! Mind you don't stop to play by the way!"

And while Harry is gone to the spring we will follow the wife into the forbidden room. Very cool and pleasant it is, with its white window-curtains, its matted floor, and displaying in the corner that draped feather bed, with its ruffled pillows and fringed curtains, which it is the great ambition of the southern cabin to attain and maintain.

The door, which opened on to a show of most brilliant flowers, was overlaid completely by the lamarque rose we have before referred to; and large clusters of its creamy blossoms, and wreaths of its dark green leaves, had been enticed in and tied to sundry nails and pegs by the small hands of the little mistress, to form an arch of flowers and roses. A little table stood in the door, draped with a spotless damask table - cloth, fine enough for the use of a princess, and only produced by the little mistress on festive occasions. On it were arranged dishes curiously trimmed with moss and vine leaves, which displayed strawberries and peaches, with a pitcher of cream and one of whey, small dishes of curd, delicate cakes and biscuit, and fresh golden butter.

After patting and arranging the table-cloth, Lisette tripped gayly around, and altered here and there the arrangement of a dish, occasionally stepping back, and cocking her little head on one side, much like a bird, singing gayly as she did so; then she would pick a bit of moss from this, and a flower from that, and retreat again, and watch the effect.

"How surprised he will be!" she said to herself. Still humming a tune in a low, gurgling undertone, she danced hither and thither, round the apartment. First she gave the curtains a little shake, and unlooping one of them, looped it up again, so as to throw the beams of the evening sun on the table.

"There, there, there! how pretty the light falls through those nasturtions! I wonder if the room smells of the mignonette. I gathered it when the dew was on it, and they say that will make it smell all day. Now, here's Harry's bookcase. Dear me! these flies! How they do get on to everything! Shoo, shoo! now, now!" and catching a gay bandana handkerchief from the drawer, she perfectly exhausted herself in flying about the room in pursuit of the buzzing intruders, who soared and dived and careered, after the manner of flies in general, seeming determined to go anywhere but out of the door, and finally were seen brushing their wings and licking their feet, with great alertness, on the very topmost height of the sacred bed-curtains; and as just this moment a glimpse was caught of Harry returning from the spring, Lisette was obliged to abandon the chase, and rush into the other room, to prevent a premature development of her little tea tableau. Then a small pug-nosed, black teakettle came on to the stage of action, from some unknown cupboard; and Harry had to fill it with water, and of course spilt the water on to the ironing-table, which made another little breezy, chattering commotion; and then the flat-irons were cleared away, and the pug-nosed kettle reigned in their stead on the charcoal brazier.

"Now, Harry, was ever such a smart wife as I am? Only think, besides all the rest that I've done, I've ironed your white linen suit, complete! Now, go put it on. Not in there! not in there!" she said, pushing him away from the door. "You can't go there, yet. You'll do well enough out here."

And away she went, singing through the garden walks; and the song, floating back behind her, seemed like an odor brushed from the flowers. The refrain came rippling in at the door —

> " Me think not what to-morrow bring;
> Me happy, so me sing! "

"Poor little thing!" said Harry to himself; "why should I try to teach her anything?"

In a few minutes she was back again, her white apron
thrown over her arm, and blossoms of yellow jessamine,
spikes of blue lavender, and buds of moss-roses peeping
out from it. She skipped gayly along, and deposited her
treasure on the ironing-table; then, with a zealous, bustling earnestness, which characterized everything she did,
she began sorting them into two bouquets, alternately talking and singing, as she did so, —

> " ' Come on, ye rosy hours,
>   All joy and gladness bring! '

"You see, Harry, you 're going to have a bouquet to
put into the buttonhole of that coat. It will make you
look so handsome! There, now — there, now, —

> ' We 'll strew the way with flowers,
>   And merrily, merrily sing. ' "

Suddenly stopping, she looked at him archly, and said,
"You can't tell, now, what I 'm doing all this for!"

"There 's never any telling what you women do anything for."

"Do hear him talk — so pompous! Well, sir, it 's for
your birthday, now. Aha! you thought, because I can't
keep the day of the month, that I did n't know anything
about it; but I did. And I have put down now a chalk-
mark every day, for four weeks, right under where I keep
my ironing-account, so as to be sure of it. And I 've been
busy about it ever since two o'clock this morning. And
now — there, the teakettle is boiling!" — and away she
flew to the door.

"Oh, dear me! — dear me, now! — I 've killed myself
now, I have!" she cried, holding up one of her hands,
and flirting it up in the air. "Dear me! who knew it
was so hot?"

"I should think a little woman that is so used to the
holder *might* have known it," said Harry, as he caressed
the little burnt hand.

VOL. I.

"Come, now, let me carry it for you," said Harry, "and I'll make the tea, if you'll let me go into that mysterious room."

"Indeed, no, Harry — I'm going to do everything myself;" and forgetting the burnt finger, Lisette was off in a moment, and back in a moment with a shining teapot in her hand, and the tea was made. And at last the mysterious door opened, and Lisette stood with her eyes fixed upon Harry, to watch the effect.

"Superb! — magnificent! — splendid! Why, this is good enough for a king! And where did you get all these things?" said Harry.

"Oh, out of our garden — all but the peaches. Those old Mist' gave me — they come from Florida. There, now, you laughed at me, last summer, when I set those strawberry vines, and made all sorts of fun of me. And what do you think now?"

"Think! I think you're a wonderful little thing — a perfect witch."

"Come, now, let's sit down, then — you there, and I here." And opening the door of the bird-cage, which hung in the lamarque rose-bush, "Little Button shall come, too."

Button, a bright yellow canary, with a smart black tuft upon his head, seemed to understand his part in the little domestic scene perfectly; for he stepped obediently upon the finger which was extended to him, and was soon sitting quite at his ease on the mossy edge of one of the dishes, pecking at the strawberries.

"And now, do tell me," said Lisette, "all about Miss Nina. How does she look?"

"Pretty and smart as ever," said Harry. "Just the same witchy, willful ways with her."

"And did she show you her dresses?"

"Oh yes; the whole."

"Oh, do tell me about them, Harry — do!"

"Well, there's a lovely pink gauze, covered with spangles, to be worn over white satin."

"With flounces?" said Lisette earnestly.

"With flounces."

"How many?"

"Really, I don't remember."

"Don't remember how many flounces? Why, Harry, how stupid! Say, Harry, don't you suppose she will let me come and look at her things?"

"Oh yes, dear, I don't doubt she will; and that will save my making a gazette of myself."

"Oh, when will you take me there, Harry?"

"Perhaps to-morrow, dear. And now," said Harry, "that you have accomplished your surprise upon me, I have a surprise, in return, for you. You can't guess, now, what Miss Nina brought for me."

"No, indeed! What?" said Lisette, springing up; "do tell me — quick."

"Patience — patience!" said Harry, deliberately fumbling in his pocket, amusing himself with her excited air. But who should speak the astonishment and rapture which widened Lisette's dark eyes when the watch was produced? She clapped her hands, and danced for joy, to the imminent risk of upsetting the table, and all the things on it.

"I do think we are the most fortunate people — you and I, Harry! Everything goes just as we want it to — does n't it, now?"

Harry's assent to this comprehensive proposition was much less fervent than suited his little wife.

"Now, what's the matter with you? What goes wrong? Why don't you rejoice as I do?" said she, coming and seating herself down upon his knee. "Come, now, you 've been working too hard, I know. I 'm going to sing to you, now; you want something to cheer you up." And Lisette took down her banjo, and sat down in the doorway under the arch of lamarque roses, and began thrumming gayly.

"This is the nicest little thing, this banjo!" she said; "I would n't change it for all the guitars in the world. Now, Harry, I 'm going to sing something specially for you." And Lisette sung: —

> " 'What are the joys of white man, here,
>   What are his pleasures, say ?
> He great, he proud, he haughty fine
>   While I my banjo play:
>   He sleep all day, he wake all night;
>   He full of care, his heart no light;
>   He great deal want, he little get ;
>   He sorry, so he fret.

> " 'Me envy not the white man here,
>   Though he so proud and gay;
> He great, he proud, he haughty fine,
>   While I my banjo play:
>   Me work all day, me sleep all night;
>   Me have no care, me heart is light;
>   Me think not what to-morrow bring;
>   Me happy, so me sing.' "

Lisette rattled the strings of the banjo, and sang with such a hearty abandon of enjoyment that it was a comfort to look at her. One would have thought that a bird's soul put into a woman's body would have sung just so.

"There," she said, throwing down her banjo, and seating herself on her husband's knee, "do you know, I think you are like white man in the song? I should like to know what is the matter with you. I can see plain enough when you are not happy; but I don't see why."

"Oh, Lisette, I have very perplexing business to manage," said Harry. "Miss Nina is a dear, good little mistress, but she does n't know anything about accounts, or money; and here she has brought me home a set of bills to settle, and I 'm sure I don't know where the money is to be got from. It's hard work to make the old place profitable in our days. The ground is pretty much worked up; it does n't bear the crops it used to. And then, our people are so childish, they don't, a soul of them, care how much they spend, or how carelessly they work. It's very expensive keeping up such an establishment. You know the Gordons must be Gordons. Things can't be done now as some other families would do them; and then, those bills which Miss Nina brings from New York are perfectly frightful."

"Well, Harry, what are you going to do?" said Lisette, nestling down close on his shoulder. "You always know how to do something."

"Why, Lisette, I shall have to do what I 've done two or three times before — take the money that I have saved, to pay these bills — our freedom money, Lisette."

"Oh, well, then, don't worry. We can get it again, you know. Why, you know, Harry, you can make a good deal with your trade, and one thing and another that you do; and then, as for me, why, you know, my ironing, and my muslins, how celebrated they are. Come, don't worry one bit; we shall get on nicely."

"Ah! But, Lisette, all this pretty house of ours, garden, and everything, is only built on air, after all, till we are free. Any accident can take it from us. Now, there 's Miss Nina; she is engaged, she tells me, to two or three lovers, as usual."

"Engaged, is she?" said Lisette eagerly, female curiosity getting the better of every other consideration; "she always did have lovers, just, you know, as I used to."

"Yes; but, Lisette, she will marry, some time, and what a thing that would be for you and me! On her husband will depend all my happiness for all my life. He may set her against me; he may not like me. Oh, Lisette! I 've seen trouble enough coming of marriages; and I was

hoping, you see, that before that time came the money for
my freedom would all be paid in, and I should be my
own man. But now, here it is. Just as the sum is
almost made up, I must pay out five hundred dollars of it,
and that throws us back two or three years longer. And
what makes me feel the most anxious is, that I'm pretty
sure Miss Nina will marry one of these lovers before long."

"Why, what makes you think so, Harry?"

"Oh, I've seen girls before now, Lisette, and I know
the signs."

"What does she do? What does she say? Tell me,
now, Harry."

"Oh, well, she runs on abusing the man, after her sort;
and she's so very earnest and positive in telling me she
don't like him."

"Just the way I used to do about you, Harry, isn't it?"

"Besides," said Harry, "I know, by the kind of character she gives of him, that she thinks of him very differently from what she ever did of any man before. Miss
Nina little knows, when she is rattling about her beaux,
what I'm thinking of. I'm saying, all the while, to
myself, 'Is that man going to be my master?' and this
Clayton, I'm very sure, is going to be my master."

"Well, isn't he a good man?"

"She says he is; but there's never any saying what
good men will do, never. Good men think it right sometimes to do the strangest things. This man may alter the
whole agreement between us, — he will have a right to do
it, if he is her husband; he may refuse to let me buy
myself; and then, all the money that I've paid will go
for nothing."

"But, certainly, Harry, Miss Nina will never consent
to such a thing."

"Lisette, Miss Nina is one thing, but Mrs. Clayton may
be quite another thing. I've seen all that, over and over

again. I tell you, Lisette, that we who live on other
people's looks and words, we watch and think a great deal!
Ah! we come to be very sharp, I can tell you. The more
Miss Nina has liked me, the less her husband may like
me; don't you know that?"

"No; Harry, you don't dislike people I like."

"Child, child, that's quite another thing."

"Well, then, Harry, if you feel so bad about it, what
makes you pay this money for Miss Nina? She don't
know anything about it; she don't ask you to. I don't
believe she would want you to, if she did know it. Just
go and pay it in, and have your freedom papers made out.
Why don't you tell her all about it?"

"No, I can't, Lisette. I've had the care of her all her
life, and I've made it as smooth as I could for her, and I
won't begin to trouble her now. Do you know, too, that
I'm afraid that, perhaps, if she knew all about it, she
wouldn't do the right thing. There's never any knowing, Lisette. Now, you see, I say to myself, 'Poor little
thing! she doesn't know anything about accounts, and she
don't know how I feel.' But if I should tell her, and
she shouldn't care, and act as I've seen women act, why,
then, you know I couldn't think so any more. I don't
believe she would mind you; but then, I don't like to try."

"Harry, what does make you love her so much?"

"Don't you know, Lisette, that Master Tom was a
dreadful bad boy, always willful and wayward, almost
broke his father's heart; and he was always ugly and contrary to her? I'm sure I don't know why; for she was
a sweet little thing, and she loves him now, ugly as he is,
and he is the most selfish creature I ever saw. And as
for Miss Nina, she isn't selfish — she is only inconsiderate. But I've known her do for him, over and over,
just what I do for her, giving him her money and her
jewels to help him out of a scrape. But then, to be sure,

it all comes upon me, at last, which makes it all the more aggravating. Now, Lisette, I'm going to tell you something, but you mustn't tell anybody. Nina Gordon is my sister!"

"Harry!"

"Yes, Lisette, you may well open your eyes," said Harry, rising involuntarily; "I'm Colonel Gordon's oldest son! Let me have the comfort of saying it once, if I never do again."

"Harry, who told you?"

"He told me, Lisette — he, himself, told me, when he was dying, and charged me always to watch over her; and I have done it! I never told Miss Nina; I wouldn't have her told for the world. It wouldn't make her love me; more likely it would turn her against me. I've seen many a man sold for nothing else but looking too much like his father, or his brothers and sisters. I was given to her, and my sister and my mother went out to Mississippi with Miss Nina's aunt."

"I never heard you speak of this sister, Harry. Was she pretty?"

"Lisette, she was beautiful, she was graceful, and she had real genius. I've heard many singers on the stage that could not sing, with all their learning, as she did by nature."

"Well, what became of her?"

"Oh, what becomes of such women always, among us! Nursed, and petted, and caressed; taught everything elegant, nothing solid. Why, the woman meant well enough that had the care of her, — Mrs. Stewart, Colonel Gordon's sister, — but she couldn't prevent her son's wanting her, and taking her, for his mistress; and when she died there she was."

"Well."

"When George Stewart had lived with her two or three

years, he was taken with smallpox. You know what perfect horror that always creates. None of his white acquaintances and friends would come near his plantation; the negroes were all frightened to death, as usual; overseer ran off. Well, then Cora Gordon's blood came up; she nursed him all through that sickness. What's more, she had influence to keep order on the place; got the people to getting the cotton crops themselves, so that when the overseer came sneaking back, things had n't all gone to ruin, as they might have done. Well, the young fellow had more in him than some of them do; for when he got well he left his plantation, took her up to Ohio, and married her, and lived with her there."

"Why did n't he live with her on his plantation?" said Lisette.

"He could n't have freed her there; it 's against the laws. But, lately, I 've got a letter from her saying that he had died and left to her and her son all his property on the Mississippi."

"Why, she will be rich, won't she?"

"Yes, if she gets it. But there 's no knowing how that will be; there are fifty ways of cheating her out of it, I suppose. But now, as to Miss Nina's estate, you don't know how I feel about it. I was trusted with it, and trusted with her. She never has known, more than a child, where the money came from, or went to; and it sha'n't be said that I 've brought the estate in debt for the sake of getting my own liberty. If I have one pride in life, it is to give it up to Miss Nina's husband in good order. But then, the trouble of it, Lisette! The trouble of getting anything like decent work from these creatures; the ways that I have to turn and twist to get round them, and manage them, to get anything done. They hate me; they are jealous of me. Lisette, I 'm just like the bat in the fable; I 'm neither bird nor beast. How often I 've

wished that I was a good, honest, black nigger, like Uncle
Pomp! Then I should know what I was; but now, I 'm
neither one thing nor another. I come just near enough
to the condition of the white to look into it, to enjoy it,
and want everything that I see. Then the way I 've
been educated makes it worse. The fact is, that when
the fathers of such as we feel any love for us, it is n't like
the love they have for their white children. They are
half ashamed of us; they are ashamed to show their love,
if they have it; and then, there 's a kind of remorse and
pity about it, which they make up to themselves by petting
us. They load us with presents and indulgences. They
amuse themselves with us while we are children, and play
off all our passions as if we were instruments to be played
on. If we show talent and smartness, we hear some one
say, aside, ' It 's rather a pity, is n't it ? ' or, ' He is too
smart for his place.' Then, we have all the family blood
and the family pride; and what to do with it ? I feel that
I am a Gordon. I feel in my very heart that I 'm like
Colonel Gordon — I know I am, and sometimes, I know I
look like him, and that 's one reason why Tom Gordon
always hated me; and then, there 's another thing, the
hardest of all, to have a sister like Miss Nina, to feel she
is my sister, and never dare to say a word of it! She
little thinks, when she plays and jokes with me, sometimes, how I feel. I have eyes and senses; I can compare
myself with Tom Gordon. I know he never would learn
anything at any of the schools he was put to; and I know
that when his tutors used to teach me, how much faster
I got along than he did. And yet he must have all the
position, and all the respect; and then, Miss Nina so
often says to me, by way of apology, when she puts up
with his ugliness, ' Ah! well, you know, Harry, he is the
only brother I have got in the world! ' Is n't it too bad ?
Colonel Gordon gave me every advantage of education,

because I think he meant me for just this place which I fill. Miss Nina was his pet. He was wholly absorbed in her, and he was frightened at Tom's wickedness; and so he left me bound to the estate in this way, only stipulating that I should buy myself on favorable terms before Miss Nina's marriage. She has always been willing enough. I might have taken any and every advantage of her inconsiderateness. And Mr. John Gordon has been willing, too, and has been very kind about it, and has signed an agreement as guardian, and Miss Nina has signed it too, that, in case of her death, or whatever happened, I 'm to have my freedom on paying a certain sum, and I have got his receipts for what I have paid. So that 's tolerably safe. Lisette, I had meant never to have been married till I was a free man; but, somehow, you bewitched me into it. I did very wrong."

"Oh, pshaw! pshaw!" interrupted Lisette. "I ain't going to hear another word of this talk! What 's the use? We shall do well enough. Everything will come out right, — you see if it don't, now. I was always lucky, and I always shall be."

The conversation was here interrupted by a loud whooping, and a clatter of horse's heels.

"What 's that?" said Harry, starting to the window. "As I live, now, if there is n't that wretch of a Tomtit, going off with that horse! How came he here? He will ruin him! Stop there! hallo!" he exclaimed, running out of doors after Tomtit.

Tomtit, however, only gave a triumphant whoop, and disappeared among the pine-trees.

"Well, I should like to know what sent him here!" said Harry, walking up and down, much disturbed.

"Oh, he 's only going round through the grove; he will be back again," said Lisette; "never fear. Is n't he a handsome little rogue?"

"Lisette, you never can see trouble anywhere!" said Harry, almost angrily.

"Ah! yes I do," said Lisette, "when you speak in that tone! Please don't, Harry. What should you want me to see trouble for?"

"I don't know, you little thing," said Harry, stroking her head fondly.

"Ah, there comes the little rascal, just as I knew he would!" said Lisette. "He only wanted to take a little race; he hasn't hurt the horse;" and tripping lightly out, she caught the reins, just as Tomtit drove up to the gate; and it seemed but a moment before he was over in the garden, with his hands full of flowers.

"Stop, there, you young rascal, and tell me what sent you here!" said Harry, seizing him, and shaking him by the shoulder.

"Laws, Massa Harry, I wants to get peaches, like other folks," said the boy, peeping roguishly in at the window, at the tea-table.

"And he shall have a peach, too," said Lisette, "and some flowers, if he'll be a good boy, and not tread on my borders."

Tomtit seized greedily at the peach she gave him, and sitting flat down where he stood, and throwing the flowers on the ground beside him, began eating it with an earnestness of devotion as if his whole being were concentrated in the act. The color was heightened in his brown cheek by the exercise, and with his long, drooping curls and eyelashes, he looked a very pretty centre to the flower-piece which he had so promptly improvised.

"Ah, how pretty he is!" said Lisette, touching Harry's elbow. "I wish he was mine!"

"You'd have your hands full, if he was," said Harry, eying the intruder discontentedly, while Lisette stood picking the hulls from a fine bunch of strawberries which she was ready to give him when he had finished the peach.

"Beauty makes fools of all you girls," said Harry cynically.

"Is that the reason I married you?" said Lisette archly. "Well, I know I could make him good, if I had the care of him. Nothing like coaxing; is there, Tom?"

"I 'll boun' there ain't!" said Tom, opening his mouth for the strawberries with much the air of a handsome, saucy robin.

"Well," said Harry, "I should like to know what brought him over here. Speak, now, Tom! Were n't you sent with some message?"

"Oh laws, yes!" said Tom, getting up and scratching his curly head. "Miss Nina sent me. She wants you to get on dat ar horse, and make tracks for home like split foot. She done got letters from two or three of her beaux, and she is dancing and tearing round there real awful. She done got scared, spects; 'feard they 'd all come together."

"And she sent you on a message, and you have n't told me, all this time!" said Harry, making a motion as though he was going to box the child's ears; but the boy glided out of his hands as if he had been water, and was gone, vanishing among the shrubbery of the garden; and while Harry was mounting his horse, he reappeared on the roof of the little cabin, caracoling and dancing, shouting at the topmost of his voice, —

> "Away down old Virginny,
> Dere I bought a yellow girl for a guinea."

"I 'll give it to you, some time!" said Harry, shaking his fist at him.

"No, he won't, either," cried Lisette, laughing. "Come down here, Tomtit, and I 'll make a good boy of you."

CHAPTER VI

THE DILEMMA

In order to understand the occasion which hurried Harry home, we must go back to Canema. Nina, after taking her letters from the hands of Tomtit, as we have related, ran back with them into Mrs. Nesbit's room, and sat herself down to read them. As she read, she evidently became quite excited and discomposed, crumpling a paper with her little hand, and tapping her foot impatiently on the carpet.

"There, now, I'm sure I don't know what I shall do, Aunt Nesbit!" addressing her aunt, because it was her outspoken habit to talk to any body or thing which happened to be sitting next to her. "I've got myself into a pretty scrape now!"

"I told you you'd get into trouble, one of these days!"

"Oh, you told me so! If there's anything I hate, it is to have anybody tell me 'I told you so!' But now, aunt, really, I know I've been foolish, but I don't know what to do. Here are two gentlemen coming together, that I wouldn't have meet each other here for the world; and I don't know really what I had better do."

"You'd better do just as you please, as you always do, and always would, ever since I knew you," said Aunt Nesbit, in a calm, indifferent tone.

"But, really, aunt, I don't know what's proper to do in such a case."

"Your and my notions of propriety, Nina, are so different, that I don't know how to advise you. You see the consequences, now, of not attending to the advice of your friends. I always knew these flirtations of yours would bring you into trouble." And Aunt Nesbit said this with that quiet, satisfied air with which precise elderly people so often edify their thoughtless young friends under difficulties.

"Well, I did n't want a sermon, now, Aunt Nesbit; but as you 've seen a great deal more of the world than I have, I thought you might help me a little, just to tell me whether it would n't be proper for me to write and put one of these gentlemen off; or make some excuse for me, or something. I 'm sure *I* never kept house before. I don't want to do anything that don't seem hospitable; and yet I don't want them to come together. Now, there, that 's flat!"

There was a long pause, in which Nina sat vexed and coloring, biting her lips, and nestling uneasily in her seat.

Mrs. Nesbit looked calm and considerate, and Nina began to hope that she was taking the case a little to heart.

At last the good old lady looked up, and said, very quietly, "I wonder what time it is."

Nina thought she was debating the expediency of sending some message; and therefore she crossed the room with great alacrity, to look at the old clock in the entry.

"It 's half past two, aunt!" and she stood, with her lips apart, looking at Mrs. Nesbit for some suggestion.

"I was going to tell Rosa," said she abstractedly, "that that onion in the stuffing does not agree with me. It rose on my stomach all yesterday morning; but it 's too late now."

Nina actually stamped with anger.

"Aunt Nesbit, you are the most selfish person I ever saw in my life!"

"Nina, child, you astonish me!" said Aunt Nesbit, with her wonted placidity. "What 's the matter?"

"I don't care!" said Nina; "I don't care a bit! I don't see how people can be so! If a dog should come to me and tell me he was in trouble, I think I should listen to him, and show some kind of interest to help him! I don't care how foolish anybody has been; if they are in trouble, I'd help them, if I could; and I think you might think enough of it to give me some little advice!"

"Oh, you are talking about that affair, yet?" said her aunt. "Why, I believe I told you I didn't know what to advise, didn't I? Shouldn't give way to this temper, Nina; it's very unladylike, besides being sinful. But then, I don't suppose it's any use for me to talk!" And Aunt Nesbit, with an abused air, got up, walked quietly to the looking-glass, took off her morning-cap, unlocked her drawer, and laid it in; took out another, which Nina could not see differed a particle from the last, held it up thoughtfully on her hand, and appeared absorbed in the contemplation of it, — while Nina, swelling with a mixture of anger and mortification, stood regarding her as she leisurely picked out each bow, and finally, with a decorous air of solemnity, arranged it upon her head, patting it tenderly down.

"Aunt Nesbit," she said suddenly, as if the words hurt her, "I think I spoke improperly, and I'm very sorry for it. I beg your pardon."

"Oh, it's no matter, child; I didn't care about it. I'm pretty well used to your temper."

Bang went the door, and in a moment Nina stood in the entry, shaking her fist at it with impotent wrath.

"You stony, stiff, disagreeable old creature! how came you ever to be my mother's sister?" And with the word mother, she burst into a tempest of tears, and rushed violently to her own chamber. The first object that she saw was Milly, arranging some clothes in her drawer; and to her astonishment, Nina rushed up to her, and throwing

her arms round her neck, sobbed and wept in such tumultuous excitement that the good creature was alarmed.

"Laws bless my soul, my dear little lamb! what's the
matter? Why, don't! Don't, honey! Why, bless the
dear little soul! bless the dear precious lamb! who's been
a-hurting of it?" And at each word of endearment,
Nina's distress broke out afresh, and she sobbed so bitterly
that the faithful creature really began to be frightened.

"Laws, Miss Nina, I hope there ain't nothing happened
to you now!"

"No, no, nothing, Milly, only I am lonesome, and I
want my mother! I haven't got any mother! Dear
me!" she said, with a fresh burst.

"Ah, the poor thing!" said Milly compassionately,
sitting down, and fondling Nina in her arms, as if she had
been a babe. "Poor chile! Laws, yes; I 'member your
ma was a beautiful woman!"

"Yes," said Nina, speaking between her sobs, "the
girls at school had mothers. And there was Mary Brooks,
she used to read to me her mother's letters, and I used
to feel so, all the while, to think nobody wrote such letters
to me! And there's Aunt Nesbit — I don't care what
they say about her being religious, she is the most selfish,
hateful creature I ever did see! I do believe, if I was
lying dead and laid out in the next room to her, she would
be thinking what she'd get next for dinner!"

"Oh, don't, my poor lamb, don't!" said Milly compassionately.

"Yes, I will, too! She's always taking it for granted
that I'm the greatest sinner on the face of the earth!
She don't scold me — she don't care enough about me to
scold! She only takes it for granted, in her hateful, quiet
way, that I'm going to destruction, and that she can't
help it, and don't care! Supposing I'm not good! —
what's to make me good? Is it going to make me good

for people to sit up so stiff, and tell me they always knew
I was a fool, and a flirt, and all that? Milly, I 've had
dreadful turns of wanting to be good, and I 've laid awake
nights and cried because I was n't good. And what makes
it worse, is that I think if mamma was alive she could
help me. She was n't like Aunt Nesbit, was she, Milly?"

"No, honey, she was n't. I 'll tell you about your ma
some time, honey."

"The worst of it is," said Nina, "when Aunt Nesbit
speaks to me in her hateful way, I get angry; then I
speak in a way that is n't proper, I know. Oh, if she
only would get angry with me back again! or if she 'd do
anything in the world but stand still, in her still way,
telling me she is astonished at me! That 's a lie, too; for
she never was astonished at anything in her life! She
has n't life enough to be!"

"Ah, Miss Nina, we must n't spect more of folks than
there is in them."

"Expect? I don't expect!"

"Well, bless you, honey, when you knows what folks
is, don't let 's worry. Ye can't fill a quart cup out of a
thimble, honey, no way you can fix it. There 's just whar
't is. I knowed your ma, and I 's knowed Miss Loo, ever
since she was a girl. 'Pears like they wa'n't no more alike
than snow is like sugar. Miss Loo, when she was a girl,
she was that pretty that everybody was wondering after
her; but to de love, dat ar went after your ma. Could n't
tell why it was, honey. 'Peared like Miss Loo wa'n't
techy, nor she wa'n't one of your bursting-out sort, scolding
round. 'Peared like she 'd never hurt nobody; and yet
our people, they could n't none of dem bar her. 'Peared
like nobody did nothing for her with a will."

"Well, good reason!" said Nina; "she never did anything for anybody else with a will! She never cared for
anybody! Now, I 'm selfish; I always knew it. I do a

great many selfish things; but it's a different kind from
hers. Do you know, Milly, she don't seem to know she
is selfish? There she sits, rocking in her old chair, so
sure she's going straight to heaven, and don't care whether
anybody else gets there or not!"

"Oh laws, now, Miss Nina, you's too hard on her.
Why, look how patient she sits with Tomtit, teaching him
his hymns and varses."

"And you think that's because she cares anything about
him? Do you know, she thinks he isn't fit to go to
heaven, and that if he dies he'll go to the bad place.
And yet, if he was to die to-morrow, she'd talk to you
about clear-starching her caps! No wonder the child don't
love her! She talks to him just as she does to me; tells
him she don't expect anything of him — she knows he'll
never come to any good; and the little wretch has got it
by heart, now. Do you know that, though I get in a passion with Tom, sometimes, and though I'm sure I should
perish sitting boring with him over those old books, yet
I really believe I care more for him than she does? And
he knows it, too. He sees through her as plain as I do.
You'll never make me believe that Aunt Nesbit has got
religion. I know there is such a thing as religion; but
she hasn't got it. It isn't all being sober, and crackling
old stiff religious newspapers, and boring with texts and
hymns, that makes people religious. She is just as
worldly minded as I am, only it's in another way. There,
now, I wanted her to advise me about something, to-day.
Why, Milly, all girls want somebody to talk with; and if
she'd only showed the least interest in what I said, she
might scold me and lecture me as much as she'd a mind
to. But to have her not even hear me! And when she
must have seen that I was troubled and perplexed, and
wanted somebody to advise me, she turned round so cool,
and began to talk about the onions and the stuffing! Got

me so angry! I suppose she is in her room, now, rocking, and thinking what a sinner I am!"

"Well, now, Miss Nina, 'pears though you 've talked enough about dat ar; 'pears like it won't make you feel no better."

"Yes it *does* make me feel better! I had to speak to somebody, Milly, or else I should have burst; and now I wonder where Harry is. He always could find a way for me out of anything."

"He is gone over to see his wife, I think, Miss Nina."

"Oh, too bad! Do send Tomtit after him, right away. Tell him that I want him to come right home, this very minute — something very particular. And, Milly, you just go and tell Old Hundred to get out the carriage and horses, and I 'll go over and drop a note in the post-office, myself. I won't trust it to Tomtit; for I know he 'll lose it."

"Miss Nina," said Milly, looking hesitatingly, "I spect you don't know how things go about round here; but the fact is, Old Hundred has got so kind of cur'ous, lately, there can't nobody do nothing with him, except Harry. Don't 'tend to do nothing Miss Loo tells him to. I 's 'feard he 'll make up some story or other about the horses; but he won't get 'em out — now, mind, I tell you, chile!"

"He won't! I should like to know if he won't, when I tell him to! A pretty story that would be! I 'll soon teach him that he has a live mistress — somebody quite different from Aunt Loo!"

"Well, well, chile, perhaps you 'd better go. He would n't mind me, I know. Maybe he 'll do it for you."

"Oh yes; I 'll just run down to his house, and hurry him up." And Nina, quite restored to her usual good humor, tripped gayly across to the cabin of Old Hundred, that stood the other side of the house.

Old Hundred's true name was, in fact, John. But he had derived the appellation, by which he was always known, from the extreme moderation of all his movements. Old Hundred had a double share of that profound sense of the dignity of his office which is an attribute of the tribe of coachmen in general. He seemed to consider the horses and carriage as a sort of family ark, of which he was the high priest, and which it was his business to save from desecration. According to his own showing, all the people on the plantation, and indeed the whole world in general, were in a state of habitual conspiracy against the family carriage and horses, and he was standing for them, single-handed, at the risk of his life. It was as much part of his duty, in virtue of his office, to show cause, on every occasion, why the carriage should not be used, as it is for state attorneys to undertake prosecutions. And it was also a part of the accomplishment of his situation to conduct his refusal in the most decorous manner; always showing that it was only the utter impossibility of the case which prevented. The available grounds of refusal Old Hundred had made a life-study, and had always a store of them cut and dried for use, all ready at a moment's notice. In the first place, there were always a number of impossibilities with regard to the carriage. Either "it was muddy, and he was laying out to wash it;" or else "he had washed it, and couldn't have it splashed;" or "he had taken out the back curtain, and had laid out to put a stitch in it, one of dese yer days;" or there was something the matter with the irons. "He reckoned they was a little bit sprung." "He 'lowed he 'd ask the blacksmith about it, some of dese yer times." And then as to the horses the possibilities were rich and abundant. What with strains, and loose shoes, and stones getting in at the hoofs, dangers of all sorts of complaints, for which he had his own vocabulary of names, it was next to an impossibility, according to any ordinary rule of computing chances, that the two should be in complete order together.

Utterly ignorant, however, of the magnitude of the undertaking which she was attempting, and buoyant with the consciousness of authority, Nina tripped singing along, and found Old Hundred tranquilly reclining in his tent-door, watching through his half-shut eyes, while the afternoon sunbeam irradiated the smoke which rose from the old pipe between his teeth. A large, black, one-eyed crow sat perching, with a quizzical air, upon his knee, and when he heard Nina's footsteps approaching, cocked his remaining eye towards her, with a smart, observing attitude, as if he had been deputed to look out for applications while his master dozed. Between this crow, who had received the sobriquet of Uncle Jeff, and his master there existed a most particular bond of friendship and amity. This was further strengthened by the fact that they were both equally disliked by all the inhabitants of the place. Like many people who are called to stand in responsible positions, Old Hundred had rather failed in the humble virtues, and become dogmatical and dictatorial to that degree that nobody but his own wife could do anything with him. And as to Jeff, if the principle of thievery could be incarnate, he might have won a temple among the Lacedemonians. In various skirmishes and battles consequent on his misdeeds, Jeff had lost an eye, and had a considerable portion of the feathers scalded off on one side of his head; while the remaining ones, discomposed by the incident, ever after stood up in a protesting attitude, imparting something still more sinister to his goblin appearance. In another rencounter he had received a permanent twist in the neck, which gave him always the appearance of looking over his shoulder, and added not a little to the oddity of the general effect. Uncle Jeff thieved with an assiduity and skill which were worthy of a better cause, and when not upon any serious enterprise of this kind, employed his time in pulling up corn, scratching up newly planted flower seeds, tangling yarn, pulling out knitting-needles, pecking the eyes of sleeping people, scratching and biting children, and any other little miscellaneous mischief which occurred to him. He was invaluable to Old Hundred, because he was a standing apology for any and all discoveries made on his premises of things which ought not to have been there. No matter what was brought to light, — whether spoons from the great house, or a pair of sleeve-buttons, or a handkerchief, or a pipe from a neighboring cabin, — Jeff was always called up to answer. Old Hundred regularly scolded, on these occasions, and declared he was enough to "spile the character of any man's house." And Jeff would look at him comically over the shoulder, and wink his remaining eye, as much as to say that the scolding was a settled thing between them, and that he was n't going to take it at all in ill part.

"Uncle John," said Nina, "I want you to get the carriage out for me, right away. I want to take a ride over the cross run."

"Laws bless you sweet face, honey, chile, I's dreadful sorry; but you can't do it dis yer day."

"Can't do it! Why not?"

"Why, bless you, chile, it ain't possible, noway. Can't have the carriage and hosses dis yer arternoon."

"But I *must* go over to cross run to the post-office. I must go this minute!"

"Law, chile, you can't do it! fur you can't walk, and it's sartain you can't ride, because dese yer hosses, nor dis yer carriage, can't stir out dis yer arternoon, no way you can fix it. Mout go, perhaps, to-morrow, or next week."

"Oh, Uncle John, I don't believe a word of it! I want them this afternoon, and I say I *must* have them!"

"No, you can't, chile," said Old Hundred, in a tender,

condescending tone, as if he was speaking to a baby. "I tell you dat ar is impossible. Why, bless your soul, Miss Nina, de curtains is all off de carriage!"

"Well, put them on again, then!"

"Ah, Miss Nina, dat ar ain't all. Pete was desperate sick, last night; took with de thumps, powerful bad. Why, Miss Nina, he was dat sick I had to be up with him most all night!" And while Old Hundred thus adroitly issued this little work of fiction, the raven nodded waggishly at Nina, as much as to say, "You hear that fellow, now!"

Nina stood quite perplexed, biting her lips, and Old Hundred seemed to go into a profound slumber.

"I don't believe but what the horses can go to-day! I mean to go and look."

"Laws, honey, chile, ye can't, now; de do's is all locked, and I've got de key in my pocket. Every one of dem critturs would have been killed forty times over 'fore now. I think everybody in dis yer world is arter dem dar critturs. Miss Loo, she's wanting 'em to go one way, and Harry's allers usin' de critturs. Got one out, dis yer arternoon, riding over to see his wife. Don't see no use in his riding round so grand, noway! Laws, Miss Nina, your pa used to say to me, says he, 'Uncle John, you knows more about dem critturs dan I do; and now I tell you what it is, Uncle John — you take care of dem critturs; don't you let nobody kill 'em for nothing.' Now, Miss Nina, I's always a-walking in the steps of the colonel's 'rections. Now, good, clar, bright weather, over good roads, I likes to trot the critturs out. Dat ar is reasonable. But den, what roads is over the cross run, I want to know? Dem dere roads is de most mis'ablest things you ever did see. Mud! Hi! Ought for to see de mud down dar by de creek! Why, de bridge all tared off! Man drowned in dat dar creek once! Was so! It

ain't no sort of road for young ladies to go over. Tell
you, Miss Nina; why don' you let Harry carry your letter
over? If he must be ridin' round de country, don't see
why he could n't do some good wid his ridin'. Why, de
carriage would n't get over before ten o'clock, dis yer
night! Now, mine, I tell you. Besides, it 's gwine fur
to rain. I 's been feeling dat ar in my corns, all dis yer
morning; and Jeff, he 's been acting like the berry debil
hisself — de way he always does 'fore it rains. Never
knowed dat ar sign to fail."

"The short of the matter is, Uncle John, you are determined not to go," said Nina. "But I tell you you *shall*
go! — there, now! Now, do you get up immediately, and
get out those horses! "

Old Hundred still sat quiet, smoking; and Nina, after
reiterating her orders till she got thoroughly angry, began,
at last, to ask herself the question, how she was going to
carry them into execution. Old Hundred appeared to
have descended into himself in a profound reverie, and
betrayed not the smallest sign of hearing anything she
said.

"I wish Harry would come back quick," she said to
herself as she pensively retraced her steps through the garden; but Tomtit had taken the commission to go for him
in his usual leisurely way, spending the greater part of the
afternoon on the road.

"Now, ain't you ashamed of yourself, you mean old
nigger! " said Aunt Rose, the wife of Old Hundred, who
had been listening to the conversation; "talking 'bout de
creek, and de mud, and de critturs, and Lor knows what
all, when we all knows it 's nothing but your laziness! "

"Well," said Old Hundred, "and what would come o'
the critturs if I was n't lazy, I want to know? Laziness!
it 's the berry best thing for the critturs can be. Where 'd
dem horses 'a' been now, if I had been one of your highfa-

lutin' sort, always driving round? Where 'd dey 'a' been, and what would dey 'a' been, hey? Who wants to see hosses all skin and bone? Lord! if I had been like some o' de coachmen, de buzzards would have had the picking of dem critturs, long ago!"

"I rally believe that you 've told dem dar lies till you begin to believe them yourself!" said Rose. "Telling our dear, sweet young lady about your being up with Pete all night, when de Lord knows you laid here snoring fit to tar de roof off!"

"Well, must say something! Folks must be 'spectful to de ladies. Course I could n't tell her I *would n't* take de critturs out; so I just trots out scuse. Ah! lots of dem scuses I keeps! I tell you, now, scuses is excellent things. Why, scuses is like dis yer grease that keeps de wheels from screaking. Lord bless you, de whole world turns round on scuses. Whar de world be if everybody was such fools to tell the raal reason for everything they are gwine fur to do, or ain't gwine fur to!"

CHAPTER VII

"OH, Harry, I'm so glad to see you back! In such trouble as I've been to-day! Don't you think, this very morning, as I was sitting in Aunt Nesbit's room, Tomtit brought up these two letters; and one of them is from Clayton, and the other from Mr. Carson; and now, see here what Clayton says: 'I shall have business that will take me in your vicinity next week; and it is quite possible, unless I hear from you to the contrary, that you may see me at Canema next Friday or Saturday.' Well, then, see here; there's another from Mr. Carson, — that hateful Carson! Now, you see, he hasn't got my letter; says he is coming. What impudence! I'm tired to death of that creature, and he'll be here just as certain! Disagreeable people always do keep their promises! He'll certainly be here!"

"Well, Miss Nina, you recollect you said you thought it would be good fun."

"Oh, Harry, don't bring that up, I beg of you! The fact is, Harry, I've altered my mind about that. You know I've put a stop to all those foolish things at once, and am done with them. You know I wrote to Carson and Emmons, both, that my sentiments had changed, and all that sort of thing, that the girls always say. I'm going to dismiss all of 'em at once, and have no more fooling."

"What, all? Mr. Clayton and all?"

"Well, I don't know, exactly, — no. Do you know, Harry, I think his letters are rather improving? — at least, they are different letters from any I've got before; and though I don't think I shall break my heart after him, yet I like to get them. But the other two I'm sick to death of; and as for having that creature boring round here, I won't! At any rate, I don't want him and Clayton here together. I would n't have them together for the world; and I wrote a letter to keep Carson off, this morning, and I've been in trouble all day. Everybody has plagued me. Aunt Nesbit only gave me one of her mopy lectures about flirting, and would n't help me in the least. And then, Old Hundred: I wanted him to get out the carriage and horses for me to go over and put this letter in the office, and I never saw such a creature in my life! I can't make him do anything! I should like to know what the use is of having servants, if you can't get anything done!"

"Oh, as to Old Hundred, I understand him, and he understands me," said Harry. "I never find any trouble with him; but he is a provoking old creature. He stands very much on the dignity of his office. But if you want your letter carried to-night, I can contrive a safer way than that, if you 'll trust it to me."

"Ah! well, do take it!"

"Yes," said Harry, "I'll send a messenger across on horseback, and I have means to make him faithful."

"Well, Harry, Harry!" said Nina, catching at his sleeve as he was going out, "come back again, won't you? I want to talk to you."

During Harry's absence, our heroine drew a letter from her bosom, and read it over.

"How well he writes!" she said to herself. "So different from the rest of them! I wish he'd keep away from here, — that's what I do! It's a pretty thing to get his letters, but I don't think I want to see him. Oh, dear! I wish I had somebody to talk to about it — Aunt Nesbit is *so* cross! I can't — no, I won't care about him! Harry is a kind soul."

"Ah, Harry, have you sent the letter?" said she eagerly as he entered.

"I have, Miss Nina; but I can't flatter you too much. I'm afraid it's too late for the mail — though there's never any saying when the mail goes out, within two or three hours."

"Well, I hope it will stay for me, once. If that stupid creature comes, why, I don't know what I shall do! He's so presuming! and he'll squeak about with those horrid shoes of his; and then, I suppose, it will all come out, one way or another; and I don't know what Clayton will think."

"But I thought you didn't care what he thought."

"Well, you know, he's been writing to me all about his family. There's his father, is a very distinguished man, of a very old family; and he's been writing to me about his sister, the most dreadfully sensible sister, he has got — good, lovely, accomplished, and pious! Oh, dear me! I don't know what in the world he ever thought of *me* for! And, do you think, there's a postscript from his sister, written elegantly as can be!"

"As to family, Miss Nina," said Harry, "I think the Gordons can hold up their heads with anybody; and then, I rather think you'll like Miss Clayton."

"Ah! but then, Harry, this talking about fathers and sisters, it's bringing the thing awfully near! It looks so much, you know, as if I really were caught. Do you know, Harry, I think I'm just like my pony? You know, she likes to have you come and offer her corn, and stroke her neck; and she likes to *make you believe* she's going to let you catch her; but when it comes to putting a bridle on her, she's off in a minute. Now, that's the way with me. It's rather exciting, you know, these beaux, and love-letters, and talking sentiment, going to the opera, and taking rides on horseback, and all that.

But when men get to talking about their fathers, and
their sisters, and to act as if they were sure of me, I'm
just like Sylphine — I want to be off. You know, Harry,
I think it's a very serious thing, this being married. It's
dreadful! I don't want to be a woman grown. I wish
I could always be a girl, and live just as I have lived, and
have plenty more girls come and see me, and have fun.
I have n't been a bit happy lately, not a bit; and I never
was unhappy before in my life."

"Well, why don't you write to Mr. Clayton, and break
it all off, if you feel so about it?"

"Well, why don't I? I don't know. I've had a great
mind to do it; but I'm afraid I should feel worse than I
do now. He's coming just like a great dark shadow over
my life, and everything is beginning to feel so real to me!
I don't want to take up life in earnest. I read a story,
once, about Undine; and, do you know, Harry, I think
I feel just as Undine did, when she felt her soul coming
in her?"

"And is Clayton Knight Heldebound?" said Harry,
smiling.

"I don't know. What if he should be? Now, Harry,
you see the fact is that sensible men get their heads turned
by such kind of girls as I am; and they pet us, and
humor us. But then, I'm afraid they're thinking, all
the while, that their turn to rule is coming, by and by.
They marry us because they think they are going to make
us over; and what I'm afraid of is, I never *can* be made
over. Don't think I was cut out right in the first place;
and there never will be much more of me than there is
now. And he'll be comparing me with his pattern sister;
and I sha'n't be any the more amiable for that. Now, his
sister is what folks call highly educated, you know, Harry.
She understands all about literature, and everything. As
for me, I've just cultivation enough to appreciate a fine

horse — that's the extent. And yet I'm proud. I
would n't wish to stand second, in his opinion, even to his
sister. So, there it is. That's the way with us girls!
We are always wanting what we know we ought not to
have, and are not willing to take the trouble to get."

"Miss Nina, if you 'll let me speak my mind out frankly,
now, I want to offer one piece of advice. Just be perfectly
true and open with Mr. Clayton; and if he and Mr. Carson should come together, just tell him frankly how the
matter stands. You are a Gordon, and they say truth
always runs in the Gordon blood; and now, Miss Nina,
you are no longer a schoolgirl, but a young lady at the
head of the estate."

He stopped, and hesitated.

"Well, Harry, you need n't stop. I understand you —
got a few grains of sense left, I hope, and have n't got so
many friends that I can afford to get angry with you for
nothing."

"I suppose," said Harry thoughtfully, "that your aunt
will be well enough to be down to the table. Have you
told her how matters stand?"

"Who? Aunt Loo? Catch me telling her anything!
No, Harry, I 've got to stand all alone. I have n't any
mother, and I have n't any sister; and Aunt Loo is worse
than nobody, because it 's provoking to have somebody
round that you feel might take an interest, and ought to,
and don't care a red cent for you. Well, I declare, if
I 'm not much, — if I 'm not such a model as Miss Clayton, there, — how could any one expect it, when I have
just come up by myself, first at the plantation, here, and
then at that French boarding-school? I tell you what,
Harry, boarding-schools are not what they 're cried up to
be. It 's good fun, no doubt, but we never learnt anything there. That is to say, we never learnt it internally,
but had it just rubbed on to us outside. A girl can't

help, of course, learning something; and I've learnt just what I happened to like and could n't help, and a deal that is n't of the most edifying nature besides."

Well! we shall see what will come!

CHAPTER VIII

"I say, Tiff, *do* you think he will come to-night?"

"Laws, laws, missis, how can Tiff tell? I's been a-gazin' out de do'. Don't see nor hear nothin'."

"It's so lonesome! — *so* lonesome! — and the nights so long!"

And the speaker, an emaciated, feeble little woman, turned herself uneasily on the ragged pallet where she was lying, and twirling her slender fingers nervously, gazed up at the rough, unplastered beams above.

The room was of the coarsest and rudest cast. The hut was framed of rough pine logs, filled between the crevices with mud and straw; the floor made of rough-split planks, unevenly jointed together; the window was formed by some single panes arranged in a row where a gap had been made in one of the logs. At one end was a rude chimney of sticks, where smouldered a fire of pine-cones and brush-wood, covered over with a light coat of white ashes. On the mantel over it was a shelf, which displayed sundry vials, a cracked teapot and tumbler, some medicinal-looking packages, a turkey's wing, much abridged and defaced by frequent usage, some bundles of dry herbs, and lastly a gayly painted mug of coarse crockery ware, containing a bunch of wild-flowers. On pegs, driven into the logs, were arranged different articles of female attire, and divers little coats and dresses, which belonged to smaller wearers, with now and then soiled and coarse articles of man's apparel.

The woman, who lay upon a coarse chaff pallet in the corner, was one who once might have been pretty. Her skin was fair, her hair soft and curling, her eyes of a beautiful blue, her hands thin and transparent as pearl. But the deep, dark circles under the eyes, the thin, white lips, the attenuated limbs, the hurried breathing, and the burning spots in the cheek told that, whatever she might have been, she was now not long for this world.

Beside her bed was sitting an old negro, in whose close-curling wool age had begun to sprinkle flecks of white. His countenance presented, physically, one of the most uncomely specimens of negro features; and would have been positively frightful, had it not been redeemed by an expression of cheerful kindliness which beamed from it. His face was of ebony blackness, with a wide, upturned nose, a mouth of portentous size, guarded by clumsy lips, revealing teeth which a shark might have envied. The only fine feature was his large black eyes, which, at the present, were concealed by a huge pair of plated spectacles, placed very low upon his nose, and through which he was directing his sight upon a child's stocking, that he was busily darning. At his foot was a rude cradle, made of a gum-tree log, hollowed out into a trough, and wadded by various old fragments of flannel, in which slept a very young infant. Another child, of about three years of age, was sitting on the negro's knee, busily playing with some pine cones and mosses.

The figure of the old negro was low and stooping; and he wore, pinned round his shoulders, a half-handkerchief or shawl of red flannel, arranged much as an old woman would have arranged it. One or two needles, with coarse, black thread dangling to them, were stuck in on his shoulder; and as he busily darned on the little stocking, he kept up a kind of droning intermixture of chanting and talking to the child on his knee.

"So, ho, Teddy! — bub dar! — my man! — sit still! — cause yer ma's sick, and sister's gone for medicine. Dar, Tiff'll sing to his little man.

> 'Christ was born in Bethlehem,
> Christ was born in Bethlehem,
> And in a manger laid.'

Take car, dar! — dat ar needle scratch yer little fingers! — poor little fingers! Ah, be still, now! — play wid yer pretty tings, and see what yer pa'll bring ye!"

"Oh, dear me! — well!" said the woman on the bed, "I shall give up!"

"Bress de Lord, no, missis!" said Tiff, laying down the stocking, and holding the child to him with one hand, while the other was busy in patting and arranging the bed-clothes. "No use in givin' up! Why, Lord bress you, missis, we'll be all up right agin in a few days. Work has been kinder pressin', lately, and chil'n's clothes ain't quite so 'speckable; but den I's doin' heaps o' mendin'. See dat ar!" said he, holding up a slip of red flannel, re-splendent with a black patch, "dat ar hole won't go no furder — and it does well enough for Teddy to wear rollin' round de do', and such like times, to save his bettermost. And de way I's put de yarn in dese yer stockings ain't slow. Den I's laid out to take a stitch in Teddy's shoes; and dat ar hole in de kiverlet, dat ar'll be stopped 'fore morning. Oh, let me alone! — he! he! he! — Ye didn't keep Tiff for nothing, missis — ho, ho, ho!" And the black face seemed really to become unctuous with the oil of gladness, as Tiff proceeded in his work of consolation.

"Oh, Tiff, Tiff! you're a good creaturc! But you don't know. Here I've been lying alone day after day, and he off, nobody knows where! And when he comes, it'll be only a day, and he's off; and all he does don't amount to anything — all miserable rubbish brought home and traded off for other rubbish. Oh, what a fool I was for being married! Oh, dear! girls little know what marriage is! I thought it was so dreadful to be an old maid, and a pretty thing to get married! But, oh, the pain, and worry, and sickness, and suffering I 've gone through! — always wandering from place to place, never settled; one thing going after another, worrying, watching, weary, — and all for nothing, for I am worn out, and I shall die!"

"Oh, Lord, no!" said Tiff earnestly. "Lor, Tiff 'll make ye some tea, and give it to ye, ye poor lamb! It 's drefful hard, so 't is; but times 'll mend, and massa 'll come round and be more settled, like, and Teddy will grow up and help his ma; and I 'm sure dere is n't a pearter young un dan dis yer puppet!" said he, turning fondly to the trough where the little fat, red mass of incipient humanity was beginning to throw up two small fists, and to utter sundry small squeaks, to intimate his desire to come into notice.

"Lor, now," said he, adroitly depositing Teddy on the floor, and taking up the baby, whom he regarded fondly through his great spectacles; "stretch away, my pretty! stretch away! ho-e-ho! Lor, if he has n't got his mammy's eye, for all dis worl'! Ah, brave! See him, missis!" said he, laying the little bundle on the bed by her. "Did ye ever see a peartier young un? He, he, he! Dar, now, his mammy should take him, so she should! and Tiff 'll make mammy some tea, so he will!" And Tiff, in a moment, was on his knees, carefully laying together the ends of the burned sticks, and blowing a cloud of white ashes, which powdered his woolly head and red shawl like snowflakes, while Teddy was busy in pulling the needles out of some knitting-work which hung in a bag by the fire.

Tiff, having started the fire by blowing, proceeded very carefully to adjust upon it a small, black porringer of water, singing, as he did so, —

" ' My way is dark and cloudy,
    So it is, so it is;
My way is dark and cloudy,
        All de day.' "

Then rising from his work, he saw that the poor, weak
mother had clasped the baby to her bosom, and was sob-
bing very quietly. Tiff, as he stood there, with his short,
square, ungainly figure, his long arms hanging out from
his side like bows, his back covered by the red shawl,
looked much like a compassionate tortoise standing on its
hind legs. He looked pitifully at the sight, took off his
glasses and wiped his eyes, and lifted up his voice in another stave: —

" '-But we 'll join de forty tousand, by and by,
        So we will, so we will.
We 'll join de forty tousand, upon de golden shore,
And our sorrows will be gone forevermore, more, more.'

"Bress my soul, Mas'r Teddy! now us been haulin'
out de needles from Miss Fanny's work! dat ar ain't
purty, now! Tiff 'll be 'shamed of ye, and ye do like dat
when yer ma 's sick! Don't ye know ye must be good,
else Tiff won't tell ye no stories! Dar, now, sit down on
dis yere log; dat ar 's just the nicest log! plenty o' moss
on it yer can be a-pickin' out! Now, yer sit still dar, and
don't be interruptin' yer ma."

The urchin opened a wide, round pair of blue eyes upon
Tiff, looking as if he were mesmerized, and sat, with a
quiet, subdued air, upon his log, while Tiff went fumbling
about in a box in the corner. After some rattling, he
produced a pine knot, as the daylight was fading fast in
the room, and driving it into a crack in another log which
stood by the chimney-corner, he proceeded busily to light
it, muttering, as he did so, —

"Want to make it more cheerful like."

Then he knelt down and blew the coals under the little
porringer, which, like pine coals in general, always sulked

and looked black when somebody was not blowing them.
He blew vigorously, regardless of the clouds of ashes which
encircled him, and which settled even on the tips of his
eyelashes, and balanced themselves on the end of his nose.

"Bress de Lord, I 's dreadful strong in my breff! Lord,
dey might have used me in blacksmissin'! I 's kep dis yer
chimney a-gwine dis many a day. I wonder, now, what
keeps Miss Fanny out so long?"

And Tiff rose up with the greatest precaution, and glan-
cing every moment towards the bed, and almost tipping
himself over in his anxiety to walk softly, advanced to the
rude door, which opened with a wooden latch and string,
opened it carefully, and looked out. Looking out with
him, we perceive that the little hut stands alone, in the
heart of a dense pine forest, which shuts it in on every
side.

Tiff held the door open a few moments to listen. No
sound was heard but the shivering wind, swaying and surging in melancholy cadences through the long pine leaves,
— a lonesome, wailing, uncertain sound.

"Ah! dese yer pine-trees! dey always a-talkin'!" said
Tiff to himself, in a sort of soliloquy. "Whisper, whisper, whisper! De Lord knows what it 's all about! dey
never tells folks what dey wants to know. Hark! dar is
Foxy, as sure as I 'm a livin' sinner! Ah! dar she is!"
as a quick, loud bark reverberated. "Ah, ha! Foxy!
you 'll bring her along!" caressing a wolfish-looking, lean
cur, who came bounding through the trees.

"Ah, yer good-for-nothing! what makes yer run so fast,
and leave yer missus behind ye? Hark! what 's dat!"

The clear voice came caroling gayly from out the pine-
trees, —

> "If you get there before I do —
> I 'm bound for the land of Canaan."

Whereupon Tiff, kindling with enthusiasm, responded, —

"Look out for me — I'm coming too —
I'm bound for the land of Canaan."

The response was followed by a gay laugh, as a childish voice shouted, from the woods, —

"Ha! Tiff, you there?"

And immediately a bold, bright, blue-eyed girl, of about eight years old, came rushing forward.

"Lors, Miss Fanny, so grad you's come! Yer ma's powerful weak dis yer arternoon!" And then, sinking his voice to a whisper, "Why, now, yer'd better b'lieve her sperits isn't the best! Why, she's that bad, Miss Fanny, she actually been a-cryin' when I put the baby in her arms. Railly, I'm consarned, and I wish yer pa'ud come home. Did yer bring de medicine?"

"Ah, yes; here 't is."

"Ah! so good! I was a-makin' of her some tea, to set her up, like, and I'll put a little drop of dis yer in 't. You gwin, now, and speak to yer ma, and I'll pick up a little light wood round here, and make up de fire. Massa Teddy'll be powerful glad to see yer. Hope you's got him something, too!"

The girl glided softly into the room, and stood over the bed where her mother was lying.

"Mother, I've come home," said she gently.

The poor, frail creature in the bed seemed to be in one of those helpless hours of life's voyage when all its waves and billows are breaking over the soul; and while the little newcomer was blindly rooting and striving at her breast, she had gathered the worn counterpane over her face, and the bed was shaken by her sobbings.

"Mother! mother! mother!" said the child, softly touching her.

"Go away! go away, child! Oh, I wish I had never been born! I wish you had never been born, nor Teddy, nor the baby! It's all nothing but trouble and sor-

row! Fanny, don't you ever marry! Mind what I tell
you!"

The child stood frightened by the bedside, while Tiff
had softly deposited a handful of pine wood near the fire-
place, had taken off the porringer, and was busily stirring
and concocting something in an old cracked china mug. As
he stirred, a strain of indignation seemed to cross his generally tranquil mind, for he often gave short sniffs and grunts,
indicative of extreme disgust, and muttered to himself, —

"Dis yer comes of quality marrying these yer poor white
folks! Never had no 'pinion on it, noway! Ah! do
hear the poor lamb now! 'nough to break one's heart!"

By this time, the stirring and flavoring being finished to
his taste, he came to the side of the bed, and began, in
a coaxing tone, —

"Come, now, Miss Sue, come! You's all worn out!
No wonder! dat ar great fellow tugging at you! Bless his
dear little soul, he's gaining half a pound a week! 'Nough
to pull down his ma entirely! Come, now; take a little
sup of this — just a little sup! Warm you up, and put a
bit of life in you; and den I spects to fry you a morsel
of der chicken, 'cause a boy like dis yer can't be nursed
on slops, dat I knows! Dere, dere, honey!" said he,
gently removing the babe, and passing his arm under the
pillow. "I's drefful strong in the back. My arm is long
and strong, and I'll raise you up just as easy! Take a
good sup on it, now, and wash dese troubles down. I
reckon the good man above is looking down on us all, and
bring us all round right, some time."

The invalid, who seemed exhausted by the burst of feeling to which she had been giving way, mechanically obeyed
a voice to which she had always been accustomed, and
drank eagerly, as if with feverish thirst; and when she
had done, she suddenly threw her arms around the neck
of her strange attendant.

"Oh, Tiff, Tiff! poor old black, faithful Tiff! What should I have done without you? So sick as I've been, and so weak, and so lonesome! But, Tiff, it's coming to an end pretty soon. I've seen, to-night, that I ain't going to live long, and I've been crying to think the children have got to live. If I could only take them all into my arms, and all lie down in the grave together, I should be so glad! I never knew what God made me for! I've never been fit for anything, nor done anything!"

Tiff seemed so utterly overcome by this appeal, his great spectacles were fairly washed down in a flood of tears, and his broad, awkward frame shook with sobs.

"Law bless you, Miss Sue, don't be talking dat ar way! Why, if de Lord *should* call you, Miss Sue, I can take care of the children. I can bring them up powerful, I tell ye! But you *won't* be a-going; you'll get better! It's just the sperits is low; and laws, why should n't dey be?"

Just at this moment a loud barking was heard outside the house, together with the rattle of wheels and the tramp of horses' feet.

"Dar's massa, sure as I'm alive!" said he, hastily laying down the invalid, and arranging her pillows.

A rough voice called, "Hallo, Tiff! here with a light!"

Tiff caught the pine knot, and ran to open the door. A strange-looking vehicle, of a most unexampled composite order, was standing before the door, drawn by a lean, one-eyed horse.

"Here, Tiff, help me out. I've got a lot of goods here. How's Sue?"

"Missis is powerful bad; been wanting to see you dis long time."

"Well, away, Tiff! take this out," indicating a long, rusty piece of stove-pipe.

"Lay this in the house; and here!" handing a cast-iron stove-door, with the latch broken.

"Law, massa, what on arth is the use of dis yer?"

"Don't ask questions, Tiff; work away. Help me out with these boxes."

"What on arth now?" said Tiff to himself, as one rough case after another was disgorged from the vehicle, and landed in the small cabin. This being done, and orders being given to Tiff to look after the horse and equipage, the man walked into the house, with a jolly, slashing air.

"Hallo, bub!" said he, lifting the two-year-old above his head. "Hallo, Fan!" imprinting a kiss on the cheek of his girl. "Hallo, Sis!" coming up to the bed where the invalid lay, and stooping down over her. Her weak, wasted arms were thrown around his neck, and she said, with sudden animation, —

"Oh, you 've come at last! I thought I should die without seeing you!"

"Oh, you ain't a-going to die, Sis! Why, what talk!" said he, chucking her under the chin. "Why, your cheeks are as red as roses!"

"Pa, see the baby!" said little Teddy, who, having climbed over the bed, opened the flannel bundle.

"Ah! Sis, I call that ar a tolerable fair stroke of business! Well, I tell you what, I 've done up a trade now that will set us up and no mistake. Besides which, I 've got something now in my coat-pocket that would raise a dead cat to life, if she was lying at the bottom of a pond, with a stone round her neck! See here! 'Dr. Puffer's Elixir of the Water of Life!' warranted to cure janders, toothache, earache, scrofula, 'spepsia, 'sumption, and everything else that ever I hearn of! A teaspoonful of that ar, morn and night, and in a week you 'll be round agin, as pert as a cricket!"

It was astonishing to see the change which the entrance of this man had wrought on the invalid. All her apprehensions seemed to have vanished. She sat up on the bed, following his every movement with her eyes, and apparently placing full confidence in the new medicine, as if it were the first time that ever a universal remedy had been proposed to her. It must be noticed, however, that Tiff, who had returned, and was building the fire, indulged himself, now and then, when the back of the speaker was turned, by snuffing at him in a particularly contemptuous manner. The man was a thick-set and not ill-looking personage, who might have been forty or forty-five years of age. His eyes, of a clear, lively brown, his close-curling hair, his high forehead, and a certain devil-may-care frankness of expression were traits not disagreeable, and which went some way to account for the partial eagerness with which the eye of the wife followed him.

The history of the pair is briefly told. He was the son of a small farmer of North Carolina. His father, having been so unfortunate as to obtain possession of a few negroes, the whole family became ever after inspired with an intense disgust for all kinds of labor; and John, the oldest son, adopted for himself the ancient and honorable profession of a loafer. To lie idle in the sun in front of some small grog-shop, to attend horse-races, cock-fights, and gander-pullings, to flout out occasionally in a new waistcoat, bought with money which came nobody knew how, were pleasures to him all satisfactory. He was as guiltless of all knowledge of common-school learning as Governor Berkley could desire, and far more clear of religious training than a Mahometan or a Hindoo.

In one of his rambling excursions through the country, he stopped a night at a worn-out and broken-down old plantation, where everything had run down, through many years of mismanagement and waste. There he stayed certain days, playing cards with the equally hopeful son of the place, and ended his performances by running away

one night with the soft-hearted daughter, only fifteen years
of age, and who was full as idle, careless, and untaught
as he.

The family, whom poverty could not teach to forget
their pride, were greatly scandalized at the marriage; and
had there been anything left in the worn-out estate where-
with to portion her, the bride, nevertheless, would have
been portionless. The sole piece of property that went
out with her from the paternal mansion was one who,
having a mind and will of his own, could not be kept from
following her. The girl's mother had come from a distant
branch of one of the most celebrated families in Virginia,
and Tiff had been her servant; and with a heart forever
swelling with the remembrances of the ancestral greatness
of the Peytons, he followed his young mistress in her
mésalliance with long-suffering devotion. He even bowed
his neck so far as to acknowledge for his master a man
whom he considered by position infinitely his inferior; for
Tiff, though crooked and black, never seemed to cherish
the slightest doubt that the whole force of the Peyton
blood coursed through his veins, and that the Peyton honor
was intrusted to his keeping. His mistress was a Peyton,
her children were Peyton children, and even the little
bundle of flannel in the gum-tree cradle was a Peyton;
and as for him, he was Tiff Peyton, and this thought
warmed and consoled him as he followed his poor mistress
during all the steps of her downward course in the world.
On her husband he looked with patronizing, civil contempt.
He wished him well; he thought it proper to put the best
face on all his actions; but in a confidential hour, Tiff
would sometimes raise his spectacles emphatically, and
give it out, as his own private opinion, "dat dere could
not be much 'spected from dat ar 'scription of people!"

In fact, the roving and unsettled nature of John Cripps's
avocations and locations might have justified the old fel-

low's contempt. His industrial career might be defined as comprising a little of everything, and a great deal of nothing. He had begun, successively, to learn two or three trades; had half made a horse-shoe, and spoiled one or two carpenter's planes; had tried his hand at stage-driving; had raised fighting-cocks, and kept dogs for hunting negroes. But he invariably retreated from every one of his avocations, in his own opinion a much-abused man. The last device that had entered his head was suggested by the success of a shrewd Yankee peddler, who, having a lot of damaged and unsalable material to dispose of, talked him into the belief that he possessed yet an undeveloped talent for trade; and poor John Cripps, guiltless of multiplication or addition table, and who kept his cock-fighting accounts on his fingers and by making chalk-marks behind the doors, actually was made to believe that he had at last received his true vocation.

In fact, there was something in the constant restlessness of this mode of life that suited his roving turn; and though he was constantly buying what he could not sell, and losing on all that he did sell, yet somehow he kept up an illusion that he was doing something, because stray coins now and then passed through his pockets, and because the circle of small taverns in which he could drink and loaf was considerably larger. There was one resource which never failed him when all other streams went dry; and that was the unceasing ingenuity and fidelity of the bondman Tiff.

Tiff, in fact, appeared to be one of those comfortable old creatures who retain such a good understanding with all created nature that food never is denied them. Fish would always bite on Tiff's hook when they would n't on anybody's else; so that he was wont confidently to call the nearest stream "Tiff's pork-barrel." Hens always laid eggs for Tiff, and cackled to him confidentially where they were deposited. Turkeys gobbled and strutted for him, and led forth for him broods of downy little ones. All sorts of wild game, squirrels, rabbits, coons, and possums, appeared to come with pleasure and put themselves into his traps and springes; so that, where another man might starve, Tiff would look round him with unctuous satisfaction, contemplating all nature as his larder, where his provisions were wearing fur coats, and walking about on four legs, only for safe keeping till he got ready to eat them. So that Cripps never came home without anticipation of something savory, even although he had drank up his last quarter of a dollar at the tavern. This suited Cripps. He thought Tiff was doing his duty, and occasionally brought him home some unsalable bit of rubbish, by way of testimonial of the sense he entertained of his worth. The spectacles in which Tiff gloried came to him in this manner; and although it might have been made to appear that the glasses were only plain window-glass, Tiff was happily ignorant that they were not the best of convex lenses, and still happier in the fact that his strong, unimpaired eyesight made any glasses at all entirely unnecessary. It was only an aristocratic weakness in Tiff. Spectacles he somehow considered the mark of a gentleman, and an appropriate symbol for one who had "been fetched up in the very fustest families of Old Virginny."

He deemed them more particularly appropriate, as, in addition to his manifold outward duties, he likewise assumed, as the reader has seen, some feminine accomplishments. Tiff could darn a stocking with anybody in the country; he could cut out children's dresses and aprons; he could patch, and he could seam; all which he did with infinite self-satisfaction.

Notwithstanding the many crooks and crosses in his lot, Tiff was, on the whole, a cheery fellow. He had an oily, rollicking fullness of nature, an exuberance of physical satisfaction in existence, that the greatest weight of adversity could only tone down to becoming sobriety. He was on the happiest terms of fellowship with himself; he *liked* himself, he believed in himself; and when nobody else would do it, he would pat himself on his own shoulder, and say, "Tiff, you 're a jolly dog, a fine fellow, and I like you!" He was seldom without a running strain of soliloquy with himself, intermingled with joyous bursts of song and quiet intervals of laughter. On pleasant days Tiff laughed a great deal. He laughed when his beans came up, he laughed when the sun came out after a storm, he laughed for fifty things that you never think of laughing at; and it agreed with him — he throve upon it. In times of trouble and perplexity, Tiff talked to himself, and found a counselor who always kept secrets. On the present occasion it was not without some inward discontent that he took a survey of the remains of one of his best-fatted chickens, which he had been intending to serve up, piecemeal, for his mistress. So he relieved his mind by a little confidential colloquy with himself.

"Dis yer," he said to himself, with a contemptuous inclination toward the newly arrived, "will be for eating like a judgment, I 'pose. Wish, now, I had killed de old gobbler! Good enough for him — raal tough, he is. Dis yer, now, was my primest chicken, and dar she 'll jist sit and see him eat it! Laws, dese yer women! Why, dey does get so sot on husbands! Pity they could n't have something like to be sot on! It jist riles me to see him gobbling down everything, and she a-looking on! Well, here goes," said he, depositing the frying-pan over the coals, in which the chicken was soon fizzling. Drawing out the table, Tiff prepared it for supper. Soon coffee was steaming over the fire, and corn-dodgers baking in the ashes. Meanwhile, John Cripps was busy explaining to his wife the celebrated wares that had so much raised his spirits.

"Well, now, you see, Sue, this yer time I've been up to Raleigh; and I met a fellow there, coming from New York, or New Orleans, or some of them northern states."

"New Orleans is n't a northern state," humbly interposed his wife, "is it?"

"Well, New something! Who the devil cares? Don't you be interrupting me, you Suse!"

Could Cripps have seen the vengeful look which Tiff gave him over the spectacles at this moment, he might have trembled for his supper. But innocent of this, he proceeded with his story.

"You see, this yer fellow had a case of bonnets just the height of the fashion. They come from Paris, the capital of Europe; and he sold them to me for a mere song. Ah, you ought to see 'em! I 'm going to get 'em out. Tiff, hold the candle, here." And Tiff held the burning torch with an air of grim skepticism and disgust, while Cripps hammered and wrenched the top boards off, and displayed to view a portentous array of bonnets, apparently of every obsolete style and fashion of the last fifty years.

"Dem 's fustrate for scarecrows, anyhow!" muttered Tiff.

"Now, what," said Cripps, — "Sue, what do you think I gave for these?"

"I don't know," said she faintly.

"Well, I gave fifteen dollars for the whole box! And there ain't one of these," said he, displaying the most singular specimen on his hand, "that is n't worth from two to five dollars. I shall clear, at least, fifty dollars on that box."

Tiff, at this moment, turned to his frying-pan, and bent over it, soliloquizing as he did so, —

"Anyway, I 's found out one ting, — where de women gets dem roosts of bonnets dey wars at camp-meetings. Laws, dey 's enough to spile a work of grace, dem ar! If

I was to meet one of dem ar of a dark night in a grave-
yard, I should tink I was sent for — not the pleasantest
way of sending, neither. Poor missis! — looking mighty
faint! — Don't wonder! — 'Nough to scarr a weakly woman
into fits!"

"Here, Tiff, help me to open this box. Hold the light,
here. Durned if it don't come off hard! Here's a lot of
shoes and boots I got of the same man. Some on 'em's
mates, and some ain't; but then, I took the lot cheap.
Folks don't always warr both shoes alike. Might like to
warr an odd one, sometimes, ef it's cheap. Now, this yer
parr of boots is lady's gaiters, all complete, 'cept there's
a hole in the lining down by the toe; body ought to be
careful about putting it on, else the foot will slip between
the outside and the lining. Anybody that bears that in
mind — just as nice a pair of gaiters as they'd want!
Bargain, there, for somebody — complete one, too. Then
I've got two or three old bureau drawers that I got cheap
at auction; and I reckon some on 'em will fit the old frame
that I got last year. Got 'em for a mere song."

"Bless you, massa, dat ar old bureau I took for de
chicken-coop! Turkeys' chickens hops in lively."

"Oh, well, scrub it up — 't will answer just as well.
Fit the drawers in. And now, old woman, we will sit
down to supper," said he, planting himself at the table,
and beginning a vigorous onslaught on the fried chicken,
without invitation to any other person present to assist
him.

"Missis can't sit up at the table," said Tiff. "She's
done been sick ever since de baby was born." And Tiff
approached the bed with a nice morsel of chicken which he
had providently preserved on a plate, and which he now
reverently presented on a board, as a waiter, covered with
newspaper.

"Now, do eat, missis; you can't live on looking, noways you can fix it.   Do eat while Tiff gets on de baby's nightgown."

To please her old friend, the woman made a feint of eating, but while Tiff's back was turned to the fire, busied herself with distributing it to the children, who had stood hungrily regarding her, as children will regard what is put on to a sick mother's plate.

"It does me good to see them eat," she said apologetically once, when Tiff, turning round, detected her in the act.

"Ah, missis, maybe! but *you've* got to eat for *two*, now.   What dey eat ain't going to dis yer little man, here.   Mind dat ar."

Cripps apparently bestowed very small attention on anything except the important business before him, which he prosecuted with such devotion that very soon coffee, chicken, and dodgers had all disappeared.   Even the bones were sucked dry, and the gravy wiped from the dish.

"Ah, that's what I call comfortable!" said he, lying back in his chair.   "Tiff, pull my boots off! and hand out that ar demijohn.   Sue, I hope you've made a comfortable meal," he said incidentally, standing with his back to her, compounding his potation of whiskey and water; which having drank, he called up Teddy, and offered him the sugar at the bottom of the glass.   But Teddy, being forewarned by a meaning glance through Tiff's spectacles, responded, very politely, —

"No, I thank you, pa.   I don't love it."

"Come here, then, and take it off like a man.   It's good for you," said John Cripps.

The mother's eyes followed the child wishfully; and she said faintly, "Don't John! — don't!"   And Tiff ended the controversy by taking the glass unceremoniously out of his master's hand.

"Laws bless you, massa, can't be bodered with dese yer

young ones dis yer time of night! Time dey 's all in bed,
and dishes washed up. Here, Tedd," seizing the child,
and loosening the buttons of his slip behind, and drawing
out a rough trundle-bed, "you crawl in dere, and curl up
in your nest; and don't you forget your prars, honey, else
maybe you 'll never wake up again."

Cripps had now filled a pipe with tobacco of the most
villainous character, with which incense he was perfuming
the little apartment.

"Laws, massa, dat ar smoke ain't good for missis," said
Tiff. "She done been sick to her stomach all day."

"Oh, let him smoke! I like to have him enjoy himself," said the indulgent wife. "But, Fanny, you had
better go to bed, dear. Come here and kiss me, child;
good-night, — good-night!"

The mother held on to her long, and looked at her wishfully; and when she had turned to go, she drew her back,
and kissed her again, and said, "Good-night, dear child,
good-night!"

Fanny climbed up a ladder in one corner of the room,
through a square hole, to the loft above.

"I say," said Cripps, taking his pipe out of his mouth,
and looking at Tiff, who was busy washing the dishes, "I
say it 's kind of peculiar that gal keeps sick so. Seemed
to have good constitution when I married her. I 'm thinking," said he, without noticing the gathering wrath in
Tiff's face, "I 'm a-thinking whether steamin' would n't
do her good. Now, I got a most dreadful cold when I
was up at Raleigh — thought I should have given up; and
there was a steam-doctor there. Had a little kind of machine, with kettle and pipes, and he put me in a bed, put
in the pipes, and set it a-going. I thought, my soul, I
should have been floated off; but it carried off the cold,
complete. I 'm thinking if something of that kind
would n't be good for Mis' Cripps."

"Laws, massa, don't go for to trying it on her! She is never no better for dese yer things you do for her."

"Now," said Cripps, not appearing to notice the interruption, "these yer stove-pipes, and the teakettle, — I should n't wonder if we could get up a steam with them!"

"It 's my private 'pinion, if you do, she 'll be sailing out of the world," said Tiff. " 'What 's one man's meat is another one's pisin,' my old mis's used to say. Very best thing you can do for her is to let her alone. Dat ar is my 'pinion."

"John," said the little woman, after a few minutes, "I wish you 'd come here, and sit on the bed."

There was something positive, and almost authoritative, in the manner in which this was said, which struck John as so unusual, that he came with a bewildered air, sat down, and gazed at her with his mouth wide open.

"I 'm so glad you 've come home, because I have had things that I 've wanted to say to you! I 've been lying here thinking about it, and I have been turning it over in my mind. I 'm going to die soon, I know."

"Ah! bah! Don't be bothering a fellow with any of your hysterics!"

"John, John! it is n't hysterics! Look at me! Look at my hand! look at my face! I 'm so weak, and sometimes I have such coughing spells, and every time it seems to me as if I should die. But it ain't to trouble you that I talk. I don't care about myself, but I don't want the children to grow up and be like what we 've been. You have a great many contrivances; do, pray, contrive to have them taught to read, and make something of them in the world."

"Bah! what 's the use? I never learnt to read, and I 'm as good a fellow as I want. Why, there 's plenty of men round here making their money, every year, that can't read or write a word. Old Hubell, there, up on the

Shad plantation, has hauled in money, hand over hand, and he always signs his mark. Got nine sons — can't a soul of them read or write, more than I. I tell you, there's nothing ever comes of this yer larning. It's all a sell — a regular Yankee hoax! I've always got cheated by them damn reading, writing Yankees, whenever I've traded with 'em. What's the good, I want to know! You was teached how to read when you was young — much good it's ever done you!"

"Sure enough! Sick day and night, moving about from place to place, sick baby crying, and not knowing what to do for it no more than a child! Oh, I hope Fanny will learn something! It seems to me, if there was some school for my children to go to, or some church, or something — now, *if there is* any such place as heaven, I should like to have them get to it."

"Ah! bah! Don't bother about that! When we get keeled up, that will be the last of us! Come, come, don't plague a fellow any more with such talk! I'm tired, and I'm going to sleep." And the man, divesting himself of his overcoat, threw himself on the bed, and was soon snoring heavily in profound slumber.

Tiff, who had been trotting the baby by the fire, now came softly to the bedside, and sat down.

"Miss Sue," he said, "it's no 'count talking to him! I don't mean nothing dis'pectful, Miss Sue, but de fac is, dem dat isn't *born* gentlemen can't be 'spected fur to see through dese yer things like us of de old families. Law, missis, don't you worry! Now, jest leave dis yer matter to old Tiff! Dere never wasn't anything Tiff couldn't do, if he tried. He! he! he! Miss Fanny, she done got de letters right smart; and I know I'll come it round mas'r, and make him buy de books for her. I'll tell you what's come into my head, to-day. There's a young lady come to de big plantation, up dere, who's been to New

York getting edicated, and I's going for to ask her about dese yer things. And about de chil'en's going to church, and dese yer things, why, preaching, you know, is mazin' unsartain round here; but I'll keep on de lookout, and do de best I can. Why, Lord, Miss Sue, I's bound for the land of Canaan, myself, the best way I ken; and I'm sartain I sha'n't go without taking the chil'en along with me. Ho! ho! ho! Dat's what I sha'n't! De chil'en will have to be with Tiff, and Tiff will have to be with the chil'en, wherever dey is! Dat's it! He! he! he!"

"Tiff," said the young woman, her large blue eyes looking at him, "I have heard of the Bible. Have you ever seen one, Tiff?"

"Oh yes, honey, dar was a big Bible that your ma brought in the family when she married; but dat ar was tore up to make wadding for de guns, one thing or another, and dey never got no more. But I's been very 'serving, and kept my ears open in a camp-meeting, and such places, and I's learnt right smart of de things that's in it."

"Now, Tiff, can you say anything?" said she, fixing her large, troubled eyes on him.

"Well, honey, dere's one thing the man said at de last camp-meeting. He preached 'bout it, and I couldn't make out a word he said, 'cause I ain't smart about preaching like I be about most things. But he said dis yer so often that I couldn't help 'member it. Says he, it was dish yer way: 'Come unto me, all ye that labor and are heavy laden, and I will give you rest.'"

"Rest, rest, rest!" said the woman thoughtfully, and drawing a long sigh. "Oh, how much I want it! Did he say that was in the Bible?"

"Yes, he said so; and I spects, by all he said, it's de good man above dat says it. It always makes me feel better to think on it. It 'peared like it was jist what I was wanting to hear."

"And I, too!" she said, turning her head wearily, and closing her eyes. "Tiff," she said, opening them, "where I'm going, maybe I shall meet the one who said that, and I'll ask him about it. Don't talk to me more, now. I'm getting sleepy. I thought I was better a little while after he came home, but I'm more tired yet. Put the baby in my arms — I like the feeling of it. There, there; now give me rest — *please* do!" and she sank into a deep and quiet slumber.

Tiff softly covered the fire, and sat down by the bed, watching the flickering shadows as they danced upward on the wall, listening to the heavy sighs of the pine-trees and the hard breathing of the sleeping man. Sometimes he nodded sleepily, and then, recovering, rose, and took a turn to awaken himself. A shadowy sense of fear fell upon him; not that he apprehended anything, for he regarded the words of his mistress only as the forebodings of a wearied invalid. The idea that she could actually die, and go anywhere, without him to take care of her, seemed never to have occurred to him. About midnight, as if a spirit had laid its hand upon him, his eyes flew wide open with a sudden start. Her thin, cold hand was lying on his; her eyes, large and blue, shone with a singular and spiritual radiance.

"Tiff," she gasped, speaking with difficulty, "I've seen the one that said *that*, and it's all true, too! and I've seen all why I've suffered so much. He — He — He is going to take me! Tell the children about Him!" There was a fluttering sigh, a slight shiver, and the lids fell over the eyes forever.

CHAPTER IX

THE DEATH

DEATH is always sudden. However gradual may be its approaches, it is, in its effects upon the survivor, always sudden at last. Tiff thought, at first, that his mistress was in a fainting-fit, and tried every means to restore her. It was affecting to see him chafing the thin, white, pearly hands, in his large, rough, black paws; raising the head upon his arm, and calling in a thousand tones of fond endearment, pouring out a perfect torrent of loving devotion on the cold, unheeding ear. But then, spite of all he could do, the face settled itself, and the hands would not be warmed; the thought of death struck him suddenly, and throwing himself on the floor by the bed, he wept with an exceeding loud and bitter cry. Something in his heart revolted against awakening that man who lay heavily breathing by her side. He would not admit to himself, at this moment, that this man had any right in her, or that the sorrow was any part of his sorrow. But the cry awoke Cripps, who sat up bewildered in bed, clearing the hair from his eyes with the back of his hand.

"Tiff, what the durned are you howling about?"

Tiff got up in a moment, and swallowing down his grief and his tears, pointed indignantly to the still figure on the bed.

"Dar! dar! Would n't b'lieve her last night! Now what you think of dat ar? See how you look now! Good Shepherd hearn you abusing de poor lamb, and he's done took her whar you 'll never see her again!"

Cripps had, like coarse, animal men generally, a stupid
and senseless horror of death; — he recoiled from the lifeless form, and sprang from the bed with an expression of
horror.

"Well, now, who would have thought it?" he said.
"That I should be in bed with a corpse! I hadn't the
least idea!"

"No, dat's plain enough, you didn't! You'll believe
it now, won't you? Poor little lamb, lying here suffering all alone! I tell you, when folks have been sick so
long, dey has to die to make folks believe anything ails
'em!"

"Well, really," said Cripps, "this is really — why, it
ain't comfortable! darned if it is! Why, I'm sorry about
the gal! I meant to steam her up, or done something
with her. What's we to do now?"

"Pretty likely you don't know! Folks like you, dat
never tends to nothing good, is always flustered when de
Master knocks at de do'! *I* knows what to do, though.
I's boun' to get up de crittur, and go up to de old plantation, and bring down a woman and do something for her,
kind of decent. You mind the chil'en till I come back."

Tiff took down and drew on over his outer garment a
coarse, light, woolen coat, with very long skirts and large
buttons, in which he always arrayed himself in cases of
special solemnity. Stopping at the door before he went
out, he looked over Cripps from head to foot, with an air
of patronizing and half-pitiful contempt, and delivered
himself as follows: —

"Now, mas'r, I's gwine up, and will be back quick as
possible; and now do pray be decent, and let dat ar whiskey alone for one day in your life, and 'member death,
judgment, and 'ternity. Just act, now, as if you'd got a
streak of something in you such as a man ought for to
have who is married to one of de very fustest families in

old Virginny. 'Flect, now, on your latter end; maybe will do your poor old soul some good; and don't you go for to waking up the chil'en before I gets back. They 'll learn de trouble soon enough."

Cripps listened to this oration with a stupid, bewildered stare, gazing first at the bed, and then at the old man, who was soon making all the speed he could towards Canema.

Nina was not habitually an early riser, but on this morning she had awaked with the first peep of dawn, and finding herself unable to go to sleep again, she had dressed herself, and gone down to the garden. She was walking up and down in one of the alleys, thinking over the perplexities of her own affairs, when her ear was caught by the wild and singular notes of one of those tunes commonly used among the slaves as dirges. The words "She ar dead and gone to heaven" seemed to come floating down upon her; and though the voice was cracked and strained, there was a sort of wildness and pathos in it, which made a singular impression in the perfect stillness of everything around her. She soon observed a singular-looking vehicle appearing in the avenue.

This wagon, which was no other than the establishment of Cripps, drew Nina's attention, and she went to the hedge to look at it. Tiff's watchful eye immediately fell upon her, and driving up to where she was standing, he climbed out upon the ground, and lifting his hat, made her a profound obeisance, and "hoped de young lady was bery well, dis morning."

"Yes, quite well, thank you, uncle," said Nina, regarding him curiously.

"We's in 'fliction to our house!" said Tiff solemnly. "Dere's been a midnight cry dere, and poor Miss Sue (dat's my young missis), she's done gone home."

"Who is your mistress?"

"Well, her name *was* Seymour 'fore she married, and her ma come from de Virginny Peytons, — great family, dem Peytons! She was so misfortunate as to get married, as gals will, sometimes," said Tiff, speaking in a confidential tone. "The man wa'n't no 'count, and she's had a drefful hard way to travel, poor thing! and dere she's a-lying at last stretched out dead, and not a woman nor nobody to do de least thing; and please, missis, Tiff comed for to see if de young lady would n't send a woman for to do for her — getting her ready for a funeral."

"And who are you, pray?"

"Please, missis, I's Tiff Peyton, I is. I's raised in Virginny, on de great Peyton place, and I's gin to Miss Sue's mother; and when Miss Sue married dis yer man, dey was all 'fended, and would n't speak to her; but I tuck up for her, 'cause what's de use of makin' a bad thing worse? I's a 'pinion, and telled 'em, dat he oughter be 'couraged to behave hisself, seein' the thing was done, and could n't be helped. But no, dey would n't; so I jest tells 'em, says I, ' You may do jis you please, but old Tiff's a-gwine with her,' says I. ' I'll follow Miss Sue to de grave's mouth,' says I; and ye see I has done it."

"Well done of you! I like you better for it," said Nina. "You just drive up to the kitchen, there, and tell Rose to give you some breakfast, while I go up to Aunt Nesbit."

"No, thank you, Miss Nina, I's noways hungry. 'Pears like, when a body's like as I be, swallerin' down, and all de old times risin' in der throat all de time, dey can't eat; dey gets filled all up to der eyes with feelin's. Lord, Miss Nina, I hope ye won't never know what 't is to stand outside de gate, when de best friend you've got 's gone in; it's hard, dat ar is!" And Tiff pulled out a decayed-looking handkerchief, and applied it under his spectacles.

"Well, wait a minute, Tiff." And Nina ran into the house, while Tiff gazed mournfully after her.

"Well, Lor; just de way Miss Sue used to run — trip, trip, trip! — little feet like mice! Lord's will be done!"

"Oh, Milly!" said Nina, meeting Milly in the entry, "here you are. Here's a poor fellow waiting out by the hedge, his mistress dead all alone in the house, with children, — no woman to do for them. Can't you go down? you could do so well! You know how better than any one else in the house."

"Why, that must be poor old Tiff!" said Milly; "faithful old creature! So that poor woman's gone, at last? the better for her, poor soul! Well, I'll ask Miss Loo if I may go — or you ask her, Miss Nina."

A quick, imperative tap on her door startled Aunt Nesbit, who was standing at her toilet, finishing her morning's dressing operations.

Mrs. Nesbit was a particularly systematic early riser. Nobody knew why; only folks who have nothing to do are often the most particular to have the longest possible time to do it in.

"Aunt," said Nina, "there's a poor fellow, out here, whose mistress is just dead, all alone in the house, and wants to get some woman to go there to help. Can't you spare Milly?"

"Milly was going to clear-starch my caps, this morning," said Aunt Nesbit. "I have arranged everything with reference to it, for a week past."

"Well, aunt, can't she do it to-morrow, or next day, just as well?"

"To-morrow she is going to rip up that black dress, and wash it. I am always systematic, and have everything arranged beforehand. Should like very much to do anything I could, if it wasn't for that. Why can't you send Aunt Katy?"

"Why, aunt, you know we are to have company to dinner, and Aunt Katy is the only one who knows where anything is, or how to serve things out to the cook. Besides, she 's so hard and cross to poor people, I don't think she would go. I don't see, I 'm sure, in such a case as this, why you could n't put your starching off. Milly is such a kind, motherly, experienced person, and they are in affliction."

"Oh, these low families don't mind such things much," said Aunt Nesbit, fitting on her cap quietly; "they never have much feeling. There 's no use doing for them — they are miserable poor creatures."

"Aunt Nesbit, do, now, as a favor to me! I don't often ask favors," said Nina. "*Do* let Milly go! she 's just the one wanted. Do, now, say yes!" And Nina pressed nearer, and actually seemed to overpower her slow-feeling, torpid relative with the vehemence that sparkled in her eyes.

"Well, I don't care, if " —

"There, Milly, she says yes!" said she, springing out the door. "She says you may. Now, hurry; get things ready. I 'll run and have Aunt Katy put up biscuits and things for the children; and you get all that you know you will want, and be off quick, and I 'll have the pony got up, and come on behind you."

CHAPTER X

THE PREPARATION

THE excitement produced by the arrival of Tiff, and the fitting out of Milly to the cottage, had produced a most favorable diversion in Nina's mind from her own especial perplexities. Active and buoyant, she threw herself at once into whatever happened to come uppermost on the tide of events. So, having seen the wagon dispatched, she sat down to breakfast in high spirits.

"Aunt Nesbit, I declare I was so interested in that old man! I intend to have the pony, after breakfast, and ride over there."

"I thought you were expecting company."

"Well, that's one reason, now, why I'd like to be off. Do I want to sit all primmed up, smiling and smirking, and running to the window to see if my gracious lord is coming? No, I won't do that, to please any of them. If I happen to fancy to be out riding, I *will* be out riding."

"I think," said Aunt Nesbit, "that the hovels of these miserable creatures are no proper place for a young lady of your position in life."

"My position in life! I don't see what that has to do with it. My position in life enables me to do anything I please — a liberty which I take pretty generally. And then, really, I couldn't help feeling rather sadly about it, because that Old Tiff, there (I believe that's his name), told me that the woman had been of a good Virginia family. Very likely she may have been just such another wild girl as I am, and thought as little about bad times, and of dying, as I do. So I could n't help feeling sad for her. It really came over me when I was walking in the garden. Such a beautiful morning as it was — the birds all singing, and the dew all glittering and shining on the flowers! Why, aunt, the flowers really seemed alive; it seemed as though I could hear them breathing, and hear their hearts beating like mine. And, all of a sudden, I heard the most wild, mournful singing, over in the woods. It was n't anything very beautiful, you know, but it was so wild, and strange! 'She is dead and gone to heaven! — she is dead and gone to heaven!' And pretty soon I saw the funniest old wagon — I don't know what to call it — and this queer old black man in it, with an old white hat and surtout on, and a pair of great, funny-looking spectacles on his nose. I went to the fence to see who he was; and he came up and spoke to me, made the most respectful bow — you ought to have seen it! And then, poor fellow, he told me how his mistress was lying dead, with the children around her, and nobody in the house! The poor old creature, he actually cried, and I felt so for him! He seemed to be proud of his dead mistress, in spite of her poverty."

"Where do they live?" said Mrs. Nesbit.

"Why, he told me over in the pine woods, near the swamp."

"Oh," said Mrs. Nesbit, "I dare say it's that Cripps family, that's squatted in the pine woods. A most miserable set — all of them liars and thieves! If I had known who it was, I'm sure I should n't have let Milly go over. Such families ought n't to be encouraged; there ought n't a thing to be done for them; we should n't encourage them to stay in the neighborhood. They always will steal from off the plantations, and corrupt the negroes, and get drunk, and everything else that's bad. There's never a woman of decent character among them, that ever I heard of; and if you were my daughter, I should n't let you go near them."

"Well, I 'm not your daughter, thank fortune!" said Nina, whose graces always rapidly declined in controversies with her aunt, "and so I shall do as I please. And I don't know what you pious people talk so for; for Christ went with publicans and sinners, I 'm sure."

"Well," said Aunt Nesbit, "the Bible says we must n't cast pearls before swine; and when you 've lived to be as old as I am, you 'll know more than you do now. Everybody knows that you can't do anything with these people. You can't give them Bibles nor tracts, for they can't read. I 've tried it, sometimes, visiting them, and talking to them; but it did n't do them any good. I always thought there ought to be a law passed to make 'em all slaves, and then there would be somebody to take care of them."

"Well, I can't see," said Nina, "how it 's their fault. There is n't any school where they could send their children, if they wanted to learn; and then, if they want to work, there 's nobody who wants to hire them. So what can they do?"

"I 'm sure I don't know," said Aunt Nesbit, in that tone which generally means "I don't care." "All I know is, that I want them to get away from the neighborhood. Giving to them is just like putting into a bag with holes. I 'm sure I put myself to a great inconvenience on their account to-day; for if there 's anything I do hate, it is having things irregular. And to-day is the day for clear-starching the caps — and such a good, bright, sunny day! — and to-morrow, or any other day of the week, it may rain. Always puts me all out to have things that I 've laid out to do put out of their regular order. I 'd been willing enough to have sent over some old things; but why they must needs take Milly's time, just as if the funeral could n't have got ready without her! These fu-

nerals are always miserable drunken times with them!
And then, who knows, she may catch the smallpox, or
something or other. There's never any knowing what
these people die of."

"They die of just such things as we do," said Nina.
"They have that in common with us, at any rate."

"Yes; but there's no reason for risking our lives, as I
know of — especially for such people — when it don't do
any good."

"Why, aunt, what do you know against these folks?
Have you ever known of their doing anything wicked?"

"Oh, I don't know that I know anything against this
family in particular; but I know the whole race. These
squatters — I've known them ever since I was a girl in
Virginia. Everybody that knows anything knows exactly
what they are. There isn't any help for them, unless, as
I said before, they were made slaves; and then they could
be kept decent. You may go to see them, if you like,
but *I* don't want my arrangements to be interfered with on
their account."

Mrs. Nesbit was one of those quietly persisting people
whose yielding is like the stretching of an india-rubber
band, giving way only to a violent pull, and going back to
the same place when the force is withdrawn. She seldom
refused favors that were urged with any degree of impor-
tunity; not because her heart was touched, but simply because she seemed not to have force enough to refuse; and
whatever she granted was always followed by a series of
subdued lamentations over the necessity which had wrung
them from her.

Nina's nature was so vehement and imperious, when
excited, that it was a disagreeable fatigue to cross her.
Mrs. Nesbit, therefore, made amends by bemoaning herself
as we have seen. Nina started up hastily, on seeing her
pony brought round to the door; and soon arrayed in her

riding-dress, she was cantering through the pine woods in high spirits. The day was clear and beautiful. The floor of the woodland path was paved with a thick and cleanly carpet of the fallen pine leaves. And Harry was in attendance with her, mounted on another horse, and riding but a very little behind; not so much so but what his mistress could, if she would, keep up a conversation with him.

"You know this Old Tiff, Harry?"

"Oh yes, very well. A very good, excellent creature, and very much the superior of his master, in most respects."

"Well, he says his mistress came of a good family."

"I shouldn't wonder," said Harry. "She always had a delicate appearance, very different from people in their circumstances generally. The children, too, are remarkably pretty, well-behaved children; and it's a pity they couldn't be taught something, and not grow up and go on the miserable ways of these poor whites!"

"Why don't anybody ever teach them?" said Nina.

"Well, Miss Nina, you know how it is: everybody has his own work and business to attend to — there are no schools for them to go to — there's no work for them to do. In fact, there don't seem to be any place for them in society. Boys generally grow up to drink and swear. And as for girls, they are of not much account. So it goes on from generation to generation."

"This is so strange, and so different from what it is in the northern states! Why, all the children go to school there — the very poorest people's children! Why, a great many of the first men, there, were poor children! Why can't there be some such thing here?"

"Oh, because people are settled in such a scattering way they can't have schools. All the land that's good for anything is taken up for large estates. And then, these poor folks that are scattered up and down in between, it's nobody's business to attend to them, and they can't attend to themselves; and so they grow up, and nobody knows how they live, and everybody seems to think it a pity they are in the world. I've seen those sometimes that would be glad to do something, if they could find anything to do. Planters don't want them on their places — they'd rather have their own servants. If one of them wants to be a blacksmith, or a carpenter, there's no encouragement. Most of the large estates have their own carpenters and blacksmiths. And there's nothing for them to do, unless it is keeping dogs to hunt negroes; or these little low stores where they sell whiskey, and take what's stolen from the plantations. Sometimes a smart one gets a place as overseer on a plantation. Why, I've heard of their coming so low as actually to sell their children to traders, to get a bit of bread."

"What miserable creatures! But do you suppose it can be possible that a woman of any respectable family can have married a man of this sort?"

"Well, I don't know, Miss Nina; that might be. You see, good families sometimes degenerate; and when they get too poor to send their children off to school, or keep any teachers for them, they run down very fast. This man is not bad looking, and he really is a person who, if he had had any way opened to him, might have been a smart man, and made something of himself and family; and when he was young and better looking, I should n't wonder if an uneducated girl, who had never been off a plantation, might have liked him; he was fully equal, I dare say, to her brothers. You see, Miss Nina, when money goes, in this part of the country, everything goes with it; and when a family is not rich enough to have everything in itself, it goes down very soon."

"At any rate, I pity the poor things," said Nina. "I don't despise them, as Aunt Nesbit does."

Here Nina, observing the path clear and uninterrupted
for some distance under the arching pines, struck her horse
into a canter, and they rode on for some distance without
speaking. Soon the horse's feet splashed and pattered on
the cool, pebbly bottom of a small, shallow stream, which
flowed through the woods. This stream went meandering
among the pines like a spangled ribbon, sometimes tying
itself into loops, leaving open spots — almost islands of
green — graced by its waters. Such a little spot now
opened to the view of the two travelers. It was something less than a quarter of an acre in extent, entirely
surrounded by the stream, save only a small neck of about
four feet, which connected it to the mainland.

Here a place had been cleared and laid off into a garden,
which, it was evident, was carefully tended. The log
cabin which stood in the middle was far from having the
appearance of wretchedness which Nina had expected. It
was almost entirely a dense mass of foliage, being covered
with the intermingled drapery of the Virginia creeper and
the yellow jessamine. Two little borders, each side of the
house, were blooming with flowers. Around the little
island the pine-trees closed in unbroken semicircle, and
the brook meandered away through them, to lose itself
eventually in that vast forest of swampy land which girdles
the whole Carolina shore. The whole air of the place was
so unexpectedly inviting, in its sylvan stillness and beauty,
that Nina could not help checking her horse, and exclaiming, —

"I'm sure, it's a pretty place. They can't be such
very forsaken people, after all."

"Oh, that's all Tiff's work," said Harry. "He takes
care of everything outside and in, while the man is off
after nobody knows what. You'd be perfectly astonished
to see how that old creature manages. He sews, and he
knits, and works the garden, does the housework, and

teaches the children. It's a fact! You'll notice that
they haven't the pronunciation or the manners of these
wild white children; and I take it to be all Tiff's watch-
fulness, for that creature hasn't one particle of selfishness
in him. He just identifies himself with his mistress and
her children."

By this time Tiff had perceived their approach, and
came out to assist them in dismounting.

"De Lord above bless you, Miss Gordon, for coming to
see my poor missis! Ah! she is lying dere just as beautiful, just as she was the very day she was married! All
her young looks come back to her; and Milly, she done
laid her out beautiful! Lord, I's wanting somebody to
come and look at her, because she has got good blood, if she
be poor. She is none of your common sort of poor whites,
Miss Nina. Just come in; come in, and look at her."

Nina stepped into the open door of the hut. The bed
was covered with a clean white sheet, and the body,
arrayed in a long white night-dress brought by Milly, lay
there so very still, quiet, and lifelike, that one could
scarcely realize the presence of death. The expression of
exhaustion, fatigue, and anxiety, which the face had lat-
terly worn, had given place to one of tender rest, shaded
by a sort of mysterious awe, as if the closed eyes were
looking on unutterable things. The soul, though sunk
below the horizon of existence, had thrown back a twilight
upon the face radiant as that of the evening heavens.

By the head of the bed the little girl was sitting, dressed
carefully, and her curling hair parted in front, apparently
fresh from the brush; and the little boy was sitting beside
her, his round blue eyes bearing an expression of subdued
wonder.

Cripps was sitting at the foot of the bed, evidently
much the worse for liquor; for spite of the exhortation of
Tiff, he had applied to the whiskey-jug immediately on

his departure. Why not? He was uncomfortable — gloomy; and every one, under such circumstances, naturally inclines towards *some* source of consolation. He who is intellectual reads and studies; he who is industrious flies to business; he who is affectionate seeks friends; he who is pious, religion; but he who is none of these — what has he but his whiskey? Cripps made a stupid, staring inclination toward Nina and Harry, as they entered, and sat still, twirling his thumbs and muttering to himself.

The sunshine fell through the panes on the floor, and there came floating in from without the odor of flowers and the song of birds. All the Father's gentle messengers spoke of comfort; but he as a deaf man heard not — as a blind man did not regard. For the rest, an air of neatness had been imparted to the extreme poverty of the room by the joint efforts of Milly and Tiff.

Tiff entered softly, and stood by Nina, as she gazed. He had in his hand several sprays of white jessamine, and he laid one on the bosom of the dead.

"She had a hard walk of it," he said, "but she's got home! Don't she look peaceful? — poor lamb!"

The little, thoughtless, gay coquette had never looked on a sight like this before. She stood with a fixed, tender thoughtfulness, unlike her usual gayety, her riding-hat hanging carelessly by its strings from her hands, her loose hair drooping over her face. She heard some one entering the cottage, but she did not look up. She was conscious of some one looking over her shoulder, and thought it was Harry.

"Poor thing! how young she looks," she said, "to have had so much trouble!" Her voice trembled, and a tear stood in her eye. There was a sudden movement; she looked up, and Clayton was standing by her.

She looked surprised, and the color deepened in her cheek, but was too ingenuously and really in sympathy with the scene before her even to smile. She retained his hand a moment, and turned to the dead, saying, in an undertone, "See here!"

"I see," he said. "Can I be of service?"

"The poor thing died last night," said Nina. "I suppose some one might help about a funeral. Harry," she said, walking softly towards the door, and speaking low, "you provide a coffin; have it made neatly."

"Uncle," she said, motioning Tiff towards her, "where would they have her buried?"

"Buried?" said Tiff. "O Lord! buried!" And he covered his face with his hard hands, and the tears ran through his fingers.

"Lord, Lord! Well, it must come, I know, but 'pears like I couldn't! Laws, she's so beautiful! Don't, to-day! don't!"

"Indeed, uncle," said Nina tenderly, "I'm sorry I grieved you; but you know, poor fellow, that must come."

"I's known her ever since she's dat high!" said Tiff. "Her har was curly, and she used to war such pretty red shoes, and come running after me in de garden. 'Tiff, Tiff,' she used to say — and dar she is now, and troubles brought her dar! Lord, what a pretty gal she was! Pretty as you be, Miss Nina. But since she married *dat ar*," pointing with his thumb over his shoulder, and speaking confidentially, "everything went wrong. I's held her up — did all I could; and now here she is!"

"Perhaps," said Nina, laying her hand on his, "perhaps she's in a better place than this."

"Oh, Lord, dat she is! She told me dat when she died. She saw de Lord at last, — she did so! Dem's her last words. 'Tiff,' she says, 'I see Him, and He will give me rest. Tiff,' she says, — I'd been asleep, you know, and I kinder felt something cold on my hand, and I woke up right sudden, and dar she was, her eyes so bright, look-

ing at me and breathing so hard; and all she says was,
'Tiff, I've seen Him, and I know now why I've suffered
so; He's gwine to take me, and give me rest!'"

"Then, my poor fellow, you ought to rejoice that she is
safe."

"'Deed I does," said Tiff; "yet I's selfish. I wants
to be dere too, I does — only I has de chil'en to care for."

"Well, my good fellow," said Nina, "we must leave
you now. Harry will see about a coffin for your poor
mistress; and whenever the funeral is to be, our carriage
will come over, and we will all attend."

"Lord bless you, Miss Gordon! Dat ar too good on
ye! My heart's been most broke, tinking nobody cared
for my poor young mistress! you's too good, dat you is!"

Then drawing near to her, and sinking his voice, he
said: "'Bout de mourning, Miss Nina. *He* ain't no
'count, you know — body can see how 't is with him very
plain. But missis was a Peyton, you know; and I's a
Peyton, too. I naturally feels a 'sponsibility he couldn't
be 'spected fur to. I's took de ribbons off of Miss
Fanny's bonnet, and done de best I could trimming it up
with black crape what Milly gave me; and I's got a band
of black crape on Master Teddy's hat; and I 'lowed to put
one on mine, but there wasn't quite enough. You know,
missis, old family servants always wars mourning. If
missis just be pleased to look over my work! Now, dis
yer is Miss Fanny's bonnet. You know I can't be 'spected
for to make it like a milliner."

"They are very well indeed, Uncle Tiff."

"Perhaps, Miss Nina, you can kind of touch it over."

"Oh, if you like, Uncle Tiff, I'll take them all home,
and do them for you."

"The Lord bless you, Miss Gordon! Dat ar was just
what I wanted, but was most 'fraid to ask you. Some
gay young ladies doesn't like to handle black."

"Ah! Uncle Tiff, I've no fears of that sort; so put it in the wagon, and let Milly take it home." So saying, she turned and passed out of the door where Harry was standing holding the horses. A third party might have seen, by the keen, rapid glance with which his eye rested upon Clayton, that he was measuring the future probability which might make him the arbiter of his own destiny — the disposer of all that was dear to him in life. As for Nina, although the day before a thousand fancies and coquetries would have colored the manner of her meeting Clayton, yet now she was so impressed by what she had witnessed, that she scarcely appeared to know that she had met him. She placed her pretty foot on his hand, and let him lift her on to the saddle, scarcely noticing the act, except by a serious, graceful inclination of her head.

One great reason of the ascendency which Clayton had thus far gained over her was that his nature, so quiet, speculative, and undemonstrative, always left her such perfect liberty to follow the more varying moods of her own. A man of a different mould would have sought to awake her out of the trance — would have remarked on her abstracted manner, or rallied her on her silence. Clayton merely mounted his horse and rode quietly by her side, while Harry, passing on before them, was soon out of sight.

CHAPTER XI

THEY rode on in silence, till their horses' feet again clattered in the clear, pebbly water of the stream. Here Nina checked her horse, and pointing round the circle of pine forests, and up the stream, overhung with bending trees and branches, said: —

"Hush! — listen!" Both stopped, and heard the swaying of the pine-trees, the babble of the waters, the cawing of distant crows, and the tapping of the woodpecker.

"How beautiful everything is!" she said. "It seems to me so sad that people must die! I never saw anybody dead before, and you don't know how it makes me feel! To think that that poor woman was just such a girl as I am, and used to be just so full of life, and never thought any more than I do that she should lie there all cold and dead! Why is it things are made so beautiful, if we must die?"

"Remember what you said to the old man, Miss Nina. Perhaps she sees more beautiful things now."

"In heaven? Yes; I wish we knew more about heaven, so that it would seem natural and homelike to us, as this world does. As for me, I can't feel that I ever want to leave this world — I enjoy living so much! I can't forget how cold her hand was! I never felt anything like that cold!"

In all the varying moods of Nina, Clayton had never seen anything that resembled this. But he understood the peculiar singleness and earnestness of nature which made any one idea, or impression, for a time absolute in her mind.   They turned their horses into the woodpath, and rode on in silence.

"Do you know," said she, "it's such a change coming from New York to live here?   Everything is so unformed, so wild, and so lonely!   I never saw anything so lonesome as these woods are.   Here you can ride miles and miles, hours and hours, and hear nothing but the swaying of the pine-trees, just as you hear it now.   Our place (you never were there, were you?) stands all by itself, miles from any other; and I've been for so many years used to a thickly settled country that it seems very strange to me.   I can't help thinking things look rather deserted and desolate, here.   It makes me rather sober and sad.   I don't know as you'll like the appearance of our place.   A great many things are going to decay about it; and yet there are some things that can't decay; for papa was very fond of trees and shrubbery, and we have a good deal more of them than usual.   Are you fond of trees?"

"Yes; I'm almost a tree-worshiper.   I have no respect for a man who can't appreciate a tree.   The only good thing I ever heard of Xerxes was, that he was so transported with the beauty of a plane-tree, that he hung it with chains of gold.   This is a little poetical island in the barbarism of those days."

"Xerxes!" said Nina.   "I believe I studied something about him in that dismal, tedious history at Mme. Ardaine's; but nothing so interesting as that, I'm sure.   But what should he hang gold chains on a tree for?"

"'T was the best way he knew of expressing his good opinion."

"Do you know," said Nina, half checking her horse suddenly, "that I never had the least idea that these men were alive that we read about in these histories, or that they had any feelings like ours?   We always studied the lessons, and learnt the hard names, and how forty thousand were killed on one side, and fifty thousand on the other; and we don't know any more about it than if we never had. That's the way we girls studied at school, except a few ' poky ' ones, who wanted to be learned, or meant to be teachers."

"An interesting résumé, certainly," said Clayton, laughing.

"But how strange it is," said Nina, "to think that all those folks we read about are alive *now*, doing something somewhere; and I get to wondering where they are — Xerxes, and Alexander, and the rest of them. Why, they were so full of life they kept everything in commotion while in this world; and I wonder if they have been keeping a-going ever since. Perhaps Xerxes has been looking round at *our* trees — nobody knows. But here we are coming now to the beginning of our grounds. There, you see that holly hedge! Mamma had that set out. She traveled in England, and liked the hedges there so much that she thought she would see what could be done with our American holly. So she had these brought from the woods, and planted. You see it all grows wild, now, because it has n't been cut for many years. And this live-oak avenue my grandfather set out. It's my pride and delight."

As she spoke, a pair of broad gates swung open, and they cantered in beneath the twilight arches of the oaks. Long wreaths of pearly moss hung swinging from the branches, and although the sun now was at high noon, a dewy, dreamy coolness seemed to rustle through all the leaves. As Clayton passed in, he took off his hat, as he had often done in foreign countries in cathedrals.

"Welcome to Canema!" said she, riding up to him, and looking up frankly into his face.

The air, half queenly, half childish, with which this

was said, was acknowledged by Clayton with a grave smile, as he replied, bowing, —

"Thank you, madam."

"Perhaps," she added in a grave tone, "you 'll be sorry that you ever came here."

"What do you mean by that?" he replied.

"I don't know; it just came into my head to say it. We none of us ever know what 's going to come of what we do."

At this instant, a violent clamor, like the cawing of a crow, rose on one side of the avenue; and the moment after Tomtit appeared, caracoling, and cutting a somerset; his curls flying, his cheeks glowing.

"Why, Tomtit, what upon earth is this for?" said Nina.

"Laws, missis, deres been a gen'leman waiting for you at the house these two hours. And missis she 's done got on her best cap, and gone down in the parlor for him."

Nina felt herself blush to the roots of her hair, and was vexed and provoked to think she did so. Involuntarily her eyes met Clayton's. But he expressed neither curiosity nor concern.

"What a pretty drapery this light moss makes!" said he. "I was n't aware that it grew so high up in the state."

"Yes; it is very pretty," said Nina abstractedly.

Clayton, however, had noticed both the message and the blush, and was not so ill informed as Nina supposed as to the whole affair, having heard from a New York correspondent of the probability that an arrival might appear upon the field about this time. He was rather curious to watch the development produced by this event. They paced up the avenue, conversing in disconnected intervals, till they came out on the lawn which fronted the mansion — a large, gray, three-story building, surrounded on the

four sides by wide balconies of wood.   Access was had to
the lower of these by a broad flight of steps.   And there
Nina saw, plain enough, her Aunt Nesbit in all the proprieties of cap and silk gown, sitting, making the agreeable to Mr. Carson.

Mr. Frederic Augustus Carson was one of those nice
little epitomes of conventional society which appear to
such advantage in factitious life, and are so out of place in
the undress, sincere surroundings of country life.   Nina
had liked his society extremely well in the drawing-rooms
and opera-houses of New York.   But in the train of
thought inspired by the lonely and secluded life she was
now leading, it seemed to her an absolute impossibility
that she could, even in coquetry and in sport, have allowed
such an one to set up pretensions to her hand and heart.
She was vexed with herself that she had done so, and
therefore not in the most amiable mood for a meeting.
Therefore, when, on ascending the steps, he rushed precipitately forward, and, offering his hand, called her Nina,
she was ready to die with vexation.   She observed, too,
a peculiar swelling and rustling of Aunt Nesbit's plumage,
— an indescribable air of tender satisfaction, peculiar to
elderly ladies who are taking an interest in an affair of the
heart, which led her to apprehend that the bachelor had
commenced operations by declaring his position to her.
'T was with some embarrassment that Nina introduced
Mr. Clayton, whom Aunt Nesbit received with a most
stately curtsy, and Mr. Carson with a patronizing bow.

"Mr. Carson has been waiting for you these two hours,"
said Aunt Nesbit.

"Very warm riding, Nina," said Mr. Carson, observing
her red cheeks.   "You've been riding too fast, I fear.
You must be careful of yourself.   I've known people bring
on very grave illnesses by overheating the blood!"

Clayton seated himself near the door, and seemed to be

intent on the scene without. And Carson, drawing his chair close to Nina, asked, in a confidential undertone, —

"Who is that gentleman?"

"Mr. Clayton, of Claytonville," said Nina, with as much *hauteur* as she could assume.

"Ah, yes! — Hem! — hem! I 've heard of the family — a very nice family — a very worthy young man — extremely, I 'm told. Shall be happy to make his acquaintance."

"I beg," said Nina, rising, "the gentlemen will excuse me a moment or two."

Clayton replied by a grave bow, while Mr. Carson, with great *empressement*, handed Nina to the door. The moment it was closed, she stamped, with anger, in the entry.

"The provoking fool! to take these airs with me! And I, too — I deserve it! What on earth could make me think I could tolerate that man?"

As if Nina's cup were not yet full, Aunt Nesbit followed her to her chamber with an air of unusual graciousness.

"Nina, my dear, he has told me all about it! and I assure you I 'm very much pleased with him!"

"Told you all about what?" said Nina.

"Why, your engagement, to be sure! I 'm delighted to think you 've done so well! I think your Aunt Maria, and all of them, will be delighted! Takes a weight of care off my mind!"

"I wish you would n't trouble yourself about me, or my affairs, Aunt Nesbit!" said Nina. "And as for this old pussy-cat, with his squeaking boots, I won't have him purring round me, that 's certain! So provoking, to take that way towards me! Call me Nina, and talk as though he were lord paramount of me, and everything here! I 'll let him know!"

"Why, Nina! Seems to me this is very strange conduct! I am very much astonished at you!"

"I dare say you are, aunt! I never knew the time I did n't astonish you! But this man I detest!"

"Well, then, my dear, what were you engaged to him for?"

"Engaged! Aunt, for pity's sake, do hush! Engaged! I should like to know what a New York engagement amounts to! Engaged at the opera! — Engaged for a joke! Why, he was my bouquet-holder! The man is just an opera libretto! He was very useful in his time. But who wants him afterwards?"

"But, my dear Nina, this trifling with gentlemen's hearts!"

"I 'll warrant his heart! It 's neither sugar nor salt, I 'll assure you. I 'll tell you what, aunt, he loves good eating, good drinking, nice clothes, nice houses, and good times generally! and he wants a pretty wife as a part of a whole; and he thinks he 'll take me. But he is mistaken. Calling me 'Nina,' indeed! Just let me have a chance of seeing him alone! I 'll teach him to call me 'Nina'! I 'll let him know how things stand!"

"But, Nina, you must confess you 've given him occasion for all this."

"Well, supposing I have? I 'll give him occasion for something else, then!"

"Why, my dear," said Aunt Nesbit, "he came on to know when you 'll fix the day to be married!"

"Married! Oh, my gracious! Just think of the creature's talking about it! Well, it *is* my fault, as you say; but I 'll do the best I can to mend it."

"Well, I 'm really sorry for him," said Aunt Nesbit.

"You are, aunt? Why don't you take him yourself, then? You are as young and good looking as he is."

"Nina, how you talk!" said Aunt Nesbit, coloring and bridling. "There was a time when I was n't bad looking, to be sure; but that 's long since past."

"Oh, that's because you always dress in stone-color and drab," said Nina, as she stood brushing and arranging her curls. "Come, now, and go down, aunt, and do the best you can till I make my appearance. After all, as you say, I'm the most to blame. There's no use in being vexed with the old soul. So, aunt, do be as fascinating as you can; see if you can't console him. Only remember how *you* used to turn off lovers, when you were of my age."

"And who is this other gentleman, Nina?"

"Oh, nothing, only he is a friend of mine. A very good man — good enough for a minister, any day, aunt, and not so stupid as good people generally are, either."

"Well, perhaps you are engaged to him?"

"No, I am not; that is to say, I won't be to anybody. This is an insufferable business! I *like* Mr. Clayton, because he can let me alone, don't look at me in that abominably delighted way all the time, and dance about, calling me *Nina!* He and I are very good friends, that's all. I'm not going to have any engagements anywhere."

"Well, Nina, I'll go down, and you make haste."

While the gentlemen and Aunt Nesbit were waiting in the saloon, Carson made himself extremely happy and at home. It was a large, cool apartment, passing, like a hall, completely through the centre of the house. Long French windows, at either end, opened on to balconies. The pillars of the balconies were draped and garlanded with wreaths of roses now in full bloom. The floor of the room was the polished mosaic of different colors to which we have formerly alluded. Over the mantelpiece was sculptured in oak the Gordon arms. The room was wainscoted with dark wood, and hung with several fine paintings, by Copley and Stuart, of different members of the family. A grand piano, lately arrived from New York, was the most modern-looking article in the room. Most of the furniture was of heavy dark mahogany, of an an-

tique pattern. Clayton sat by the door, still admiring the
avenue of oaks which were to be seen across the waving
green of the lawn.

In about half an hour Nina reappeared in a flossy cloud
of muslin, lace, and gauzy ribbons. Dress was one of
those accomplishments for which the little gypsy had a
natural instinct; and without any apparent thought, she
always fell into that kind of color and material which
harmonized with her style of appearance and character.
There was always something floating and buoyant about
the arrangement of her garments and drapery; so that to
see her move across the floor gave one an airy kind of
sensation, like the gambols of thistle-down. Her brown
eyes had a peculiar resemblance to a bird's; and this effect
was increased by a twinkling motion of the head, and a
fluttering habit of movement peculiar to herself; so that
when she swept by in rosy gauzes, and laid one ungloved
hand lightly on the piano, she seemed to Clayton much
like some saucy bird — very good indeed if let alone, but
ready to fly on the slightest approach.

Clayton had the rare faculty of taking in every available
point of observation, without appearing to stare.

"'Pon my word, Nina," said Mr. Carson, coming towards
her with a most delighted air, "you look as if you had
fallen out of a rainbow!"

Nina turned away very coolly, and began arranging her
music.

"Oh, that's right!" said Carson; "give us one of your
songs. Sing something from the 'Favorita.' You know
it's my favorite opera," said he, assuming a most sentimental expression.

"Oh, I'm entirely out of practice — I don't sing at all.
I'm sick of all those opera-songs!" And Nina skimmed
across the floor, and out of the open door by which Clayton was lounging, and began busying herself amid the

flowers that wreathed the porch. In a moment Carson was at her heels; for he was one of those persons who seem to think it a duty never to allow any one to be quiet, if they can possibly prevent it.

"Have you ever studied the language of flowers, Nina?" said he.

"No, I don't like to study languages."

"You know the signification of a full-blown rose?" said he, tenderly presenting her with one.

Nina took the rose, coloring with vexation, and then, plucking from the bush a rose of two or three days' bloom, whose leaves were falling out, she handed it to him, and said, —

"Do you understand the signification of this?"

"Oh, you have made an unfortunate selection! This rose is all falling to pieces!" said Mr. Carson innocently.

"So I observed," said Nina, turning away quickly; then making one of her darting movements, she was in the middle of the saloon again, just as the waiter announced dinner.

Clayton rose gravely, and offered his arm to Aunt Nesbit; and Nina found herself obliged to accept the delighted escort of Mr. Carson, who, entirely unperceiving, was in the briskest possible spirits, and established himself comfortably between Aunt Nesbit and Nina.

"You must find it very dull here — very barren country, shockingly so! What do you find to interest yourself in?" said he.

"Will you take some of this gumbo?" replied Nina.

"I always thought," said Aunt Nesbit, "it was a good plan for girls to have a course of reading marked out to them when they left school."

"Oh, certainly," said Carson. "I shall be happy to mark out one for her. I've done it for several young ladies."

At this moment Nina accidentally happened to catch Clayton's eye, which was fixed upon Mr. Carson with an air of quiet amusement greatly disconcerting to her.

"Now," said Mr. Carson, "I have no opinion of making blues of young ladies; but still, I think, Mrs. Nesbit, that a little useful information adds greatly to their charms. Don't you?"

"Yes," said Mrs. Nesbit. "I've been reading Gibbon's 'Decline and Fall of the Roman Empire,' lately."

"Yes," said Nina, "aunt's been busy about that ever since I can remember."

"That's a very nice book," said Mr. Carson, looking solemnly at Nina; "only, Mrs. Nesbit, ain't you afraid of the infidel principle? I think, in forming the minds of the young, you know, one cannot be too careful."

"Why, he struck me as a very pious writer!" said Aunt Nesbit innocently. "I'm sure, he makes the most religious reflections, all along. I liked him particularly on that account."

It seemed to Nina that, without looking at Clayton, she was forced to meet his eye. No matter whether she directed her attention to the asparagus or the potatoes, it was her fatality always to end by a rencounter with his eye; and she saw, for some reason or other, the conversation was extremely amusing to him.

"For my part," said Nina, "I don't know what sort of principles Aunt Nesbit's history, there, has; but one thing I'm pretty certain of, — that *I*'m not in any danger from any such thick, close-printed, old, stupid-looking books as that. I hate reading, and I don't intend to have my mind formed; so that nobody need trouble themselves to mark out courses for me! What is it to me what all these old empires have been, a hundred years ago? It is as much as I can do to attend to what is going on now."

"For my part," said Aunt Nesbit, "I've always regretted that I neglected the cultivation of my mind when I was young. I was like Nina, here, immersed in vanity and folly."

"People always talk," said Nina, reddening, "as if there was but one kind of vanity and folly in the world. I think there can be as much learned vanity and folly as we girls have!" And she looked at Clayton indignantly, as she saw him laughing.

"I agree with Miss Gordon, entirely. There is a great deal of very stupid respectable trifling, which people pursue under the head of courses of reading," he said. "And I don't wonder that most compends of history which are studied in schools should inspire any lively young lady with a lifelong horror, not only of history, but of reading."

"Do you think so?" said Nina, with a look of inexpressible relief.

"I do, indeed," said Clayton. "And it would have been a very good thing for many of our historians if they had been obliged to have shaped their histories so that they would interest a lively schoolgirl. We literary men, then, would have found less sleepy reading. There is no reason why a young lady, who would sit up all night reading a novel, should not be made to sit up all night with a history. I'll venture to say there's no romance can come up to the gorgeousness and splendor, and the dramatic power, of things that really have happened. All that's wanting is to have it set before us with an air of reality."

"But, then," said Nina, "you'd have to make the history into a romance."

"Well, a good historical romance is generally truer than a dull history, because it gives some sort of conception of the truth, whereas the dull history gives none."

"Well, then," said Nina, "I'll confess, now, that about all the history I do know has been got from Walter Scott's novels. I always told our history teacher so; but she insisted upon it that it was very dangerous reading."

"For my part," said Mrs. Nesbit, "I've a great horror of novel-reading, particularly for young ladies. It did me a great deal of harm when I was young. It dissipates the mind; it gives false views of life."

"Oh, law!" said Nina. "We used to write compositions about that, and I've got it all by heart — how it raises false expectations, and leads people to pursue phantoms, rainbows, and meteors, and all that sort of thing!"

"And yet," said Clayton, "all these objections would lie against perfectly true history, and the more so just in proportion to its truth. If the history of Napoleon Bonaparte were graphically and minutely given, it would lie open to the very same objections. It would produce the very same cravings for something out of the commonplace course of life. There would be the same dazzling mixture of bad and good qualities in the hero, and the same lassitude and exhaustion after the story was finished. And common history does not do this, simply because it is not true — does not produce a vivid impression of the reality as it happened."

Aunt Nesbit only got an indefinite impression, from this harangue, that Clayton was defending novel-reading, and felt herself called to employ her own peculiar line of reasoning to meet it, which consisted in saying the same thing over and over, at regular intervals, without appearing to hear or notice anything said in reply. Accordingly, she now drew herself up, with a slightly virtuous air, and said to Mr. Clayton, —

"I must say, after all, that I don't approve of novel-reading. It gives false views of life, and disgusts young people with their duties."

"I was only showing, madam, that the same objection would apply to the best written history," said Clayton.

"I think novel-reading does a great deal of harm," rejoined Aunt Nesbit. "I never allow myself to read any work of fiction. I'm principled against it."

"For my part," said Nina, "I wish I could find that kind of history you are speaking of; I believe I could read that."

"'T would be very interesting history, certainly," said Mr. Carson. "I should think it would prove a very charming mode of writing. I wonder somebody don't produce one."

"For my part," said Aunt Nesbit, "I confine myself entirely to what is practically useful. Useful information is all I desire."

"Well, I suppose, then, I'm very wicked," said Nina; "but I don't like anything useful. Why, I've sometimes thought, when I've been in the garden, that the summer-savory, sage, and sweet-marjoram were just as pretty as many other flowers; and I couldn't see any reason why I shouldn't like a sprig of one of them for a bouquet, except that I've seen them used for stuffing turkeys. Well, now, that seems very bad of me, don't it?"

"That reminds me," said Aunt Nesbit, "that Rose has been putting sage into this turkey again, after all that I said to her. I believe she does it on purpose."

At this moment Harry appeared at the door, and requested to speak to Nina.

After a few moments' whispered conversation she came back to the table, apparently disconcerted.

"I'm so sorry — so very sorry!" she said. "Harry has been riding all round the country to find a minister to attend the funeral, this evening. It will be such a disappointment to that poor fellow! You know the negroes think so much of having prayers at the grave!"

"If no one else can be found to read prayers, I will," said Clayton.

"Oh, thank you! will you, indeed?" said Nina. "I'm glad of it, now, for poor Tiff's sake. The coach will be out at five o'clock, and we'll ride over together, and make as much of a party as we can."

"Why, child," said Aunt Nesbit to Nina, after they returned to the parlor, "I did not know that Mr. Clayton was an Episcopalian."

"He isn't," said Nina. "He and his family all attend the Presbyterian church."

"How strange that he should offer to read prayers!" said Aunt Nesbit. "I don't approve of such things, for my part."

"Such things as what?"

"Countenancing Episcopal errors. If we are right, they are wrong, and we ought not to countenance them."

"But, aunt, the burial service is beautiful."

"Don't approve of it!" said Aunt Nesbit.

"Why, you know, as Clayton isn't a minister, he would not feel like making an extempore prayer."

"Shows great looseness of religious principle," said Aunt Nesbit. "Don't approve of it!"

CHAPTER XII

THE golden arrows of the setting sun were shooting hither and thither through the pine woods, glorifying whatever they touched with a life not its own. A chorus of birds were pouring out an evening melody, when a little company stood around an open grave. With instinctive care for the feeling of the scene Nina had arrayed herself in a black silk dress, and plain straw bonnet with black ribbon — a mark of respect to the deceased remembered and narrated by Tiff for many a year after.

Cripps stood by the head of the grave, with that hopeless, imbecile expression with which a nature wholly gross and animal often contemplates the symbols of the close of mortal existence. Tiff stood by the side of the grave, his white hat conspicuously draped with black crape, and a deep weed of black upon his arm. The baby, wrapped in an old black shawl, was closely fondled in his bosom, while the two children stood weeping bitterly at his side. The other side of the grave stood Mr. Carson and Mr. Clayton, while Milly, Harry, and several plantation slaves were in a group behind.

The coffin had been opened, that all might take that last look, so coveted, yet so hopeless, which the human heart will claim on the very verge of the grave. It was but a moment since the coffin had been closed; and the burst of grief which shook the children was caused by that last farewell. As Clayton, in a musical voice, pronounced the words, "I am the resurrection and the life," Nina wept and sobbed as if the grief had been her own; nor did she cease to weep during the whole touching service. It was the same impulsive nature which made her so gay in other scenes that made her so sympathetic 'here. When the whole was over she kissed the children, and shaking hands with Old Tiff, promised to come and see them on the morrow. After which, Clayton led her to the carriage, into which he and Carson followed her.

"Upon my word," said Carson briskly, "this has been quite solemn! Really, a very interesting funeral, indeed! I was delighted with the effect of our Church service; in such a romantic place, too! 'T was really very interesting. It pleases me, also, to see young ladies in your station, Nina, interest themselves in the humble concerns of the poor. If young ladies knew how much more attractive it made them to show a charitable spirit, they would culti-vate it more. Singular-looking person, that old negro! Seems to be a good creature. Interesting children, too! I should think the woman must have been pretty when she was young. Seen a great deal of trouble, no doubt, poor thing! It's a comfort to hope she is better off now."

Nina was filled with indignation at this monologue; not considering that the man was giving the very best he had in him, and laboring assiduously at what he considered his vocation, the prevention of half an hour of silence in any spot of earth where he could possibly make himself heard. The same excitement which made Nina cry made him talk. But he was not content with talking, but insisted upon asking Nina, every moment, if she didn't think it an interesting occasion, and if she had not been much im-pressed.

"I don't feel like talking, Mr. Carson," said Nina.

"Oh — ah — yes, indeed! You've been so deeply affected — yes. Naturally does incline one to silence. Understand your feelings perfectly. Very gratifying to me to see you take such a deep interest in your fellow creatures."

Nina could have pushed him out of the carriage.

"For my part," continued Carson, "I think we don't reflect enough about this kind of things — I positively don't. It really is useful sometimes to have one's thoughts turned in this direction. It does us good."

Thus glibly did Carson proceed to talk away the impression of the whole scene they had witnessed. Long before the carriage reached home Nina had forgotten all her sympathy in a tumult of vexation. She discovered an increasing difficulty in making Carson understand, by any degree of coolness, that he was not acceptable; and saw nothing before her but explanations in the very plainest terms, mortifying and humiliating as that might be. His perfect self-complacent ease, and the air with which he constantly seemed to appropriate her as something which of right belonged to himself, filled her with vexation. But yet her conscience told her that she had brought it upon herself.

"I won't bear this another hour!" she said to herself, as she ascended the steps toward the parlor. "All this before Clayton, too! What must he think of me?" But they found tea upon the table and Aunt Nesbit waiting.

"It's a pity, madam, you were not with us. Such an interesting time!" said Mr. Carson, launching, with great volubility, into the tide of discourse.

"It wouldn't have done for me at all," said Mrs. Nesbit. "Being out when the dew falls always brings on hoarseness. I have been troubled in that way these two or three years. Now I have to be very careful. Then I'm timid about riding in a carriage with John's driving."

"I was amused enough," said Nina, "with Old Hundred's indignation at having to get out the carriage and horses to go over to what he called a 'cracker funeral.' I really believe, if he could have upset us without hurting himself, he would have done it."

"For my part," said Aunt Nesbit, "I hope that family will move off before long. It's very disagreeable having such people round."

"The children look very pretty and bright," said Nina.

"Oh, there's no hope for them! They'll grow up and be just like their parents. I've seen that sort of people all through and through. I don't wish them any evil; only I don't want to have anything to do with them!"

"For my part," said Nina, "I'm sorry for them. I wonder why the legislature, or somebody, don't have schools, as they do up in New York State? There isn't anywhere there where children can't go to school, if they wish to. Besides, aunt, these children really came from an old family in Virginia. Their old servant-man says that their mother was a Peyton."

"I don't believe a word of it! They'll lie — all of them. They always do."

"Well," said Nina, "I shall do something for these children, at any rate."

"I quite agree with you, Nina. It shows a very excellent spirit in you," said Mr. Carson. "You'll always find me ready to encourage everything of that sort."

Nina frowned and looked indignant. But to no purpose. Mr. Carson went on remorselessly with his really good-hearted rattle, till Nina, at last, could bear it no longer.

"How dreadfully warm this room is!" said she, springing up. "Come, let's go back into the parlor."

Nina was as much annoyed at Clayton's silence, and his quiet, observant reserve, as with Carson's forth-putting. Rising from table, she passed on before the company, with a half-flying trip, into the hall, which lay now cool, calm, and breezy, in the twilight, with the odor of the pillar-

roses floating in at the window. The pale white moon,
set in the rosy belt of the evening sky, looked in at the
open door. Nina would have given all the world to be
still; but well aware that stillness was out of the question she determined to select her own noise, and sitting
down at the piano, began playing very fast, in a rapid,
restless, disconnected manner. Clayton threw himself on
a lounge by the open door; while Carson busied himself
fluttering the music, opening and shutting music-books,
and interspersing running commentaries and notes of admiration on the playing.

At last, as if she could bear it no longer, she rose, with
a very decided air, from the piano, and facing about towards Mr. Carson, said: —

"It looks very beautiful outdoors. Don't you want to
come out? There's a point of view at the end of one
of the paths, where the moon looks on the water, that I
should like to show you."

"Won't you catch cold, Nina?" said Aunt Nesbit.

"No, indeed! I never catch cold," said Nina, springing into the porch, and taking the delighted Mr. Carson's
arm. And away she went with him, with almost a skip
and a jump, leaving Clayton *tête-à-tête* with Aunt Nesbit.

Nina went so fast that her attendant was almost out of
breath. They reached a little knoll, and there Nina
stopped suddenly, and said, "Look here, Mr. Carson; I
have something to say to you."

"I should be delighted, my dear Nina! I'm perfectly
charmed!"

"No — no — if you please — don't!" said Nina, putting up her hand to stop him. "Just wait till you hear
what I have to say. I believe you did not get a letter
which I wrote you a few days ago, did you?"

"A letter! no, indeed. How unfortunate!"

"Very unfortunate for me!" said Nina; "and for you,

too. Because, if you had, it would have saved you and
me the trouble of this interview. I wrote that letter to
tell you, Mr. Carson, that I cannot *think* of such a thing
as an engagement with you! That I 've acted very wrong
and very foolishly; but that I cannot do it. In New
York, where everybody and everything seemed to be trifling, and where the girls all trifled with these things, I was
engaged — just for frolic — nothing more. I had no idea
what it would amount to; no idea what I was saying, nor
how I should feel afterwards. But every hour since I 've
been home, here, since I 've been so much alone, has made
me feel how wrong it is. Now, I 'm very sorry, I 'm sure.
But I must speak the truth, this time. But it is — I
can't tell you how — disagreeable to me to have you treat
me as you have since you 've been here!"

"Miss Gordon!" said Mr. Carson, "I am positively
astonished! I — I don't know what to think!"

"Well, I only want you to think I am in earnest; and
that, though I can like you very well as an acquaintance,
and shall always wish you well, yet anything else is just
as far out of the question as that moon there is from us.
I can't tell you how sorry I am that I 've made you all
this trouble. I really am," said she good naturedly;
"but please now to understand how we stand." She
turned, and tripped away.

"There!" said she to herself, "at any rate, I 've done
one thing!"

Mr. Carson stood still, gradually recovering from the
stupor into which this communication had thrown him.
He stretched himself, rubbed his eyes, took out his watch
and looked at it, and then began walking off with a very
sober pace in the opposite direction from Nina. Happily
constituted mortal that he was, nothing ever could be sub-
tracted from his sum of complacence that could not be
easily balanced by about a quarter of an hour's considera-

tion. The walk through the shrubbery in which he was
engaged was an extremely pretty one, and wound along on
the banks of the river through many picturesque points of
view, and finally led again to the house by another approach. During the course of this walk Mr. Carson had
settled the whole question for himself. In the first place,
he repeated the comfortable old proverb, that there were as
good fish in the sea as ever were caught. In the second
place, as Mr. Carson was a shrewd business man, it occurred to him, in this connection, that the plantation was
rather run down, and not a profitable acquisition. And
in the third place, contemplating Nina as the fox of old
did his bunch of sour grapes, he began to remember that,
after all, she was dressy, expensive, and extravagant.
Then, as he did not want that imperturbable good nature
which belongs to a very shallow capability of feeling, he
said to himself that he should n't like the girl a bit the
less. In fact, when he thought of his own fine fortune,
his house in New York, and all the accessories which
went to make up himself, he considered her, on the whole,
as an object of pity; and by the time that he ascended
the balcony steps again, he was in as charitable and Christian a frame as any rejected suitor could desire.

He entered the drawing-room. Aunt Nesbit had ordered
candles, and was sitting up with her gloves on, alone.
What had occurred during his walk he did not know; but
we will take our readers into confidence.

Nina returned to the house with the same decided air
with which she went out, and awakened Mr. Clayton from
a reverie with a brisk little tap of her fan on his shoulder.

"Come up here with me," she said, "and look out of
the library window, and see this moonlight."

And up she went, over the old oaken staircase, stopping
on each landing, and beckoning to Clayton, with a whim-
sically authoritative gesture, threw open the door of a

large, black-wainscoted room, and ushered him in. The
room lay just above the one where they had been sitting,
and, like that, opened on to the veranda by long-sashed
windows, through which, at the present moment, a flood
of moonlight was pouring. A large mahogany writing-
table, covered with papers, stood in the middle of the
room, and the moon shone in so brightly that the pattern
of the bronze inkstand and the color of the wafers and
sealing-wax were plainly revealed. The window commanded a splendid view of the river over the distant treetops, as it lay shimmering and glittering in the moonlight.

"Is n't that a beautiful sight?" said Nina in a hurried
voice.

"Very beautiful!" said Clayton, sitting down in the
large lounging-chair before the window, and looking out
with the abstracted air which was habitual with him.

After a moment's thought, Nina added, with a sudden
effort, —

"But, after all, that was not what I wanted to speak to
you about. I wanted to see you somewhere, and say a
few words which it seems to me it is due to you that I
should say. I got your last letter, and I 'm sure I am
very much obliged to your sister for all the kind things
she says; but I think you must have been astonished at
what you have seen since you have been here."

"Astonished at what?" said Clayton quietly.

"At Mr. Carson's manners towards me."

"I have not been astonished at all," replied Clayton
quietly.

"I think, at all events," said Nina, "I think it is no
more than honorable that I should tell you exactly how
things have stood. Mr. Carson has thought that he had
a right to me and mine; and I was so foolish as to give
him reason to think so. The fact is, that I have been
making a game of life, and saying and doing anything and

everything that came into my head, just for frolic. It don't seem to me that there has been anything serious or real about me, until very lately. Somehow, my acquaintance with you has made things seem more real to me than they ever did before; and it seems to me now perfectly incredible, the way we girls used to play and trifle with everything in the world. Just for sport, I was engaged to that man; just for sport, too, I have been engaged to another one."

"And," said Clayton, breaking the silence, "just for sport have you been engaged to me?"

"No," said Nina, after a few moments' silence, "not in sport, certainly; but yet, not enough in earnest. I think I am about half waked up. I don't know myself. I don't know where or what I am, and I want to go back into that thoughtless dream. I do really think it's too hard to take up the responsibility of living in good earnest. Now, it seems to me just this, — that I cannot be bound to anybody. I want to be free. I have positively broken all connection with Mr. Carson; I have broken with another one, and I wish" —

"To break with me?" said Clayton.

"I don't really know as I can say what I do wish. It is a very different thing from any of the others, but there's a feeling of dread, and responsibility, and constraint, about it; and though I think I should feel very lonesome now without you, and though I like to get your letters, yet it seems to me that I cannot be engaged, — that is a most dreadful feeling to me."

"My dear friend," said Clayton, "if that is all, make yourself easy. There's no occasion for our being engaged. If you can enjoy being with me and writing to me, why, do it in the freest way, and to-morrow shall take care for the things of itself. You shall say what you please, do what you please, write when you please, and not write

when you please, and have as many or as few letters as
you like.   There can be no true love without liberty."

"Oh, I'm sure I'm much obliged to you!" said Nina,
with a sigh of relief.' "And now, do you know, I like
your sister's postscript very much; but I can't tell what it
is in it, for the language is as kind as can be, that would
give me the impression that she is one of those very proper
kind of people, that would be dreadfully shocked if she
knew of all my goings on in New York."

Clayton could hardly help laughing at the instinctive
sagacity of this remark.

"I'm sure I don't know," said he, "where you could
have seen that, — in so short a postscript, too."

"Do you know, I never take anybody's handwriting into
my hand that I don't feel an idea of them come over me,
just as you have when you see people?   And that idea
came over me when I read your sister's letter."

"Well, Nina, to tell you the truth, sister Anne is a
little bit conventional — a little set in her ways; but,
after all, a large-hearted, warm-hearted woman.   You
would like each other, I know."

"I don't know about that," said Nina.   "I am very
apt to shock proper people.   Somehow or other, they have
a faculty of making me contrary."

"Well, but, you see, Anne isn't merely a conventional
person; there's only the slightest crust of conventionality,
and a real warm heart under it."

"Whereas," said Nina, "most conventional people are
like a shallow river, frozen to the bottom.   But now,
really, I should like very much to have your sister come
and visit us, if I could think that she would come as any
other friend; but, you know, it isn't very agreeable to
have anybody come to look one over to see if one will do."

Clayton laughed at the naïve undisguised frankness of
this speech.

"You see," said Nina, "though I'm nothing but an ignorant schoolgirl, I'm as proud as if I had everything to be proud of. Now, do you know, I don't much like writing to your sister, because I don't think I write very good letters! I never could sit still long enough to write."

"Write exactly as you talk," said Clayton. "Say just what comes into your head, just as you would talk it. I hope you will do that much, for it will be very dull writing all on one side."

"Well," said Nina, rising, with animation, "now, Mr. Edward Clayton, if we have settled about this moonlight, we may as well go down into the parlor, where Aunt Nesbit and Mr. Carson are *tête-à-tête*."

"Poor Carson!" said Clayton.

"Oh, don't pity him! Good soul! he's a man that one night's rest would bring round from anything in creation. He's so thoroughly good natured! Besides, I shall like him better, now. He did not use to seem to me so intrusive and disagreeable. We girls used to like him very well, he was such a comfortable, easy-tempered, agreeable creature, always brisk and in spirits, and knowing everything that went on. But he is one of those men that I think would be really insufferable, if anything serious were the matter with me. Now, you heard how he talked coming from that funeral! Do you know, that if he had been coming from *my* funeral it would have been just so?"

"Oh no, not quite so bad," said Clayton.

"Indeed he is," said Nina. "That man! why, he just puts me in mind of one of these brisk blue-flies, whirring and whisking about, marching over pages of books, and alighting on all sorts of things. When he puts on that grave look, and begins to talk about serious things, he actually looks to me just as a fly does when he stands brushing his wings on a Bible! But come, let's go down to the good soul."

Down they went, and Nina seemed like a person en-
franchised. Never had she seemed more universally gracious. She was chatty and conversable with Carson, and
sang over for him all her old opera-songs, with the better
grace that she saw that Clayton was listening intently.

As they were sitting and conversing together, the sound
of a horse's heels was heard coming up the avenue.

"Who can that be, this time of night?" said Nina,
springing to the door, and looking out.

She saw Harry hastening in advance to meet her, and
ran down the veranda steps to speak to him.

"Harry, who is coming?"

"Miss Nina, it's Master Tom," said Harry in a low
voice.

"Tom! Oh, mercy!" said Nina in a voice of apprehension. "What sent him here, now?"

"What sends him anywhere?" said Harry.

Nina reascended the steps, and stood looking apprehensively towards the horseman, who approached every moment
nearer. Harry came up on the veranda, and stood a little
behind her. In a few moments the horse was up before
the steps.

"Hallo, there!" said the rider. "Come, take my
horse, you rascal!"

Harry remained perfectly still, put his arms by his side,
and stood with a frowning expression on his forehead.

"Don't you hear?" said the horseman, throwing himself off, with an oath. "Come here, boy, and take my
horse!"

"For pity's sake," said Nina, turning and looking in
Harry's face, "don't have a scene here! Do take his
horse, quick! Anything to keep him quiet!"

With a sudden start, Harry went down the steps, and
took the bridle from the hand of the newly arrived in
silence.

The horseman sprang up the steps.

"Hallo, Nin, is this you?" And Nina felt herself roughly seized in the arms of a shaggy greatcoat, and kissed by lips smelling of brandy and tobacco. She faintly said, as she disengaged herself, —

"Tom, is it you?"

"Yes, to be sure! Who did you think it was? Devil-ish glad to see me, ain't you? Suppose you was in hopes I would n't come!"

"Hush, Tom, do! I *am* glad to see you. There are gentlemen in there; don't speak so loud!"

"Some of your beaux, hey? Well, I am as good a fel-low as any of 'em! Free country, I hope! No, I ain't going to whisper, for any of them. So now, Nin — If there is n't old Starchy, to be sure!" said he, as Aunt Nesbit came to the door. "Hallo, old girl, how are you?"

"Thomas!" said Mrs. Nesbit softly, "Thomas!"

"None of your Thomasing me, you old pussy-cat! Don't you be telling me, neither, to hush! I won't hush, neither! I know what I am about, I guess! It's my house as much as it is Nin's, and I'm going to do as I have a mind to here! I ain't going to have my mouth shut on account of her beaux! So, clear out, I tell you, and let me come in!" and Aunt Nesbit gave back. He pushed his way into the apartment.

He was a young man, about twenty-five years old, who evidently had once possessed advantages of face and figure; but every outline in the face was bloated and rendered un-meaning by habits of constant intemperance. His dark eyes had that muddy and troubled expression which in a young man too surely indicates the habitual consciousness of inward impurity. His broad, high forehead was flushed and pim-pled, his lips swollen and tumid, and his whole air and manner gave painful evidence that he was at present too far under the influence of stimulants justly to apprehend what he was about.

Nina followed him, and Clayton was absolutely shocked at the ghastly paleness of her face. She made an uncertain motion towards him, as if she would have gone to him for protection. Clayton rose; Carson, also; and all stood for a moment in silent embarrassment.

"Well, this is a pretty business, to be sure! Nina," said he, turning to her, with a tremendous oath, "why don't you introduce me? Pretty way to meet a brother you have n't seen for three or four years! You act as if you were ashamed of me! Confound it all! introduce me, I say!"

"Tom, don't speak so!" said Nina, laying her hand on his arm, in a soothing tone. "This gentleman is Mr. Clayton; and Mr. Clayton," she said, lifting her eyes to him, and speaking in a trembling voice, "this is my brother."

Mr. Clayton offered his hand, with the ordinary expressions of civility.

"Mr. Carson," said Nina, "my brother."

There was something inexpressibly touching and affecting in the manner in which this was said. One other person noticed it. Harry, who had given the horse to a servant, stood leaning against the doorway, looking on. A fiery gleam, like that of a steel blade, seemed to shoot from his blue eyes; and each time that Nina said "my brother," he drew in his breath, as one who seeks to restrain himself in some violent inward emotion.

"I suppose you don't any of you want to see me much," said the newcomer, taking a chair, and sitting down doggedly in the centre of the group, with his hat on his head.

"Well, I have as good a right as anybody to be here!" he continued, spitting a quid of tobacco at Aunt Nesbit's feet.

"For my part, I think relations ought to have natural affection, and be glad to see one another. Well, now, you can see, gentlemen, with your own eyes, just how it is here! There's my sister, there. You better believe me, she hasn't seen me for three years! Instead of appearing glad, or anything, there she sits, all curled up in a corner! Won't come near me, more than if I had the plague! Come here, now, you little kit, and sit in my lap!"

He made a movement to pull Nina towards him, which she resisted with an air of terror, looking at her aunt, who, more terrified still, sat with her feet drawn up on the sofa, as if he had been a mad dog. There was reason enough for the terror which seemed to possess them both. Both had too vivid recollections of furious domestic hurricanes that had swept over the family when Tom Gordon came home. Nina remembered the storms of oaths and curses that had terrified her when a child; the times that she had seen her father looking like death, leaning his head on his hand, and sighing as only those sigh who have an only son worse than dead. It is no wonder, therefore, that Nina, generally courageous and fearless as she was, should have become fearful and embarrassed at his sudden return.

"Tom," she said softly, coming up to him, "you haven't been to supper. Hadn't you better come out?"

"No you don't!" said he, catching her round the waist, and drawing her on his knee. "You won't get me out of the room, now! I know what I am about! Tell me," continued he, still holding her on his knee, "which of them is it, Nin? — which is the favored one?"

Clayton rose and went out on the veranda, and Mr. Carson asked Harry to show him into his room.

"Hallo! shelling out there, are they? Well, Nin, to tell the truth, I am deuced hungry. For my part, I don't see what the thunder keeps my Jim out so long. I sent him across to the post-office. He ought to have been back certainly as soon as I was. Oh, here he comes! Hallo! you dog, there!" said he, going to the door, where a very black negro was dismounting. "Any letters?"

"No, mas'r. I spect de mails have gin up. Der ain't been no letters dere, for no one, for a month. It is some 'quatic disorganization of dese yer creeks, I s'pose. So de letter-bags goes anywhere 'cept der right place."

"Confound it all! I say, you Nin," turning round, "why don't you offer a fellow some supper? Coming home, here, in my own father's house, everybody acts as if they were scared to death! No supper!"

"Why, Tom, I've been asking you, these three or four times."

"Bless us!" said Jim, whispering to Harry. "De mischief is, he ain't more than half primed! Tell her to give him a little more brandy, and after a little we will get him into bed as easy as can be!"

And the event proved so; for on sitting down to supper, Tom Gordon passed regularly through all the stages of drunkenness; became as outrageously affectionate as he had been before surly, kissed Nina and Aunt Nesbit, cried over his sins and confessed his iniquities, laughed and cried feebly, till at last he sank in his chair asleep.

"Dar, he is done for, now!" said Jim, who had been watching the gradual process. "Now, just you and I, let's tote him off," said he to Harry.

Nina, on her part, retired to a troubled pillow. She foresaw nothing before her but mortification and embarrassment, and realized more than ever the peculiar loneliness of her situation. For all purposes of consultation and aid, Aunt Nesbit was nobody in her esteem, and Nina was always excited and vexed by every new attempt that she made to confide in her.

"Now, to-morrow," she said to herself, as she lay down, "no one knows what will turn up. He will go round as usual, interfering with everything — threatening and frightening my servants, and getting up some difficulty with Harry. Dear me! it seems to me life is coming over me hard enough, and all at once, too!"

As Nina said this she saw some one standing by her bed. It was Milly, who stooped tenderly over her, smoothing and arranging the bedclothes in a motherly way. "Is that you, Milly? Oh, sit down here a minute! I am so troubled! It seems to me I've had so much trouble to-day! Do you know, Tom came home to-night *so* drunk! Oh, dear Milly, it was horrid! Do you know, he took me in his arms and kissed me; and though he is my only brother, it's perfectly dreadful to me! And I feel so worried and so anxious!"

"Yes, lamb, I knows all about dese yer things," said Milly. "I's seen him many and many times."

"The worst of it is," said Nina, "that I don't know what he will do to-morrow — and before Mr. Clayton, too! It makes me feel so helpless, ashamed, and mortifies me so!"

"Yes, yes, chile," said Milly, gently stroking her head.

"I stand so much alone!" said Nina. "Other girls have some friend or relation to lean on; but I have nobody!"

"Why don't you ask your *Father* to help you?" said Milly to Nina in a gentle tone.

"Ask *who?*" said Nina, lifting up her head from the pillow.

"Your Father!" said Milly, with a voice of solemnity. "Don't you know ' Our Father who art in Heaven '? You have n't forgot your prayers, I hope, honey."

Nina looked at her with surprise. And Milly continued, "Now, if I was you, lamb, I would tell my Father

all about it. Why, chile, He loves you! He would n't
like nothing better, now, than to have you just come to Him
and tell Him all about your troubles, and He 'll make 'em
all straight. That 's the way I does, and I 's found it
come out right many and many a time."

"Why, Milly, you would n't have me go to God about
my little foolish affairs ? "

"Laws, chile, what should you go to Him 'bout, den ?
Sure dese are all de 'fairs you 's got."

"Well, but, Milly," said Nina apprehensively, "you
know I 've been a very bad girl about religion. It 's years
and years since I 've said any prayers. At school, the
girls used to laugh at anybody who said prayers; and so I
never did. And since I 've neglected my heavenly Father
when things went well with me, it would n't be fair to call
on Him now, just because I 've got into trouble. I don't
think it would be honorable."

"De Lord bless dis yer chile! Do hear her talk! Just
as if de heavenly Father did n't know all about you, and
had n't been a loving and watching you de whole time!
Why, chile, He knows what poor foolish creatures we be;
and He ain't noways surprised, nor put out. Why, laws,
don't you know He 's de good shepherd? And what you
suppose dey has shepherds fur, 'cept de sheeps are all de
time running away, and getting into trouble? Why,
honey, dat 's what dey 's fur."

"Well, but it is so long since I prayed, that I don't
know anything how to pray, Milly."

"Bless you, chile, who wanted you to pray? I never
prays myself. Used to try, but I made such drefful poor
work on it that I gin it up. Now, I just goes and talks
to de Father, and tells Him anything and everything; and
I think He likes it a great deal better. Why, He is just
as willing to hear me now as if I was the greatest lady in
the land. And He takes such an interest in all my poor

'fairs! Why, sometimes I go to Him when my heart is *so* heavy; and when I tells Him all about it, I comes away as light as a feather!"

"Well, but after I 've forgotten Him so many years!"

"Why, honey, now just look yere! I 'member once, when you was a little weety thing, that you toddles down dem steps dere, and you slips away from dem dat was watching you, and you toddles away off into de grove, yonder, and dere you got picking flowers, and one thing and another, mighty tickled and peart. You was down dere 'joying yourself, till, by and by, your pa missed you; and den such another hunt as dere was! Dere was a hurrying here, and a looking dere; and finally your pa run down in de woods, and dere you 'd got stuck fast in de mud! both your shoes off, and well scratched with briers; and dere you stood a-crying, and calling your pa. I tell you he said dat ar was de sweetest music he ever heard in his life. I 'member he picked you up, and came up to de house kissing you. Now, dere 't was, honey! You did n't call on your pa till you got into trouble. And laws, laws, chile, dat 's de way with us all. We never does call on de Father till we gets into trouble; and it takes heaps and heaps of trouble, sometimes, to bring us round. Some time, chile, I 'll tell you my sperence. I 's got a sperence on this point. But now, honey, don't trouble yourself no more; but just ask your Father to take care of your 'fairs, and turn over and go to sleep. And He 'll do it. Now you mind."

So saying, Milly smoothed the pillow with anxious care, and kissing Nina on the forehead, departed.

CHAPTER XIII

"I say, Nina," said her brother, coming in, the day after, from a survey he had been taking round the premises, "you want me here to manage this place. Everything going at sixes and sevens; and that nigger of a Harry riding round with his boots shining. That fellow cheats you, and feathers his own nest well. I know! These white niggers are all deceitful."

"Come, Tom, you know the estate is managed just as father left word to have it; and Uncle John says that Harry is an excellent manager. I'm sure nobody could have been more faithful to me; and I am very well satisfied."

"Yes, I dare say. All left to you and the executors, as you call them; as if *I* were not the natural guardian of my sister! Then I come here to put up with that fellow's impudence!"

"Whose? — Harry's? He is never impudent. He is always gentlemanly. Everybody remarks it."

"Gentlemanly! There it is, Nin! What a fool you are to encourage the use of that word in connection with any of your niggers! Gentleman, forsooth! And while he plays gentleman, who takes care? I tell you what, you'll find one of these days how things are going on. But that's just the way! You never would listen to me, or pay the least attention to my advice."

"Oh, Tom, don't talk about that — don't! I never interfere about your affairs. Please leave me the right to manage mine in my own way."

"And who is this Clayton that's hanging about here? Are you going to have him, or he you — hey?"

"I don't know," said Nina.

"Because *I*, for one, don't like him; and I sha'n't give my consent to let him have you. That other one is worth twice as much. He has one of the largest properties in New York. Joe Snider has told me about him. You shall have him."

"I shall not have him, say what you please; and I shall have Mr. Clayton, if I choose!" said Nina, with a heightened color. "You have no right to dictate to me of my own affairs; and I sha'n't submit to it, I tell you frankly."

"Highty-tighty! We are coming up, to be sure!" said Tom.

"Moreover," said Nina, "I wish you to let everything on this place entirely alone; and remember that my servants are not your servants, and that you have no control over them whatever."

"Well, we will see how you'll help yourself! I am not going to go skulking about on my father's own place as if I had no right or title there; and if your niggers don't look sharp, they'll find out whether I am the master here or not, especially that Harry. If the dog dares so much as to lift his fingers to countermand any one of my orders, I'd put a bullet through his head as soon as I would through a buck's. I give you warning!"

"Oh, Tom, pray don't talk so!" said Nina, who really began to be alarmed. "What do you want to make me such trouble for?"

The conversation was here suspended by the entrance of Milly. "If you please, Miss Nina, come and show me which of your muslins you wish to be done up, as I's starching for Miss Loo."

Glad of an opportunity to turn the conversation, Nina

ran up to her room, whither she was followed by Milly,
who shut the door, and spoke to her in mysterious tones.
"Miss Nina, can't you make some errand to get Harry off
the place for two or three days, while Mas'r Tom's
round?"

"But what right," said Nina, with heightened color,
"has he to dictate to my servants, or me? or to interfere
with any of our arrangements here?"

"Oh, dere's no use talking about *rights*, honey. We
must all do jest what we *ken*. Don't make much odds
whether our rights is one way or t'other. You see, chile,
it's just here. Harry's your right hand. But you see, he
ain't learnt to bend 'fore the wind, like the rest of us. He
is spirity; he is just as full now as a powder-box; and
Mas'r Tom is bent on aggravating him. And, laws, chile,
dere may be bloody work — dere may so!"

"Why, do you think he'd *dare*" —

"Chile, don't talk to me! Dare! — yes; sure 'nough
he will dare! Besides, dere's fifty ways young gentlemen
may take to aggravate and provoke. And when flesh and
blood can't bear it no longer, if Harry raises his hand,
why, den shoot him down! Nothing said — nothing done.
You can't help yourself. You won't want to have a lawsuit with your own brother; and if you did, 't wouldn't
bring Harry to life! Laws, chile, ef I could tell you what
I've seen — you don't know nothing 'bout it. Now, I
tell you, get up some message to your uncle's plantation;
send him off for anything or nothing; only have him
gone! And then speak your brother fair, and then maybe
he will go off. But don't you quarrel! don't you cross
him, come what may! Dere ain't a soul on the place that
can bar de sight on him. But then, you see, the rest dey
all bends! But, chile, you must be quick about it! Let
me go right off and find him. Just you come in the little
back room, and I'll call him in."

Pale and trembling, Nina descended into the room; and in a few moments after Milly appeared, followed by Harry.

"Harry!" said Nina in a trembling voice, "I want you to take your horse and go over to Uncle John's plantation, and carry a note for me."

Harry stood with his arms folded, and his eyes fixed upon the ground, and Nina continued, —

"And, Harry, I think you had better make some business or errand to keep you away two or three days, or a week."

"Miss Nina," said Harry, "the affairs of the place are very pressing now, and need overlooking. A few days' neglect now may produce a great loss, and then it will be said that I neglected my business to idle and ride round the country."

"Well, but, if I send you, I take the responsibility, and I'll bear the loss. The fact is, Harry, I'm afraid that you won't have patience to be here, now Tom is at home. In fact, Harry, I'm afraid for your life! And now, if you have any regard for me, make the best arrangement with the work you can, and be off. I'll tell him that I sent you on business of my own, and I am going to write a letter for you to carry. It's the only safe way. He has so many ways in which he can provoke and insult you, that, at last, you may say or do something that will give him occasion against you; and I think he is determined to drive you to this."

"Isn't this provoking, now? isn't this outrageous!" said Harry between his teeth, looking down, "that everything must be left, and all because I haven't the right to stand up like a man, and protect you and yours!"

"It is a pity! it is a shame!" said Nina. "But, Harry, don't stop to think upon it; do go!" She laid her hand softly on his. "For my sake, now, be good — be good!"

The room where they were standing had long windows,

which opened, like those of the parlor, on the veranda, and commanded a view of a gravel walk bordered with shrubbery. As Harry stood, hesitating, he started at seeing Lisette come tripping up the walk, balancing on her head a basket of newly ironed muslins and linens. Her trim little figure was displayed in a close-fitting gown of blue, a snowy handkerchief crossed upon her bust, and one rounded arm raised to steady the basket upon her head. She came tripping forward, with her usual airy motion, humming a portion of a song; and attracted, at the same moment, the attention of Tom Gordon and of her husband.

"'Pon my word, if that is n't the prettiest concern!" said Tom, as he started up and ran down the walk to meet her.

"Good-morning, my pretty girl!" he said.

"Good-morning, sir," returned Lisette in her usual tone of gay cheerfulness.

"Pray, who do you belong to, my pretty little puss! I think I 've never seen you on this place."

"Please, sir, I 'm Harry's wife."

"Indeed! you are, hey? Devilish good taste he has!" said he, laying his hand familiarly on her shoulder.

The shoulder was pulled away, and Lisette moved rapidly on to the other side of the path, with an air of vexation which made her look rather prettier.

"What, my dear, don't you know that I am your husband's young master? Come, come!" he said, following her, and endeavoring to take hold of her arm.

"Please let me alone!" said Lisette, coloring, and in a pettish, vexed tone.

"Let you alone? No, that I sha'n't, not while you ask it in such a pretty way as that!" And again the hand was laid upon her shoulder.

It must be understood that Harry had witnessed so far, in pantomime, this scene. He had stood with compressed lips, and eyes slowly dilating, looking at it. Nina, who was standing with her back to the window, wondered at the expression of his countenance.

"Look there, Miss Nina!" he said. "Do you see my wife and your brother?"

Nina turned, and in an instant the color mounted to her cheeks; her little form seemed to dilate, and her eyes flashed fire; and before Harry could see what she was doing, she was down in the gravel walk, and had taken Lisette's hand.

"Tom Gordon," she said, "I'm ashamed of you! Hush! hush!" she continued, fixing her eyes on him, and stamping her foot. "Dare to come to my place, and take such liberties here! You shall not be allowed to while *I* am mistress; and I am mistress! Dare to lay a finger on this girl while she is here under my protection! Come, Lisette!" And she seized the trembling girl by the hand, and drew her along towards the house.

Tom Gordon was so utterly confused at this sudden burst of passion in his sister that he let them go off without opposition. In a few moments he looked after her, and gave a long, low whistle.

"Ah! Pretty well up for her! But she'll find it's easier said than done, I fancy!" And he sauntered up to the veranda, where Harry stood with his arms folded, and the veins in his forehead swelling with repressed emotion.

"Go in, Lisette," said Nina; "take the things into my room, and I'll come to you."

"'Pon my word, Harry," said Tom, coming up, and addressing Harry in the most insulting tone, "we are all under the greatest obligations to you for bringing such a pretty little fancy article here!"

"My wife does not belong to this place," said Harry, forcing himself to speak calmly. "She belongs to a Mrs. Le Clere, who has come into Belleville plantation."

"Ah! thank you for the information! I may take a fancy to buy her, and I 'd like to know who she belongs to. I 've been wanting a pretty little concern of that sort. She 's a good housekeeper, is n't she, Harry? Does up shirts well? What do you suppose she could be got for? I must go and see her mistress."

During this cruel harangue Harry's hands twitched and quivered, and he started every now and then, looking first at Nina, and then at his tormentor. He turned deadly pale; even his lips were of ashy whiteness; and with his arms still folded, and making no reply, he fixed his large blue eyes upon Tom; and, as it sometimes happened in moments of excitement and elevation, there appeared on the rigid lines of his face, at that moment, so strong a resemblance to Colonel Gordon, that Nina noticed and was startled by it. Tom Gordon noticed it also. It added fuel to the bitterness of his wrath; and there glared from his eyes a malignancy of hatred that was perfectly appalling. The two brothers seemed like thunder-clouds opposing each other, and ready to dart lightning. Nina hastened to interfere.

"Hurry, hurry, Harry! I want that message carried. Do, pray, go directly!"

"Let me see," said Tom, "I must call Jim, and have my horse. Which is the way to that Belleville plantation? I think I 'll ride over." And he turned and walked indolently down the steps.

"For shame, Tom! you won't! you can't! How can you want to trouble me so?" said Nina.

He turned and looked upon her with an evil smile, turned again, and was gone.

"Harry, Harry, go quick! Don't you worry; there 's no danger!" she added in a lower voice. "Mme. Le Clere never would consent."

"There 's no knowing!" said Harry, "never any knowing! People act about money as they do about nothing else."

"Then — then I 'll send and buy her myself!" said Nina.

"You don't know how our affairs stand, Miss Nina," said Harry hurriedly. "The money could n't be raised now for it, especially if I have to go off this week. It will make a great difference, my being here or not being here; and very likely Master Tom may have a thousand dollars to pay down on the spot. I never knew him to want money when his will was up. Great God! have n't I borne this yoke long enough?"

"Well, Harry," said Nina, "I 'll sell everything I 've got — my jewels — everything. I 'll mortgage the plantation, before Tom Gordon shall do this thing! I 'm not quite so selfish as I 've always seemed to be. I know you 've made the sacrifice of body and soul to my interest; and I 've always taken it because I loved my ease, and was a spoiled child. But, after all, I know I 've as much energy as Tom has, when I am roused, and I 'll go over this very morning and make an offer for her. Only you be off. You can't stand such provocation as you get here; and if you yield, as any man will do, at last, then everything and everybody will go against you, and I can't protect you. Trust to *me*. I 'm not so much of a child as I have seemed to be! You 'll find I can act for myself, and you, too! There comes Mr. Clayton through the shrubbery — that 's right! Order two horses round to the door immediately, and we 'll go over there this morning."

Nina gave her orders with a dignity as if she had been a princess, and in all his agitation Harry could not help marveling at the sudden air of womanliness which had come over her.

"I could serve you," he said in a low voice, "to the last drop of my blood! But," he added in a tone which

made Nina tremble, "I hate everybody else! I hate your
country! I hate your laws!"

"Harry," said Nina, "you do wrong — you forget yourself!"

"Oh, I do wrong, do I? We are the people that are
never to do wrong! People may stick pins in us, and
stick knives in us, wipe their shoes on us, spit in our face
— *we* must be amiable! we must be models of Christian
patience! I tell you, your father should rather have put
me into quarters and made me work like a field-negro,
than to have given me the education he did, and leave me
under the foot of every white man that dares tread on
me!"

Nina remembered to have seen her father in transports
of passion, and was again shocked and startled to see the
resemblance between his face and the convulsed face before
her.

"Harry," she said in a pitying, half-admonitory tone,
"do think what you are saying! If you love me, be
quiet!"

"Love you? You have always held my heart in your
hand. That has been the clasp upon my chain. If it
had n't been for you, I should have fought my way to the
North before now, or I would have found a grave on the
road!"

"Well, Harry," said Nina, after a moment's thought,
"my love shall not be a clasp upon any chain; for as there
is a God in heaven, I will set you free! I 'll have a bill
introduced at the very next legislature, and I know what
friend will see to it. So go, now, Harry, go!"

Harry stood a moment, then suddenly raised the hand
of his little mistress to his lips, turned, and was gone.

Clayton, who had been passing through the shrubbery,
and who had remarked that Nina was engaged in a very
exciting conversation, had drawn off, and stood waiting for

her at the foot of the veranda steps. As soon as Nina saw him, she reached out her hand frankly, saying, "Oh, there, Mr. Clayton, you are just the person! Wouldn't you like to take a ride with me?"

"Of course I should," said he.

"Wait here a moment," said she, "till I get ready. The horses will be here immediately." And running up the steps, she passed quickly by him, and went into the house.

Clayton had felt himself in circumstances of considerable embarrassment ever since the arrival of Tom Gordon, the evening before. He had perceived that the young man had conceived an instinctive dislike of himself, which he was at no particular pains to conceal; and he had found it difficult to preserve the appearance of one who does not notice. He did not wish to intrude upon Nina any embarrassing recognition of her situation, even under the guise of sympathy and assistance; and waited, therefore, till some word from her should authorize him to speak. He held himself, therefore, ready to meet any confidence which she might feel disposed to place in him; not doubting, from the frankness of her nature, that she would soon find it impossible not to speak of what was so deeply interesting to her.

Nina soon reappeared, and mounting their horses, they found themselves riding through the same forest road that led to the cottage of Tiff, from which a divergent path went to the Belleville plantation.

"I'm glad to see you alone this morning, for many reasons," said Nina; "for I think I never needed a friend's help more. I'm mortified that you should have seen what you did last night; but since you have, I may as well speak of it. The fact is, that my brother, though he is the only one I have, never did treat me as if he loved me. I can't tell what the reason is: whether he was jealous of

my poor father's love for me, or whether it was because I
was a willful, spoiled girl, and so gave him reason to be set
against me, or whatever the reason might be, — he never
has been kind to me long at a time. Perhaps he would
be, if I would always do exactly as he says; but I am
made as positive and willful as he is. I never have been
controlled, and I can't recognize the right which he seems
to assume to control me, and to dictate as to my own
private affairs. He was not left my guardian; and though
I do love him, I sha'n't certainly take him as one. Now,
you see, he has a bitter hatred, and a most unreasonable
one, towards my Harry; and I had no idea, when I came
home, in how many ways he had the power to annoy me.
It does seem as if an evil spirit possessed them both when
they get together; they seem as full of electricity as they
can be, and I am every instant afraid of an explosion.
Unfortunately for Harry, he has had a much superior education to the generality of his class and station, and the
situation of trust in which he has been placed has given
him more the feelings of a free man and a gentleman than
is usual; for, except Tom, there is n't one of our family
circle that has n't always treated him with kindness, and
even with deference; and I think this very thing angers
Tom the more, and makes him take every possible occasion
of provoking and vexing. I believe it is his intention to
push Harry up to some desperate action; and when I see
how frightfully they look at each other, I tremble for the
consequences. Harry has lately married a very pretty
wife, with whom he lives in a little cottage on the extrem-
ity of the Belleville estate; and this morning Tom happened to spy her, and it seemed to inspire him with a most
ingenious plan to trouble Harry. He threatened to come
over and buy her of Mme. Le Clere; and so, to quiet
Harry, I promised to come over here before him, and make
an offer for her."

"Why," said Clayton, "do you think her mistress would sell her?"

"I can't say," said Nina. "She is a person I am acquainted with only by report. She is a New Orleans creole who has lately bought the place. Lisette, I believe, hired her time of her. Lisette is an ingenious, active creature, and contrives, by many little arts and accomplishments, to pay a handsome sum, monthly, to her mistress. Whether the offer of a large sum at once would tempt her to sell her is more than I know until it's tried. I should like to have Lisette, for Harry's sake."

"And do you suppose your brother was really serious?"

"I shouldn't be at all surprised if he were. But, serious or not serious, I intend to make the matter sure."

"If it be necessary to make an immediate payment," said Clayton, "I have a sum of money which is lying idle in the bank, and it's but drawing a check which will be honored at sight. I mention this, because the ability to make an immediate payment may make the negotiation easier. You ought to allow me the pleasure of joining you in a good work."

"Thank you," said Nina frankly. "It may not be necessary; but if it should be, I will take it in the same spirit in which it is offered."

After a ride of about an hour they arrived in the boundaries of Belleville plantation. In former days, Nina had known this as the residence of an ancient rich family, with whom her father was on visiting terms. She was therefore uncomfortably struck with the air of poverty, waste, and decay, everywhere conspicuous through the grounds.

Nothing is more depressing and disheartening than the sight of a gradual decay of what has been arranged and constructed with great care; and when Nina saw the dilapidated gateway, the crushed and broken shrubbery, the gaps in the fine avenue where the trees had been improvidently cut down for fire-wood, she could not help a feeling of depression.

"How different this place used to be when I came here as a child!" said she. "This madam, whatever her name is, can't be much of a manager."

As she said this their horses came to the front of the house, in which the same marks of slovenly neglect were apparent. Blinds were hanging by one hinge; the door had sunk down into the rotten sill; the wooden pillars that supported it were decayed at the bottom; and the twining roses which once climbed upon them laid trailing, dishonored, upon the ground. The veranda was littered with all kinds of rubbish, — rough boxes, saddles, bridles, overcoats; and various nondescript articles formed convenient hiding-places and retreats, in which a troop of negro children and three or four dogs were playing at hide-and-go-seek with great relish and noise. On the alighting of Nina and Clayton at the door they all left their sports, and arranged themselves in a grinning row, to see the new-comers descend. Nothing seemed to be further from the minds of the little troop than affording the slightest assistance in the way of holding horses or answering questions. All they did was alternately to look at each other and the travelers, and grin.

A tattered servant-man, with half a straw hat on his head, was at length raised by a call of Clayton, who took their horses — having first distributed a salutation of kicks and cuffs among the children, asking where their manners were that they didn't show the gentleman and lady in. And Nina and Clayton were now marshaled by the whole seven of them into an apartment on the right of the great hall. Everything in the room appeared in an unfinished state. The curtains were half put up at the windows, and part lying in a confused heap on the chairs. The damp, mouldy paper, which hung loosely from the wall, had been torn away in some places, as if to prepare for repapering; and certain half-opened rolls of costly wall-paper lay on the table, on which appeared the fragment of some ancient luncheon; to wit, plates, and pieces of bread and cheese, dirty tumblers, and an empty bottle. It was difficult to find a chair sufficiently free from dust to sit down on. Nina sent up her card by one of the small fry, who, having got halfway up the staircase, was suddenly taken with the desire to slide down the banisters with it in his hand. Of course he dropped the card in the operation; and the whole group precipitated themselves briskly on to it, all in a heap, and fought, tooth and nail, for the honor of carrying it upstairs. They were aroused, however, by the entrance of the man with half a hat; who, on Nina's earnest suggestion, plunged into the troop, which ran, chattering and screaming like so many crows, to different parts of the hall, while he picked up the card, and with infinite good will beaming on his shining black face, went up with it, leaving Nina and Clayton waiting below. In a few moments he returned.

"Missis will see de young lady upstairs."

Nina tripped promptly after him, and left Clayton the sole tenant of the parlor for an hour. At length she returned, skipping down the stairs, and opening the door with great animation.

"The thing is done!" she said. "The bill of sale will be signed as soon as we can send it over."

"I had better bring it over myself," said Clayton, "and make the arrangement."

"So be it!" said Nina. "But pray let us be delivered from this place! Did you ever see such a desolate-looking house? I remember when I've seen it a perfect paradise — full of the most agreeable people."

"And pray what sort of a person did you find?" said Clayton, as they were riding homeward.

"Well," said Nina, "she's one of the tow-string order of women. Very slack-twisted, too, I fancy — tall, snuffy, and sallow. Clothes looked rough-dry, as if they had been pulled out of a bag. She had a bright-colored Madras handkerchief tied round her head, and spoke French a little more through her nose than French people usually do. Flourished a yellow silk pocket-handkerchief. Poor soul! She said she had been sick for a week with tooth-ache, and kept awake all night! So, one mustn't be critical! One comfort about these French people is, that they are always *ravis de vous voir*, let what will turn up. The good soul was really polite, and insisted on clearing all the things off from a dusty old chair for me to sit down in. The room was as much at sixes and sevens as the rest of the house. She apologized for the whole state of things by saying that they could not get workmen out there to do anything for her; and so everything is left in the second future tense; and the darkeys, I imagine, have a general glorification in the chaos. She is one of the indulgent sort, and I suspect she'll be eaten up by them like the locusts. Poor thing! she is shockingly homesick, and longing for Louisiana again. For notwithstanding her snuffy appearance, and yellow pocket-handkerchief, she really has a genuine taste for beauty; and spoke most feelingly of the oleanders, crape myrtles, and cape jessamines, of her native state."

"Well, how did you introduce your business?" said Clayton, laughing at this description.

"Me? — Why, I flourished out the little French I have at command, and she flourished her little English; and I think I rather prepossessed the good soul, to begin with. Then I made a sentimental story about Lisette and Harry's amours; because I know French people always have a taste for the sentimental. The old thing was really quite affected, wiped her little black eyes, pulled her hooked nose as a tribute to my eloquence, called Lisette her *enfant mignon,* and gave me a little lecture on the tender passion, which I am going to lay up for future use."

"Indeed!" said Clayton. "I should be charmed to have you repeat it. Can't you give us a synopsis?"

"I don't know what synopsis means. But if you want me to tell you what she said, I sha'n't do it. Well, now, do you know I am in the best spirits in the world, now that I 've got this thing off my mind, and out of that desolate house? Did you ever see such a direful place? What is the reason, when we get down South, here, every-thing seems to be going to destruction, so? I noticed it all the way down through Virginia. It seems as if every-thing had stopped growing, and was going backwards. Well, now, it 's so different at the North! I went up, one vacation, into New Hampshire. It 's a dreadfully poor, barren country; nothing but stony hills and poor soil. And yet the people there seem to be so well off! They live in such nice, tight, clean-looking white houses! Everything around them looks so careful and comfortable; and yet their land is n't half so good as ours, down here. Why, actually, some of those places seem as if there were nothing but rock! And then, they have winter about nine months in the year, I do believe! But these Yankees turn everything to account. If a man's field is covered with rock, he 'll find some way to sell it, and make money out of it; and if they freeze up all winter, they sell the ice, and make money out of that. They just live by sell-ing their disadvantages!"

"And we grow poor by wasting our advantages," said Clayton.

"Do you know," said Nina, "people think it 's a dread-ful thing to be an Abolitionist? But for my part, I 've a great inclination to be one. Perhaps because I have a contrary turn, and always have a little spite against what

everybody else believes.   But if you won't tell anybody,
I 'll tell you — I don't believe in slavery! "

"Nor I, either! " said Clayton.

"You don't!   Well, really, I thought I was saying something original.   Now, the other day, Aunt Nesbit's minister
was at our house, and they sat crooning together, as they
always do; and among other things, they said, ' What a
blessed institution it was to bring these poor Africans over
here to get them Christianized! '   So, by way of saying
something to give them a start, I told them I thought they
came nearer to making heathen of us than we to making
Christians of them. "

"That 's very true, " said Clayton.   "There 's no doubt
that the kind of society which is built up in this way constantly tends to run back towards barbarism.   It prevents
general education of the whites, and keeps the poorer
classes down to the lowest point, while it enriches a
few. "

"Well, what do we have it for? " said Nina.   "Why
don't we blow it up, right off? "

"That 's a question easier asked than answered.   The
laws against emancipation are very stringent.   But I think
it is every owner's business to contemplate this as a future
resort, and to educate his servants in reference to it.   That
is what I am trying to do on my plantation. "

"Indeed! " said Nina, looking at him with a good deal
of interest.   "Well, now, that reminds me of what I was
going to say to you.   Generally speaking, my conscience
don't trouble me much about my servants, because I think
they are doing about as well with me as they would be
likely to do anywhere else.   But now, there 's Harry!
He is well educated, and I know that he could do for
himself, anywhere, better than he does here.   I have
always had a kind of sense of this; but I 've thought of it
more lately, and I 'm going to try to have him set free at

the next legislature. And I shall want you to help me about all the what-do-you-call-'ems."

"Of course, I shall be quite at your service," said Clayton.

"There used to be some people, when I was up at the North, who talked as if all of us were no better than a pack of robbers and thieves. And, of course, when I was there I was strong for our institutions, and would not give them an inch of ground. It set me to thinking, though; and the result of my thinking is, that we have no right to hold those to work for us who clearly can do better. Now, there's Aunt Nesbit's Milly — there's Harry and Lisette. Why, it's clear enough, if they can support themselves and us too, they certainly can support themselves alone. Lisette has paid eight dollars a month to her mistress, and supported herself besides. I'm sure it's *we* that are the helpless ones!"

"Well, do you think your Aunt Nesbit is going to follow your example?"

"No! catch her at it! Aunt Nesbit is doubly fortified in her religion. She is so satisfied with something or other about 'cursed be Canaan,' that she'd let Milly earn ten dollars a month for her, all the year round, and never trouble her head about taking every bit of it. Some folks, you know, have a way of calling everything they want to do a dispensation of Providence! Now, Aunt Nesbit is one of 'em. She always calls it a dispensation that the negroes were brought over here, and a dispensation that we are the mistresses. Ah! Milly will not get free while Aunt Nesbit is alive! And do you know, though it does not seem very generous in me, yet I'm resigned to it, because Milly is such a good soul, and such a comfort to me? Do you know she seems a great deal more like a mother to me than Aunt Nesbit? Why, I really think, if Milly had been educated as we are, she would have made a most splendid woman — been a perfect Candace queen of Ethiopia. There's a vast deal that is curious and interesting in some of these old Africans. I always did love to be with them; some of them are so shrewd and original! But I wonder, now, what Tom will think of my cutting him out so neatly? 'T will make him angry, I suppose."

"Oh, perhaps, after all, he had no real intention of doing anything of the kind," said Clayton. "He may have said it merely for bravado."

"I should have thought so, if I hadn't known that he always had a grudge against Harry."

At this moment the galloping of a horse was heard in the woodland path before them; and very soon Tom Gordon appeared in sight, accompanied by another man, on horseback, with whom he was in earnest conversation. There was something about the face of this man which, at the first glance, Nina felt to be very repulsive. He was low, thick-set, and yet lean; his features were thin and sharp; his hair and eyebrows bushy and black, and a pair of glassy, pale blue eyes formed a peculiar contrast to their darkness. There was something in the expression of the eye which struck Nina as hard and cold. Though the man was habited externally as a gentleman, there was still about him an underbred appearance, which could be detected at the first glance, as the coarseness of some woods will reveal themselves through every varnish.

"Good-morrow, Nina," said her brother, drawing his horse up to meet hers, and signing to his companion to arrest his also. "Allow me to present to you my friend, Mr. Jekyl. We are going out to visit the Belleville plantation."

"I wish you a pleasant ride!" said Nina. And touching her horse, she passed them in a moment. Looking back almost fiercely, a moment, she turned and said to Clayton:

"I hate that man!"

"Who is it?" said Clayton.

"I don't know!" said Nina. "I never saw him before. But I hate him! He is a bad man! I'd as soon have a serpent come near me as that man!"

"Well, the poor fellow's face isn't prepossessing," said Clayton. "But I should not be prepared for such an anathema."

"Tom's badness," continued Nina, speaking as if she were following out a train of thought, without regarding her companion's remark, "is good turned to bad. It's wine turned to vinegar. But this man don't even know what good is!"

"How can you be so positive about a person that you've only seen once!" said Clayton.

"Oh," said Nina, resuming her usual gay tones, "don't you know that girls and dogs, and other inferior creatures, have the gift of seeing what's in people? It doesn't belong to highly cultivated folks like you, but to us poor creatures, who have to trust to our instincts. So, beware!" And as she spoke, she turned to him with a fascinating air of half-saucy defiance.

"Well," said Clayton, "have you seen, then, what is in me?"

"Yes, to be sure!" said Nina with energy; "I knew what you were the very first time I saw you. And that's the reason why" —

Clayton made an eager gesture, and his eye met hers with a sudden flash of earnestness. She stopped, and blushed, and then laughed.

"What, Nina?"

"Oh, well, I always thought you were a grandfatherly body, and that you wouldn't take advantage of ' us girls,' as some of the men do. And so I've treated you with confidence, as you know. I had just the same feeling that you could be trusted, as I have that that other fellow cannot!"

"Well," said Clayton, "that deduction suits me so well that I should be sorry to undermine your faith. Nevertheless, I must say such a way of judging is n't always safe. Instinct may be a greater matter than we think; yet it is n't infallible, any more than our senses. We try the testimony even of our eyesight by reason. It will deceive us, if we don't. Much more we ought to try this more subtle kind of sight."

"Maybe so," said Nina; "yet I don't think I shall like that man, after all. But I 'll give him a chance to alter my feeling, by treating him civilly if Tom brings him back to dinner. That 's the best I can do."

CHAPTER XIV

AUNT NESBIT'S LOSS

ON entering the house, Nina was met at the door by Milly, with a countenance of some anxiety.

"Miss Nina," she said, "your aunt has heard bad news this morning."

"Bad news!" said Nina quickly — "what?"

"Well, honey, ye see dere has been a lawyer here," said Milly, following Nina as she was going upstairs; "and she has been shut up with him all de mornin'; and when he come out I found her taking on quite dreadful! And she says she has lost all her property."

"Oh! is that all?" said Nina. "I didn't know what dreadful thing might have happened. Why, Milly, this isn't so very bad. She hadn't much to lose."

"Oh, bless you, chile! nobody wants to lose all they got, much or little!"

"Yes; but," said Nina, "you know she can always live here with us; and what little money she wants to fuss with, to buy new caps, and paregoric for her cough, and all such little matters, we can give her, easily enough."

"Ah, Miss Nina, your heart is free enough; you'd give away both ends of the rainbow, if you had 'em to give. But the trouble is, chile, you haven't got 'em. Why, chile, dis yer great place, and so many mouths opened to eat and eat, chile, I tell you it takes heaps to keep it a-going. And Harry, I tell you, finds it hard work to bring it even all the year round, though he never says nothing to you about his troubles, — wants you always to walk on flowers, with both hands full, and never think where they come from. I tell you what, chile, we's boun' to think for you a little; and I tell you what, I's jist a-going to hire out."

"Why, Milly, how ridiculous!"

"It ain't ridiculous, now. Why, just look on it, Miss Nina. Here's Miss Loo, dat's one; here's me, dat's two; here's Polly, — great grown girl, — three; dere's Tomtit, four; all on us eating your bread, and not bringing in a cent to you, 'cause all on us together ain't done much more than wait on Miss Loo. Why, you's got servants enough of your own to do every turn that wants doing in dis yer house. I know, Miss Nina, young ladies don't like to hear about dese things; but the fac' is, victuals cost something, and dere must be some on us to bring in something. Now, dat ar gentleman what talked with your aunt, he said he could find me a right good place up dar to the town, and I was jest a-going. Sally, she is big enough now to do everything that I have been used to doing for Miss Loo, and I am jest a-going; besides, to tell you the truth, I think Miss Loo has kind o' set her heart upon it. You know she is a weakly kind of thing, — don't know how to do much 'cept sit in her chair and groan. She has always been so used to having me make a way for her; and when I told her about dis yer, she kind o' brightened up."

"But, Milly, what shall I do? I can't spare you at all," said Nina.

"Law bless you, chile! don't you suppose I's got eyes? I tell you, Miss Nina, I looked that gen'leman over pretty well for you, and my opinion is he'll do."

"Oh, come, you hush!" said Nina.

"You see, chile, it wouldn't be everybody that our people would be willing to have come on to de place, here, but there ain't one of 'em that wouldn't go in for dis yar, now I tell you. Dere's Old Hundred, as you calls him, told me 't was just as good as a meeting to hear him reading de prayers dat ar day at de funeral. Now, you see, I's seen gen'lemen handsome, and rich, and right pleasant, too, dat de people would n't want at all; 'cause why? dey has dere frolics and drinks, and de money flies one way for dis ting and one way for dat, till by and by it's all gone. Den comes de sheriff, and de people is all sold, some one way and some another way. Now, Mr. Clayton, he ain't none of dem."

"But, Milly, all this may be very well; but if I could n't love him?"

"Law sakes, Miss Nina! You look me in the face and tell me dat ar? Why, chile, it's plain enough to see through *you.* 'T is so! The people's all pretty sure, by this time. Sakes alive, we's used to looking out for the weather; and we knows pretty well what's coming. And now, Miss Nina, you go right along and give him a good word, 'cause you see, dear lamb, you *need* a good husband to take care of you, — dat's what you want, chile. Girls like you has a hard life being at the head of a place, especially your brother being just what he is. Now, if you had a husband here, Mas'r Tom 'ud be quiet, 'cause he knows he could n't do nothing. But just as long as you's alone he'll plague you. But, now, chile, it's time for you to be getting ready for dinner."

"Oh, but, do you know, Milly," said Nina, "I've something to tell you, which I had liked to have forgotten! I have been out to the Belleville plantation, and bought Harry's wife."

"You has, Miss Nina! Why, de Lord bless you! Why, Harry was dreadful worked, dis yer morning, 'bout what Mas'r Tom said. 'Peared like he was most crazy."

"Well," said Nina, "I've done it. I've got the receipt here."

"Why, but, chile, where alive did you get all the money to pay right sudden so?"

"Mr. Clayton lent it to me," said Nina.

"Mr. Clayton! Now, chile, didn't I tell you so? Do you suppose, now, you'd a let him lend you dat ar money if you hadn't liked him? But, come, chile, hurry! Dere's Mas'r Tom and dat other gen'leman coming back, and you must be down to dinner."

The company assembled at the dinner-table was not particularly enlivening. Tom Gordon, who, in the course of his morning ride, had discovered the march which his sister had stolen upon him, was more sulky and irritable than usual, though too proud to make any allusion to the subject. Nina was annoyed by the presence of Mr. Jekyl, whom her brother insisted should remain to dinner. Aunt Nesbit was uncommonly doleful, of course. Clayton, who in mixed society generally took the part of a listener rather than a talker, said very little; and had it not been for Carson, there's no saying whether any of the company could have spoken. Every kind of creature has its uses, and there are times when a lively, unthinking chatterbox is a perfect godsend. Those unperceiving people, who never notice the embarrassment of others, and who walk with the greatest facility into the gaps of conversation, simply because they have no perception of any difficulty there, have their hour; and Nina felt positively grateful to Mr. Carson for the continuous and cheerful rattle which had so annoyed her the day before. Carson drove a brisk talk with the lawyer about the value of property, percentage, etc.; he sympathized with Aunt Nesbit on her last-caught cold, rallied Tom on his preoccupation, complimented Nina on her improved color from her ride, and seemed on such excellent terms both with himself and everybody else that the thing was really infectious.

"What do you call your best investments, down here, — land, eh?" he said to Mr. Jekyl.

Mr. Jekyl shook his head.

"Land deteriorates too fast. Besides, there's all the trouble and risk of overseers, and all that. I've looked this thing over pretty well, and I always invest in niggers."

"Ah!" said Mr. Carson, "you do?"

"Yes, sir, I invest in niggers; that's what I do; and I hire them out, sir, — hire them out. Why, sir, if a man has a knowledge of human nature, knows where to buy and when to buy, and watches his opportunity, he gets a better percentage on his money that way than any other. Now, that was what I was telling Mrs. Nesbit, this morning. Say, now, that you give one thousand dollars for a man, — and I always buy the best sort, that's economy, — well, and he gets — put it at the lowest figure — ten dollars a month wages, and his living. Well, you see there, that gives you a pretty handsome sum for your money. I have a good talent of buying. I generally prefer mechanics. I have got now working for me three bricklayers. I own two firstrate carpenters, and last month I bought a perfect jewel of a blacksmith. He is an uncommonly ingenious man; a fellow that will make, easy, his fifteen dollars a month; and he is the more valuable because he has been religiously brought up. Why, some of them, now, will cheat you, if they can; but this fellow has been brought up in a district where they have a missionary, and a great deal of pains has been taken to form his religious principles. Now, this fellow would no more think of touching a cent of his earnings than he would of stealing right out of my pocket. I tell people about him, sometimes, when I find them opposed to religious instruction. I tell them, 'See there, now — you see how godliness is profitable to the life that now is.' You know the Scriptures, Mrs. Nesbit?"

"Yes," said Aunt Nesbit, "I always believed in religious education."

"Confound it all!" said Tom, "I don't! I don't see the use of making a set of hypocritical sneaks of them! I'd make niggers bring me my money; but, hang it all, if he came snuffling to me, pretending 't was his duty, I'd choke him! They never think so, — they don't and they can't, — and it's all hypocrisy, this religious instruction, as you call it!"

"No, it is n't," said the undiscouraged Mr. Jekyl, "not when you found it on right principles. Take them early enough, and work them right, you'll get it ground into them. Now, when they begun religious instruction, there was a great prejudice against it in our part of the country. You see they were afraid that the niggers would get *uppish*. Ah, but you see the missionaries are pretty careful; they put it in strong in the catechisms about the rights of the master. You see the instruction is just grounded on this, that the master stands in God's place to them."

"D—d bosh!" said Tom Gordon.

Aunt Nesbit looked across the table as if she were going to faint. But Mr. Jekyl's composure was not in the slightest degree interrupted.

"I can tell you," he said, "that, in a business, practical view, — for I am used to investments, — that, since the publishing of those catechisms, and the missionaries' work among the niggers, the value of that kind of property has risen ten per cent. They are better contented. They don't run away, as they used to. Just that simple idea that their master stands in God's place to them. Why, you see, it cuts its way."

"I have a radical objection to all that kind of instruction," said Clayton.

Aunt Nesbit opened her eyes, as if she could hardly believe her hearing.

"And pray what is your objection?" said Mr. Jekyl, with an unmoved countenance.

"My objection is that it is all a lie," said Clayton in such a positive tone that everybody looked at him with a start.

Clayton was one of those silent men who are seldom roused to talk, but who go with a rush when they are. Not seeming to notice the startled looks of the company, he went on: "It's a worse lie, because it's told to bewilder a simple, ignorant, confiding creature. I never could conceive how a decent man could ever look another man in the face and say such things. I remember reading, in one of the missionary reports, that when this doctrine was first propounded in an assembly of negroes somewhere, all the most intelligent of them got up and walked deliberately out of the house; and I honor them for it."

"Good for them!" said Tom Gordon. "I can keep my niggers down without any such stuff as that!"

"I have no doubt," said Clayton, "that these missionaries are well-intending, good men, and that they actually think the only way to get access to the negroes at all is to be very positive in what will please the masters. But I think they fall into the same error that the Jesuits did when they adulterated Christianity with idolatry in order to get admission in Japan. A lie never works well in religion, nor in morals."

"That's what I believe," said Nina warmly.

"But then, if you can't teach them this, what can you teach them?" said Mr. Jekyl.

"Confound it all!" said Tom Gordon, "teach them that you've got the power! — teach them the weight of your fist! That's enough for them. I am bad enough, I know; but I can't bear hypocrisy. I show a fellow my pistol. I say to him, You see that, sir! I tell him, You do so and so, and you shall have a good time with me. But you do that, and I'll thrash you within an inch of your life! That's my short method with niggers, and

poor whites, too. When one of these canting fellows
comes round to my plantation, let him see what he'll get,
that's all!"

Mr. Jekyl appeared properly shocked at this declaration.
Aunt Nesbit looked as if it was just what she had expected, and went on eating her potato with a mournful air,
as if nothing could surprise her. Nina looked excessively
annoyed, and turned a sort of appealing glance upon Clayton.

"For my part," said Clayton, "I base my religious instruction to my people on the ground that every man and
every woman must give an account of themselves to God
alone; and that God is to be obeyed first, and before
me."

"Why," said Mr. Jekyl, "that would be destructive of
all discipline. If you are going to allow every fellow to
judge for himself, among a parcel of ignorant, selfish
wretches, what the will of God is, one will think it's one
thing, another will think it's another; and there will be
an end of all order. It would be absolutely impossible to
govern a place in that way."

"They must not be left an ignorant set," said Clayton.
"They must be taught to read the Scriptures for themselves, and be able to see that my authority accords with
it. If I command anything contrary to it, they ought to
oppose it!"

"Ah! I should like to see a plantation managed in
that way!" said Tom Gordon scornfully.

"Please God, you shall see such an one, if you'll come
to mine," said Clayton, "where I should be very happy
to see you, sir."

The tone in which this was said was so frank and sincere that Tom was silenced, and could not help a rather
sullen acknowledgment.

"I think," said Mr. Jekyl, "that you'll find such a

course, however well it may work at first, will fail at last.
You begin to let people think, and they won't stop where
you want them to; they 'll go too far; it 's human nature.
The more you give, the more you may give. You once
get your fellows to thinking, and asking all sorts of questions, and they get discontented at once. I 've seen that
thing tried in one or two instances, and it did n't turn out
well. Fellows got restless and discontented. The more
was given to them, the more dissatisfied they grew, till
finally they put for the free states."

"Very well," said Clayton; "if that 's to be the result,
they may all ' put ' as soon as they can get ready. If my
title to them won't bear an intelligent investigation, I
don't wish to keep them. But I never will consent to
keep them by making false statements to them in the name
of religion, and presuming to put myself as an object of
obedience before my Maker."

"I think," said Mr. Carson, "Mr. Clayton shows an
excellent spirit — excellent spirit! On my word, I think
so. I wish some of our northern agitators, who make
such a fuss on the subject, could hear him. I 'm always
disgusted with these Abolitionists producing such an un-
pleasantness between the North and the South, interrupting
trade, and friendship, and all that sort of thing."

"He shows an excellent spirit," said Mr. Jekyl; "but
I must think he is mistaken if he thinks that he can bring
up people in that way, under our institutions, and not do
them more harm than good. It 's a notorious fact that the
worst insurrections have arisen from the reading of the
Bible by these ignorant fellows. That was the case with
Nat Turner, in Virginia. That was the case with Denmark Vesey, and his crew, in South Carolina. I tell you,
sir, it will never do, this turning out a set of ignorant
people to pasture in the Bible! That blessed book is a
savor of life unto life when it 's used right; but it 's a

savor of death unto death when ignorant people take hold
of it.   The proper way is this: administer such portions
only as these creatures are capable of understanding.   This
admirable system of religious instruction keeps the matter
in our own hands, by allowing us to select for them such
portions of the word as are best fitted to keep them quiet,
dutiful, and obedient; and I venture to predict that whoever undertakes to manage a plantation on any other system will soon find it getting out of his hands."

"So you are afraid to trust the Lord's word without
holding the bridle!" said Tom, with a sneer.   "That's
pretty well for you!"

"*I* am not!" said Clayton.   "I'm willing to resign
any rights to any one that I am not able to defend in
God's word — any that I cannot make apparent to any
man's cultivated reason.   I scorn the idea that I must
dwarf a man's mind, and keep him ignorant and childish,
in order to make him believe any lie I choose to tell him
about my rights over him!   I intend to have an educated,
intelligent people, who shall submit to me because they
think it clearly for their best interests to do so; because
they shall feel that what I command is right in the sight
of God."

"It's my opinion," said Tom, "that both these ways
of managing are humbugs.   One way makes hypocrites,
and the other makes rebels.   The best way of educating
is, to show folks that they can't help themselves.   All the
fussing and arguing in the world is n't worth one dose of
certainty on that point.   Just let them know that there
are no two ways about it, and you'll have all still
enough."

From this point the conversation was pursued with considerable warmth, till Nina and Aunt Nesbit rose and
retired to the drawing-room.   Perhaps it did not materially
discourage Clayton, in the position he had taken, that

Nina, with the frankness usual to her, expressed the most eager and undisguised admiration of all that he said.

"Did n't he talk beautifully? Was n't it noble?" she said to Aunt Nesbit, as she came in the drawing-room. "And that hateful Jekyl! is n't he mean?"

"Child!" said Aunt Nesbit, "I 'm surprised to hear you speak so! Mr. Jekyl is a very respectable lawyer, an elder in the church, and a very pious man. He has given me some most excellent advice about my affairs; and he is going to take Milly with him, and find her a good place. He 's been making some investigations, Nina, and he 's going to talk to you about them, after dinner. He 's discovered that there 's an estate in Mississippi worth a hundred thousand dollars, that ought properly to come to you!"

"I don't believe a word of it!" said Nina. "Don't like the man! — think he is hateful! — don't want to hear anything he has to say! — don't believe in him!"

"Nina, how often have I warned you against such sudden prejudices — against such a good man, too!"

"You won't make me believe he is good, not if he were elder in twenty churches!"

"Well, but, child, at any rate you must listen to what he has got to say. Your brother will be very angry if you don't, and it 's really very important. At any rate, you ought not to offend Tom, when you can help it."

"That 's true enough," said Nina; "and I 'll hear, and try and behave as well as I can. I hope the man will go, some time or other! I don't know why, but his talk makes me feel worse than Tom's swearing! That 's certain."

Aunt Nesbit looked at Nina as if she considered her in a most hopeless condition.

CHAPTER XV

AFTER the return of the gentlemen to the drawing-room, Nina, at the request of Tom, followed him and Mr. Jekyl into the library.

"Mr. Jekyl is going to make some statements to us, Nina, about our property in Mississippi, which, if they turn out as he expects, will set us up in the world," said Tom.

Nina threw herself carelessly into the leather armchair by the window, and looked out of it.

"You see," said Mr. Jekyl, also seating himself, and pulling out the stiff points of his collar, "having done law business for your father, and known, in that way, a good deal about the family property, I have naturally always felt a good deal of interest in it; and you remember your father's sister, Mrs. Stewart, inherited, on the death of her husband, a fine estate in Mississippi."

"I remember," said Tom, — "well, go on."

"Well, she died, and left it all to her son. Well, he, it seems like some other young men, lived in a very reprehensible union with a handsome quadroon girl, who was his mother's maid; and she, being an artful creature, I suppose, as a great many of them are, got such an ascendency over him that he took her up to Ohio, and married her, and lived there with her some years, and had two children by her. Well, you see, he had a deed of emancipation recorded for her in Mississippi, and just taking her into Ohio, set her free by the laws of that state. Well, you see, he thought he'd fixed it so that the thing couldn't

be undone, and she thought so too; and I understand
she's a pretty shrewd woman — has a considerable share
of character, or else she would n't have done just what she
has; for, you see, he died about six months ago, and left
the plantation and all the property to her and her children,
and she has been so secure that she has actually gone and
taken possession.   You see, she is so near white, you
must know that there is n't one in twenty would think
what she was, — and the people round there, actually,
some of them, had forgotten all about it, and did n't know
but what she was a white woman from Ohio; and so, you
see, the thing never would have been looked into at all, if
I had n't happened to have been down there.   But, you
see, she turned off an overseer that had managed the place,
because the people complained of him; and I happened to
fall in with the man, and he began telling me his story,
and after a little inquiry, I found who these people were.
Well, sir, I just went to one of the first lawyers, for I
suspected there was false play; and we looked over the
emancipation laws together, and we found out that, as the
law stood, the deed of emancipation was no more than so
much waste paper.   And so, you see, she and her children
are just as much slaves as any on her plantation; and the
whole property, which is worth a hundred thousand dollars, belongs to your family.   I rode out with him, and
looked over the place, and got introduced to her and her
children, and looked them over.   Considered as property,
I should call them a valuable lot.   She is past forty, but
she don't look older than twenty-seven or twenty-eight, I
should say.   She is a very good-looking woman, and then,
I'm told, a very capable woman.   Well, her price in the
market might range between one thousand and fifteen hundred dollars.   Smalley said he had seen no better article
sold for two thousand dollars; but then, he said, they
had to give a false certificate as to the age, — and that I

could n't hear of, for I never countenance anything like untruth. Then, the woman's children: she has got two fine-looking children as I have ever seen — almost white. The boy is about ten years old; the little girl, about four. You may be sure I was pretty careful not to let on, because I consider the woman and children are an important part of the property, and, of course, nothing had better be said about it, lest she should be off before we are ready to come down on them. Now, you see, you Gordons are the proper owners of this whole property; there is n't the slightest doubt in my mind that you ought to put in your claim immediately. The act of emancipation was contrary to law, and though the man meant well, yet it amounted to a robbery of the heirs. I declare, it rather raised my indignation to see that creature so easy in the possession of property which of right belongs to you. Now, if I have only the consent of the heirs, I can go on and commence operations immediately."

Nina had been sitting regarding Mr. Jekyl with a fixed and determined expression of countenance. When he had finished, she said to him, —

"Mr. Jekyl, I understand you are an elder in the church; is that true?"

"Yes, Miss Gordon, I have that privilege," said Mr. Jekyl, his sharp, business tone subsiding into a sigh.

"Because," said Nina, "I am a wild young girl, and don't profess to know much about religion; but I want you to tell me, as a Christian, if you think it would be right to take this woman and children, and her property."

"Why, certainly, my dear Miss Gordon; is n't it right that every one should have his own property? I view things simply with the eye of the law; and in the eye of the law that woman and her children are as much your property as the shoe on your foot; there is no manner of doubt of it."

"I should think," said Nina, "that you might see with the eye of the gospel, sometimes! Do you think, Mr. Jekyl, that doing this is doing as I should wish to be done by, if I were in the place of this woman?"

"My dear Miss Gordon, young ladies of fine feeling, at your time of life, are often confused on this subject by a wrong application of the Scripture language. Suppose I were a robber, and had possession of your property? Of course, I shouldn't wish to be made to give it up. But would it follow that the golden rule obliged the lawful possessor not to take it from me? This woman is your property; this estate is your property, and she is holding it as unlawfully as a robber. Of course, she won't want to give it up; but right is right, notwithstanding."

Like many other young persons, Nina could feel her way out of sophistry much sooner than she could think it out; and she answered to all this reasoning, —

"After all, I can't think it would be right."

"Oh, confound the humbug!" said Tom; "who cares whether it is right or not? The fact is, Nin, to speak plain sense to you, you and I both are deuced hard up for money, and want all we can get; and what's the use of being more religious than the very saints themselves at our time of day? Mr. Jekyl is a pious man — one of the tallest kind! He thinks this is all right, and why need we set ourselves all up? He has talked with Uncle John, and he goes in for it. As for my part, I am free to own I don't care whether it's right or not! I'll do it if I can. Might makes right, — that's my doctrine!"

"Why," said Mr. Jekyl, "I have examined the subject, and I haven't the slightest doubt that slavery is a divinely appointed institution, and that the rights of the masters are sanctioned by God; so however much I may naturally feel for this woman, whose position is, I must say, an unfortunate one, still it is my duty to see that the law is properly administered in the case."

"All I have to say, Mr. Jekyl," said Nina, "is just this: that I won't have anything to do with this matter; for, if I can't prove it's wrong, I shall always feel it is."

"Nina, how ridiculous!" said Tom.

"I have said my say," said Nina, as she rose and left the room.

"Very natural, — fine feelings, but uninstructed," said Mr. Jekyl.

"Certainly, we pious folks know a trick worth two of that, don't we?" said Tom. "I say, Jekyl, this sister of mine is a pretty rapid little case, I can tell you, as you saw by the way she circumvented us this morning. She is quite capable of upsetting the whole dish, unless we go about it immediately. You see, her pet nigger, this Harry, is this woman's brother; and if she gave him the word, he'd write at once, and put her on the alarm. You and I had better start off to-morrow, before this Harry comes back. I believe he is to be gone a few days. It's no matter whether she consents to the suit or not. She don't need to know anything about it."

"Well," said Jekyl, "I advise you to go right on, and have the woman and children secured. It's a perfectly fair, legal proceeding. There has been an evident evasion of the law of the state, by means of which your family are defrauded of an immense sum. At all events, it will be tried in an open court of justice, and she will be allowed to appear by her counsel. It's a perfectly plain, above-board proceeding; and as the young lady has shown such fine feelings, there's the best reason to suppose that the fate of this woman would be as good in her hands as in her own."

Mr. Jekyl was not now talking to convince Tom Gordon, but himself; for spite of himself, Nina's questions had awakened in his mind a sufficient degree of misgiving to make it necessary for him to pass in review the arguments by which he generally satisfied himself. Mr. Jekyl was a theologian, and a man of principle. His metaphysical talent, indeed, made him a point of reference among his Christian brethren; and he spent much of his leisure time in reading theological treatises. His favorite subject of all was the nature of true virtue; and this, he had fixed in his mind, consisted in a love of the greatest good. According to his theology, right consisted in creating the greatest amount of happiness; and every creature had rights to be happy in proportion to his capacity of enjoyment or being. He whose capacity was ten pounds had a right to place his own happiness before that of him who had five, because, in that way, five pounds more of happiness would exist in the general whole. He considered the right of the Creator to consist in the fact that he had a greater amount of capacity than all creatures put together, and, therefore, was bound to promote his own happiness before all of them put together. He believed that the Creator made himself his first object in all that He did; and, descending from Him, all creatures were to follow the same rule, in proportion to their amount of being; the greater capacity of happiness always taking precedence of the less. Thus, Mr. Jekyl considered that the Creator brought into the world yearly myriads of human beings with no other intention than to make them everlastingly miserable; and that this was right, because his capacity of enjoyment being greater than all theirs put together, He had a right to gratify himself in this way.

Mr. Jekyl's belief in slavery was founded on his theology. He assumed that the white race had the largest amount of being; therefore, it had a right to take precedence of the black. On this point he held long and severe arguments with his partner, Mr. Israel McFogg, who, belonging to a different school of theology, referred the whole matter to no natural fitness, but to a divine decree, by which it pleased the Creator in the time of Noah to pronounce a curse upon Canaan. The fact that the African race did *not* descend from Canaan was, it is true, a slight difficulty in the chain of the argument; but theologians are daily in the habit of surmounting much greater ones. Either way, whether by metaphysical fitness or divine decree, the two partners attained the same practical result.

Mr. Jekyl, though a coarse-grained man, had started from the hands of nature no more hard hearted or unfeeling than many others; but his mind, having for years been immersed in the waters of law and theology, had slowly petrified into such a steady consideration of the greatest general good, that he was wholly inaccessible to any emotion of particular humanity. The trembling, eager tone of pity, in which Nina had spoken of the woman and children who were about to be made victims of a legal process, had excited but a moment's pause. What considerations of temporal loss and misery can shake the constancy of the theologian who has accustomed himself to contemplate and discuss, as a cool intellectual exercise, the eternal misery of generations? — who worships a God that creates myriads only to glorify himself in their eternal torments?

CHAPTER XVI

MILLY'S STORY

NINA spent the evening in the drawing-room; and her brother, in the animation of a new pursuit, forgetful of the difference of the morning, exerted himself to be agreeable, and treated her with more consideration and kindness than he had done any time since his arrival. He even made some off-hand advances towards Clayton, which the latter received with good humor, and which went further than she supposed to raise the spirits of Nina; and so, on the whole, she passed a more than usually agreeable evening. On retiring to her room, she found Milly, who had been for some time patiently waiting for her, having dispatched her mistress to bed some time since.

"Well, Miss Nina, I am going on my travels in de morning. Thought I must have a little time to see you, lamb, 'fore I goes."

"I can't bear to have you go, Milly! I don't like that man you are going with."

"I spects he's a nice man," said Milly. "Of course he'll look me out a nice place, because he has always took good care of Miss Loo's affairs. So you never trouble yourself 'bout me! I tell you, chile, I never gets where I can't find de Lord; and when I finds Him, I gets along. 'De Lord is my shepherd, I shall not want.'"

"But you have never been used to living except in our family," said Nina, "and, somehow, I feel afraid. If they don't treat you well, come back, Milly; will you?"

"Laws, chile, I isn't much 'feard but what I'll get

along well enough. When people keep about dere business, doing de best dey ken, folks does n't often trouble
dem. I never yet seed de folks I could n't suit," she
added, with a glow of honest pride. "No, chile, it is n't
for myself I's fearing; it's just for you, chile. Chile,
you don't know what it is to live in dis yer world, and
I wants you to get de Best Friend to go with you. Why,
dear lamb, you wants somebody to go to and open your
heart; somebody dat 'll love you, and always stand by
you; somebody dat 'll always lead you right, you know.
You has more cares than such a young thing ought for to
have; great many looking to you, and 'pending on you.
Now, if your ma was alive, it would be different; but
just now, I see how 't is; dere 'll be a hundred things
you 'll be thinking and feeling, and nobody to say 'em to.
And now, chile, you must learn to go to de Lord. Why,
chile, He loves you! Chile, He loves you *just as you
be ;* if you only saw how much, it would melt your heart
right down. I told you I was going some time fur to tell
you my sperience — how I first found Jesus. Oh Lord,
Lord! but it is a long story."

Nina, whose quick sympathies were touched by the
earnestness of her old friend, and still more aroused by the
allusion to her mother, answered, —

"Oh yes, come, tell me about it!" And drawing a
low ottoman, she sat down, and laid her head on the lap
of her humble friend.

"Well, well, you see, chile," said Milly, her large dark
eyes fixing themselves on vacancy, and speaking in a slow
and dreamy voice, "a body's life, in dis yer world, is a
mighty strange thing! You see, chile, my mother — well,
dey brought her from Africa; my father, too. Heaps and
heaps my mother has told me about dat ar. Dat ar was
a mighty fine country, where dey had gold in the rivers,
and such great, big, tall trees, with de strangest beautiful

flowers on them you ever did see! Laws, laws! well, dey
brought my mother and my father into Charleston, and
dere Mr. Campbell, — dat was your ma's father, honey, —
he bought dem right out of de ship; but dey had five children, and dey was all sold, and dey never knowed where
dey went to. Father and mother could n't speak a word
of English when dey come ashore; and she told me often
how she could n't speak a word to nobody, to tell 'em how
it hurt her.

"Laws, when I was a chile, I 'member how often,
when de day's work was done, she used to come out and
sit and look up at de stars, and groan, groan, and groan!
I was a little thing, playing round; and I used to come
up to her, dancing, and saying, —

"' Mammy, what makes you groan so? what 's de matter
of you?'

"' Matter enough, chile!' she used to say. ' I 's a-thinking of my poor children. I likes to look at de stars, because dey sees de same stars dat I do. 'Pears like we was
in one room; but I don't know where dey is! Dey don't
know where I be!'

"Den she 'd say to me, —

"' Now, chile, you may be sold away from your mammy.
Der 's no knowing what may happen to you, chile; but
if you gets into any trouble, as I does, you mind, chile,
you ask God to help you.'

"' Who is God, mammy,' says I, ' anyhow?'

"' Why, chile,' says she, ' He made dese yer stars.'

"And den I wanted mammy to tell me more about it;
only she says, —

"' He can do anything he likes; and if .ye are in any
kind of trouble, He can help you.'

"Well, to be sure, I did n't mind much about it — all
dancing round, because pretty well don't need much help.
But she said dat ar to me so many times, I could n't help

'member it. 'Chile, troubles will come; and when dey does come, you ask God, and He will help you.'

"Well, sure enough, I was n't sold from her, but she was took from me, because Mr. Campbell's brother went off to live in Orleans, and parted de hands. My father and mother was took to Orleans, and I was took to Virginny. Well, you see, I growed up along with de young ladies, — your ma, Miss Harrit, Miss Loo, and de rest on 'em, — and I had heaps of fun. Dey all like Milly. Dey could n't nobody run, nor jump, nor ride a horse, nor row a boat, like Milly; and so it was Milly here, and Milly dere, and whatever de young ladies wanted, it was Milly made de way for it.

"Well, dere was a great difference among dem young ladies. Dere was Miss Loo — she was de prettiest, and she had a great many beaux; but den, dere was your ma — everybody loved her; and den dere was Miss Harrit — she had right smart of life in her, and was always for *doing* something — always right busy 'tending to something or other, and she liked me because I 'd always go in with her. Well, well! dem dar was pleasant times enough; but when I got to be about fourteen or fifteen, I began to feel kind o' bad — sort of strange and heavy. I really did n't know why, but 'peared like 's when I got older, I felt I was in bondage.

"'Member one day your ma came in, and seed me looking out of window, and she says to me, —

"' Milly, what makes you so dull lately ? '

"' Oh,' says I, ' I, somehow, I don't have good times.'

"' Why ? ' says she; ' why not ? Don't everybody make much of you, and don't you have everything that you want ? '

"' Oh, well,' says I, ' missis, I 's a poor slave-girl, for all dat.'

"Chile, your ma was a weety thing, like you. I 'mem-

ber just how she looked dat minute. I felt sorry, 'cause
I thought I'd hurt her feelings. But says she, —

"'Milly, I don't wonder you feel so. I know I should
feel so myself, if I was in your place.'

"Afterwards, she told Miss Loo and Miss Harrit; but
dey laughed, and said dey guessed der was n't many girls
who were as well off as Milly. Well, den, Miss Harrit,
she was married de first. She married Mr. Charles Blair;
and when she was married, nothing was to do but she
must have me to go with her. I liked Miss Harrit; but
den, honey, I'd liked it much better if it had been your
ma. I'd always counted that I wanted to belong to your
ma, and I think your ma wanted me; but den, she was
still, and Miss Harrit she was one of de sort dat never lost
nothing by not asking for it. She was one of de sort dat
always *got things* by hook or by crook. She always had
more clothes, and more money, and more everything, dan
de rest of them, 'cause she was always wide awake, and
looking out for herself.

"Well, Mr. Blair's place was away off in another part
of Virginny, and I went dere with her. Well, she wa'n't
very happy, noways, she wa'n't; because Mr. Blair, he
was a high fellow. Laws, Miss Nina, when I tells you
dis yere one you've got here is a good one, and I 'vise
you to take him, it's because I knows what comes o' girls
marrying high fellows. Don't care how good looking dey
is, nor what dere manners is, — it's just de ruin of girls
that has them. Law, when he was a-courting Miss Harrit,
it was all nobody but her. She was going to be his angel,
and he was going to give up all sorts of bad ways, and
live *such* a good life! Ah! she married him; it all went
to smoke! 'Fore de month was well over he got a-going
in his old ways; and den it was go, go, all de time, carous-
ing and drinking, — parties at home, parties abroad, —
money flying like de water.

"Well, dis made a great change in Miss Harrit. She did n't laugh no more; she got sharp and cross, and she wa'n't good to me like what she used to be. She took to be jealous of me and her husband. She might have saved herself de trouble. I should n't have touched him with a pair of tongs. But he was always running after everything that came in his way; so no wonder. But 'tween them both I led a bad life of it.

"Well, things dragged kind along in this way. She had three children, and at last he was killed, one day, falling off his horse when he was too drunk to hold the bridle. Good riddance, too, I thought. And den, after he 's dead, Miss Harrit, she seemed to grow more quiet like, and setting herself picking up what pieces and crumbs was left for her and de children. And I 'member she had one of her uncles dere a good many days helping her in counting up de debts. Well, dey was talking one day in missis' room, and dere was a little light closet on one side, where I got set down to do some fine stitching; but dey was too busy in their 'counts to think anything 'bout me. It seemed dat de place and de people was all to be sold off to pay de debts, — all 'cept a few of us, who were to go off with missis, and begin again on a small place, — and I heard him telling her about it.

" ' While your children are small,' he says, ' you can live small, and keep things close, and raise enough on the place for ye all; and den you can be making the most of your property. Niggers is rising in de market. Since Missouri came in, they 's worth double; and so you can just sell de increase of 'em for a good sum. Now, there 's that black girl Milly, of yourn.' — You may be sure, now, I pricked up my ears, Miss Nina. — ' You don't often see a girl of finer breed than she is,' says he, just as if I 'd been a cow, you know. ' Have you got her a husband ? '

"'No,' said Miss Harrit; and then says she, 'I believe Milly is something of a coquette among the young men. She's never settled on anybody yet,' says she.

"'Well,' says he, 'that must be attended to, 'cause that girl's children will be an estate of themselves. Why, I've known women to have twenty! and her children wouldn't any of 'em be worth less than eight hundred dollars. There's a fortune at once. If dey's like her, dey'll be as good as cash in the market, any day. You can send out and sell one, if you happen to be in any straits, just as soon as you can draw a note on the bank.'

"Oh, laws, Miss Nina, I tell you dis yer fell on me like so much lead. 'Cause, you see, I'd been keeping company with a very nice young man, and I was going to ask Miss Harrit about it dat very day; but, dere — I laid down my work dat minute, and thinks, says I, 'True as de Lord's in heaven I won't never be married in dis world!' And I cried 'bout it, off and on, all day, and at night I told Paul 'bout it. He was de one, you know. But Paul, he tried to make it all smooth. He guessed it wouldn't happen; he guessed missis would think better on 't. At any rate, we loved each other, and why shouldn't we take as much comfort as we could? Well, I went to Miss Harrit, and told her just what I thought 'bout it. Allers had spoke my mind to Miss Harrit 'bout everything, and I wa'n't going to stop den. And she laughed at me, and told me not to cry 'fore I's hurt. Well, things went on so two or three weeks, and finally Paul he persuaded me. And so we was married. When our first child was born, Paul was so pleased, he thought strange that I wa'n't.

"'Paul,' said I, 'dis yer child ain't ourn; it may be took from us, and sold, any day.'

"'Well, well,' says he, 'Milly, it may be God's child, anyway, even if it ain't ourn.'

"'Cause, you see, Miss Nina, Paul, he was a Christian. Ah, well, honey, I can't tell you; after dat I had a great many chil'en, girls and boys, growing up round me. Well, I's had fourteen chil'en, dear, and dey's all been sold from me, every single one of 'em. Lord, it's a heavy cross! heavy, heavy! None knows but dem dat bears it!"

"What a shame!" said Nina. "How could Aunt Harriet be such a wicked woman! — an aunt of mine do so!"

"Chile, chile," said Milly, "we does n't none of us know what's in us. When Miss Harrit and I was gals together, hunting hens' eggs and rowing de boat in de river, — well, I would n't have thought it would have been so, and she would n't have thought so, neither. But den, what little 's bad in girls when dey's young and handsome, and all de world smiling on 'em — Oh, honey, it gets drefful strong when dey gets grown women, and de wrinkles comes in der faces! Always, when she was a girl, — whether it was eggs, or berries, or chincapins, or what, — it was Miss Harrit's nature to *get* and to *keep*; and when she got old, dat all turned to money."

"Oh! but," said Nina, "it does seem impossible that a woman — a lady born, too, and my aunt — could do such a thing!"

"Ah, ah, honey! ladies born have some bad stuff in dem, sometimes, like de rest of us. But den, honey, it was de most natural thing in de world, come to look on 't; for now, see here, honey, dere was your aunt — she was poor, and she was pestered for money. Dere was Mas'r George's bills and Peter's bills to pay, and Miss Susy's; and every one of 'em must have everything, and dey was all calling for money, money; and dere has been times she did n't know which way to turn. Now, you see, when a woman is pestered to pay two hundred here and tree hun-

dred dere, and when she has got more niggers on her place
dan she can keep, and den a man calls in and lays down
eight hundred dollars in gold and bills before her, and
says, ' I want dat ar Lucy or George of yourn,' why, don't
you see ?   Dese yer soul-drivers is always round, tempting
folks dey know is poor; and dey always have der money
as handy as de devil has his.   But den, I ought n't fur
to be hard upon dem poor soul-drivers, neither, 'cause dey
ain't taught no better.   It 's dese yer Christians, dat profess Christ, dat makes great talks 'bout religion, dat has
der Bibles, and turns der backs upon swearing soul-drivers,
and tinks dey ain't fit to speak to — it 's *dem*, honey,
dat 's de root of de whole business.   Now, dere was dat
uncle of hern, — mighty great Christian he was, with his
prayer-meetings, and all dat! — he was always a-putting
her up to it.   Oh, dere 's been times — dere was times
'long first, Miss Nina, when my first chil'en was sold —
dat, I tell you, I poured out my soul to Miss Harrit, and
I 've seen dat ar woman cry so dat I was sorry for her.
And she said to me, ' Milly, I 'll never do it again.'   But,
Lord! I did n't trust her, — not a word on 't, — 'cause I
knowed she would.   I knowed dere was dat in her heart
dat de devil would n't let go of.   I knowed he 'd no kind
of objection to her 'musing herself with meetin's, and
prayers, and all dat; but he 'd no notion to let go his grip
on her heart.

"But, Lord! she was n't *quite* a bad woman, — poor
Miss Harrit was n't, — and she would n't have done so
bad, if it had n't been for *him*.   But he 'd come and have
prayers, and exhort, and den come prowling round my
place like a wolf, looking at my chil'en.

"' And, Milly,' he 'd say, ' how do you do now ?   Lucy
is getting to be a right smart girl, Milly.   How old is
she ?   Dere 's a lady in Washington has advertised for a
maid, — a nice woman, a pious lady.   I suppose you

would n't object, Milly? Your poor mistress is in great trouble for money.'

"I never said nothing to that man. Only once, when he asked me what I thought my Lucy would be worth, when she was fifteen years old, says I to him: —

"'Sir, she is worth to me just what your daughter is worth to you.'

"Den I went in and shut de door. I did n't stay to see how he took it. Den he'd go up to de house, and talk to Miss Harrit. 'Twas her duty, he'd tell her, to take proper care of her goods. And dat ar meant selling my chil'en. I 'member, when Miss Susy came home from boarding-school, she was a pretty girl: but I did n't look on her very kind, I tell you, 'cause three of my chil'en had been sold to keep her at school. My Lucy, — ah, honey! — she went for a lady's maid. I knowed what dat ar meant, well enough. De lady had a son grown, and he took Lucy with him to Orleans, and dere was an end of dat. Dere don't no letters go 'tween us. Once gone, we can't write, and it is good as being dead. Ah, no, chile, not so good! Paul used to teach Lucy little hymns, nights, 'fore she went to sleep. And if she 'd 'a' died right off after one of dem, it would have been better for her. Oh, honey, 'long dem times I used to rave and toss like a bull in a net — I did so!

"Well, honey, I was n't what I was. I got cross and ugly. Miss Harrit, she grew a great Christian, and joined de church, and used to have heaps of ministers and elders at her house; and some on 'em used to try and talk to me. I told 'em I'd seen enough of der old religion, and I did n't want to hear no more. But Paul, he was a Christian; and when he talked to me, I was quiet, like, though I could n't be like what he was. Well, last, my missis promised me one. She'd give me my youngest child, sure and certain. His name was Alfred. Well, dat boy — I

loved dat child better dan any of de rest of 'em. He was
all I 'd got left to love; for when he was a year old,
Paul's master moved away down to Louisiana, and took
him off, and I never heard no more of him. So it 'peared
as if dis yer child was all I had left. Well, he *was* a
bright boy. Oh, he was most uncommon! He was so
handy to anything, and saved me so many steps! Oh,
honey, he had such ways with him — dat boy! — would
always make me laugh. He took after larnin' mighty,
and he larned himself to read; and he 'd read de Bible to
me, sometimes. I just brought him up and teached him
de best way I could. All dat made me 'fraid for him was,
dat he was so spirity. I 's 'fraid 't would get him into
trouble.

"He wa'n't no more spirity dan white folks would like
der chil'en fur to be. When white chil'en holds up der
heads, and answers back, den de parents laugh, and say,
' He 's got it in him! He 's a bright one! ' But if one
of ourn does so, it 's a drefful thing. I was allers talking
to Alfred 'bout it, and told him to keep humble. It
'peared like there was so much in him, you couldn't keep
it down. Laws, Miss Nina, folks may say what dey like
about de black folks, dey 'll never beat it out of my head;
— dere 's some on 'em can be as smart as any white folks,
if dey could have de same chance. How many white boys
did you ever see would take de trouble for to teach their
selves to read? And dat 's what my Alfred did. Laws,
I had a mighty heap of comfort in him, 'cause I was
thinkin' to get my missis to let me hire my time; den I
was going to work over-hours, and get money, and buy
him; because, you see, chile, I knowed he was too spirity
for a slave. You see he couldn't *learn to stoop ;* he
wouldn't let nobody impose on him; and he always had
a word back again to give anybody as good as dey sent.
Yet for all dat, he was a dear, good boy to me; and when

I used to talk to him, and tell him dese things was dangerous, he'd always promise fur to be kerful. Well, things
went on pretty well while he was little, and I kept him
with me till he got to be about twelve or thirteen years
old. He used to wipe de dishes, and scour de knives,
and black de shoes, and such like work. But by and by,
dey said it was time dat he should go to de reg'lar work;
and dat ar was de time I felt 'feard. Missis had an overseer, and he was real aggravating, and I felt 'feard dere'd
be trouble; and sure enough dere was, too. Dere was
always somethin' brewing 'tween him and Alfred; and he
was always running to missis with tales, and I was talking
to Alfred. But 'peared like he aggravated de boy so, dat
he couldn't do right. Well, one day, when I had been
up to town for an errand, I come home at night, and I
wondered Alfred didn't come home to his supper. I
thought something was wrong; and I went to de house,
and dere sat Miss Harrit by a table covered with rolls of
money, and dere she was a-counting it.

"'Miss Harrit,' says I, 'I can't find Alfred. Ain't
you seen him?' says I.

"At first she didn't answer, but went on counting —
fifty-one, fifty-two, fifty-three. Finally I spoke again.

"'I hope there ain't nothing happened to Alfred, Miss
Harrit?'

"She looked up, and says she to me, —

"'Milly,' says she, 'de fact is, Alfred has got too much
for me to manage, and I had a great deal of money offered
for him; and I sold him.'

"I felt something strong coming up in my throat, and I
just went up and took hold of her shoulders, and said I, —

"'Miss Harrit, you took de money for thirteen of my
chil'en, and you promised me, sure enough, I should have
dis yer one. You call dat being a Christian?' says I.

"'Why,' says she, 'Milly, he ain't a great way off;

you can see him about as much. It's only over to Mr.
Jones's plantation. You can go and see him, and he can
come and see you. And you know you didn't like the
man who had the care of him here, and thought he was
always getting him into trouble.'

"'Miss Harrit,' says I, 'you may cheat yourself saying
dem things; but you don't cheat me, nor de Lord neither.
You folks have de say all on your side, with your ministers
preaching us down out of de Bible; you won't teach us to
read. But I'm going straight to de Lord with dis yer
case. I tell you, if de Lord is to be found, I'll find him;
and I'll ask him to look on 't, — de way you've been
treating me, — selling *my* chil'en, all de way 'long, to
pay for *your* chil'en, and now breaking your word to me,
and taking dis yer boy, de last drop of blood in my heart!
I'll pray de Lord to curse every cent of dat ar money to
you and your chil'en!'

"Dat ar was de way I spoke to her, child. I was poor,
ignorant cretur, and didn't know God, and my heart was
like a red-hot coal. I turned and walked right straight
out from her. I didn't speak no more to her, and she
didn't speak no more to me. And when I went to bed
at night, dar, sure 'nough, was Alfred's bed in de corner,
and his Sunday coat hanging up over it, and his Sunday
shoes I had bought for him with my own money; 'cause
he was a handsome boy, and I wanted him always to look
nice. Well, so, come Sunday morning, I took his coat
and his shoes, and made a bundle of 'em, and I took my
stick, and says I, 'I'll just go over to Jones's place and
see what has 'come of Alfred.' All de time, I hadn't
said a word to missis, nor she to me. Well, I got about
halfway over to de place, and dere I stopped under a big
hickory-tree, to rest me a bit, and I looked along and seed
some one a-coming; and pretty soon I knowed it was Huldah. She was one that married Paul's cousin, and she

lived on Jones's place. And so I got up and went to meet her, and told her I was going over to see 'bout Alfred.

"'Lord!' says she, 'Milly, have n't you heard dat Alfred 's dead?'

"Well, Miss Nina, it seemed as if my heart and everything in it stopped still. And said I, 'Huldah, has dey killed him?'

"And said she, 'Yes.' And she told me it was dis yer way. Dat Stiles — he dat was Jones's overseer — had heard dat Alfred was dreadful spirity; and when boys is so, sometimes dey aggravates 'em to get 'em riled, and den dey whips 'em to break 'em in. So Stiles, when he was laying off Alfred's task, was real aggravating to him; and dat boy — well, he answered back, just as he allers would be doing, 'cause he was smart, and it 'peared like he could n't keep it in. And den dey all laughed round dere, and den Stiles was mad, and swore he 'd whip him; and den Alfred, he cut and run. And den Stiles he swore awful at him, and he told him to 'come here, and he 'd give him hell, and pay him de cash.' Dem is de very words he said to my boy. And Alfred said he would n't come back; he was n't going to be whipped. And just den young Master Bill come along, and wanted to know what was de matter. So Stiles told him, and he took out his pistol, and said, 'Here, young dog, if you don't come back before I count five, I 'll fire!'

"'Fire ahead!' says Alfred; 'cause, you see, dat boy never knowed what fear was. And so he fired. And Huldah said he just jumped up and give one scream, and fell flat. And dey run up to him, and he was dead; 'cause, you see, de bullet went right through his heart. Well, dey took off his jacket and looked, but it wa'n't of no use; his face settled down still. And Huldah said dat dey just dug a hole and put him in. Nothing on him —

nothing round him — no coffin; like he 'd been a dog.
Huldah showed me de jacket. Dere was de hole, cut
right round in it, like it was stamped, and his blood running out on it. I did n't say a word. I took up de
jacket, and wrapped it up with his Sunday clothes, and
I walked straight — straight home. I walked up into
missis' room, and she was dressed for church, sure enough,
and sat dere reading her Bible. I laid it right down
under her face, dat jacket. 'You see dat hole!' said I;
'you see dat blood! Alfred 's killed! *You* killed him;
his blood be on you and your chil'en! O Lord God in
heaven, hear me, and render unto her double!' "

Nina drew in her breath hard, with an instinctive shudder. Milly had drawn herself up, in the vehemence of
her narration, and sat leaning forward, her black eyes
dilated, her strong arms clenched before her, and her powerful frame expanding and working with the violence of
her emotion. She might have looked, to one with myth-
ological associations, like the figure of a black marble
Nemesis in a trance of wrath. She sat so for a few
minutes, and then her muscles relaxed, her eyes gradually
softened ; she looked tenderly but solemnly down on
Nina. "Dem was awful words, chile; but I was in
Egypt den. I was wandering in de wilderness of Sinai.
I had heard de sound of de trumpet, and de voice of
words; but, chile, I had n't seen de Lord. Well — I
went out, and I did n't speak no more to Miss Harrit.
Dere was a great gulf fixed 'tween us; and dere did n't no
words pass over it. I did my work — I scorned not to do
it; but I did n't speak to her. Den it was, chile, dat I
thought of what my mother told me, years ago; it came
to me, all fresh — ' Chile, when trouble comes, you ask de
Lord to help you;' and I saw dat I had n't asked de Lord
to help me; and now, says I to myself, de Lord can't
help me; 'cause he could n't bring back Alfred, no way

you could fix it; and yet I wanted to find de Lord, 'cause I was so tossed up and down. I wanted just to go and say, 'Lord, you see what dis woman has done.' I wanted to put it to him, if he'd stand up for such a thing as that. Lord, how de world, and everything, looked to me in dem times! Everything goin' on in de way it did; and dese yer Christians, dat said dat dey was going into de kingdom, doing as dey did! I tell you, I sought de Lord early and late. Many nights I have been out in de woods and laid on de ground till morning, calling and crying, and 'peared like nobody heerd me. Oh, how strange it used to look, when I looked up to de stars! winking at me, so kind of still and solemn, but never saying a word! Sometimes I got dat wild, it seemed as if I could tear a hole through de sky, 'cause I must find God; I had an errand to him, and I must find him.

"Den I heard 'em read out de Bible, 'bout how de Lord met a man on a threshing-floor, and I thought maybe if I had a threshing-floor he would come to me. So I threshed down a place just as hard as I could under de trees; and den I prayed dere — but he didn't come. Den dere was coming a great camp-meeting; and I thought I'd go and see if I could find de Lord dere; because, you see, missis, she let her people go Sunday to de camp-meeting. Well, I went into de tents and heerd dem sing; and I went afore de altar, and I heerd preaching; but it 'peared like it was no good. It didn't touch me nowhere; and I couldn't see nothing to it. I heerd 'em read out of de Bible, 'Oh, dat I knew where I might find him. I would come even to his seat. I would order my cause before him. I would fill my mouth with arguments;' and I thought, sure enough, dat ar's just what I want. Well, came on dark night, and dey had all de camp-fires lighted up, and dey was singing de hymns round and round, and I went for to hear de preaching. And dere

was a man, — pale, lean man he was, with black eyes and
black hair. Well, dat ar man, he preached a sermon, to
be sure, I never shall forget. His text was, ' He that
spared not his own Son, but freely delivered him up for
us all, how shall he not with him freely give us all
things?' Well, you see, the first sound of dis took me,
because I'd lost my son. And the man, he told us who
de son of God was, — Jesus, — Oh, how sweet and beautiful he was! How he went round doing for folks. O
Lord, what a story dat ar was! And den, how dey took
him, and put de crown of thorns on his head, and hung
him up bleeding, bleeding, and bleeding! God so loved
us dat he let his own dear Son suffer all dat for us.
Chile, I got up, and I went to de altar, and I kneeled
down with de mourners; and I fell flat on my face, and
dey said I was in a trance. Maybe I was. Where I
was, I don't know; but I saw de Lord! Chile, it seemed
as if my very heart was still. I saw him, suffering, bearing with us, year in and year out — bearing — bearing —
bearing so patient! 'Peared like, it wa'n't just on de
cross; but, bearing always, everywhar! Oh, chile, I saw
how he loved us! — us *all* — all — every one on us! —
we dat hated each other so! 'Peared like he was using
his heart up for us, all de time — bleedin' for us like he
did on Calvary, and willin' to bleed! Oh, chile, I saw
what it was for me to be hatin', like I'd hated. ' O
Lord,' says I, ' I give up! O Lord, never see you afore;
I didn't know. Lord, I's a poor sinner! I won't hate
no more!' And oh, chile, den dere come such a rush of
love in my soul! Says I, ' Lord, I ken love even de
white folks!' And den came another rush; and says I,
' Yes, Lord, I love poor Miss Harrit, dat's sole all my
chil'en, and been de death of my poor Alfred! I loves
her.' Chile, I overcome — I did so — I overcome by de
blood of de *Lamb* — de Lamb! — Yes, de Lamb, chile! —

'cause if he 'd been a lion I could 'a' kept in; 't was de
Lamb dat overcome.

"When I come to, I felt like a chile. I went home to
Miss Harrit; and I had n't spoke peaceable to her since
Alfred died. I went in to her. She 'd been sick, and
she was in her room, looking kinder pale and yaller, poor
thing; 'cause her son, honey, he got drunk and 'bused
her awful. I went in, and says I, 'Oh, Miss Harrit, I 's
seen de Lord! Miss Harrit, I ain't got no more hard
feelin's; I forgive ye, and loves ye with all my heart, just
as de Lord does.' Honey, ye ought to see how dat
woman cried! Says she, 'Milly, I 's a great sinner.'
Says I, 'Miss Harrit, we 's sinners, both on us, but de
Lord gives hisself for us both; and if he loves us poor
sinners, we must n't be hard on each other. Ye was
tempted, honey,' says I (for you see I felt like makin'
scuses for her); 'but de Lord Jesus has got a pardon for
both on us.'

"After dat, I did n't have no more trouble with Miss
Harrit. Chile, we was sisters in Jesus. I bore her burdens, and she bore mine. And, dear, de burdens was
heavy; for her son he was brought home a corpse; he shot
hisself right through de heart trying to load a gun when
he was drunk. Oh, chile, I thought den how I 'd prayed
de Lord to render unto her double; but I had a better
mind den. Ef I could have brought poor Mas'r George to
life, I 'd 'a' done it; and I held de poor woman's head on
my arm all dat ar night, and she a-screamin' every hour.
Well, dat ar took her down to de grave. She did n't live
much longer; but she was ready to die. She sent and
bought my daughter Lucy's son, dis here Tom, and gin
him to me. Poor thing! she did all she could.

"I watched with her de night she died. Oh, Miss
Nina, if ever ye 're tempted to hate anybody, think how
't 'll be with 'em when dey comes to die.

"She died hard, poor thing! and she was cast down 'bout her sins. 'Oh, Milly,' says she, 'the Lord and you may forgive me, but I *can't* forgive myself.'

"'And,' says I to her, 'oh, missis, don't think of it no more! *de Lord's hid it in his own heart!*' Oh, but she struggled long, honey; she was all night dyin', and 't was 'Milly! Milly!' all de time; 'Oh, Milly, stay with me!'

"And, chile, I felt I loved her like my own soul; and when de day broke de Lord set her free, and I laid her down like she'd been one o' my babies. I took up her poor hand. It was warm, but the strength was all gone out on 't; and, 'Oh,' I thought, 'ye poor thing, how could I ever have hated ye so?' Ah, chile, we must n't hate nobody; we's all poor creatures, and de dear Lord he loves us all."

CHAPTER XVII

UNCLE JOHN

ABOUT four miles east of Canema lay the plantation of Nina's uncle, whither Harry had been sent on the morning which we have mentioned. The young man went upon his errand in no very enviable mood of mind. Uncle Jack, as Nina always called him, was the nominal guardian of the estate, and a more friendly and indulgent one Harry could not have desired. He was one of those joyous, easy souls whose leading desire seemed to be that everybody in the world should make himself as happy as possible, without fatiguing him with consultations as to particulars. His confidence in Harry was unbounded; and he esteemed it a good fortune that it was so, as he was wont to say, laughingly, that his own place was more than he could manage. Like all gentlemen who make the study of their own ease a primary consideration, Uncle Jack found the whole course of nature dead-set against him. For as all creation is evidently organized with a view to making people work, it follows that no one has so much care as the man who resolves not to take any. Uncle Jack was systematically, and as a matter of course, cheated and fleeced by his overseers, by his negroes, and the poor whites of his vicinity, and worst of all, continually hectored and lectured by his wife therefor. Nature, or Destiny, or whoever the lady may be that deals the matrimonial cards, with her usual thoughtfulness in balancing opposites, had arranged that jovial, easy, care-hating Uncle John should have been united to a most undaunted

and ever-active spirit of enterprise and resolution, who
never left anything quiet in his vicinity. She it was who
continually disturbed his repose, by constantly ferreting
out, and bringing before his view, all the plots, treasons,
and conspiracies with which plantation life is ever abound-
ing; bringing down on his devoted head the necessity of
discriminations, decisions, and settlements, most abhorrent
to an easy man.

The fact was, that responsibility, aggravated by her
husband's negligence, had transformed the worthy woman
into a sort of domestic dragon of the Hesperides; and her
good helpmeet declared that he believed she never slept,
nor meant anybody else should. It was all very well, he
would observe. He wouldn't quarrel with her for walking the whole night long, or sleeping with her head out of
the window, watching the smoke-house; for stealing out
after one o'clock to convict Pompey, or circumvent Cuff,
if she only wouldn't bother him with it. Suppose the
half of the hams were carried off, between two and three,
and sold to Abijah Skinflint for rum? — He must have his
sleep; and if he had to pay for it in ham, why, he'd pay
for it in ham; but sleep he must, and would. And supposing he really believed, in his own soul, that Cuffy, who
came in the morning, with a long face, to announce the
theft, and to propose measures of discovery, was in fact
the main conspirator — what then? He couldn't prove it
on him. Cuff had gone astray from the womb, speaking
lies ever since he was born; and what would be the use of
his fretting and sweating himself to death to get truth out
of Cuff? No, no! Mrs. G., as he commonly called his
helpmeet, might do that sort of thing, but she mustn't
bother him about it. Not that Uncle Jack was invariable
in his temper; human nature has its limits, and a personage who finds "mischief still for idle hands to do" often
seems to take a malicious pleasure in upsetting the temper

of idle gentlemen. So Uncle Jack, though confessedly
the best fellow in the world, was occasionally subject to a
tropical whirlwind of passion, in which he would stamp,
tear, and swear, with most astounding energy; and in those
ignited moments all the pent-up sorrows of his soul would
fly about him, like red-hot shot, in every direction. And
then he would curse the negroes, curse the overseers, curse
the plantation, curse Cuff and Pomp and Dinah, curse the
poor white folks round, curse Mr. Abijah Skinflint, and
declare that he would send them and the niggers all sev-
erally to a department which politeness forbids us to mention. He would pour out awful threats of cutting up,
skinning alive, and selling to Georgia. To all which commotion and bluster the negroes would listen, rolling the
whites of their eyes, and sticking their tongues in their
cheeks, with an air of great satisfaction and amusement;
because experience had sufficiently proved to them that
nobody had ever been cut up, skinned alive, or sent to
Georgia, as the result of any of these outpourings. So
when Uncle Jack had one of these fits, they treated it as
hens do an approaching thunderstorm, — ran under cover,
and waited for it to blow over.

As to Madam Gordon, her wrath was another affair.
And her threats they had learned to know generally meant
something; though it very often happened that, in the
dispensation of most needed justice, Uncle Jack, if in an
extra good humor, would rush between the culprit and his
mistress, and bear him off in triumph, at the risk of most
serious consequences to himself afterwards. Our readers
are not to infer from this that Madam Gordon was really
and naturally an ill-natured woman. She was only one
of that denomination of vehement housekeepers who are
to be found the world over — women to whom is appointed
the hard mission of combating, single handed, for the principles of order and exactness, against a whole world in

arms. Had she had the good fortune to have been born in Vermont or Massachusetts, she would have been known through the whole village as a woman who couldn't be cheated half a cent on a pound in meat, and had an instinctive knowledge whether a cord of wood was too short, or a pound of butter too light. Put such a woman at the head of the disorderly rabble of a plantation, with a cheating overseer, surrounded by thieving poor whites, to whom the very organization of society leaves no resource but thieving, with a never-mind husband, with land that has seen its best days, and is fast running to barrenness, and you must not too severely question her temper, if it should not be at all times in perfect subjection. In fact, Madam Gordon's cap habitually bristled with horror, and she was rarely known to sit down. Occasionally, it is true, she alighted upon a chair, but was in a moment up again, to pursue some of her household train, or shout, at the top of her lungs, some caution toward the kitchen.

When Harry reined up his horse before the plantation, the gate was thrown open for him by old Pomp, a superannuated negro, who reserved this function as his peculiar sinecure.

"Lord bress you, Harry, dat you? Bress you, you ought fur to see mas'r! Such a gale up to de house!"

"What's the matter, Pomp?"

"Why, mas'r, he done got one of he fits! Tarin' round dar, fit to split! — stompin' up and down de 'randy, swarin' like mad! Lord, if he ain't! He done got Jake tied up, dar! — swars he's goin' to cut him to pieces! He! he! he! Has so! Got Jake tied up dar! Ho! ho! ho! Real curus! And he's blowin' hisself out dere mighty hard, I tell you! So, if you want to get word wid him, you can't do it till he done got through wid dis yer!" And the old man ducked his pepper-and-salt-colored head, and chuckled with a lively satisfaction.

As Harry rode slowly up the avenue to the house, he caught sight of the portly figure of its master, stamping up and down the veranda, vociferating and gesticulating in the most violent manner. He was a corpulent man, of middle age, with a round, high forehead, set off with grizzled hair. His blue eyes, fair, rosy, fat face, his mouth adorned with brilliant teeth, gave him, when in good humor, the air of a handsome and agreeable man. At present his countenance was flushed almost to purple, as he stood storming, from his rostrum, at a saucy, ragged negro, who, tied to the horse-post, stood the picture of unconcern; while a crowd of negro men, women, and children were looking on.

"I 'll teach you!" he vociferated, shaking his fist. "I won't — won't bear it of you, you dog, you! You won't take my orders, won't you? I 'll kill you — that I will! I 'll cut you up into inch pieces!"

"No, you won't, and you know you won't!" interposed Mrs. Gordon, who sat at the window behind him. "You won't, and you know you won't! and they know you won't, too! It will all end in smoke, as it always does. I only wish you would n't talk and threaten, because it makes you ridiculous!"

"Hold your tongue, too! I 'll be master in my own house, I say! Infernal dog! — I say, Cuff, cut him up! — Why don't you go at him? — Give it to him! — What you waiting for?"

"If mas'r pleases!" said Cuff, rolling up his eyes, and making a deprecating gesture.

"If I please! Well, blast you, I *do* please! Go at him! — thrash away ! Stay, I 'll come myself." And seizing a cowhide, which lay near him, he turned up his cuffs, and ran down the steps, but missing his footing in his zeal, came head-first against the very post where the criminal was tied.

"There! I hope, now, you are satisfied! You have killed me! — you have broke my head, you have! I shall be laid up a month, all for you, you ungrateful dog!"

Cuffy and Sambo came to the rescue, raised him up carefully, and began brushing the dust off his clothes, smothering the laughter with which they seemed ready to explode, while the culprit at the post seemed to consider this an excellent opportunity to put in his submission.

"Please, mas'r, do forgive me! I tole 'em to go out, and dey said dey would n't. I did n't mean no harm when I said 'Mas'r had better go hisself;' 'cause I thinks so now. Mas'r had better go! Dem folks is curus, and dey won't go for none of us. Dey just acts ridiculous, dey does! And I did n't mean fur to be sarcy, nor nothin'. I say 'gin, if mas'r 'll take his horse and go over dar, mas'r drive dose folks out; and nobody else can't do it! We done can't do it — dey jest sarce us. Now, 'fore my Heavenly Master, all dis yere is de truth I 've been telling. De Lord, de Master, knows it is; and if mas'r 'll take his horse, and ride down dere, he 'd see so; so dere, jest as I 've been telling mas'r. I did n't mean no harm at all, I did n't!"

The quarrel, it must be told, related to the ejecting of a poor white family which had *squatted*, as the phrase is, in a deserted cabin, on a distant part of the Gordon plantation. Mrs. Gordon's untiring assiduity having discovered this fact, she had left her husband no peace till something was undertaken in the way of ejectment. He accordingly commissioned Jake, a stout negro, on the morning of the present day, to go over and turn them off. Now, Jake, who inherited to the full the lofty contempt with which the plantation negro regards the poor white folks, started upon his errand, nothing loath, and whistled his way in high feather, with two large dogs at his heels. But when he found a miserable, poor, sick woman, sur-

rounded by four starving children, Jake's mother's milk
came back to him, and instead of turning them out, he
actually pitched a dish of cold potatoes in among them,
which he picked up in a neighboring cabin, with about the
same air of contemptuous pity with which one throws
scraps to a dog.   And then, meandering his way back to
the house, informed his master that "he could n't turn de
white trash out, and if he wanted them turned out, he
would have to go hisself."

Now, we all know that a fit of temper has very often
nothing to do with the thing which appears to give rise
to it.   When a cloud is full charged with electricity, it
makes no difference which bit of wire is put in.   The
flash and the thunder come one way as well as another.
Mr. Gordon had received troublesome letters on business,
a troublesome lecture from his wife, his corn-cake had been
overdone at breakfast, and his coffee burned bitter; besides which, he had a cold in his head coming on, and
there was a settlement brewing with the overseer.   In consequence of all which things, though Jake's mode of
delivering himself was n't a whit more saucy than ordinary,
the storm broke upon him then and there, and raged as
we have described.   The heaviest part of it, however,
being now spent, Mr. Gordon consented to pardon the
culprit on condition that he would bring him up his horse
immediately, when he would ride over and see if he
could n't turn out the offending party.   He pressed Harry,
who was rather a favorite of his, into the service; and in
the course of a quarter of an hour they were riding off in
the direction of the squatter's cabin.

"It 's perfectly insufferable, what we proprietors have
to bear from this tribe of creatures!" he said.   "There
ought to be hunting-parties got up to chase them down,
and exterminate 'em, just as we do rats.   It would be a
kindness to them; the only thing you can do for them is

to kill them. As for charity, or that kind of thing, you might as well throw victuals into the hollow logs as to try to feed 'em. The government ought to pass laws, — we will have laws, somehow or other, — and get them out of the state."

And so discoursing, the good man at length arrived before the door of a miserable, decaying log cabin, out of whose glassless windows dark emptiness looked, as out of the eyeholes of a skull. Two scared, cowering children disappeared round the corner as he approached. He kicked open the door, and entered. Crouched on a pile of dirty straw sat a miserable, haggard woman, with large, wild eyes, sunken cheeks, disheveled, matted hair, and long, lean hands, like bird's claws. At her skinny breast an emaciated infant was hanging, pushing, with its little skeleton hands, as if to force the nourishment which nature no longer gave; and two scared-looking children, with features wasted and pinched blue with famine, were clinging to her gown. The whole group huddled together, drawing as far as possible away from the newcomer, looked up with large, frightened eyes, like hunted wild animals.

"What you here for?" was the first question of Mr. Gordon, put in no very decided tone; for if the truth must be told, his combativeness was oozing out.

The woman did not answer, and after a pause, the youngest child piped up in a shrill voice, —

"Ain't got nowhere else to be!"

"Yes," said the woman, "we camped on Mr. Durant's place, and Bobfield — him is the overseer — pulled down the cabin right over our head. 'Pears like we could n't get nowhere."

"Where is your husband?"

"Gone looking for work. 'Pears like he could n't get none nowhere. 'Pears like nobody wants us. But we have got to be somewhere, though!" said the woman in a melancholy, apologetic tone. "We can't die, as I see! — wish we could!"

Mr. Gordon's eye fell upon two or three cold potatoes in a piece of broken crock, over which the woman appeared keeping jealous guard.

"What you doing with those potatoes?"

"Saving them for the children's dinner."

"And is that all you 've got to eat, I want to know?" said Mr. Gordon in a high, sharp tone, as if he were getting angry very fast.

"Yes," said the woman.

"What did you have to eat yesterday?"

"Nothing!" said the woman.

"And what did you eat the day before?"

"Found some old bones round the nigger houses; and some on 'em give us some corn-cake."

"Why the devil did n't you send up to *my* house, and get some bacon? Picking up bones, slop, and swill, round the nigger huts? Why did n't you send up for some ham, and some meal? Lord bless you, you don't think Madam Gordon is a dog to bite you, do you? Wait here till I send you down something fit to eat. Just end in my having to take care of you, I see! And if you are going to stay here, there will be something to be done to keep the rain out!"

"There, now," he said to Harry, as he was mounting his horse, "just see what 't is to be made with hooks in one's back, like me! Everybody hangs on to me, of course! Now, there 's Durant turns off these folks; there 's Peters turns them off! Well, what 's the consequence? They come and litter down on me, just because I am an easy, soft-hearted old fool! It 's too devilish bad! They breed like rabbits! What God Almighty makes such people for, I don't know! I suppose He does. But there 's these poor, miserable trash have children like

sixty; and there's folks living in splendid houses, dying
for children, and can't have any. If they manage one or
two, the scarlet fever or whooping-cough makes off with
'em. Lord bless me, things go on in a terrible mixed-up
way in this world! And then, what upon earth I'm to
say to Mrs. G.! I know what she'll say to me. She'll
tell me she told me so — that's what she always says. I
wish she'd go and see them herself — I do so! Mrs. G.
is the nicest kind of a woman — no mistake about that;
but she has an awful deal of energy, that woman! It's
dreadful fatiguing to a quiet man, like me — dreadful!
But I'm sure I don't know what I should do without her.
She'll be down upon me about this woman; but the
woman must have some ham, that's flat! Cold potatoes
and old bones! Pretty story! Such people have no business to live at all; but if they will live, they ought to
eat Christian things! There goes Jake. Why couldn't
he turn 'em off before I saw 'em? It would have saved
me all this plague! Dog knew what he was about when
he got me down here! Jake! Oh, Jake, Jake! come
here!"

Jake came shambling along up to his master, with an
external appearance of the deepest humility, under which
was too plainly seen to lurk a facetious air of waggish satisfaction.

"Here, you, Jake; you get a basket" —

"Yes, mas'r!" said Jake, with an air of provoking
intelligence.

"Be still saying 'Yes, mas'r,' and hear what I've got
to say! Mind yourself!"

Jake gave a side glance of inexpressible drollery at
Harry, and then stood like an ebony statue of submission.

"You go to your missis, and ask her for the key of the
smoke-house, and bring it to me."

"Yes, sir."

"And you tell your missis to send me a peck of meal. Stay — a loaf of bread, or some biscuit, or corn-cake, or anything else which may happen to be baked up. Tell her I want them sent out right away."

Jake bowed and disappeared.

"Now we may as well ride down this path, while he is gone for the things. Mrs. G. will blow off on him first, so that rather less of it will come upon me. I wish I could get her to see them herself. Lord bless her, she is a kind-hearted woman enough! but she thinks there's no use doing, — and there ain't. She is right enough about it. But then, as the woman says, there must be some place for them to *be* in the world. The world is wide enough, I'm sure! Plague take it! why can't we pass a law to take them all in with our niggers, and then they'd have some one to take care of them! Then we'd do something for them, and there'd be some hope of keeping 'em comfortable."

Harry felt in nowise inclined to reply to any of this conversation, because he knew that, though nominally addressed to him, the good gentleman was talking merely for the sake of easing his mind, and that he would have opened his heart just as freely to the next hickory bush, if he had not happened to be present. So he let him expend himself, waiting for an opportunity to introduce subjects which lay nearer his heart.

In a convenient pause he found opportunity to say, —

"Miss Nina sent me over here, this morning."

"Ah, Nin! my pretty little Nin! Bless the child! She did? Why couldn't she come over herself, and comfort an old fellow's heart? Nin is the prettiest girl in the county! I tell you that, Harry!"

"Miss Nina is in a good deal of trouble. Master Tom came home last night drunk, and to-day he is so cross and contrary she can't do anything with him."

"Drunk? Oh, what a sad dog! Tom gets drunk too often! Carries that too far, altogether! Told him that, the last time I talked to him. Says I, 'Tom, it does very well for a young man to have a spree once in one or two months. I did it myself, when I was young. But,' says I, 'Tom, to spree *all* the time won't do, Tom!' says I. 'Nobody minds a fellow being drunk occasionally; but he ought to be moderate about it, and know where to stop,' says I; 'because, when it comes to that, that he is drunk every day, or every other day, why, it's my opinion that he may consider the devil's got him!' I talked to Tom just so, right out square; because, you see, I'm in a father's place to him. But, Lord, it don't seem to have done him a bit of good! Good Lord! they tell me he is drunk one half his time, and acts like a crazy creature! Goes too far, Tom does, altogether. Mrs. G. ain't got any patience with him. She blasts at him every time he comes here, and he blasts at her; so it ain't very comfortable having him here. Good woman at heart, Mrs. Gordon, but a little strong in her ways, you know; and Tom is strong, too. So it's fire fight fire when they get together. It's noways comfortable to a man wanting to have everybody happy around him. Lord bless me! I wish Nin were my daughter! Why can't she come over here, and live with me? She hasn't got any more spirit in her than just what I like. Just enough fizz in her to keep one from flatting out. What about those beaux of hers? Is she going to be married? Hey?"

"There's two gentlemen there, attending upon Miss Nina. One is Mr. Carson, of New York" —

"Hang it all! she isn't going to marry a d—d Yankee! Why, brother would turn over in his grave!"

"I don't think it will be necessary to put himself to that trouble," said Harry, "for I rather think it's Mr. Clayton who is to be the favored one."

VOL. I.

"Clayton! good blood! — like that! Seems to be a gentlemanly good fellow, does n't he?"

"Yes, sir. He owns a plantation, I 'm told, in South Carolina."

"Ah! ah! that 's well! But I hate to spare Nin! I never half liked sending her off to New York. Don't believe in boarding-schools. I 've seen as fine girls grown on plantations as any man need want. What do we want to send our girls there, to get fipenny-bit ideas? I thank the Lord I never was in New York, and I never mean to be! Carolina born and raised, I am; and my wife is Virginia — pure breed! No boarding-school about her! And when I stood up to be married to her, there was n't a girl in Virginia could stand up with her. Her cheeks were like damask roses! A tall, straight, lively girl, she was! Knew her own mind, and had a good notion of speaking it, too. And there is n't a woman, now, that can get through the business she can, and have her eyes always on everything. If it does make me uncomfortable, every now and then, I ought to take it, and thank the Lord for it. For if it wa'n't for her, what with the overseer, and the niggers, and the poor white trash, we should all go to the devil in a heap!"

"Miss Nina sent me over here to be out of Master Tom's way," said Harry, after a pause. "He is bent upon hectoring me, as usual. You know, sir, that he always had a spite against me, and it seems to grow more and more bitter. He quarrels with her about the management of everything on the place; and you know, sir, that I try to do my very best, and you and Mrs. Gordon have always been pleased to say that I did well."

"So we did, Harry, my boy! So we did! Stay here as long as you like. Just suit yourself about that. Maybe you 'd like to go out shooting with me."

"I 'm worried," said Harry, "to be obliged to be away

just at the time of putting in the seed. Everything depends upon my overseeing."

"Why don't you go back, then? Tom's ugliness is nothing but because he is drunk. There's where it is! I see through it! You see, when a fellow has had a drunken spree, why, the day after it he is all at loose ends and cross — nerves all raveled out, like an old stocking. Then fellows are sulky and surly like. I've heard of their having temperance societies up in those northern states, and I think something of that sort would be good for our young men. They get drunk too often. Full a third of them, I should reckon, get the delirium tremens before they are fifty. If we could have a society like them, and that sort of thing, and agree to be moderate! Nobody expects young men to be old before their time; but if they'd agree not to blow out more than once a month, or something in that way!"

"I'm afraid," said Harry, "Master Tom's too far gone for that."

"Oh, ay! yes! Pity, pity! Suppose it is so. Why, when a fellow gets so far, he's like a nigger's old patched coat — you can't tell where the real cloth is. Now, Tom; I suppose he never is himself — always up on a wave, or down in the trough! Heigho! I'm sorry!"

"It's very hard on Miss Nina," said Harry. "He interferes, and I have no power to stand for her. And, yesterday, he began talking to my wife in a way I can't bear, nor won't! He must let her alone!"

"Sho! sho!" said Mr. Gordon. "See what a boy that is, now! That ain't in the least worth while — that ain't! I shall tell Tom so. And, Harry, mind your temper! Remember, young men will be young; and if a fellow will treat himself to a pretty wife, he must expect trials. But Tom ought not to do so. I shall tell him. High! there comes Jake, with the basket and the smoke-house key. Now for something to send down to those poor hobgoblins. If people are going to starve, they must n't come on to my place to do it. I don't mind what I don't see — I would n't mind if the whole litter of 'em was drowned to-morrow; but, hang it, I can't stand it if I know it! So, here, Jake, take this ham and bread, and look 'em up an old skillet, and see if you can't tinker up the house a bit. I 'd set the fellow to work, when he comes back, only we have two hands to every turn, now, and the niggers always plague 'em. Harry, you go home, and tell Nin Mrs. G. and I will be over to dinner."

CHAPTER XVIII

DRED

HARRY spent the night at the place of Mr. John Gordon, and arose the next morning in a very discontented mood of mind. Nothing is more vexatious to an active and enterprising person than to be thrown into a state of entire idleness; and Harry, after lounging about for a short time in the morning, found his indignation increased by every moment of enforced absence from the scene of his daily labors and interest. Having always enjoyed substantially the privileges of a free man in the ability to regulate his time according to his own ideas, to come and go, to buy and sell, and transact business unfettered by any felt control, he was the more keenly alive to the degradation implied in his present position.

"Here I must skulk around," said he to himself, "like a partridge in the bushes, allowing everything to run at loose ends, preparing the way for my being found fault with for a lazy fellow by and by; and all for what? Because my younger brother chooses to come, without right or reason, to domineer over me, to insult my wife; and because the laws will protect him in it, if he does it! Ah! ah! that's it. They are all leagued together! No matter how right I am — no matter how bad he is! Everybody will stand up for him, and put me down; all because my grandmother was born in Africa, and his grandmother was born in America. Confound it all, I won't stand it! Who knows what he'll be saying and doing to Lisette while I am gone? I'll go back and face him, like a man!

I 'll keep straight about my business, and if he crosses
me, let him take care! He has n't got but one life, any
more than I have. Let him look out! "

And Harry jumped upon his horse, and turned his head
homeward. He struck into a circuitous path, which led
along that immense belt of swampy land to which the name
of Dismal has been given. As he was riding along
immersed in thought, the clatter of horses' feet was heard
in front of him. A sudden turn of the road brought him
directly facing to Tom Gordon and Mr. Jekyl, who had
risen early and started off on horseback, in order to reach
a certain stage depot before the heat of the day. There
was a momentary pause on both sides; when Tom Gordon,
like one who knows his power, and is determined to use it
to the utmost, broke out scornfully: —

"Stop, you d—d nigger, and tell your master where
you are going! "

"You are not my master! " said Harry, in words whose
concentrated calmness conveyed more bitterness and wrath
than could have been given by the most violent outburst.

"You d—d whelp! " said Tom Gordon, striking him
across the face twice with his whip, "take that, and that!
We 'll see if I 'm not your master! There, now, help
yourself, won't you? Is n't that a master's mark? "

It had been the lifelong habit of Harry's position to
repress every emotion of anger within himself. But at
this moment his face wore a deadly and frightful expression. Still, there was something majestic and almost
commanding in the attitude with which he reined back
his horse, and slowly lifted his hand to heaven. He
tried to speak, but his voice was choked with repressed
passion. At last he said: —

"You may be sure, Mr. Gordon, this mark will *never*
be forgotten! "

There are moments of high excitement, when all that is in a human being seems to be roused, and to concentrate itself in the eye and the voice. And in such moments *any* man, apparently by virtue of his mere humanity, by the mere awfulness of the human soul that is in him, gains power to overawe those who in other hours scorn him. There was a minute's pause in which neither spoke; and Mr. Jekyl, who was a man of peace, took occasion to touch Tom's elbow, and say: —

"It seems to me this is n't worth while — we shall miss the stage." And as Harry had already turned his horse and was riding away, Tom Gordon turned his, shouting after him, with a scornful laugh: —

"I called on your wife before I came away this morning, and I liked her rather better the second time than I did the first!"

This last taunt flew like a Parthian arrow backward, and struck into the soul of the bondman with even a keener power than the degrading blow. The sting of it seemed to rankle more bitterly as he rode along, till at last he dropped the reins on his horse's neck, and burst into a transport of bitter cursing.

"Aha! aha! it has come nigh thee, has it? It toucheth thee, and thou faintest!" said a deep voice from the swampy thicket beside him.

Harry stopped his horse and his imprecations. There was a crackling in the swamp, and a movement among the copse of briers; and at last the speaker emerged, and stood before Harry. He was a tall black man, of magnificent stature and proportions. His skin was intensely black, and polished like marble. A loose shirt of red flannel, which opened very wide at the breast, gave a display of a neck and chest of herculean strength. The sleeves of the shirt, rolled up nearly to the shoulders, showed the muscles of a gladiator. The head, which rose with an imperial air from the broad shoulders, was large and massive, and developed with equal force both in the reflective and perceptive department. The perceptive organs jutted like dark ridges over the eyes, while that part of the head which phrenologists attribute to the moral and intellectual sentiments rose like an ample dome above them. The large eyes had that peculiar and solemn effect of unfathomable blackness and darkness which is often a striking characteristic of the African eye. But there burned in them, like tongues of flame in a black pool of naphtha, a subtle and restless fire that betokened habitual excitement to the verge of insanity. If any organs were predominant in the head, they were those of ideality, wonder, veneration, and firmness; and the whole combination was such as might have formed one of the wild old warrior prophets of the heroic ages. He wore a fantastic sort of turban, apparently of an old scarlet shawl, which added to the outlandish effect of his appearance. His nether garments, of coarse negro-cloth, were girded round the waist by a strip of scarlet flannel, in which were thrust a bowie-knife and hatchet. Over one shoulder he carried a rifle, and a shot-pouch was suspended to his belt. A rude game-bag hung upon his arm. Wild and startling as the apparition might have been, it appeared to be no stranger to Harry; for after the first movement of surprise, he said in a tone of familiar recognition, in which there was blended somewhat of awe and respect: —

"Oh, it is you, then, Dred! I did n't know that you were hearing me!"

"Have I not heard?" said the speaker, raising his arm, and his eyes gleaming with wild excitement. "How long wilt thou halt between two opinions? Did not Moses refuse to be called the son of Pharaoh's daughter? How long wilt thou cast in thy lot with the oppressors of Israel, who say unto thee, 'Bow down that we may walk over thee'? Shall not the Red Sea be divided? 'Yea,' saith the Lord, ' it shall.' "

"Dred! I know what you mean!" said Harry, trembling with excitement.

"Yea, thou dost!" said the figure. "Yea, thou dost! Hast thou not eaten the fat and drunk the sweet with the oppressor, and hid thine eyes from the oppression of thy people? Have not our wives been for a prey, and thou hast not regarded? Hath not our cheek been given to the smiter? Have we not been counted as sheep for the slaughter? But thou saidst, 'Lo! I knew it not,' and didst hide thine eyes! Therefore, the curse of Meroz is upon thee, saith the Lord. And thou shalt bow down to the oppressor, and his rod shall be upon thee; and thy wife shall be for a prey!"

"Don't talk in that way!—don't!" said Harry, striking out his hands with a frantic gesture, as if to push back the words. "You are raising the very devil in me!"

"Look here, Harry," said the other, dropping from the high tone he at first used to that of common conversation, and speaking in bitter irony, "did your master strike you? It's sweet to kiss the rod, isn't it? Bend your neck and ask to be struck again!— won't you? Be meek and lowly! that's the religion for you! You are a slave, and you wear broadcloth, and sleep soft. By and by he will give you a fip to buy salve for those cuts! Don't fret about your wife! Women always like the master better than the slave! Why shouldn't they? When a man licks his master's foot, his wife scorns him, — serves him right. Take it meekly, my boy! 'Servants, obey your masters.' Take your master's old coats — take your wife when he's done with her — and bless God that brought you under the light of the gospel! Go! you are a slave! But as for me," he said, drawing up his head, and throwing back his shoulders with a deep inspiration, "*I* am a free man!

Free by this," holding out his rifle. "Free by the Lord of hosts, that numbereth the stars, and calleth them forth by their names. Go home — that's all I have to say to you! You sleep in a curtained bed. — I sleep on the ground, in the swamps! You eat the fat of the land. I have what the ravens bring me! But no man whips me! — no man touches my wife! — no man says to me, 'Why do ye so?' Go! you are a slave! — I am free!" And with one athletic bound, he sprang into the thicket, and was gone.

The effect of this address on the already excited mind of the bondman may be better conceived than described. He ground his teeth and clenched his hands.

"Stop!" he cried; "Dred, I will — I will — I'll do as you tell me — I will not be a slave!"

A scornful laugh was the only reply, and the sound of crackling footsteps retreated rapidly. He who retreated struck up, in a clear, loud voice, one of those peculiar melodies in which vigor and spirit are blended with a wild, inexpressible mournfulness. The voice was one of a singular and indescribable quality of tone; it was heavy as the sub-bass of an organ, and of a velvety softness, and yet it seemed to pierce the air with a keen dividing force which is generally characteristic of voices of much less volume. The words were the commencement of a wild camp-meeting hymn, much in vogue in those parts: —

> "Brethren, don't you hear the sound ?
>   The martial trumpet now is blowing;
> Men in order listing round,
>   And soldiers to the standard flowing."

There was a wild, exultant fullness of liberty that rolled in the note; and, to Harry's excited ear, there seemed in it a fierce challenge of contempt to his imbecility, and his soul at that moment seemed to be rent asunder with a pang such as only those can know who have felt what it

is to be a slave. There was an uprising within him,
vague, tumultuous, overpowering; dim instincts, heroic
aspirations; the will to do, the soul to dare; and then, in
a moment, there followed the picture of all society leagued
against him, the hopeless impossibility of any outlet to
what was burning within him. The waters of a nature
naturally noble, pent up, and without outlet, rolled back
upon his heart with a suffocating force; and in his hasty
anguish he cursed the day of his birth. The spasm of
his emotion was interrupted by the sudden appearance of
Milly coming along the path.

"Why, bless you, Milly," said Harry in sudden surprise, "where are you going?"

"Oh, bless you, honey, chile, I's gwine on to take de
stage. Dey wanted to get up de wagon for me; but, bless
you, says I, what you s'pose de Lord gin us legs for? I
never wants no critturs to tug me round, when I can walk
myself. And den, honey, it's so pleasant like, to be
a-walking along in de bush here, in de morning; 'pears
like de voice of de Lord is walking among de trees. But
bless you, chile, honey, what's de matter o' yer face?"

"It's Tom Gordon, d—n him!" said Harry.

"Don't talk dat ar way, chile!" said Milly, using the
freedom with Harry which her years and weight of character had gradually secured for her among the members of
the plantation.

"I will talk that way! Why shouldn't I? I am not
going to be good any longer."

"Why, 't won't help de matter to be bad, will it,
Harry? 'Cause you hate Tom Gordon, does you want to
act just like him?"

"No!" said Harry, "I won't be like him, but I'll
have my revenge! Old Dred has been talking to me again,
this morning. He always did stir me up so that I could
hardly live; and I won't stand it any longer!"

"Chile," said Milly, "you take care! Keep clear on him! He's in de wilderness of Sinai; he is with de blackness and darkness and tempest. He hain't come to de heavenly Jerusalem. Oh! Oh! honey! dere's a blood of sprinkling dat speaketh better things dan dat of Abel. Jerusalem above is free — is free, honey; so, don't you mind, now, what happens in dis yer time."

"Ah, ah, Aunt Milly! this may do well enough for old women like you; but stand opposite to a young fellow like me, with good strong arms, and a pair of doubled fists, and a body and soul just as full of fight as they can be; it don't answer to go to telling about a heavenly Jerusalem! We want something here. We'll have it, too! How do you know there is any heaven, anyhow?"

"Know it?" said Milly, her eye kindling, and striking her staff on the ground. "Know it? I knows it by de hankering arter it I got in here," giving her broad chest a blow which made it resound like a barrel. "De Lord knowed what he was 'bout when he made us. When he made babies rooting round, with der poor little mouths open, he made milk and de mammies for 'em too. Chile, we's nothing but great babies, dat ain't got our eyes opened — rooting round and round; but de Father 'll feed us yet — he will so."

"He's a long time about it," said Harry sullenly.

"Well, chile, ain't it a long time 'fore your corn sprouts — a long time 'fore it gets into de ears? — but you plants for all dat. What's dat to me what I is here? — Sha'n't I reign with de Lord Jesus?"

"I don't know," said Harry.

"Well, honey, *I does!* Jest so sure as I's standing on dis yer ground, I knows in a few years I shall be reigning with de Lord Jesus, and a-casting my crown at his feet. Dat's what I knows. Flesh and blood didn't reveal it unto me, but de Spirit of de Father. It's no odds to me what I does here; every road leads straight to glory, and de glory ain't got no end to it!" And Milly uplifted her voice in a favorite stave: —

> "'When we've been dere ten thousand years,
>   Bright shining like de sun,
>   We've no less days to sing God's praise
>   Than when we first begun.'

"Chile," said she to him solemnly, "I ain't a fool. Does ye s'pose dat I thinks folks has any business to be sitting on der cheers all der life long, and working me, and living on my money? Why, I knows dey hain't! Ain't it all wrong, from fust to last, de way dey makes merchandise o' us! Why, I knows it is; but I's still about it, for de Lord's sake. I don't work for Miss Loo; I works for de Lord Jesus; and he is good pay — no mistake, now I tell you."

"Well," said Harry, a little shaken, but not convinced, "after all, there isn't much use in trying to do any other way. But you're lucky in feeling so, Aunt Milly; but I can't."

"Well, chile, anyway, don't you do nothing rash and don't you hear *him*. Dat ar way out is through seas of blood. Why, chile, would you turn against Miss Nina? Chile, if they get a-going, they won't spare nobody. Don't you start up dat ar tiger; 'cause, I tell ye, ye can't chain him, if ye do!"

"Yes," said Harry, "I see it's all madness, perfect madness; there's no use thinking, no use talking. Well, good-morning, Aunt Milly. Peace go with you!" And the young man started his horse, and was soon out of sight.

CHAPTER XIX

THE CONSPIRATORS

WE owe our readers now some words of explanation respecting the new personage who has been introduced into our history; therefore we must go back somewhat, and allude to certain historical events of painful significance.

It has been a problem to many, how the system of slavery in America should unite the two apparent inconsistencies of a code of slave-laws more severe than that of any other civilized nation with an average practice at least as indulgent as any other; for bad as slavery is at the best, it may yet be admitted that the practice, as a whole, has been less cruel in this country than in many. An examination into history will show us that the cruelty of the laws resulted from the effects of indulgent practice. During the first years of importation of slaves into South Carolina, they enjoyed many privileges. Those who lived in intelligent families, and had any desire to learn, were instructed in reading and writing. Liberty was given them to meet in assemblies of worship, in class-meetings, and otherwise, without the presence of white witnesses; and many were raised to situations of trust and consequence. The result of this was the development of a good degree of intelligence and manliness among the slaves. There arose among them grave, thoughtful, energetic men, with their ears and eyes open, and their minds constantly awake to compare and reason.

When minds come into this state, in a government professing to be founded on principles of universal equality, it follows that almost every public speech, document, or newspaper becomes an incendiary publication.

Of this fact the southern slave states have ever exhibited the most singular unconsciousness. Documents containing sentiments most dangerous for slaves to hear have been publicly read and applauded among them. The slave has heard, amid shouts, on the Fourth of July, that his masters held the truth to be self-evident that all men were born equal, and had an *inalienable right* to life, liberty, and the pursuit of happiness; and that all governments derive their just power from the consent of the governed. Even the mottoes of newspapers have embodied sentiments of the most insurrectionary character.

Such inscriptions as "Resistance to tyrants is obedience to God" stand, to this day, in large letters, at the head of southern newspapers; while speeches of senators and public men, in which the principles of universal democracy are asserted, are constant matters of discussion. Under such circumstances, it is difficult to induce the servant, who feels that he is a man, to draw those lines which seem so obvious to masters, by whom this fact has been forgotten. Accordingly we find that when the discussions for the admission of Missouri as a slave state produced a wave whose waters undulated in every part of the Union, there were found among the slaves men of unusual thought and vigor, who were no inattentive witnesses and listeners. The discussions were printed in the newspapers; and what was printed in the newspapers was further discussed at the post-office door, in the tavern, in the bar-room, at the dinner-party, where black servants were listening behind the chairs. A free colored man in the city of Charleston, named Denmark Vesey, was the one who had the hardihood to seek to use the electric fluid in the cloud thus accumulated. He conceived the hopeless project of imitating the example set by the American race, and achieving independence for the blacks.

Our knowledge of this man is derived entirely from the printed reports of the magistrates who gave an account of the insurrection of which he was the instigator, and who will not, of course, be supposed to be unduly prejudiced in his favor. They state that he was first brought to the country by one Captain Vesey, a young lad, distinguished for personal beauty and great intelligence, and that he proved, for twenty years, a most faithful slave; but on drawing a prize of fifteen hundred dollars in the lottery, he purchased his freedom of his master, and worked as a carpenter in the city of Charleston. He was distinguished for strength and activity, and, as the accounts state, maintained such an irreproachable character, and enjoyed so much the confidence of the whites, that when he was accused, the charge was not only discredited, but he was not even arrested for several days after, and not till the proof of his guilt had become too strong to be doubted. His historians go on, with considerable *naïveté*, to remark: —

"It is difficult to conceive what motive he had to enter into such a plot, unless it was the one mentioned by one of the witnesses, who said that Vesey had several children who were slaves, and that he said, on one occasion, he wished he could see them free, as he himself artfully remarked in his defense on his trial."

It appears that the project of rousing and animating the blacks to this enterprise occupied the mind of Vesey for more than four years, during which time he was continually taking opportunities to animate and inspire the spirits of his countrymen. The account states that the speeches in Congress of those opposed to the admission of Missouri into the Union, perhaps garbled and misrepresented, furnished him with ample means for inflaming the minds of the colored population.

"Even while walking in the street," the account goes
on to say, "he was not idle; for if his companion bowed
to a white person, as slaves universally do, he would
rebuke him, and observe, 'that all men were born equal,
and that he was surprised that any one would degrade
himself by such conduct; that he would never cringe to
the whites nor ought any one to who had the feelings of
a man.'[1] When answered, 'We are slaves,' he would
say sarcastically and indignantly, 'You deserve to remain
slaves!' And if he were further asked, 'What can we
do?' he would remark, 'Go and buy a spelling-book, and
read the fable of "Hercules and the Wagoner."' He also
sought every opportunity of entering into conversation with
white persons, during which conversation he would artfully
introduce some bold remark on slavery; and sometimes,
when, from the character he was conversing with, he found
he might be still bolder, he would go so far that, had not
his declarations been clearly proved, they would scarcely
have been credited."

But his great instrument of influence was a book that
has always been prolific of insurrectionary movements,
under all systems of despotism.

"He rendered himself perfectly familiar with all those
parts of Scripture which he thought he could pervert to
his purpose, and would readily quote them to prove that
slavery was contrary to the laws of God, and that slaves
were bound to attempt their emancipation, however shocking and bloody might be the consequences; that such
efforts would not only be pleasing to the Almighty, but
were absolutely enjoined."

Vesey, in the course of time, associated with himself
five slave men of marked character — Rolla, Ned, Peter,
Monday, and Gullah Jack. Of these, the account goes on
to say: —

---

[1] These extracts are taken from the official report.

"In the selection of his leaders, Vesey showed great penetration and sound judgment. Rolla was plausible, and possessed uncommon self-possession; bold and ardent, he was not to be deterred from his purpose by danger. Ned's appearance indicated that he was a man of firm nerves and desperate courage. Peter was intrepid and resolute, true to his engagements, and cautious in observing secrecy where it was necessary; he was not to be daunted nor impeded by difficulties, and though confident of success, was careful in providing against any obstacles or casualties which might arise, and intent upon discovering every means which might be in their power, if thought of beforehand. Gullah Jack was regarded as a sorcerer, and, as such, feared by the natives of Africa, who believed in witchcraft. He was not only considered invulnerable, but that he could make others so by his charms, and that he could, and certainly would, provide all his followers with arms. He was artful, cruel, bloody; his disposition, in short, was diabolical. His influence among the Africans was inconceivable. Monday was firm, resolute, discreet, and intelligent.

"It is a melancholy truth that the general good conduct of all the leaders, except Gullah Jack, was such as rendered them objects least liable to suspicion. Their conduct had secured them, not only the unlimited confidence of their owners, but they had been indulged in every comfort, and allowed every privilege compatible with their situation in the community; and though Gullah Jack was not remarkable for the correctness of his deportment, he by no means sustained a bad character. But," adds the report, "not only were the leaders of good character, and very much indulged by their owners, but this was very generally the case with all who were convicted, many of them possessing the highest confidence of their owners, and not one a bad character.

"The conduct and behavior of Vesey and his five leaders during their trial and imprisonment may be interesting to many. When Vesey was tried, he folded his arms, and seemed to pay great attention to the testimony given against him, but with his eyes fixed on the floor. In this situation he remained immovable until the witnesses had been examined by the court, and cross-examined by his counsel, when he requested to be allowed to examine the witnesses himself, which he did. The evidence being closed, he addressed the court at considerable length. When he received his sentence, tears trickled down his cheeks.

"Rolla, when arraigned, affected not to understand the charge against him, and when, at his request, it was explained to him, assumed, with wonderful adroitness, astonishment and surprise. He was remarkable throughout his trial for composure and great presence of mind. When he was informed that he was convicted, and was advised to prepare for death, he appeared perfectly confounded, but exhibited no signs of fear.

"In Ned's behavior there was nothing remarkable. His countenance was stern and immovable, even while he was receiving sentence of death. From his looks it was impossible to discover or conjecture what were his feelings. Not so with Peter Poyes. In his countenance were strongly marked disappointed ambition, revenge, indignation, and an anxiety to know how far the discoveries had extended. He did not appear to fear personal consequences, for his whole behavior indicated the reverse, but exhibited an evident anxiety for the success of their plan, in which his whole soul was embarked. His countenance and behavior were the same when he received his sentence, and his only words were, on retiring, ' I suppose you 'll let me see my wife and family before I die,' and that in no supplicating tone. When he was asked, a day or two after, 'If it was possible that he could see his master and family murdered, who had treated him so kindly?' he replied to the question only by a smile.   In their prison, the convicts resolutely refused to make any confessions or communications which might implicate others; and Peter Poyes sternly enjoined it upon them to maintain this silence, — 'Do not open your lips; die silent, as you will see me do!' and in this resolute silence they met their fate.   Twenty-two of the conspirators were executed upon one gallows."

The account says that "Peter Poyes was one of the most active of the recruiting agents.   All the principal conspirators kept a list of those who had consented to join them, and Peter was said, by one of the witnesses, to have had six hundred names on his list; but so resolutely to the last did he observe his pledge of secrecy to his associates, that, of the whole number arrested and tried, not one of them belonged to his company.   In fact, in an insurrection in which thousands of persons were supposed to have been implicated, only thirty-six were convicted."

Among the children of Denmark Vesey was a boy by a Mandingo slave woman, who was his father's particular favorite.   The Mandingos are one of the finest of African tribes, distinguished for intelligence, beauty of form, and an indomitable pride and energy of nature.   As slaves, they are considered particularly valuable by those who have tact enough to govern them, because of their great capability and their proud faithfulness; but they resent a government of brute force, and under such are always fractious and dangerous.

This boy received from his mother the name of Dred; a name not unusual among the slaves, and generally given to those of great physical force.

The development of this child's mind was so uncommon as to excite astonishment among the negroes.   He early acquired the power of reading, by an apparent instinctive faculty, and would often astonish those around him with things which he had discovered in books. Like other children of a deep and fervent nature, he developed great religious ardor, and often surprised the older negroes by his questions and replies on this subject. A son so endowed could not but be an object of great pride and interest to a father like Denmark Vesey. The impression seemed to prevail universally among the negroes that this child was born for extraordinary things; and perhaps it was the yearning to acquire liberty for the development of such a mind which first led Denmark Vesey to reflect on the nature of slavery, and the terrible weights which it lays on the human intellect, and to conceive the project of liberating a race.

The Bible, of which Vesey was an incessant reader, stimulated this desire. He likened his own position of comparative education, competence, and general esteem among the whites to that of Moses among the Egyptians; and nourished the idea that, like Moses, he was sent as a deliverer. During the process of the conspiracy, this son, though but ten years of age, was his father's confidant; and he often charged him, though he should fail in the attempt, never to be discouraged. He impressed it upon his mind that he should never submit tamely to the yoke of slavery; and nourished the idea already impressed, that some more than ordinary destiny was reserved for him. After the discovery of the plot, and the execution of its leaders, those more immediately connected with them were sold from the state, even though not proved to have participated. With the most guarded caution, Vesey had exempted this son from suspicion. It had been an agreed policy with them both, that in the presence of others they should counterfeit alienation and dislike. Their confidential meetings with each other had been stolen and secret.

At the time of his father's execution, Dred was a lad of fourteen. He could not be admitted to his father's prison, but he was a witness of the undaunted aspect with which he and the other conspirators met their doom. The memory dropped into the depths of his soul, as a stone drops into the desolate depths of a dark mountain lake.

Sold to a distant plantation, he became noted for his desperate, unsubduable disposition. He joined in none of the social recreations and amusements of the slaves, labored with proud and silent assiduity, but on the slightest rebuke or threat, flashed up with a savage fierceness which, supported by his immense bodily strength, made him an object of dread among overseers. He was one of those of whom they gladly rid themselves, and like a fractious horse, was sold from master to master. Finally, an overseer, hardier than the rest, determined on the task of subduing him. In the scuffle that ensued Dred struck him to the earth, a dead man, made his escape to the swamps, and was never afterwards heard of in civilized life.

The reader who consults the map will discover that the whole eastern shore of the southern states, with slight interruptions, is belted by an immense chain of swamps, regions of hopeless disorder, where the abundant growth and vegetation of nature, sucking up its forces from the humid soil, seem to rejoice in a savage exuberance, and bid defiance to all human efforts either to penetrate or subdue. These wild regions are the homes of the alligator, the moccasin, and the rattlesnake. Evergreen trees, mingling freely with the deciduous children of the forest, form here dense jungles, verdant all the year round, and which afford shelter to numberless birds, with whose warbling the leafy desolation perpetually resounds. Climbing vines and parasitic plants, of untold splendor and boundless exuberance of growth, twine and interlace, and hang from the heights of the highest trees pennons of gold and purple, — triumphal banners, which attest the solitary majesty of nature. A species of parasitic moss wreathes its abundant draperies from tree to tree, and hangs in pearly festoons through which shine the scarlet berry and green leaves of the American holly.

What the mountains of Switzerland were to the persecuted Vaudois, this swampy belt has been to the American slave. The constant effort to recover from thence fugitives has led to the adoption, in these states, of a separate profession, unknown at this time in any other Christian land — hunters, who train and keep dogs for the hunting of men, women, and children. And yet, with all the convenience of this profession, the reclaiming of the fugitives from these fastnesses of nature has been a work of such expense and difficulty that the near proximity of the swamp has always been a considerable check on the otherwise absolute power of the overseer. Dred carried with him to the swamp but one solitary companion — the Bible of his father. To him it was not the messenger of peace and good will, but the herald of woe and wrath!

As the mind, looking on the great volume of nature, sees there a reflection of its own internal passions, and seizes on that in it which sympathizes with itself, — as the fierce and savage soul delights in the roar of torrents, the thunder of avalanches, and the whirl of ocean storms, — so is it in the great answering volume of revelation. There is something there for every phase of man's nature; and hence its endless vitality and stimulating force. Dred had heard read in the secret meetings of conspirators the wrathful denunciations of ancient prophets against oppression and injustice. He had read of kingdoms convulsed by plagues; of tempest, and pestilence, and locusts; of the sea cleft in twain, that an army of slaves might pass through and of their pursuers whelmed in the returning waters. He had heard of prophets and deliverers, armed with supernatural powers, raised up for oppressed people; had pondered on the nail of Jael, the goad of Shamgar, the pitcher and lamp of Gideon; and thrilled with fierce joy as he read how Samson, with his two strong arms, pulled down the pillars of the festive temple, and whelmed his triumphant persecutors in one grave with himself.

In the vast solitudes which he daily traversed, these things entered deep into his soul. Cut off from all human companionship, often going weeks without seeing a human face, there was no recurrence of every-day and prosaic ideas to check the current of the enthusiasm thus kindled. Even in the soil of the cool Saxon heart the Bible has thrown out its roots with an all-pervading energy, so that the whole framework of society may be said to rest on soil held together by its fibres. Even in cold and misty England, armies have been made defiant and invincible by the incomparable force and deliberate valor which it breathes into men. But when this Oriental seed, an exotic among us, is planted back in the fiery soil of a tropical heart, it bursts forth with an incalculable ardor of growth.

A stranger cannot fail to remark the fact that, though the slaves of the South are unable to read the Bible for themselves, yet most completely have its language and sentiment penetrated among them, giving a Hebraistic coloring to their habitual mode of expression. How much greater, then, must have been the force of the solitary perusal of this volume on so impassioned a nature! — a nature, too, kindled by memories of the self-sacrificing ardor with which a father and his associates had met death at the call of freedom; for none of us may deny that, wild and hopeless as this scheme was, it was still the same in kind with the more successful one which purchased for our fathers a national existence.

A mind of the most passionate energy and vehemence, thus awakened, for years made the wild solitudes of the swamp its home. That book, so full of startling symbols and vague images, had for him no interpreter but the silent courses of nature. His life passed in a kind of dream. Sometimes, traversing for weeks these desolate regions, he would compare himself to Elijah traversing for forty days and nights the solitudes of Horeb; or to John the Baptist in the wilderness, girding himself with camel's hair, and eating locusts and wild honey. Sometimes he would fast and pray for days; and then voices would seem to speak to him, and strange hieroglyphics would be written upon the leaves. In less elevated moods of mind, he would pursue, with great judgment and vigor, those enterprises necessary to preserve existence. The negroes lying out in the swamps are not so wholly cut off from society as might at first be imagined. The slaves of all the adjoining plantations, whatever they may pretend, to secure the good will of their owners, are at heart secretly disposed, from motives both of compassion and policy, to favor the fugitives. They very readily perceive that, in the event of any difficulty occurring to themselves, it might be quite necessary to have a friend and protector in the swamp; and therefore they do not hesitate to supply these fugitives, so far as they are able, with anything which they may desire. The poor whites, also, who keep small shops in the neighborhood of plantations, are never particularly scrupulous, provided they can turn a penny to their own advantage, and willingly supply necessary wares in exchange for game, with which the swamp abounds.

Dred, therefore, came in possession of an excellent rifle, and never wanted for ammunition, which supplied him with an abundance of food. Besides this, there are here and there elevated spots in the swampy land, which, by judicious culture, are capable of great productiveness. And many such spots Dred had brought under cultivation, either with his own hands, or from those of other fugitives,

whom he had received and protected.   From the restlessness of his nature, he had not confined himself to any particular region, but had traversed the whole swampy belt of
both the Carolinas, as well as that of Southern Virginia;
residing a few months in one place, and a few months in
another.   Wherever he stopped, he formed a sort of retreat, where he received and harbored fugitives.   On one
occasion, he rescued a trembling and bleeding mulatto
woman from the dogs of the hunters, who had pursued
her into the swamp.   This woman he made his wife, and
appeared to entertain a very deep affection for her.   He
made a retreat for her, with more than common ingenuity,
in the swamp adjoining the Gordon plantation; and after
that, he was more especially known in that locality.   He
had fixed his eye upon Harry, as a person whose ability,
address, and strength of character might make him at
some day a leader in a conspiracy against the whites.
Harry, in common with many of the slaves on the Gordon
plantation, knew perfectly well of the presence of Dred in
the neighborhood, and had often seen and conversed with
him.   But neither he nor any of the rest of them ever
betrayed before any white person the slightest knowledge
of the fact.

This ability of profound secrecy is one of the invariable
attendants of a life of slavery.   Harry was acute enough
to know that his position was by no means so secure that
he could afford to dispense with anything which might
prove an assistance in some future emergency.   The low
white traders in the neighborhood also knew Dred well;
but as long as they could drive an advantageous trade
with him he was secure from their intervention.   So
secure had he been, that he had been even known to
mingle in the motley throng of a camp-meeting unmolested.
Thus much with regard to one who is to appear often on
the stage before our history is done.

CHAPTER XX

SUMMER TALK AT CANEMA

In the course of a few days the family circle at Canema was enlarged by the arrival of Clayton's sister; and Carson, in excellent spirits, had started for a northern watering-place. In answer to Nina's letter of invitation, Anne had come with her father, who was called to that vicinity by the duties of his profession. Nina received her with her usual gay frankness of manner; and Anne, like many others, soon found herself liking her future sister much better than she had expected. Perhaps, had Nina been in any other situation than that of hostess, her pride might have led her to decline making the agreeable to Anne, whom, notwithstanding, she very much wished to please. But she was mistress of the mansion, and had an Arab's idea of the privileges of a guest; and so she chatted, sang, and played for her; she took her about, showed her the walks, the arbors, the flower-garden; waited on her in her own apartment, with a thousand little attentions, all the more fascinating from the kind of careless independence with which they were rendered. Besides, Nina had vowed a wicked little vow in her heart that she would ride rough-shod over Anne's dignity; that she would n't let her be grave or sensible, but that she should laugh and frolic with her. And Clayton could scarce help smiling at the success that soon crowned her exertions. Nina's gayety, when in full tide, had a breezy infectiousness in it, that seemed to stir up every one about her and carry them on the tide of her own spirits; and Anne, in her company, soon found herself laughing at everything and nothing, simply because she felt gay.

To crown all, Uncle John Gordon arrived, with his cheery, jovial face; and he was one of those fearless, hit-or-miss talkers, that are invaluable in social dilemmas, because they keep something or other all the while in motion.

With him came Madam Gordon, or, as Nina commonly called her, Aunt Maria. She was a portly, finely formed, middle-aged woman, who might have been handsome, had not the lines of care and nervous anxiety ploughed themselves so deeply in her face. Her bright, keen, hazel eyes, fine teeth, and the breadth of her ample form attested the vitality of the old Virginia stock from whence she sprung.

"There," said Nina to Anne Clayton, as they sat in the shady side of the veranda, "I've marshaled Aunt Maria up into Aunt Nesbit's room, and there they will have a comfortable dish of lamentation over me."

"Over you?" said Anne.

"Yes — over me, to be sure! — that's the usual order of exercises. Such a setting down as I shall get! They'll count up on their fingers all the things I ought to know and don't, and ought to do and can't. I believe that's the way relatives always show their affection — aunts in particular — by mourning over you."

"And what sort of a list will they make out?" said Anne.

"Oh, bless me, that's easy enough. Why, there's Aunt Maria is a perfectly virulent housekeeper — really insane, I believe, on that subject. Why, she chases up every rat and mouse and cockroach, every particle of dust, every scrap of litter. She divides her hours, and is as punctual as a clock. She rules her household with a rod of iron, and makes everybody stand round; and tells each one how many times a day one may wink. She keeps accounts like a very dragon, and always is sure to pounce on anybody that is in the least out of the way. She cuts out clothes by the bale; she sews, and she knits, and she jingles keys. And all this kind of bustle she calls house-keeping! Now, what do you suppose she must think of me, who just put on my hat in the morning, and go sail-ing down the walks, looking at the flowers, till Aunt Katy calls me back, to know what my orders are for the day?"

"Pray, who is Aunt Katy?" said Anne.

"Oh, she is my female prime minister; and she is very much like some prime ministers I have studied about in history, who always contrive to have their own way, let what will come. Now, when Aunt Katy comes and wants to know, so respectfully, 'What Miss Nina is going to have for dinner,' do you suppose she has the least expecta-tion of getting anything that I order? She always has fifty objections to anything that I propose. For sometimes the fit comes over me to try to be *housekeepy*, like Aunt Maria; but it's no go, I can tell you. So, when she has proved that everything that I propose is the height of absurdity, and shown conclusively that there's nothing fit to be eaten in the neighborhood, by that time I am reduced to a proper state of mind. And when I humbly say, 'Aunt Katy, what *shall* we do?' then she gives a little cough, and out comes the whole programme, just as she had arranged it the night before. And so it goes. As to accounts, why Harry has to look after them. I detest everything about money, except the spending of it — I have rather a talent for that. Now, just think how awfully all this must impress poor Aunt Maria! What sighings, and rollings up of eyes, and shakings of heads, there are over me! And then, Aunt Nesbit is always dinging at me about improving my mind! And improving my mind means reading some horrid, stupid, boring old book, just as she does! Now, I like the idea of improv-

ing my mind.   I am sure it wants improving, bad enough;
but then, I can't help thinking that racing through the
garden, and cantering through the woods, improves it faster
than getting asleep over books.   It seems to me that books
are just like dry hay — very good when there is n't any
fresh grass to be had.   But I'd rather be out and eat
what's growing.   Now, what people call nature never
bores me; but almost every book I ever saw does.   Don't
you think people are made differently?   Some like books,
and some like things; don't you think so?"

"I can give you a good fact on your side of the argument," said Clayton, who had come up behind them during
the conversation.

"I didn't know I was arguing; but I shall be glad to
have anything on my side," said Nina, "of course."

"Well, then," said Clayton, "I'll say that the books
that have influenced the world the longest, the widest, and
deepest have been written by men who attended to things
more than to books; who, as you say, eat what was growing, instead of dry hay.   Homer couldn't have had much
to read in his time, nor the poets of the Bible; and they
have been fountains for all ages.   I don't believe Shakespeare was much of a reader."

"Well, but," said Anne, "don't you think that, for us
common folks, who are not going to be either Homers or
Shakespeares, that it's best to have two strings to our bow,
and to gain instruction both from books and things?"

"To be sure," said Clayton, "if we only use books
aright.   With many people, reading is only a form of
mental indolence, by which they escape the labor of thinking for themselves.   Some persons are like Pharaoh's lean
kine; they swallow book upon book, but remain as lean as
ever."

"My grandfather used to say," said Anne, "that the
Bible and Shakespeare were enough for a woman's library."

"Well," said Nina, "I don't like Shakespeare, there! I 'm coming out flat with it. In the first place, I don't understand half he says; and then, they talk about his being so very natural! I 'm sure I never heard people talk as he makes them. Now, did you ever hear people talk in blank verse, with every now and then one or two lines of rhyme, as his characters do when they go off in long speeches? Now, did you?"

"As to that," said Clayton, "it 's about half and half. His conversations have just about the same resemblance to real life that acting at the opera has. It is not natural for Norma to burst into a song when she discovers the treachery of her husband. You make that concession to the nature of the opera, in the first place; and then, with that reserve, all the rest strikes you as natural, and the music gives an added charm to it. So in Shakespeare, you concede that the plays are to be poems, and that the people are to talk in rhythm, and with all the exaltation of poetic sentiment; and that being admitted, their conversations may seem natural."

"But I can't understand a great deal that Shakespeare says," said Nina.

"Because so many words and usages are altered since he wrote," said Clayton. "Because there are so many allusions to incidents that have passed, and customs that have perished, that you have, as it were, to acquire his language before you can understand him. Suppose a poem were written in a foreign tongue; you could n't say whether you liked it or disliked it till you could read the language. Now, my opinion is, that there is a liking for Shakespeare hidden in your nature, like a seed that has not sprouted."

"What makes you think so?"

"Oh, I see it in you, just as a sculptor sees a statue in a block of marble."

"And are you going to chisel it out?" said Nina.

"With your leave," said Clayton. "After all, I like your sincerity in saying what you do think. I have often heard ladies profess an admiration for Shakespeare that I knew couldn't be real. I knew that they had neither the experience of life nor the insight into human nature really to appreciate what is in him; and that their liking for him was all a worked-up affair, because they felt it would be very shocking not to like him."

"Well," said Nina, "I'm much obliged to you for all the sense you find in my nonsense. I believe I shall keep you to translate my fooleries into good English."

"You know I'm quite at your disposal," said Clayton, "for that or anything else."

At this moment the attention of Nina was attracted by loud exclamations from that side of the house where the negro cottages were situated.

"Get along off! don't want none o' yo' old trash here! No, no, Miss Nina don't want none o' yo' old fish! She's got plenty of niggers to ketch her own fish."

"Somebody taking my name in vain in those regions," said Nina, running to the other end of the veranda. "Tomtit," she said to that young worthy, who lay flat on his back, kicking up his heels in the sun, waiting for his knives to clean themselves, "pray tell me what's going on there!"

"Laws, missis," said Tom, "it's just one of dese yer poor white trash, coming round here trying to sell one thing o' 'nother. Miss Loo says it won't do 'courage 'em, and I's de same 'pinion."

"Send him round here to me," said Nina, who, partly from humanity, and partly from a spirit of contradiction, had determined to take up for the poor white folks, on all occasions. Tomtit ran accordingly, and soon brought to the veranda a man whose wretchedly tattered clothing scarcely formed a decent covering. His cheeks were

sunken and hollow, and he stood before Nina with a cring-
ing, half-ashamed attitude; and yet one might see that,
with better dress and better keeping, he might be made to
assume the appearance of a handsome, intelligent man.
"What do you ask for your fish?" she said to him.

"Anything ye pleases!"

"Where do you live?" said Nina, drawing out her
purse.

"My folks 's staying on Mr. Gordon's place."

"Why don't you get a place of your own to stay on?"
said Nina.

There was an impatient glance flashed from the man's
eye, but it gave place immediately to his habitual cowed
expression, as he said, —

"Can't get work — can't get money — can't get nothing."

"Dear me," said her Uncle John, who had been standing for a moment listening to the conversation. "This
must be husband of that poor hobgoblin that has lighted
down on my place lately. Well, you may as well pay him
a good price for his fish. Keep them from starving one
day longer, maybe." And Nina paid the man a liberal
sum and dismissed him.

"I suppose, now, all my eloquence would n't make Rose
cook those fish for dinner," said Nina.

"Why not, if you told her to?" said Aunt Maria, who
had also descended to the veranda.

"Why not? — Just because, as she would say, she
had n't *laid out* to do it."

"That 's not the way *my* servants are taught to do!"
said Aunt Maria.

"I 'll warrant not," said Nina. "But yours and mine
are quite different affairs, aunt. They all do as they have
a mind to, in my *diggings*. All I stipulated for is a little
of the same privilege."

"That man's wife and children have come and squatted down on my place," said Mr. Gordon, laughing; "and so, Nin, all you paid for his fish is just so much saving to me."

"Yes, to be sure! Mr. Gordon is just one of those men that will have a tribe of shiftless hangers-on at his heels!" said Mrs. Gordon.

"Well, bless my soul! what's a fellow to do? Can't see the poor heathen starve, can we? If society could only be organized over, now, there would be hope for them. The brain ought to control the hands; but among us the hands try to set up for themselves; — and see what comes of it!"

"Who do you mean by brain?" said Nina.

"Who? — Why, *we* upper crust, to be sure! We educated people! We ought to have an absolute sway over the working classes, just as the brain rules the hand. It must come to that, at last — no other arrangement is possible. The white working classes can't take care of themselves, and must be put into a condition for us to take care of them. What is liberty to them? — Only a name — liberty to be hungry and naked, that's all. It's the strangest thing in the world, how people stick to names! I suppose that fellow, up there, would flare up terribly at being put in with my niggers; and yet he and his children are glad of the crumbs that fall from their table! It's astonishing to me how, with such examples before them, any decent man can be so stone-blind as to run atilt against slavery. Just compare the free working classes with our slaves! Dear me! the blindness of people in this world! It's too much for my patience, particularly in hot weather!" said Mr. John, wiping his face with a white pocket-handkerchief.

"Well, but, Uncle John," said Nina, "my dear old gentleman, you haven't traveled, as I have."

"No, child! I thank the Lord I never stepped my foot out of a slave state, and I never mean to," said Uncle John.

"But you ought to see the northern working people," said Nina. "Why, the governors of the states are farmers, sometimes, and work with their own men. The brain and the hand go together, in each one — not one great brain to fifty pair of hands. And, I tell you, work is done up there very differently from what's done here! Just look at our ploughs and our hoes! — the most ridiculous things that I ever saw. I should think one of them would weigh ten pounds!"

"Well, if you don't have 'em heavy enough to go into the ground by their own weight, these cussed lazy nigs won't do anything with them. They'd break a dozen Yankee hoes in a forenoon," said Uncle John.

"Now," said Nina, "Uncle John, you dear old heathen, you! do let me tell you a little how it is there. I went up into New Hampshire, once, with Livy Ray, to spend a vacation. Livy's father is a farmer; works part of every day with his own men; hoes, digs, plants; but he is governor of the state. He has a splendid farm — all in first-rate order; and his sons, with two or three hired men, keep it in better condition than our places ever saw. Mr. Ray is a man who reads a great deal; has a fine library, and he's as much of a gentleman as you'll often see. There are no high and low *classes* there. Everybody works; and everybody seems to have a good time. Livy's mother has a beautiful dairy, spring-house, and two strong women to help her; and everything in the house looks beautifully; and, for the greater part of the day, the house seems so neat and still, you wouldn't know anything had been done in it. Seems to me this is better than making slaves of all the working classes, or having any working classes at all."

"How wise young ladies always are!" said Uncle John. "Undoubtedly the millennium is begun in New Hampshire! But, pray, my dear, what part do young ladies take in all this? Seems to me, Nin, you have n't picked up much of this improvement in person."

"Oh, as to that, I labor in my vocation," said Nina; "that is, of enlightening dull, sleepy old gentlemen, who never traveled out of the state they were born in, and don't know what can be done. I come as a missionary to them; I 'm sure that 's work enough for one."

"Well," said Aunt Maria, "I know I am as great a slave as any of the poor whites, or negroes either. There is n't a soul in my whole troop that pretends to take any care, except me, either about themselves or their children, or anything else."

"I hope that is n't a slant at me!" said Uncle John, shrugging his shoulders.

"I must say you are as bad as any of them," said Aunt Maria.

"There it goes! — now, I 'm getting it!" said Uncle John. "I declare, the next time we get a preacher out here, I 'm going to make him hold forth on the duties of wives!"

"And husbands, too!" said Aunt Maria.

"Do," said Nina; "I should like a little prospective information."

Nina, as often, spoke before she thought. Uncle John gave a malicious look at Clayton. Nina could not recall the words. She colored deeply, and went on hastily to change the subject.

"At any rate, I know that aunt, here, has a much harder time than housekeepers do in the free states. Just the shoes she wears out chasing up her negroes would hire help enough to do all her work. They used to have an idea up there, that all the southern ladies did was to lie on the sofa. I used to tell them it was as much as they knew about it."

"Your cares don't seem to have worn you much!" said Uncle John.

"Well, they will, Uncle John, if you don't behave better. It's enough to break anybody down to keep you in order."

"I wish," said Uncle John, shrugging up his shoulders, and looking quizzically at Clayton, "somebody would take warning!"

"For my part," said Aunt Maria, "I know one thing: I'd be glad to get rid of my negroes. Sometimes I think life is such a burden that I don't think it's worth having."

"Oh no, you don't, mother!" said Uncle John; "not with such a charming husband as you've got, who relieves you from all care so perfectly!"

"I declare," said Nina, looking along the avenue, "what's that? Why, if there isn't Old Tiff, coming along with his children!"

"Who is he?" said Aunt Maria.

"Oh, he belongs to one of these miserable families," said Aunt Nesbit, "that have squatted in the pine woods somewhere about here — a poor, worthless set! but Nina has a great idea of patronizing them."

"Clear Gordon, every inch of her!" said Aunt Maria, as Nina ran down to meet Tiff. "Just like her uncle!"

"Come, now, old lady, I'll tell of you, if you don't take care!" said Mr. Gordon. "Didn't I find you putting up a basket of provisions for those folks you scolded me so for taking in?"

"Scold, Mr. Gordon? I never scold!"

"I beg pardon — that you reproved me for!"

Ladies generally are not displeased for being reproached for their charities; and Aunt Maria, whose bark, to use

a vulgar proverb, was infinitely worse than her bite, sat
fanning herself, with an air of self-complacency.   Meanwhile, Nina had run down the avenue, and was busy in a
confidential communication with Tiff.   On her return, she
came skipping up the steps, apparently in high glee.

"Oh, Uncle John! there's the greatest fun getting up!
You must all go, certainly!   What do you think?   Tiff
says there's to be a camp-meeting in the neighborhood,
only about five miles off from his place.   Let's make up
a party, and all go!"

"That's the time of day!" said Uncle John.   "I enroll
myself under your banner at once.   I am open to improvement!   Anybody wants to convert me, here I am!"

"The trouble with you, Uncle John," said Nina, "is
that you don't stay converted.   You are just like one of
these heavy fishes — you bite very sharp; but before anybody can get you fairly on to the bank, you are flapping
and floundering back into the water, and down you go into
your sins again.   I know at least three ministers who
thought they had hooked you out; but they were mistaken."

"For my part," said Aunt Maria, "I think these camp-
meetings do more harm than good.   They collect all the
scum and the riff-raff of the community, and I believe
there's more drinking done at camp-meetings in one week
than is done in six anywhere else.   Then, of course, all
the hands will want to be off; and Mr. Gordon has brought
them up so that they feel dreadfully abused if they are not
in with everything that's going on.   I shall set down my
foot, this year, that they sha'n't go any day except Sunday."

"My wife knows that she was always celebrated for
having the handsomest foot in the country, and so she is
always setting it down at me!" said Mr. Gordon; "for
she knows that a pretty foot is irresistible with me."

"Mr. Gordon, how can you talk so? I should think that you'd got old enough not to make such silly speeches!" said Aunt Maria.

"Silly speeches! It's a solemn fact, and you won't hear anything truer at the camp-meeting!" said Uncle John. "But come, Clayton, will you go? My dear fellow, your grave face will be an appropriate ornament to the scene, I can assure you; and as to Miss Anne, it won't do for an old fellow like me, in this presence, to say what a happiness it would be."

"I suspect," said Anne, "Edward is afraid he may be called on for some of the services. People are always taking him for a clergyman, and asking him to say grace at meals, and to conduct family prayers, when he is traveling among strangers."

"It's a comment on our religion, that these should be thought peculiar offices of clergymen," said Clayton. "Every Christian man ought to be ready and willing to take them."

"I honor that sentiment!" said Uncle John. "A man ought not to be ashamed of his religion anywhere, no more than a soldier of his colors. I believe there's more religion hid in the hearts of honest laymen, now, than is plastered up behind the white cravats of clergymen; and they ought to come out with it. Not that I have any disrespect for the clergy, either," said Uncle John. "Fine men — a little stiffish, and don't call things by good English names. Always talking about dispensation, and sanctification, and edification, and so forth; but I like them. They are sincere. I suppose they wouldn't any of them give me a chance for heaven, because I rip out with an oath, every now and then. But the fact is, what with niggers and overseers and white trash, my chances of salvation are dreadfully limited. I can't help swearing, now and then, if I was to die for it. They say it's dread-

fully wicked; but I feel more Christian when I let out
than when I keep in!"

"Mr. Gordon," said Aunt Maria reprovingly, "do consider what you're saying!"

"My dear, I am considering. I am considering all the
time! I never do anything else but consider — except, as
I said before, every now and then, when what-'s-his-name
gets the advantage over me. And, hark you, Mrs. G.,
let's have things ready at our house, if any of the clergy
would like to spend a week or so with us; and we could
get them up some meetings, or any little thing in their
line. I always like to show respect for them."

"Our beds are always prepared for company, Mr. Gordon," said Aunt Maria, with a stately air.

"Oh yes, yes, I don't doubt that! I only meant some
special preparation — some little fatted-calf killing, and so
on."

"Now," said Nina, "shall we set off to-morrow morning?"

"Agreed!" said Uncle John.

CHAPTER XXI

THE announcement of the expected camp-meeting produced a vast sensation at Canema in other circles beside
the hall. In the servants' department, everybody was
full of the matter, from Aunt Katy down to Tomtit. The
women were thinking over their available finery; for these
gatherings furnish the negroes with the same opportunity
of display that Grace Church does to the Broadway belles.
And so, before Old Tiff, who had brought the first intelligence to the plantation, had time to depart, Tomtit had
trumpeted the news through all the cluster of negro houses
that skirted the right side of the mansion, proclaiming that
"dere was gwine to be a camp-meeting, and tip-top work
of grace, and Miss Nina was going to let all de niggers
go." Old Tiff, therefore, found himself in a prominent
position in a group of negro women, among whom Rose,
the cook, was conspicuous.

"Law, Tiff, ye gwine? and gwine to take your chil'en?
Ha! ha! ha!" said she. "Why, Miss Fanny, dey'll tink
Tiff's yer mammy! Ho! ho! ho!"

"Yah! yah! Ho! ho! ho!" roared in a chorus of
laughter on all sides, doing honor to Aunt Rose's wit;
and Tomtit, who hung upon the skirts of the crowd, threw
up the fragment of a hat in the air, and kicked it in an
abandon of joy, regardless of the neglected dinner-knives.
Old Tiff, mindful of dignities, never failed to propitiate
Rose, on his advents to the plantation, with the gift which
the "wise man saith maketh friends;" and on the present

occasion he had enriched her own peculiar stock of domestic fowl by the present of a pair of young partridge-chicks, a nest of which he had just captured, intending to bring them up by hand, as he did his children. By this discreet course Tiff stood high where it was of most vital consequence that he should so stand; and many a choice morsel did Rose cook for him in secret, besides imparting to him most invaluable recipes on the culture and raising of sucking babies. Old Hundred, like many other persons, felt that general attention lavished on any other celebrity was so much taken from his own merits, and, therefore, on the present occasion, sat regarding Tiff's evident popularity with a cynical eye. At last, coming up, like a wicked fellow as he was, he launched his javelin at Old Tiff, by observing to his wife, —

"I 's 'stonished at you, Rose! *You*, cook to de Gordons, and making youself so cheap — so familiar with de poor white folks' niggers!"

Had the slant fallen upon himself, personally, Old Tiff would probably have given a jolly crow, and laughed as heartily as he generally did if he happened to be caught out in a rainstorm; but the reflection on his family connection fired him up like a torch, and his eyes flashed through his big spectacles like firelight through windows.

"You go 'long, talking 'bout what you don' know nothing 'bout! I like to know what you knows 'bout de old Virginny fam'lies? Dem 's de real old stock! You Car'lina folks come from dem, stick and stock, every blest one of you! De Gordons is a nice family, — ain't nothing to say agin de Gordons, — but whar was you raised, dat ye did n't hear 'bout de Peytons? Why, old Gen'al Peyton, did n't he use to ride with six black horses afore him, as if he 'd been a king? Dere wa'n't one of dem horses dat had n't a tail as long as my arm. *You* never see no such critters in your life!"

"I hain't, hain't I?" said Old Hundred, now, in his turn, touched in a vital point. "Bless me, if I hain't seen de Gordons riding out with der eight horses, any time o' day!"

"Come, come, now, dere was n't so many!" said Rose, who had her own reasons for staying on Tiff's side. "Nobody never rode with eight horses!"

"Did too! You say much more, I 'll make sixteen on 'em! 'Fore my blessed Master, how dese yer old niggers will lie! Dey 's always zaggerating der families. Makes de very har rise on my head, to hear dese yer old niggers talk, dey lie so!" said Old Hundred.

"You tink folks dat take to lying is using up your business, don't ye?" said Tiff. "But, I tell you, any one dat says a word agin de Peytons got me to set in with!"

"Laws, dem chil'en ain't Peytons!" said Old Hundred; "dey 's Crippses; and I like to know who ever hearn of de Crippses? Go 'way! don't tell me nothing about dem Crippses! Dey 's poor white folks! A body may see dat sticking out all over 'em!"

"You shut up!" said Tiff. "I don't b'lieve you was born on de Gordon place, 'cause you ain't got no manners. I spects you some old, second-hand nigger, Colonel Gordon must a took for debt, some time, from some of dese yer mean Tennessee families, dat don' know how to keep der money when dey gets it. Der niggers is allers de meanest kind. 'Cause all de real Gordon niggers is ladies and gen'lemen — every one of 'em!" said Old Tiff, like a true orator, bent on carrying his audience along with him.

A general shout chorused this compliment; and Tiff, under cover of the applause, shook up his reins, and rode off in triumph.

"Dar, now, you aggravating old nigger," said Rose, turning to her bosom lord, "I hope yer got it now! De plaguest old nigger dat ever I see! And you, Tom, go 'long and clean your knives, if yer don't mean to be cracked over!"

Meanwhile Tiff, restored to his usual tranquillity, ambled along homeward behind his one-eyed horse, singing "I'm bound for the land of Canaan," with some surprising variations.

At last Miss Fanny, as he constantly called her, interposed with a very pregnant question.

"Uncle Tiff, where is the land of Canaan?"

"De Lord-a-mercy, chile, dat ar's what I'd like to know myself."

"Is it heaven?" said Fanny.

"Well, I reckon so," said Tiff dubiously.

"Is it where ma is gone?" said Fanny.

"Chile, I reckon it is," said Tiff.

"Is it down under ground?" said Fanny.

"Why, no! ho! ho! honey!" said Tiff, laughing heartily. "What put dat ar in your head, Miss Fanny?"

"Didn't ma go that way?" said Fanny; "down through the ground?"

"Lordy, no, chile! Heaven's up!" said Tiff, pointing up to the intense blue sky which appeared through the fringy hollows of the pine-trees above them.

"Is there any stairs anywhere? or any ladder to get up by?" said Fanny. "Or do they walk to where the sky touches the ground, and get up? Perhaps they climb up on the rainbow."

"I don' know, chile, how dey works it," said Uncle Tiff. "Dey gets dar somehow. I's studdin' upon dat ar. I's gwine to camp-meeting to find out. I's been to plenty of dem ar, and I never could quite see clar. 'Pears like dey talks about everything else more 'n dey does about dat. Dere's de Methodists, dey cuts up de Presbyter'ans; and de Presbyter'ans pitches into de Methodists; and den, both on 'em's down on de 'Piscopals. My ole mist' was 'Piscopal, and I never seed no harm in 't. And de Baptists think dey ain't none on 'em right; and while dey's all a-blowing out at each other, dat ar way, I's a wondering whar's de way to Canaan. It takes a mighty heap o' larning to know about dese yer things, and I ain't got no larning. I don' know nothing, only de Lord, He 'peared to your ma, and He knows de way, and He took her. But now, chile, I's gwine to fix you up right smart, and take you, Teddy, and de baby to dis yer camp-meeting, so you can seek de Lord in yer youth."

"Tiff, if you please, I'd rather not go!" said Fanny in an apprehensive tone.

"Oh, bress de Lord, Miss Fanny, why not? Fustrate times dere."

"There'll be too many people. I don't want them to see us."

The fact was, that Rose's slant speech about Tiff's maternal relationship, united with the sneers of Old Hundred, had their effect upon Fanny's mind. Naturally proud, and fearful of ridicule, she shrank from the public display which would thus be made of their family condition; yet she would not for the world have betrayed to her kind old friend the real reason of her hesitation. But Old Tiff's keen eye had noticed the expression of the child's countenance at the time. If anybody supposes that the faithful old creature's heart was at all wounded by the perception, he is greatly mistaken.

To Tiff it appeared a joke of the very richest quality; and as he rode along in silence for some time, he indulged himself in one of his quiet, long laughs, actually shaking his old sides till the tears streamed down his cheeks.

"What's the matter with you, Tiff?" said Fanny.

"Oh, Miss Fanny, Tiff knows! — Tiff knows de reason ye don't want to go to camp-meeting. Tiff's seen it in yer face — ye ho! ho! ho! Miss Fanny, is you 'fraid dey'll take Old Tiff for yer mammy? — ye ho! ho! ho! — for yer mammy? — and Teddy's, and de baby's? —

bless his little soul!" And the amphibious old creature rollicked over the idea with infinite merriment. "Don't I look like it, Miss Fanny? Lord, ye por dear lamb, can't folks see ye 's a born lady, with yer white, little hands? Don't ye be 'feard, Miss Fanny!"

"I know it 's silly," said Fanny; "but, beside, I don't like to be called *poor white folksy!*"

"Oh, chile, it 's only dem mean niggers! Miss Nina 's allers good to ye, ain't she? Speaks to ye so handsome. Ye must memorize dat ar, Miss Fanny, and talk like Miss Nina. I 's 'feard, now yer ma 's dead, ye 'll fall into some o' my nigger ways of talking. 'Member you must n't talk like Old Tiff, 'cause young ladies and gen'lemen must n't talk like niggers. Now I says 'dis and dat, dis yer and dat ar.' Dat ar is nigger talk, and poor white folksy, too. Only de por white folks, dey 's mis'able, 'cause niggers knows what 's good talk, but dey does n't. Lord, chile, Old Tiff knows what good talk is. Ain't he heard de greatest ladies and gen'lemen in de land talk? But he don't want de trouble to talk dat ar way, 'cause he 's a nigger! Tiff likes his own talk — it 's good enough for Tiff. Tiff's talk sarves him mighty well, I tell yer. But den, white children must n't talk so. Now, you see, Miss Nina has got de prettiest way of saying her words. Dey drops out one after another, one after another, so pretty! Now, you mind, 'cause she 's coming to see us off and on — she promised so. And den, you keep a good lookout how she walks, and how she holds her pocket-handker-chief. And when she sits down she kind o' gives a little flirt to her clothes, so dey all set out round her like ruffles. Dese yer little ways ladies have! Why, dese yer por white folks, did yer ever mind der settin' down? Why, dey jist slaps down into a chair like a spoonful o' mush, and der clothes all stick tight about 'em. I don't want nothing *poor white folksy* 'bout you. Den, if you don't

understand what people's a-saying to you, any time, you
must n't star, like poor white chil'en, and say, 'what?'
but you must say 'I beg pardon, sir,' or, 'I beg pardon,
ma'am.' Dat ar's de way. And, Miss Fanny, you and
Teddy, you must study yer book; 'cause, if you can't
read, den dey 'll be sure to say yer poor white folks. And
den, Miss Fanny, you see dat ladies don't demean dem-
selves with sweeping and scrubbing, and dem tings; and
yet dey does work, honey! Dey sews, and dey knits; and
it would be good for you to larn how to sew and knit;
'cause, you know, I can't allers make up all de clothes;
'cause, you see, young ladies haves ways wid 'em dat
niggers can't get. Now, you see, Miss Fanny, all dese
yer tings I was telling you, you must 'bserve. Now, you
see, if you was one of dese yer poor white folks, dere be
no use of your trying; 'cause dat ar 'scription o' people
could n't never be ladies, if dey was waring themselves out
a-trying. But you see, you 's got it in you; you was born
to it, honey. It 's in de blood; and what 's in de blood
must come out — ho! ho! ho!" And with this final
laugh, Tiff drew up to his dwelling.

A busy day was before Old Tiff; for he was to set his
house in order for a week's campaign. There was his corn
to be hoed, his parsley to be weeded; there was his orphan
family of young partridges to be cared for. And Tiff,
after some considerable consideration, resolved to take
them along with him in a basket; thinking, in the intervals of devotion, he should have an abundant opportunity
to minister to their wants, and superintend their education.
Then he went to one of his favorite springes, and brought
from thence, not a fatted calf, to be sure, but a fatted
coon, which he intended to take with him, to serve as the
basis of a savory stew on the camp-ground. Tiff had a
thriving company of pot-herbs, and a flourishing young
colony of onions; so that, whatever might be true of the

sermons, it was evident that the stew would lack no savor. Teddy's clothes, also, were to be passed in review; washing and ironing to be done; the baby fitted up to do honor to his name, or rather to the name of his grandfather. With all these cares upon his mind, the old creature was even more than usually alert. The day was warm, and he resolved, therefore, to perform his washing operations in the magnificent kitchen of nature. He accordingly kindled a splendid bonfire, which was soon crackling at a short distance from the house, slung over it his kettle, and proceeded to some other necessary avocations. The pine wood, which had been imperfectly seasoned, served him the ungracious trick that pine wood is apt to do: it crackled and roared merrily while he was present, but while he was down examining his traps in the woods went entirely out, leaving only the blackened sticks.

"Uncle Tiff," said Teddy, "the fire is all gone out!"

"Ho! ho! ho! — Has it?" said Tiff, coming up. "Curus enough! Well, bress de Lord, got all de wood left, anyway; had a real bright fire, beside," said Tiff, intent on upholding the sunniest side of things. "Lord, it's de sun dat puts de fire out o' countenance. Did you ever see fire dat wouldn't go out when de sun's shining right in its face? Dat ar is a curus fact. I's minded it heaps o' times. Well, I'll jist have to come out wid my light-wood kindlings, dat's all. Bress de Lord, ho! ho! ho!" said Tiff, laughing to himself "if dese yer ain't the very sp'rit of de camp-meeting professors! Dey blazes away at de camp-meeting, and den dey's black all de year round! See 'em at de camp-meetings, you'd say dey war gwine right into de kingdom, sure enough! Well, Lord have marcy on us all! Our 'ligion's drefful poor stuff! We don't know but a despert leetle, and what we does know we don' do. De good Mas'r above must have his hands full with us!"

CHAPTER XXII

THE WORSHIPERS

THE camp-meeting is one leading feature in the American development of religion, peculiarly suited to the wide extent of country, and to the primitive habits which generally accompany a sparse population. Undoubtedly its general effects have been salutary. Its evils have been only those incident to any large gatherings, in which the whole population of a country are brought promiscuously together. As in many other large assemblies of worship, there are those who go for all sorts of reasons; some from curiosity, some from love of excitement, some to turn a penny in a small way of trade, some to scoff, and a few to pray. And so long as the heavenly way remains straight and narrow, so long the sincere and humble worshipers will ever be the minority in all assemblies. We can give no better idea of the difference of motive which impelled the various worshipers, than by taking our readers from scene to scene, on the morning when different attendants of the meeting were making preparations to start.

Between the grounds of Mr. John Gordon and the plantation of Canema stood a log cabin, which was the trading establishment of Abijah Skinflint. The establishment was a nuisance in the eyes of the neighboring planters, from the general apprehension entertained that Abijah drove a brisk underhand trade with the negroes, and that the various articles which he disposed for sale were many of them surreptitiously conveyed to him in nightly installments from off their own plantations. But of this nothing could be proved.

Abijah was a shrewd fellow, long, dry, lean, leathery, with a sharp nose, sharp, little, gray eyes, a sharp chin, and fingers as long as bird's claws. His skin was so dry that one would have expected that his cheeks would crackle whenever he smiled or spoke; and he rolled in them a never-failing quid of tobacco.

Abijah was one of those over-shrewd Yankees who leave their country for their country's good, and who exhibit, wherever they settle, such a caricature of the thrifty virtue of their native land as to justify the aversion which the native-born Southerner entertains for the Yankee. Abijah drank his own whiskey, — prudently, however, — or, as he said, "never so as not to know what he was about."

He had taken a wife from the daughters of the land, who also drank whiskey, but less prudently than her husband, so that sometimes she did *not* know what she was about. Sons and daughters were born unto this promising couple, white-headed, forward, dirty, and ill mannered. But amid all domestic and social trials, Abijah maintained a constant and steady devotion to the main chance — the acquisition of money. For money he would do anything; for money he would have sold his wife, his children, even his own soul, if he had happened to have one. But that article, had it ever existed, was now so small and dry, that one might have fancied it to rattle in his lean frame like a shriveled pea in a last year's peascod. Abijah was going to the camp-meeting for two reasons. One, of course, was to make money; and the other was to know whether his favorite preacher, Elder Stringfellow, handled the doctrine of election according to his views; for Abijah had a turn for theology, and could number off the five points of Calvinism on his five long fingers with unfailing accuracy.

It is stated in the Scriptures that the devils believe and tremble. The principal difference between their belief and Abijah's was, that he believed and did *not* tremble. Truths awful enough to have shaken the earth and veiled the sun, he could finger over with as much unconcern as a practiced anatomist the dry bones of a skeleton.

"You, Sam!" said Abijah to his only negro helot, "you mind, you steady that ar bar'l, so that it don't roll out, and pour a pailful of water in at the bung. It won't do to give it to 'em too strong. Mis' Skinflint, you make haste! If you don't, I sha'n't wait for you; 'cause, whatever the rest may do, it's important I should be on the ground early. Many a dollar lost for not being in time, in this world. Hurry, woman!"

"I am ready, but Polly ain't!" said Mrs. Skinflint. "She's busy a-plastering down her hair."

"Can't wait for her!" said Abijah, as he sallied out of the house to get into the wagon, which stood before the door, into which he had packed a copious supply of hams, eggs, dressed chickens, corn-meal, and green summer vegetables, to say nothing of the barrel of whiskey aforesaid.

"I say, dad, you stop!" called Polly, from the window. "If you don't, I'll make work for you 'fore you come home; you see if I don't! Durned if I won't!"

"Come along, then, can't you? Next time we go anywhere, I'll shut you up overnight to begin to dress!"

Polly hastily squeezed her fat form into a red calico dress, and seizing a gay summer shawl, with her bonnet in her hand, rushed to the wagon and mounted, the hooks of her dress successively exploding, and flying off, as she stooped to get in.

"Durned if I knows what to do!" said she; "this yer old durned gear coat's all off my back!"

"Gals is always fools!" said Abijah consolingly.

"Stick in a pin, Polly," said her mother in an easy, sing-song drawl.

"Durn you, old woman, every hook is off!" said the promising young lady.

"Stick in more pins, then," said the mamma; and the vehicle of Abijah passed onward.

On the verge of the swamp, a little beyond Tiff's cabin, lived Ben Dakin.

Ben was a mighty hunter; he had the best pack of dogs within thirty miles round; and his advertisements, still to be seen standing in the papers of his native state, detailed with great accuracy the precise terms on which he would hunt down and capture any man, woman, or child, escaping from service and labor in that country. Our readers must not necessarily suppose Ben to have been a monster for all this, when they recollect that, within a few years, both the great political parties of our Union solemnly pledged themselves, as far as in them lay, to accept a similar vocation; and as many of them were in good and regular standing in churches, and had ministers to preach sermons to the same effect, we trust they'll entertain no unreasonable prejudice against Ben on this account.

In fact, Ben was a tall, broad-shouldered, bluff, hearty-looking fellow, who would do a kind turn for a neighbor with as much good will as anybody; and except that he now and then took a little too much whiskey, as he himself admitted, he considered himself quite as promising a candidate for the kingdom as any of the company who were going up to camp-meeting. Had any one ventured to remonstrate with Ben against the nature of his profession, he would probably have defended it by pretty much the same arguments by which modern theologians defend the institution of which it is a branch.

Ben was just one of those jovial fellows who never could bear to be left behind in anything that was going on in the community, and was always one of the foremost in a camp-meeting. He had a big, loud voice, and could roll out the chorus of hymns with astonishing effect. He was generally converted at every gathering of this kind; though through the melancholy proclivity to whiskey, before alluded to, he usually fell from grace before the year was out. Like many other big and hearty men, he had a little, pale, withered moonshiny wisp of a wife, who hung on his elbow much like an empty work-bag; and Ben, to do him justice, was kind to the wilted little mortal, as if he almost suspected that he had absorbed her vitality into his own exuberant growth. She was greatly given to eating clay, cleaning her teeth with snuff, and singing Methodist hymns, and had a very sincere concern for Ben's salvation. The little woman sat resignedly on the morning we speak of, while a long-limbed, broad-shouldered child, of two years, with bristly white hair, was pulling her by her ears and hair, and otherwise maltreating her, to make her get up to give him a piece of bread and molasses; and she, without seeming to attend to the child, was giving earnest heed to her husband.

"There's a despit press of business now!" said Ben. "There's James's niggers, and Smith's Polly, and we ought to be on the trail, right away!"

"Oh, Ben, you ought to 'tend to your salvation afore anything else!" said his wife.

"That's true enough!" said Ben; "meetings don't come every day. But what are we to do with dis yer un?" pointing to the door of an inner room.

"Dis yer un" was no other than a negro woman, named Nance, who had been brought in by the dogs, the day before.

"Laws!" said his wife, "we can set her something to eat, and leave the dogs in front of the door. She can't get out."

Ben threw open the door, and displayed to view a low kind of hutch, without any other light than that between the crevices of the logs. On the floor, which was of hard-trodden earth, sat a sinewy, lean negro woman, drawing up her knees with her long arms, and resting her chin upon them.

"Hollo, Nance, how are you?" said Ben, rather cheer-ily.

"Po'rly, mas'r," said the other in a sullen tone.

"Nance, you think your old man will whale you, when he gets you?" said Ben.

"I reckons he will," said Nance; "he allers does."

"Well, Nance, the old woman and I want to go to a camp-meeting; and I'll just tell you what it is, — you stay here quiet, while we are gone, and I'll make the old fellow promise not to wallop you. I wouldn't mind tak-ing off something of the price — that's fair, ain't it?"

"Yes, mas'r!" said the woman in the same subdued tone.

"Does your foot hurt you much?" said Ben.

"Yes, mas'r!" said the woman.

"Let me look at it," said Ben.

The woman put out one foot, which had been loosely bound up in old rags, now saturated in blood.

"I declar, if that ar dog ain't a pealer!" said Ben. "Nance, you ought ter have stood still; then he wouldn't have hurt you so."

"Lord, he hurt me so I couldn't stand still!" said the woman. "It ain't natur to stand still with a critter's teeth in yer foot."

"Well, I don't know as it is," said Ben good naturedly. "Here, Mis' Dakin, you bind up this here gal's foot. Stop your noise, sir-ee!" he added, to the young aspirant for bread and molasses, who, having dispatched one piece, was clamoring vigorously for another.

"I'll tell you what!" said Ben to his wife, "I am going to talk to that ar old Elder Settle. I runs more

niggers for him than any man in the county, and I know
there 's some reason for it. Niggers don't run into swamps
when they 's treated well. Folks that professes religion,
I think, ought n't to starve their niggers, noway ! "

Soon the vehicle of Ben was also on the road. He
gathered up the reins vigorously, threw back his head to
get the full benefit of his lungs, and commenced a vehement camp-meeting melody, to the tune of

> " Am I a soldier of the cross,
> A follower of the Lamb ? "

A hymn, by the bye, which was one of Ben's particular
favorites.

We come next to Tiff's cottage, of which the inmates
were astir, in the coolness of the morning, bright and
early. Tiff's wagon was a singular composite article, principally of his own construction. The body of it consisted
of a long packing-box. The wheels were all odd ones,
that had been brought home at different times by Cripps.
The shafts were hickory-poles, thinned at one end, and
fastened to the wagon by nails. Some barrel-hoops bent
over the top, covered by coarse white cotton cloth, formed
the curtains, and a quantity of loose straw dispersed inside
was the only seat. The lean, one-eyed horse was secured
to this vehicle by a harness made of old ropes; but no
millionaire, however, ever enjoyed his luxuriantly cushioned coach with half the relish with which Tiff enjoyed
his equipage. It was the work of his hands, the darling
of his heart, the delight of his eyes. To be sure, like
other mortal darlings, it was to be admitted that it had its
weak points and failings. The wheels would now and
then come off, the shafts get loose, or the harness break;
but Tiff was always prepared, and on occasion of any such
mishaps would jump out and attend to them with such
cheerful alacrity, that, if anything, he rather seemed to
love it better for the accident. There it stands now,

before the inclosure of the little cabin; and Tiff and
Fanny and Teddy, with bustling assiduity, are packing
and arranging it. The gum-tree cradle-trough took precedence of all other articles. Tiff, by the private advice of
Aunt Rose, had just added to this an improvement, which
placed it, in his view, tip-top among cradles. He had
nailed to one end of it a long splint of elastic hickory,
which drooped just over the baby's face. From this was
suspended a morsel of salt pork, which this young scion of
a noble race sucked with a considerate relish, while his
large, round eyes opened and shut with sleepy satisfaction.
This arrangement Rose had recommended, in mysterious
tones, as all powerful in making sucking babies forget
their mammies, whom otherwise they might pine for in a
manner prejudicial to their health.

Although the day was sultry, Tiff was arrayed in his
long-skirted white greatcoat, as his nether garments were
in too dilapidated a state to consist with the honor of the
family. His white felt hat still bore the band of black
crape.

"It's a 'mazin' good day, bless de Lord!" said Tiff.
"'Pears like dese yer birds would split der troats, praising
de Lord! It's a mighty good zample to us, anyway.
You see, Miss Fanny, you never see birds put out, nor
snarly like, rain or shine. Dey's allers a-praising de
Lord. Lord, it seems as if critters is better dan we be!"
And as Tiff spoke, he shouldered into the wagon a mighty
bag of corn; but failing in what he meant to do, the bag
slid over the side, and tumbled back into the road. Being
somewhat of the oldest, the fall burst it asunder, and the
corn rolled into the sand, with that provoking alacrity
which things always have when they go the wrong way.
Fanny and Teddy both uttered an exclamation of lamentation; but Tiff held on to his sides and laughed till the
tears rolled down his cheeks.

"He! he! he! ho! ho! ho! Why, dat ar is de last bag we's got, and dar's all de corn a-running out in de sand! Ho! ho! ho! Lord, it's so curus!"

"Why, what are you going to do?" said Fanny.

"Oh, bress you, Miss Fanny," said Tiff, "I's bound to do something, anyhow. 'Clare for it, now, if I hain't got a box!" And Tiff soon returned with the article in question, which proved too large for the wagon. The corn, however, was emptied into it *pro tem.*, and Tiff, producing his darning-needle and thimble, sat down seriously to the task of stitching up the hole.

"De Lord's things ain't never in a hurry," said Tiff. "Corn and 'tatoes will have der time, and why should n't I? Dar," he said, after having mended the bag and replaced the corn, "dat ar's better now nor 't was before."

Besides his own store of provisions, Tiff prudently laid into his wagon enough of garden stuff to turn a penny for Miss Fanny and the children, on the camp-ground. His commissariat department, in fact, might have provoked appetite, even among the fastidious. There were dressed chickens and rabbits, the coon aforesaid, bundles of savory herbs, crisp, dewy lettuce, bunches of onions, radishes, and green peas.

"Tell ye what, chil'en," said Tiff, "we'll live like princes! And you mind, order me round well. Let folks har ye; 'cause what's de use of having a nigger, and nobody knowing it?"

And everything being arranged, Tiff got in, and jogged comfortably along. At the turn of the cross-road, Tiff, looking a little behind, saw, on the other road, the Gordon carriage coming, driven by Old Hundred, arrayed in his very best ruffled shirt, white gloves, and gold hat-band.

If ever Tiff came near having a pang in his heart, it was at that moment; but he retreated stoutly upon the idea that, however appearances might be against them, his family was no less ancient and honorable for that; and, therefore, putting on all his dignity, he gave his beast an extra cut, as who should say, "I don't care."

But as ill luck would have it, the horse, at this instant, giving a jerk, wrenched out the nails that fastened the shaft on one side, and it fell, trailing dishonored on the ground. The rope harness pulled all awry, and just at this moment the Gordon carriage swept up.

"'Fore I'd drive sich old trash!" said Old Hundred scornfully; "pulls all to pieces every step! If dat ar ain't a poor white folksy 'stablishment, I never seed one!"

"What's the matter?" said Nina, putting her head out. "Oh, Tiff! good-morning, my good fellow. Can we help you, there? John, get down and help him."

"Please, Miss Nina, de hosses is so full o' tickle, dis yer mornin', I couldn't let go, noways!" said Old Hundred.

"Oh, laws bless you, Miss Nina," said Tiff, restored to his usual spirits, "'t ain't nothin'. Broke in a strordinary good place dis yer time. I ken hammer it up in a minute."

And Tiff was as good as his word; for a round stone and big nail made all straight.

"Pray," said Nina, "how are little Miss Fanny, and the children?"

Miss Fanny! If Nina had heaped Tiff with presents, she could not have conferred the inexpressible obligation conveyed in these words. He bowed low to the ground, with the weight of satisfaction, and answered that "Miss Fanny and the chil'en were well."

"There," said Nina, "John, you may drive on. Do you know, friends, I've set Tiff up for six weeks, by one word? Just saying *Miss* Fanny has done more for him than if I'd sent him six bushels of potatoes."

.   .   .   .

We have yet to take our readers to one more scene before we finish the review of those who were going to the camp-

meeting. The reader must follow us far beyond the abodes
of man, into the recesses of that wild desolation known as
the "Dismal Swamp." We pass over vast tracts where
the forest seems growing out of the water. Cypress, red
cedar, sweet-gum, tulip, poplar, beech, and holly form a
goodly fellowship, waving their rustling boughs above.
The trees shoot up in vast columns, fifty, seventy-five, and
a hundred feet in height; and below are clusters of evergreen gall-bushes, with their thick and glossy foliage,
mingled in with swamp honeysuckles, grapevines, twining
brier, and laurels, and other shrubs, forming an impenetrable thicket. The creeping plants sometimes climb sev-
enty or eighty feet up the largest tree, and hang in heavy
festoons from their branches. It would seem impossible
that human foot could penetrate the wild, impervious
jungle; but we must take our readers through it, to a
cleared spot, where trunks of fallen trees, long decayed,
have formed an island of vegetable mould, which the art
of some human hand has extended and improved. The
clearing is some sixty yards long by thirty broad, and is
surrounded with a natural rampart, which might well bid
defiance to man or beast. Huge trees have been felled,
with all their branches lying thickly one over another, in
a circuit around; and nature, seconding the efforts of the
fugitives who sought refuge here, has interlaced the framework thus made with thorny cat-briers, cables of grapevine, and thickets of Virginia creeper, which, running wild
in their exuberance, climb on to the neighboring trees,
and swinging down, again lose themselves in the mazes
from which they spring, so as often to form a verdurous
wall fifty feet in height. In some places the laurel, with
its glossy green leaves, and its masses of pink-tipped snowy
blossoms, presents to the eye, rank above rank, a wilderness of beauty. The pendants of the yellow jessamine
swing to and fro in the air like censers, casting forth clouds

of perfume. A thousand twining vines, with flowers of
untold name, perhaps unknown as yet to the botanist, help
to fill up the mosaic.   The leafy ramparts sweep round on
all the sides of the clearing, for the utmost care has been
taken to make it impenetrable; and in that region of heat
and moisture, nature, in the course of a few weeks, admi-
rably seconds every human effort.   The only egress from
it is a winding path cut through with a hatchet, which can
be entered by only one person at a time; and the water
which surrounds this island entirely cuts off the trail from
the scent of dogs.   It is to be remarked that the climate,
in the interior of the swamp, is far from being unhealthy.
Lumbermen, who spend great portions of the year in it,
cutting shingles and staves, testify to the general salubrity
of the air and water.   The opinion prevails among them
that the quantity of pine and other resinous trees that
grow there impart a balsamic property to the water, and
impregnate the air with a healthy, resinous fragrance,
which causes it to be an exception to the usual rule of the
unhealthiness of swampy land.   The soil also, when
drained sufficiently for purposes of culture, is profusely
fertile.   Two small cabins stood around the border of the
clearing, but the centre was occupied with patches of corn
and sweet potatoes, planted there to secure as much as
possible the advantage of sun and air.

At the time we take our readers there, the afternoon
sun of a sultry June day is casting its long shadows over
the place, and a whole choir of birds is echoing in the
branches.   On the ground, in front of one of the cabins,
lies a negro man, covered with blood; two women, with
some little children, are grouped beside him; and a wild
figure, whom we at once recognize as Dred, is kneeling by
him, busy in efforts to stanch a desperate wound in the
neck.   In vain! The red blood spurts out at every pulsation of the heart, with a fearful regularity, telling too

plainly that it is a great life-artery which has been laid
open. The negro woman, kneeling on the other side, is
anxiously holding some bandages, which she has stripped
from a portion of her raiment.

"Oh, put these on, quick — do!"

"It's no use," said Dred; "he is going!"

"Oh, do! — don't, don't let him go! *Can't* you save
him?" said the woman in tones of agony.

The wounded man's eyes opened, and first fixed themselves, with a vacant stare, on the blue sky above; then,
turning on the woman, he seemed to try to speak. He
had had a strong arm; he tries to raise it, but the blood
wells up with the effort, the eye glazes, the large frame
shivers for a few moments, and then all is still. The blood
stops flowing now, for the heart has stopped beating, and
an immortal soul has gone back to Him who gave it.

The man was a fugitive from a neighboring plantation
— a simple-hearted, honest fellow, who had fled, with his
wife and children, to save her from the licentious persecu-
tion of the overseer. Dred had received and sheltered
him; had built him a cabin, and protected him for months.

A provision of the Revised Statutes of North Carolina
enacts that slaves thus secreted in the swamps, not returning within a given time, shall be considered outlawed; and
that "it shall be lawful for any person or persons whatso-
ever to kill and destroy such slaves, by such ways and
means as they shall think fit, without any accusation or
impeachment of crime for the same." It also provides
that, when any slave shall be killed in consequence of such
outlawry, the value of such slave shall be ascertained by
a jury, and the owner entitled to receive two thirds of the
valuation from the sheriff of the county wherein the slave
was killed.

In olden times, the statute provided that the proclamation of outlawry should be published on a Sabbath day, at

the door of any church or chapel, or place where divine
service should be performed, immediately after divine service, by the parish clerk or reader.   In the spirit of this
permission, a party of negro-hunters, with dogs and guns,
had chased this man, who, on this day, had unfortunately
ventured out of his concealment.   He succeeded in outrun-
ning all but one dog, which sprang up, and fastening his
fangs in his throat, laid him prostrate within a few paces
of his retreat.   Dred came up in time to kill the dog, but
the wound, as appeared, had proved a mortal one.

As soon as the wife perceived that her husband was
really dead, she broke into a loud wail.   "Oh, dear, he's
gone! and 't was all for me he did it!   Oh, he was so good,
such a good man!   Oh, do tell me, *is* he dead, is he?"

Dred lifted the yet warm hand in his a moment, and
then dropped it heavily.   "Dead!" he said, in a deep
undertone of suppressed emotion.   Suddenly kneeling
down beside him, he lifted his hands, and broke forth
with wild vehemence: "O Lord God, to whom vengeance
belongeth, show thyself!   Lift up thyself, thou Judge of
the earth, render a reward to the proud!   Doubtless thou
art our Father, though Abraham be ignorant of us, and
Israel acknowledge us not.   Thou, O Lord, art our Father,
our Redeemer; thy ways are everlasting — where is thy
zeal and thy strength, and the sounding of thy bowels
towards us?   Are they restrained?"   Then, tossing his
hands to heaven, with a yet wilder gesture, he almost
screamed: "O Lord! O Lord! how long?   Oh, that thou
wouldst rend the heavens and come down!   Oh, let the
sighings of the prisoner come before thee!   Our bones are
scattered at the grave's mouth, as when one cutteth and
cleaveth wood!   We are given as sheep to the slaughter!
We are killed all the day long!   O Lord, avenge us of our
adversaries!"

These words were spoken with a vehement earnestness

of gesture and voice, that hushed the lamentation of the mourners. Rising up from his knees, he stood a moment looking down at the lifeless form before him. "See here," he said, "what harm had this man done? Was he not peaceable? Did he not live here in quietness, tilling the ground in the sweat of his brow? Why have they sent the hunters upon him? Because he wanted to raise his corn for himself, and not for another. Because he wanted his wife for himself, and not for another. Was not the world wide enough? Isn't there room enough under the sky? Because this man wished to eat the fruit of his own labor, the decree went forth against him, even the curse of Cain, so that whosoever findeth him shall kill him. Will not the Lord be avenged on such a people as this? To-night they will hold their solemn assembly, and blow the trumpet in their new moon, and the prophets will prophesy falsely, and the priests will speak wickedly concerning oppression. The word of the Lord saith unto me, ' Go unto this people, and break before them the staff beauty and the staff bands, and be a sign unto this people of the terror of the Lord. Behold, saith the Lord, therefore have I raised thee up and led thee through the wilderness, through the desolate places of the land not sown.' "

As Dred spoke, his great black eye seemed to enlarge itself and roll with a glassy fullness, like that of a sleepwalker in a somnambulic dream. His wife, seeing him prepare to depart, threw herself upon him.

"Oh, don't, don't leave us! You'll be killed, some of these times, just as they killed him!"

"Woman! the burden of the Lord is upon me. The word of the Lord is as a fire shut up in my bones. The Lord saith unto me, ' Go show unto this people their iniquity, and be a sign unto this evil nation!' "

Breaking away from his wife, he precipitated himself through an opening into the thicket, and was gone.

CHAPTER XXIII

THE CAMP-MEETING

THE place selected for the camp-meeting was in one of the most picturesque portions of the neighborhood. It was a small, partially cleared spot, in the midst of a dense forest, which stretched away in every direction, in cool, green aisles of checkered light and shade. In the central clearing, a sort of rude amphitheatre of seats was formed of rough pine slabs. Around on the edges of the forest the tents of the various worshipers were pitched; for the spending of three or four days and nights upon the ground is deemed an essential part of the service. The same clear stream which wound round the dwelling of Tiff prattled its way, with a modest gurgle, through this forest, and furnished the assembly with water.

The Gordons, having come merely for the purposes of curiosity, and having a residence in the neighborhood, did not provide themselves with a tent. The servants, however, were less easily satisfied. Aunt Rose shook her head, and declared, oracularly, that "de blessing was sure to come down in de night, and dem dat wanted to get a part of it would have to be dar!"

Consequently, Nina was beset to allow her people to have a tent, in which they were to take turns in staying all night, as candidates for the blessing. In compliance with that law of good-humored indulgence which had been the traditionary usage of her family, Nina acceded; and the Gordon tent spread its snowy sails, to the rejoicing of their hearts. Aunt Rose predominated about the door, alternately slapping the children and joining the chorus of hymns which she heard from every part of the camp-ground. On the outskirts were various rude booths, in which whiskey and water, and sundry articles of provision, and fodder for horses, were dispensed for a consideration. Abijah Skinflint here figured among the money-changers, while his wife and daughter were gossiping through the tents of the women. In front of the seats, under a dense cluster of pines, was the preacher's stand: a rude stage of rough boards, with a railing around it, and a desk of small slabs, supporting a Bible and a hymn-book.

The preachers were already assembling; and no small curiosity was expressed with regard to them by the people, who were walking up and down among the tents. Nina, leaning on the arm of Clayton, walked about the area with the rest. Anne Clayton leaned on the arm of Uncle John. Aunt Nesbit and Aunt Maria came behind. To Nina the scene was quite new, for a long residence in the northern states had placed her out of the way of such things; and her shrewd insight into character, and her love of drollery, found an abundant satisfaction in the various little points and oddities of the scene. They walked to the Gordon tent, in which a preliminary meeting was already in full course. A circle of men and women, interspersed with children, were sitting, with their eyes shut, and their heads thrown back, singing at the top of their voices. Occasionally, one or other would vary the exercises by clapping of hands, jumping up straight into the air, falling flat on the ground, screaming, dancing, and laughing.

"Oh, set me up on a rock!" screamed one.

"I's sot up!" screamed another.

"Glory!" cried the third, and a tempest of "amens" poured in between.

"I's got a sperience!" cried one, and forthwith began piping it out in a high key, while others kept on singing.

VOL. I.

"I's got a sperience!" shouted Tomtit, whom Aunt Rose, with maternal care, had taken with her.

"No, you ain't neither! Sit down!" said Aunt Rose, kneading him down as if he had been a batch of biscuits, and going on at the same time with her hymn.

"I's on the Rock of Ages!" screamed a neighbor.

"I want to get on a rock edgeways!" screamed Tomtit, struggling desperately with Aunt Rose's great fat hands.

"Mind yourself! — I'll crack you over!" said Aunt Rose. And Tomtit, still continuing rebellious, *was* cracked over accordingly, with such force as to send him head-foremost on the straw at the bottom of the tent; an indignity which he resented with loud howls of impotent wrath, which, however, made no impression in the general whirlwind of screaming, shouting, and praying.

Nina and Uncle John stood at the tent-door laughing heartily. Clayton looked on with his usual thoughtful gravity of aspect. Anne turned her head away with an air of disgust.

"Why don't you laugh?" said Nina, looking round at her.

"It doesn't make me feel like it," said Anne. "It makes me feel melancholy."

"Why so?"

"Because religion is a sacred thing with me, and I don't like to see it travestied," said she.

"Oh," said Nina, "I don't respect religion any the less for a good laugh at its oddities. I believe I was born without any organ of reverence, and so don't feel the incongruity of the thing as you do. The distance between laughing and praying isn't so very wide in my mind as it is in some people's."

"We must have charity," said Clayton, "for every religious manifestation. Barbarous and half-civilized people always find the necessity for outward and bodily demonstration in worship; I suppose because the nervous excitement wakes up and animates their spiritual natures, and gets them into a receptive state, just as you have to shake up sleeping persons and shout in their ears to put them in a condition to understand you. I have known real conversions to take place under just these excitements."

"But," said Anne, "I think we might teach them to be decent. These things ought not to be allowed!"

"I believe," said Clayton, "intolerance is a rooted vice in our nature. The world is as full of different minds and bodies as the woods are of leaves, and each one has its own habit of growth. And yet our first impulse is to forbid everything that would not be proper for us. No, let the African scream, dance, and shout, and fall in trances. It suits his tropical lineage and blood as much as our thoughtful inward ways do us."

"I wonder who that is!" said Nina, as a general movement on the ground proclaimed the arrival of some one who appeared to be exciting general interest. The stranger was an unusually tall, portly man, apparently somewhat past the middle of life, whose erect carriage, full figure, and red cheeks, and a certain dashing frankness of manner, might have indicated him as belonging rather to the military than the clerical profession. He carried a rifle on his shoulder, which he set down carefully against the corner of the preacher's stand, and went around shaking hands among the company with a free and jovial air that might almost be described by the term rollicking.

"Why," said Uncle John, "that's Father Bonnie! How are you, my fine fellow?"

"What! you, Mr. Gordon? — How do you do?" said Father Bonnie, grasping his hand in his, and shaking it heartily. "Why, they tell me," he said, looking at him with a jovial smile, "that you have fallen from grace!"

"Even so!" said Uncle John. "I am a sad dog, I dare say."

"Oh, I tell you what," said Father Bonnie, "but it takes a strong hook and a long line to pull in you *rich* sinners! Your money-bags and your niggers hang round you like millstones! You are too tough for the gospel! Ah!" said he, shaking his fist at him playfully, "but I'm going to come down upon you, to-day, with the law, I can tell you! You want the thunders of Sinai! You must have a dose of the law!"

"Well," said Uncle John, "thunder away! I suppose we need it, all of us. But now, Father Bonnie, you ministers are always preaching to us poor dogs on the evils of riches; but, somehow, I don't see any of you that are much afraid of owning horses, or niggers, or any other good thing that you can get your hands on. Now, I hear that you've got a pretty snug little place, and a likely drove to work it. You'll have to look out for your own soul, Father Bonnie!"

A general laugh echoed this retort; for Father Bonnie had the reputation of being a shrewder hand at a bargain, and of having more expertness in swapping a horse or trading a negro, than any other man for six counties round.

"He's into you, now, old man!" said several of the bystanders laughingly.

"Oh, as to that," said Father Bonnie, laughing, also, "I go in with Paul, — they that preach the gospel must live of the gospel. Now, Paul was a man that stood up for his rights to live as other folks do. 'Isn't it right,' says he, 'that those that plant a vineyard should first eat of the fruit? Haven't we power to lead about a sister, a wife?' says he. And if Paul had lived in our time he would have said a drove of niggers, too! No danger about us ministers being hurt by riches, while you laymen are so slow about supporting the gospel!"

At the elbow of Father Bonnie stood a brother minister, who was in many respects his contrast. He was tall, thin,

and stooping, with earnest black eyes, and a serene sweetness of expression. A threadbare suit of rusty black, evidently carefully worn, showed the poverty of his worldly
estate. He carried in his hand a small portmanteau, probably containing a change of linen, his Bible, and a few
sermons. Father Dickson was a man extensively known
through all that region. He was one of those men among
the ministers of America who keep alive our faith in
Christianity, and renew on earth the portrait of the old
apostle: "In journeyings often, in weariness and painfulness, in watchings often, in hunger and thirst, in fastings
often, in cold and nakedness. Besides those things that
are without, that which cometh upon them daily, the care
of all the churches. Who is weak, and they are not weak?
who is offended, and they burn not?"

Every one in the state knew and respected Father Dickson; and like the generality of the world, people were
very well pleased, and thought it extremely proper and
meritorious for him to bear weariness and painfulness,
hunger and cold, in their spiritual service, leaving to them
the right of attending or not attending to him, according
to their own convenience. Father Dickson was one of
those who had never yielded to the common customs and
habits of the country in regard to the holding of slaves.
A few, who had been left him by a relation, he had at
great trouble and expense transported to a free state, and
settled there comfortably. The world need not trouble
itself with seeking to know or reward such men; for the
world cannot know and has no power to reward them.
Their citizenship is in heaven, and all that can be given
them in this life is like a morsel which a peasant gives in his
cottage to him who to-morrow will reign over a kingdom.

He had stood listening to the conversation thus far with
the grave yet indulgent air with which he generally listened
to the sallies of his ministerial brothers. Father Bonnie,

though not as much respected or confided in as Father Dickson, had, from the frankness of his manners, and a certain rude but effective style of eloquence, a more general and apparent popularity. He produced more sensation on the camp-ground; could sing louder and longer, and would often rise into flights of eloquence both original and impressive. Many were offended by the freedom of his manner out of the pulpit; and the stricter sort were known to have said of him, "that when out he never ought to be in, and when in never out." As the laugh that rose at his last sally died away, he turned to Father Dickson, and said: —

"What do you think?"

"I don't think," said Father Dickson mildly, "that you would ever have found Paul leading a drove of negroes."

"Why not, as well as Abraham, the father of the faithful? Did n't he have three hundred trained servants?"

"Servants, perhaps; but not slaves!" said Father Dickson, "for they all bore arms. For my part, I think that the buying, selling, and trading of human beings, for purposes of gain, is a sin in the sight of God."

"Well, now, Father Dickson, I would n't have thought you had read your Bible to so little purpose as that! I would n't believe it! What do you say to Moses?"

"He led out a whole army of fugitive slaves through the Red Sea," said Father Dickson.

"Well, I tell you, now," said Father Bonnie, "if the buying, selling, or holding of a slave for the sake of gain is, as you say, a sin, then three fourths of all the Episcopalians, Methodists, Baptists, and Presbyterians, in the slave states of the Union, are of the devil!"

"I think it is a sin, notwithstanding," said Father Dickson quietly.

"Well, but does n't Moses say expressly, 'Ye shall buy of the heathen round about you?'"

"There's into him!" said a Georgia trader, who, having camped with a coffle of negroes in the neighborhood, had come up to camp-meeting.

"All those things," said Father Dickson, "belong to the old covenant, which Paul says was annulled for the weakness and unprofitableness thereof, and have nothing to do with us, who have risen with Christ. We have got past Mount Sinai and the wilderness, and have come unto Mount Zion; and ought to seek the things that are above, where Christ sitteth."

"I say, brother," said another of the ministers, tapping him on the shoulder, "it's time for the preaching to begin. You can finish your discussion some other time. Come, Father Bonnie, come forward, here, and strike up the hymn."

Father Bonnie accordingly stepped to the front of the stand, and with him another minister, of equal height and breadth of frame, and standing with their hats on, they uplifted, in stentorian voices, the following hymn: —

> "Brethren don't you hear the sound ?
>   The martial trumpet now is blowing ;
> Men in order listing round,
>   And soldiers to the standard flowing."

As the sound of the hymn rolled through the aisles and arches of the wood, the heads of different groups, who had been engaged in conversation, were observed turning toward the stand, and voices from every part of the camp-ground took up the air, as, suiting the action to the words, they began flowing to the place of preaching. The hymn went on, keeping up the same martial images: —

> "Bounty offered, life and peace;
>   To every soldier this is given,
> When the toils of life shall cease,
>   A mansion bright, prepared in heaven."

As the throng pressed up, and came crowding from the distant aisles of the wood, the singers seemed to exert themselves to throw a wilder vehemence into the song, stretching out their arms and beckoning eagerly. They went on singing: —

> "You need not fear ; the cause is good,
>   Let who will to the crown aspire:
> In this cause the martyrs bled,
>   And shouted victory in the fire.

> "In this cause let 's follow on,
>   And soon we 'll tell the pleasing story,
> How by faith we won the crown,
>   And fought our way to life and glory.

> "Oh, ye rebels, come and 'list !
>   The officers are now recruiting:
> Why will you in sin persist,
>   Or waste your time in vain disputing ?

> "All excuses now are vain;
>   For, if you do not sue for favor,
> Down you 'll sink to endless pain,
>   And bear the wrath of God forever."

There is always something awful in the voice of the multitude. It would seem as if the breath that a crowd breathed out together, in moments of enthusiasm, carried with it a portion of the dread and mystery of their own immortal natures. The whole area before the pulpit, and in the distant aisles of the forest, became one vast, surging sea of sound, as negroes and whites, slaves and free men, saints and sinners, slave-holders, slave-hunters, slave-traders, ministers, elders, and laymen, alike joined in the pulses of that mighty song. A flood of electrical excitement seemed to rise with it, as, with a voice of many waters, the rude chant went on: —

> "Hark ! the victors singing loud!
>   Emanuel's chariot wheels are rumbling;
> Mourners weeping through the crowd,
>   And Satan's kingdom down is tumbling!"

Our friend, Ben Dakin, pressed to the stand, and with tears streaming down his cheeks, exceeded all others in the energy of his vociferations. Ben had just come from almost a fight with another slave-hunter, who had boasted a better-trained pack of dogs than his own; and had broken away to hurry to the camp-ground, with the assurance that he 'd "give him fits when the preachin' was over;" and now he stood there, tears rolling down his cheeks, singing with the heartiest earnestness and devotion. What shall we make of it? Poor heathen Ben! is it any more out of the way for him to think of being a Christian in this manner than for some of his more decent brethren, who take Sunday passage for eternity in the cushioned New York or Boston pews, and solemnly drowse through very sleepy tunes, under a dim, hazy impression that they are going to heaven? Of the two, we think Ben's chance is the best; for in some blind way he does think himself a sinner, and in need of something he calls salvation; and, doubtless, while the tears stream down his face, the poor fellow makes a new resolve against the whiskey-bottle, while his more respectable sleepy brethren never think of making one against the cotton-bale.

Then there was his rival, also, Jim Stokes, — a surly, foul-mouthed, swearing fellow, — he joins in the chorus of the hymn, and feels a troublous, vague yearning, deep down within him, which makes him for the moment doubt whether he had better knock down Ben at the end of the meeting.

As to Harry, who stood also among the crowd, the words and tune recalled but too vividly the incidents of his morning's interview with Dred, and with it the tumultuous boiling of his bitter controversy with the laws of the society in which he found himself. In hours of such high excitement, a man seems to have an intuitive perception of the whole extent and strength of what is within himself; and if there be anything unnatural or false in his position, he realizes it with double intensity.

Mr. John Gordon, likewise, gave himself up, without resistance, to be swayed by the feeling of the hour. He sang with enthusiasm, and wished he was a soldier of somebody, going somewhere, or a martyr shouting victory in the fire; and if the conflict described had been with any other foe than his own laziness and self-indulgence — had there been any outward, tangible enemy at the moment — he would doubtless have enlisted, without loss of time.

When the hymn was finished, however, there was a general wiping of eyes, and they all sat down to listen to the sermon. Father Bonnie led off in an animated strain. His discourse was like the tropical swamp, bursting out with a lush abundance of every kind of growth — grave, gay, grotesque, solemn, fanciful, and even coarse caricature, provoking the broadest laughter. The audience were swayed by him like trees before the wind. There were not wanting touches of rude pathos as well as earnest appeals. The meeting was a union one of Presbyterians and Methodists, in which the ministers of both denominations took equal part; and it was an understood agreement among them, of course, that they were not to venture upon polemic ground, or attack each other's peculiarities of doctrine. But Abijah's favorite preacher could not get through a sermon without some quite pointed exposition of Scripture bearing on his favorite doctrine of election, which caused the next minister to run a vehement tilt on the correlative doctrines of free grace, with a eulogy on John Wesley. The auditors, meanwhile, according to their respective sentiments, encouraged each preacher with a cry of "Amen!" "Glory be to God!" "Go on, brother!" and other similar exclamations.

About noon the services terminated, *pro tem.*, and the audience dispersed themselves to their respective tents through the grove, where there was an abundance of chat-

ting, visiting, eating, and drinking, as if the vehement
denunciations and passionate appeals of the morning had
been things of another state of existence. Uncle John, in
the most cheery possible frame of mind, escorted his party
into the woods, and assisted them in unpacking a hamper
containing wine, cold fowls, cakes, pies, and other delica-
cies which Aunt Katy had packed for the occasion.

Old Tiff had set up his tent in a snug little nook on the
banks of the stream, where he informed passers-by that it
was his young mas'r and missis's establishment, and that
he, Tiff, had come to wait on them. With a good-natured
view of doing him a pleasure, Nina selected a spot for their
nooning at no great distance, and spoke in the most gracious and encouraging manner to them, from time to time.

"See, now, can't you, how real quality behaves dem-
selves!" he said grimly to Old Hundred, who came up
bringing the carriage-cushions for the party to sit down
upon. "Real quality sees into things! I tell ye what,
blood sees into blood. Miss Nina sees dese yer chil'en
ain't de common sort — dat 's what she does!"

"Umph!" said Old Hundred, "such a muss as ye keep
up about yer chil'en! Tell you what, dey ain't no better
dan oder white trash!"

"Now, you talk dat ar way, I 'll knock you down!"
said Old Tiff, who, though a peaceable and law-abiding
creature, in general, was driven, in desperation, to the last
resort of force.

"John, what are you saying to Tiff?" said Nina, who
had overheard some of the last words. "Go back to your
own tent, and don't you trouble him! I have taken him
under my protection."

The party enjoyed their dinner with infinite relish, and
Nina amused herself in watching Tiff's cooking preparations. Before departing to the preaching-ground, he had
arranged a slow fire, on which a savory stew had been all

the morning simmering, and which, on the taking off of
the pot-lid, diffused an agreeable odor through the place.

"I say, Tiff, how delightfully that smells!" said Nina,
getting up, and looking into the pot. "Would n't Miss
Fanny be so kind as to favor us with a taste of it?"

Fanny, to whom Tiff punctiliously referred the question,
gave a bashful consent. But who shall describe the pride
and glory that swelled the heart of Tiff as he saw a bowl
of his stew smoking among the Gordon viands, praised and
patronized by the party? And when Nina placed on their
simple board — literally a board, and nothing more — a
small loaf of frosted cake, in exchange, it certainly required
all the grace of the morning exercises to keep Tiff within
due bounds of humility. He really seemed to dilate with
satisfaction.

"Tiff, how did you like the sermon?" said Nina.

"Dey's pretty far, Miss Nina. Dere's a good deal o'
quality preaching."

"What do you mean by quality preaching, Tiff?"

"Why, dat ar kind dat's good for quality — full of long
words, you know. I spects it's very good; but poor
nigger like me can't see his way through it. You see, Miss
Nina, what I's studdin' on, lately, is, how to get dese yer
chil'en to Canaan; and I hars fus with one ear, and den
with t'oder, but 'pears like ain't clar 'bout it, yet. Dere's
a heap about mose everything else, and it's all very good;
but 'pears like I ain't clar, arter all, about dat ar. Dey
says, 'Come to Christ;' and I says, 'Whar is he, anyhow?' Bress you, I *want* to come! Dey talks 'bout
going in de gate, and knocking at de do', and 'bout marching on de road, and 'bout fighting and being soldiers of de
cross; and de Lord knows, now, I'd be glad to get de
chil'en through any gate; and I could take 'em on my
back and travel all day, if dere was any road; and if dere
was a do', bless me, if dey would n't hear Old Tiff a-rap-

ping! I spects de Lord would have fur to open it —
would so. But, arter all, when de preaching is done, dere
don't 'pear to be nothing to it. Dere ain't no gate, dere
ain't no do', nor no way; and dere ain't no fighting, 'cept
when Ben Dakin and Jim Stokes get jawing about der
dogs; and everybody comes back eating der dinner quite
comf'table, and 'pears like dere wa'n't no such ting dey 's
been preaching 'bout. Dat ar troubles me — does so —
'cause I wants fur to get dese yer chil'en in de kingdom,
some way or oder. I did n't know but some of de quality
would know more 'bout it."

"Hang me, if I have n't felt just so!" said Uncle John.
"When they were singing that hymn about enlisting and
being a soldier, if there had been any fighting doing anywhere, I should have certainly gone right into it; and the
preaching always stirs me up terribly. But then, as Tiff
says, after it 's all over, why, there 's dinner to be eaten,
and I can't see anything better than to eat it; and then,
by the time I have drank two or three glasses of wine,
it 's all gone. Now, that 's just the way with me!"

"Dey says," said Tiff, "dat we must wait for de blessing to come down upon us, and Aunt Rose says it 's dem
dat shouts dat gets de blessing; and I 's been shouting till
I 's most beat out, but I has n't got it. Den, one of dem
said none of dem could get it but de 'lect; but den,
t'oder one, he seemed to tink different; and in de meeting
dey tells about de scales falling from der eyes, — and I
wished dey fall from mine — I do so! Perhaps, Miss
Nina, now, you could tell me something."

"Oh, don't ask me!" said Nina; "I don't know anything about these things. I think I feel a little like Uncle
John," she said, turning to Clayton. "There are two
kinds of sermons and hymns; one gets me to sleep, and
the other excites and stirs me up in a general kind of way;
but they don't either seem to do me real good."

"For my part, I am such an enemy to stagnation," said
Clayton, "that I think there is advantage in everything
that stirs up the soul, even though we see no immediate
results.   I listen to music, see pictures, as far as I can,
uncritically.   I say, 'Here I am; see what you can do
with me.'   So I present myself to almost all religious
exercises.   It is the most mysterious part of our nature.
I do not pretend to understand it, therefore never criti-
cise."

"For my part," said Anne, "there is so much in the
wild freedom of these meetings that shocks my taste and
sense of propriety, that I am annoyed more than I am
benefited."

"There spoke the true, well-trained conventionalist,"
said Clayton.   "But look around you.   See, in this wood,
among these flowers, and festoons of vine, and arches of
green, how many shocking, unsightly growths!   *You*
would not have had all this underbrush, these dead limbs,
these briers running riot over trees, and sometimes chok-
ing and killing them.   You would have well-trimmed
trees and velvet turf.   But I love briers, dead limbs, and
all, for their very savage freedom.   Every once in a while
you see in a wood a jessamine, or a sweet-brier, or a grapevine, that throws itself into a gracefulness of growth which
a landscape gardener would go down on his knees for,
but cannot get.   Nature resolutely denies it to him.   She
says, 'No! I keep this for my own.   You won't have
my wildness — my freedom; very well, then you shall not
have the graces that spring from it.'   Just so it is with
men.   Unite any assembly of common men in a great enthusiasm, — work them up into an abandon, and let every
one 'let go,' and speak as nature prompts, — and you will
have brush, underwood, briers, and all grotesque growths;
but, now and then, some thought or sentiment will be
struck out with a freedom or power such as you cannot get

in any other way. You cultivated people are much mistaken when you despise the enthusiasms of the masses. There is more truth than you think in the old *Vox populi, vox Dei.*"

"What's that?" said Nina.

"'The voice of the people is the voice of God.' There is truth in it. I never repent my share in a popular excitement, provided it be of the higher sentiments; and I do not ask too strictly whether it has produced any tangible result. I reverence the people, as I do the woods, for the wild, grand freedom with which their humanity develops itself."

"I'm afraid, Nina," said Aunt Nesbit, in a low tone, to the latter, "I'm afraid he isn't orthodox."

"What makes you think so, aunt?"

"Oh, I don't know; his talk hasn't the real sound."

"You want something that ends in 'ation,' don't you, aunt? — justification, sanctification, or something of that kind."

. . . .

Meanwhile, the department of Abijah Skinflint exhibited a decided activity. This was a long, low booth, made of poles, and roofed with newly cut green boughs. Here the whiskey-barrel was continually pouring forth its supplies to customers who crowded around it. Abijah sat on the middle of a sort of rude counter, dangling his legs, and chewing a straw, while his negro was busy in helping his various customers. Abijah, as we said, being a particularly high Calvinist, was recreating himself by carrying on a discussion with a fat, little, turnipy brother of the Methodist persuasion.

"I say," he said, "Stringfellow put it into you Methodists this morning! Hit the nail on the head, I thought!"

"Not a bit of it!" said the other contemptuously.

"Why, Elder Baskum chawed him up completely! There wa'n't nothin' left of him!"

"Well," said Abijah, "strange how folks will see things! Why, it's just as clar to me that all things is decreed! Why, that ar nails everything up tight and handsome. It gives a fellow a kind of comfort to think on it. Things is just as they have got to be. All this free-grace stuff is drefful loose talk. If things is been decreed 'fore the world was made, well, there seems to be some sense in their coming to pass. But if everything kind of turns up whenever folks think on 't, it's a kind of shaky business."

"I don't like this tying up things so tight," said the other, who evidently was one of the free, jovial order. "I go in for the freedom of the will. Free gospel, and free grace."

"For my part," said Abijah, rather grimly, "if things was managed my way, I should n't commune with nobody that did n't believe in election, up to the hub."

"You strong electioners think you's among the elect!" said one of the bystanders. "You would n't be so crank about it, if you did n't! Now, see here: if everything is decreed, how am I going to help myself?"

"That ar is none of my lookout," said Abijah. "But there's a pint my mind rests upon — everything is fixed as it can be, and it makes a man mighty easy."

. . . .

In another part of the camp-ground Ben Dakin was sitting in his tent-door, caressing one of his favorite dogs, and partaking his noontide repast with his wife and child.

"I declar," said Ben, wiping his mouth, "wife, I intend to go into it, and sarve the Lord, now, full chisel! If I catch the next lot of niggers, I intend to give half the money towards keeping up preaching somewhere round here. I'm going to enlist, now, and be a soldier."

"And," said his wife, "Ben, just keep clear of Abijah Skinflint's counter, won't you?"

"Well, I will, durned if I won't!" said Ben. "I'll be moderate. A fellow wants a glass or two, to strike up the hymn on, you know; but I'll be moderate."

The Georgia trader, who had encamped in the neighborhood, now came up.

"Do you believe, stranger," said he, "one of them durned niggers of mine broke loose and got in the swamps, while I was at meeting this morning! Couldn't you take your dog, here, and give 'em a run? I just gave nine hundred dollars for that fellow, cash down."

"Ho! what you going to him for?" said Jim Stokes, a short, pursy, vulgar-looking individual, dressed in a hunting-shirt of blue Kentucky jean, who just then came up. "Why, durn ye, his dogs ain't no breed 't all! Mine's the true grit, I can tell you; they's the true Florida bloodhounds! I's seen one of them ar dogs shake a nigger in his mouth like he'd been a sponge."

Poor Ben's new-found religion could not withstand this sudden attack of his spiritual enemy; and rousing himself, notwithstanding the appealing glances of his wife, he stripped up his sleeves, and squaring off, challenged his rival to a fight.

A crowd gathered round, laughing and betting, and cheering on the combatants with slang oaths and expressions such as we will not repeat, when the concourse was routed by the approach of Father Bonnie on the outside of the ring.

"Look here, boys, what works of the devil have you got round here? None of this on the camp-ground! This is the Lord's ground, here; so shut up your swearing, and don't fight."

A confused murmur of voices now began to explain to Father Bonnie the cause of the trouble.

"Ho, ho!" said he, "let the nigger run; you can catch him fast enough when the meetings are over. You come here to 'tend to your salvation. Ah, don't you be swearing and blustering round! Come, boys, join in a hymn with me." So saying he struck up a well-known air: —

"When Israel went to Jericho,
O good Lord, in my soul!"

in which one after another joined, and the rising tumult was soon assuaged.

"I say," said Father Bonnie to the trader, in an undertone, as he was walking away, "you got a good cook in your lot, hey?"

"Got a prime one," said the trader; "an A number one cook, and no mistake! Picked her up real cheap, and I'll let you have her for eight hundred dollars, being as you are a minister."

"You must think the gospel a better trade than it is," said Father Bonnie, "if you think a minister can afford to pay at that figure!"

"Why," said the trader, "you haven't seen her; it's dirt cheap for her, I can tell you! A sound, strong, hearty woman; a prudent, careful housekeeper; a real pious Methodist, a member of a class-meeting! Why, eight hundred dollars ain't anything! I ought to get a thousand for her; but I don't hear preaching for nothing, — always think right to make a discount to ministers!"

"Why couldn't you bring her in?" said Father Bonnie. "Maybe I'll give you seven hundred and fifty for her."

"Couldn't do that, noway!" said the trader. "Couldn't, indeed!"

"Well, after the meetings are over I'll talk about it."

"She's got a child, four years old," said the trader, with a little cough; "healthy, likely child; I suppose I shall want a hundred dollars for him!"

"Oh, that won't do!" said Father Bonnie. "I don't

want any more children round my place than I've got now!"

"But I tell you," said the trader, "it's a likely boy. Why, the keeping of him won't cost you anything, and before you think of it you'll have a thousand-dollar hand grown on your own place."

"Well," said Father Bonnie, "I'll think of it!"

In the evening the scene on the camp-ground was still more picturesque and impressive. Those who conduct camp-meetings are generally men who, without much reasoning upon the subject, fall into a sort of tact in influencing masses of mind, and pressing into the service all the great life forces and influences of nature. A kind of rude poetry pervades their minds, colors their dialect, and influences their arrangements. The solemn and harmonious grandeur of night, with all its mysterious power of exalting the passions and intensifying the emotions, has ever been appreciated, and used by them with even poetic skill. The day had been a glorious one in June; the sky of that firm, clear blue, the atmosphere of that crystalline clearness, which often gives to the American landscape such a sharply defined outline, and to the human system such an intense consciousness of life. The evening sun went down in a broad sea of light, and even after it had sunk below the purple horizon, flashed back a flood of tremulous rose-colored radiance, which, taken up by a thousand filmy clouds, made the whole sky above like a glowing tent of the most ethereal brightness. The shadows of the forest aisles were pierced by the rose-colored rays; and as they gradually faded, star after star twinkled out, and a broad moon, ample and round, rose in the purple zone of the sky. When she had risen above the horizon but a short space, her light was so resplendent and so profuse, that it was decided to conduct the evening service by that alone; and when, at the sound of the hymn, the assembly poured in and arranged themselves before the preaching-stand, it is probable that the rudest heart present was somewhat impressed with the silent magnificence by which God was speaking to them through his works. As the hymn closed, Father Bonnie, advancing to the front of the stage, lifted his hands, and pointing to the purple sky, and in a deep and not unmelodious voice, repeated the words of the Psalmist: —

"The heavens declare the glory of God, and the firmament showeth his handy-work; day unto day uttereth speech, and night unto night showeth knowledge."

"Oh, ye sinners!" he exclaimed, "look up at the moon, there, walking in her brightness, and think over your oaths, and your cursings, and your drinkings! Think over your backbitings, and your cheatings! think over your quarrelings and your fightings! How do they look to you now, with that blessed moon shining down upon you? Don't you see the beauty of our Lord God upon her? Don't you see how the saints walk in white with the Lord, like her? I dare say some of you, now, have had a pious mother, or a pious wife, or a pious sister, that's gone to glory? and there they are walking with the Lord! — walking with the Lord, through the sky, and looking down on you, sinners, just as that moon looks down! And what does she see you doing, your wife, or your mother, or sister, that's in glory? Does she see all your swearings, and your drinkings, and your fightings, and your hankerings after money, and your horse-racings, and your cock-fightings? Oh, sinners, but you are a bad set! I tell you the Lord is looking now down on you, out of that moon! He is looking down in mercy! But, I tell you, he'll look down quite another way, one of these days! Oh, there'll be a time of wrath, by and by, if you don't repent! Oh, what a time there was at Sinai, years ago, when the voice of the trumpet waxed louder and louder, and the mountain was all of a smoke, and there were thunderings and lightnings, and the Lord descended on Sinai! That's nothing to what you'll see, by and by! No more moon looking down on you! No more stars, but the heavens shall pass away with a great noise, and the elements shall melt with fervent heat! Ah! did you ever see a fire in the woods? I have; and I've seen the fire on the prairies, and it rolled like a tempest, and men and horses and everything had to run before it. I have seen it roaring and crackling through the woods, and great trees shriveled in a minute like tinder! I have seen it flash over trees seventy-five and a hundred feet high, and in a minute they'd be standing pillars of fire, and the heavens were all ablaze, and the crackling and roaring was like the sea in a storm. There's a judgment-day for you! Oh, sinner, what will become of you in that day? Never cry, Lord, Lord! Too late — too late, man! You wouldn't take mercy when it was offered, and now you shall have wrath! No place to hide! The heavens and earth are passing away, and there shall be no more sea! There's no place for you now in God's universe."

By this time there were tumultuous responses from the audience of groans, cries, clapping of hands, and mingled shouts of Glory and Amen.

The electric shout of the multitude acted on the preacher again, as he went on, with a yet fiercer energy. "Now is your time, sinners! Now is your time! Come unto the altar, and God's people will pray for you! Now is the day of grace! Come up! Come up, you that have got pious fathers and mothers in glory! Come up, father! come up, mother! come up, brother! Come, young man! we want you to come! Ah, there's a hardened sinner, off there! I see his lofty looks! Come up, come up! Come up, you rich sinners! You'll be poor enough in the day of the Lord, I can tell you! Come up, you young women!

You daughters of Jerusalem, with your tinkling ornaments!
Come, saints of the Lord, and labor with me in prayer.
Strike up a hymn, brethren, strike up the hymn!" And
a thousand voices commenced the hymn, —

> "Stop, poor sinner, stop and think,
> Before you further go!"

And, meanwhile, ministers and elders moved around the
throng, entreating and urging one and another to come and
kneel before the stand. Multitudes rushed forward, groans
and sobs were heard, as the speaker continued, with redou-
bled vehemence.

"I don't care," said Mr. John Gordon, "who sees me;
I'm going up! I am a poor old sinner, and I ought to be
prayed for, if anybody."

Nina shrank back, and clung to Clayton's arm. So
vehement was the surging feeling of the throng around her
that she wept with a wild, tremulous excitement.

"Do take me out, — it's dreadful!" she said.

Clayton passed his arm round her, and opening a way
through the crowd, carried her out beyond the limits,
where they stood together alone, under the tree.

"I know I am not good as I ought to be," she said,
"but I don't know how to be any better. Do you think
it would do me any good to go up there? Do you believe
in these things?"

"I sympathize with every effort that man makes to
approach his Maker," said Clayton; "these ways do not
suit me, but I dare not judge them. I cannot despise
them. I must not make myself a rule for others."

"But don't you think," said Nina, "that these things
do harm sometimes?"

"Alas, child, what form of religion does not? It is our
fatality that everything that does good must do harm.
It's the condition of our poor, imperfect life here."

"I do not like these terrible threats," said Nina. "Can

fear of fire make me love? Besides, I have a kind of courage in me that always rises up against a threat. It isn't my nature to fear."

"If we may judge our Father by his voice in nature," said Clayton, "he deems severity a necessary part of our training. How inflexibly and terribly regular are all his laws! Fire and hail, snow and vapor, stormy wind, fulfilling his word — all these have a crushing regularity in their movements, which show that he is to be feared as well as loved."

"But I want to be religious," said Nina, "entirely apart from such considerations. Not driven by fear, but drawn by love. You can guide me about these things, for you are religious."

"I fear I should not be accepted as such in any church," said Clayton. "It is my misfortune that I cannot receive any common form of faith, though I respect and sympathize with all. Generally speaking, preaching only weakens my faith; and I have to forget the sermon in order to recover my faith. I do not *believe* — I *know* that our moral nature needs a thorough regeneration; and I believe this must come through Christ. This is all I am certain of."

"I wish I were like Milly," said Nina. "She is a Christian, I know; but she has come to it by dreadful sorrows. Sometimes I'm afraid to ask my heavenly Father to make me good, because I think it will come by dreadful trials, if he does."

"And I," said Clayton, speaking with great earnestness, "would be willing to suffer anything conceivable, if I could only overcome all evil, and come up to my highest ideas of good." And as he spoke, he turned his face up to the moonlight with an earnest fervor of expression, that struck Nina deeply.

"I almost shudder to hear you say so! You don't know what it may bring on you!"

He looked at her with a beautiful smile, which was a peculiar expression of his face in moments of high excitement.

"I say it again!" he said.   "Whatever it involves, let it come!"

.   .   .   .

The exercises of the evening went on with a succession of addresses, varied by singing of hymns and prayers.   In the latter part of the time many declared themselves converts, and were shouting loudly.   Father Bonnie came forward.

"Brethren," he shouted, "we are seeing a day from the Lord!   We've got a glorious time!   Oh, brethren, let us sing glory to the Lord!   The Lord is coming among us!"

The excitement now became general.   There was a confused sound of exhortation, prayers, and hymns, all mixed together, from different parts of the ground.   But all of a sudden, every one was startled by a sound which seemed to come pealing down directly from the thick canopy of pines over the heads of the ministers.

"Woe unto you that desire the day of the Lord!   To what end shall it be for you?   The day of the Lord shall be darkness, and not light!   Blow ye the trumpet in Zion!   Sound an alarm in my holy mountain!   Let all the inhabitants of the land tremble! for the day of the Lord cometh!"

There was deep, sonorous power in the voice that spoke, and the words fell pealing down through the air like the vibrations of some mighty bell.   Men looked confusedly on each other; but in the universal license of the hour, the obscurity of the night, and the multitude of the speakers, no one knew exactly whence it came.   After a moment's pause, the singers were recommencing, when again the same deep voice was heard.

"Take away from me the noise of thy songs, and the

melody of thy viols; for I will not hear them, saith the Lord. I hate and despise your feast-days! I will not smell in your solemn assemblies; for your hands are defiled with blood, and your fingers are greedy for violence! Will ye kill, and steal, and commit adultery, and swear falsely, and come and stand before *me*, saith the Lord? Ye oppress the poor and needy, and hunt the stranger; also in thy skirts is found the blood of poor innocents! and yet ye say, Because I am clean shall his anger pass from me! Hear this, ye that swallow up the needy, and make the poor of the land to fail, saying, When will the new moon be gone, that we may sell corn? that we may buy the poor for silver, and the needy for a pair of shoes? The Lord hath sworn, saying, I will never forget their works. I will surely visit you!"

The audience, thus taken, in the obscurity of the evening, by an unknown speaker, whose words seemed to fall apparently from the clouds, in a voice of such strange and singular quality, began to feel a creeping awe stealing over them. The high state of electrical excitement under which they had been going on, predisposed them to a sort of revulsion of terror; and a vague, mysterious panic crept upon them, as the boding, mournful voice continued to peal from the trees.

"Hear, oh ye rebellious people! The Lord is against this nation! The Lord shall stretch out upon it the line of confusion, and the stones of emptiness! For thou saidst, I will ascend into the stars; I will be as God! But thou shalt be cast out as an abominable branch, and the wild beasts shall tread thee down! Howl, fir-tree, for thou art spoiled! Open thy doors, O Lebanon, that the fire may devour thy cedars! for the Lord cometh out of his place to punish the inhabitants of the land! The Lord shall utter his voice before his army, for his camp is very great! Multitudes! multitudes! in the valley of decision!

For the day of the Lord is near in the valley of decision!
The sun and the moon shall be dark, and the stars with-
draw their shining; for the Lord shall utter his voice from
Jerusalem, and the heavens and earth shall shake! In
that day I will cause the sun to go down at noon, and
darken the whole earth! And I will turn your feasts into
mourning, and your songs into lamentation! Woe to the
bloody city! It is full of lies and robbery! The noise of
a whip!—the noise of the rattling of wheels!—of the
prancing horses, and the jumping chariot! The horseman
lifteth up the sword and glittering spear! and there is a
multitude of slain! There is no end of their corpses!—
They are stumbling upon the corpses! For, Behold, I am
against thee, saith the Lord, and I will make thee utterly
desolate!"

There was a fierce, wailing earnestness in the sound of
these dreadful words, as if they were uttered in a paroxysm
of affright and horror, by one who stood face to face with
some tremendous form. And when the sound ceased,
men drew in their breath, and looked on each other, and
the crowd began slowly to disperse, whispering in low
voices to each other. So extremely piercing and so wildly
earnest had the voice been, that it actually seemed, in the
expressive words of Scripture, to make every ear to tingle.
And as people of rude and primitive habits are always
predisposed to superstition, there crept through the different groups wild legends of prophets strangely commissioned
to announce coming misfortunes. Some spoke of the predictions of the judgment-day; some talked of comets, and
strange signs that had preceded wars and pestilences. The
ministers wondered, and searched around the stand in vain.
One auditor alone could, had he desired it, make an explanation. Harry, who stood near the stand, had recognized
the voice. But though he searched, also, around, he
could find no one.

He who spoke was one whose savage familiarity with nature gave him the agility and stealthy adroitness of a wild animal. And during the stir and commotion of the dispersing audience, he had silently made his way from tree to tree, over the very heads of those who were yet wondering at his strange, boding words, till at last he descended in a distant part of the forest.

After the service, as Father Dickson was preparing to retire to his tent, a man pulled him by the sleeve. It was the Georgia trader.

"We have had an awful time, to-night!" said he, looking actually pale with terror. "Do you think the judgment-day really is coming?"

"My friend," said Father Dickson, "it surely is! Every step we take in life is leading us directly to the judgment-seat of Christ!"

"Well," said the trader, "but do you think that was from the Lord, the last one that spoke? Durned if he did n't say awful things!—'nough to make the hair rise! I tell you what, I 've often had doubts about my trade. The ministers may prove it 's all right out of the Old Testament; but I 'm durned if I think they know all the things that we do! But then, I ain't so bad as some of 'em. But now, I 've got a gal out in my gang that 's dreadful sick, and I partly promised her I 'd bring a minister to see her."

"I 'll go with you, friend," said Father Dickson; and forthwith he began following the trader to the racks where their horses were tied. Selecting, out of some hundred who were tied there, their own beasts, the two midnight travelers soon found themselves trotting along under the shadow of the forest's boughs.

"My friend," said Father Dickson, "I feel bound in conscience to tell you that I think your trade a ruinous one to your soul. I hope you 'll lay to heart the solemn warning you've heard to-night. Why, your own sense can show you that a trade can't be right that you'd be afraid to be found in if the great judgment-day were at hand."

"Well, I rather spect you speak the truth; but then, what makes Father Bonnie stand up for 't?"

"My friend, I must say that I think Father Bonnie upholds a soul-destroying error. I must say that, as conscience-bound. I pray the Lord for him and you both. I put it right to your conscience, my friend, whether you think you could keep to your trade, and live a Christian life."

"No; the fact is, it's a d—d bad business, that's just where 't is. We ain't fit to be trusted with such things that come to us — gals and women. Well, I feel pretty bad, I tell you, to-night; 'cause I know I haven't done right by this yer gal. I ought fur to have let her alone; but then, the devil or something possessed me. And now she has got a fever, and screeches awfully. I declar, some things she says go right through me!"

Father Dickson groaned in spirit over this account, and felt himself almost guilty for belonging ostensibly and outwardly to a church which tolerated such evils. He rode along by the side of his companion, breaking forth into occasional ejaculations and snatches of hymns. After a ride of about an hour, they arrived at the encampment. A large fire had been made in a cleared spot, and smouldering fragments and brands were lying among the white ashes. One or two horses were tied to a neighboring tree, and wagons were drawn up by them. Around the fire, in different groups, lay about fifteen men and women, with heavy iron shackles on their feet, asleep in the moonlight. At a little distance from the group, and near to one of the wagons, a blanket was spread down on the ground under a tree, on which lay a young girl of seventeen, tossing and moaning in a disturbed stupor. A respectable-looking mulatto woman was sitting beside her, with a gourd full of water, with which from time to time she moistened her forehead. The woman rose as the trader came up.

"Well, Nance, how does she do now?" said the trader.

"Mis'able enough!" said Nance. "She done been tossing, a-throwing round, and crying for her mammy, ever since you went away!"

"Well, I've brought the minister," said he. "Try, Nance, to wake her up; she'll be glad to see him."

The woman knelt down, and took the hand of the sleeper.

"Emily! Emily!" she said, "wake up!"

The girl threw herself over with a sudden, restless toss. "Oh, how my head burns!—Oh, dear!—Oh, my mother! Mother!—mother!—mother!—why don't you come to me?"

Father Dickson approached and knelt the other side of her. The mulatto woman made another effort to bring her to consciousness.

"Emily, here's the minister you was wanting so much! Emily, wake up!"

The girl slowly opened her eyes—large, tremulous, dark eyes. She drew her hand across them, as if to clear her sight, and looked wistfully at the woman.

"Minister!—minister!" she said.

"Yes, minister! You said you wanted to see one."

"Oh yes, I did!" she said heavily.

"My daughter!" said Father Dickson, "you are very sick!"

"Yes!" she said, "very! And I'm glad of it! I'm going to die!—I'm glad of that, too! That's all I've got left to be glad of! But I wanted to ask you to write to my mother. She is a free woman; she lives in New York. I want you to give my love to her, and tell her

not to worry any more. Tell her I tried all I could to
get to her; but they took us, and mistress was so angry
she sold me! I forgive her, too. I don't bear her any
malice, 'cause it's all over, now! She used to say I was
a wild girl, and laughed too loud. I sha'n't trouble any
one that way any more! So that's no matter!"

The girl spoke these sentences at long intervals, occasionally opening her eyes and closing them again in a
languid manner. Father Dickson, however, who had
some knowledge of medicine, placed his finger on her
pulse, which was rapidly sinking. It is the usual instinct,
in all such cases, to think of means of prolonging life.
Father Dickson rose, and said to the trader: —

"Unless some stimulant be given her, she will be gone
very soon!"

The trader produced from his pocket a flask of brandy,
which he mixed with a little water in a cup, and placed it
in Father Dickson's hand. He kneeled down again, and
calling her by name, tried to make her take some.

"What is it?" said she, opening her wild, glittering
eyes.

"It's something to make you feel better."

"I don't want to feel better! I want to die!" she said,
throwing herself over. "What should I want to live for?"

What should she? The words struck Father Dickson
so much that he sat for a while in silence. He meditated
in his mind how he could reach, with any words, that
dying ear, or enter with her into that land of trance and
mist, into whose cloudy circle the soul seemed already to
have passed. Guided by a subtle instinct, he seated himself by the dying girl, and began singing, in a subdued,
plaintive air, the following well-known hymn: —

> "Hark, my soul! it is the Lord,
> 'T is thy Saviour, hear his word;
> Jesus speaks — he speaks to thee!
> Say, poor sinner, lov'st thou me?"

The melody is one often sung among the negroes; and
one which, from its tenderness and pathos, is a favorite
among them.   As oil will find its way into crevices where
water cannot penetrate, so song will find its way where
speech can no longer enter.   The moon shone full on the
face of the dying girl, only interrupted by flickering shadows of leaves; and as Father Dickson sang, he fancied
he saw a slight, tremulous movement of the face, as if the
soul, so worn and weary, were upborne on the tender
pinions of the song.   He went on singing: —

> "Can a mother's tender care
> Cease toward the child she bare ?
> Yes, she may forgetful be:
> Still will I remember thee."

By the light of the moon, he saw a tear steal from
under the long lashes, and course slowly down her cheek.
He continued his song: —

> "Mine is an eternal love,
> Higher than the heights above,
> Deeper than the depths beneath,
> True and faithful — strong as death.

> "Thou shalt see my glory soon,
> When the work of faith is done;
> Partner of my throne shalt be!
> Say, poor sinner, lov'st thou me ? "

Oh, love of Christ! which no sin can weary, which no
lapse of time can change; from which tribulation, perse-
cution, and distress cannot separate — all-redeeming, all-
glorifying, changing even death and despair to the gate of
heaven!   Thou hast one more triumph here in the wilderness, in the slave-coffle, and thou comest to bind up the
broken hearted.

As the song ceased, she opened her eyes.

"Mother used to sing that!" she said.

"And can you believe in it, daughter?"

"Yes," she said, "I see Him now! He loves me!
Let me go!"

There followed a few moments of those strugglings and shiverings which are the birth-pangs of another life, and Emily lay at rest.

Father Dickson, kneeling by her side, poured out the fullness of his heart in an earnest prayer. Rising, he went up to the trader, and taking his hand, said to him, —

"My friend, this may be the turning-point with your soul for eternity. It has pleased the Lord to show you the evil of your ways; and now my advice to you is, break off your sins at once, and do works meet for repentance. Take off the shackles of these poor creatures, and tell them they are at liberty to go."

"Why, bless your soul, sir, this yer lot's worth ten thousand dollars!" said the trader, who was not prepared for so close a practical application.

Do not be too sure, friend, that the trader is peculiar in this. The very same argument, though less frankly stated, holds in the bonds of Satan many extremely well-bred, refined, respectable men, who would gladly save their souls if they could afford the luxury.

"My friend," said Father Dickson, using the words of a very close and uncompromising preacher of old, "what shall it profit a man if he should gain the whole world, and lose his own soul?"

"I know that," said the trader doubtfully; "but it's a very hard case, this. I'll think about it, though. But there's Father Bonnie wants to buy Nance. It would be a pity to disappoint him. But I'll think it over."

Father Dickson returned to the camp-ground between one and two o'clock at night, and putting away his horse, took his way to the ministers' tent. Here he found Father Bonnie standing out in the moonlight. He had been asleep within the tent; but it is to be confessed that the interior of a crowded tent on a camp-ground is anything but favorable to repose. He therefore came out into the

fresh air, and was there when Father Dickson came back
to enter the tent.

"Well, brother, where have you been so late?" said
Father Bonnie.

"I have been looking for a few sheep in the wilderness,
whom everybody neglects," said Father Dickson.   And
then, in a tone tremulous from agitation, he related to him
the scene he had just witnessed.

"Do you see," he said, "brother, what iniquities you
are countenancing?   Now here, right next to our camp,
a slave-coffle encamped!   Men and women, guilty of no
crime, driven in fetters through our land, shaming us in
the sight of every Christian nation!   What horrible,
abominable iniquities are these poor traders tempted to
commit!   What perfect hells are the great trading-houses,
where men, women, and children are made merchandise
of, and where no light of the gospel ever enters!   And
when this poor trader is convicted of sin, and wants to
enter into the kingdom, you stand there to apologize for
his sins!   Brother Bonnie, I much fear you are the stum-
bling-block over which souls will stumble into hell.   I
don't think you believe your argument from the Old Testament, yourself.   You must see that it has no kind of relation to such kind of slavery as we have in this country.
There's an awful Scripture which saith: ' He feedeth on
ashes; a deceived heart hath turned him aside, so that he
cannot deliver his soul, nor say, Is there not a lie in my
right hand?' "

The earnestness with which Father Dickson spoke, com-
bined with the reverence commonly entertained for his
piety, gave great force to his words.   The reader will not
therefore wonder to hear that Father Bonnie, impulsive
and easily moved as he was, wept at the account, and was
moved by the exhortation.   Nor will he be surprised to

learn that, two weeks after, Father Bonnie drove a brisk bargain with the same trader for three new hands.

The trader had discovered that the judgment-day was not coming yet a while; and Father Bonnie satisfied himself that Noah, when he awoke from his wine, said, "Cursed be Canaan."

.   .   .   .

We have one scene more to draw before we dismiss the auditors of the camp-meeting.

At a late hour the Gordon carriage was winding its way under the silent, checkered, woodland path. Harry, who came slowly on a horse behind, felt a hand laid on his bridle. With a sudden start, he stopped. "Oh, Dred, is it you? How dared you — how *could* you be so imprudent? How dared you come here, when you know you risk your life?"

"Life!" said the other, "what is life? He that loveth his life shall lose it. Besides, the Lord said unto me, Go! The Lord is with me as a mighty and terrible one! Harry, did you mark those men? Hunters of men, their hands red with the blood of the poor, all seeking unto the Lord! Ministers who buy and sell us! Is this a people prepared for the Lord? I left a man dead in the swamps, whom their dogs have torn! His wife is a widow — his children, orphans! They eat and wipe their mouth, and say, 'What have I done?' The temple of the Lord, the temple of the Lord, are we!"

"I know it," said Harry gloomily.

"And you join yourself unto them?"

"Don't speak to me any more about that! I won't betray you, but I won't consent to have blood shed. My mistress is my sister."

"Oh yes, to be sure! They read Scripture, don't they? Cast out the children of the bondwoman! That's Scripture for them!"

"Dred," said Harry, "I love her better than I love myself. I will fight for her to the last, but never against her, nor hers!"

"And you will serve Tom Gordon?" said Dred.

"Never!" said Harry.

Dred stood still a moment. Through an opening among the branches the moonbeams streamed down on his wild, dark figure. Harry remarked his eye fixed before him on vacancy, the pupil swelling out in glassy fullness, with a fixed, somnambulic stare. After a moment, he spoke, in a hollow, altered voice, like that of a sleep-walker: —

"Then shall the silver cord be loosed, and the golden bowl be broken. Yes, cover up the grave — cover it up! Now, hurry! come to me, or he will take thy wife for a prey!"

"Dred, what do you mean?" said Harry. "What's the matter?" He shook him by the shoulder.

Dred rubbed his eyes, and stared on Harry.

"I must go back," he said, "to my den. 'Foxes have holes, the birds of the air have nests,' and in the habitation of dragons the Lord hath opened a way for his outcasts!"

He plunged into the thickets, and was gone.

CHAPTER XXIV

LIFE IN THE SWAMPS

OUR readers will perhaps feel an interest to turn back with us, and follow the singular wanderings of the mysterious personage, whose wild denunciations had so disturbed the minds of the worshipers at the camp-meeting.

There is a twilight-ground between the boundaries of the sane and insane, which the old Greeks and Romans regarded with a peculiar veneration. They held a person whose faculties were thus darkened as walking under the awful shadow of a supernatural presence; and as the mysterious secrets of the stars only become visible in the night, so in these eclipses of the more material faculties they held there was often an awakening of supernatural perceptions.

The hot and positive light of our modern materialism, which exhales from the growth of our existence every dewdrop, which searches out and dries every rivulet of romance, which sends an unsparing beam into every cool grotto of poetic possibility, withering the moss, and turning the dropping cave to a dusty den — this spirit, so remorseless, allows us no such indefinite land. There are but two words in the whole department of modern anthropology — the sane and the insane; the latter dismissed from human reckoning almost with contempt. We should find it difficult to give a suitable name to the strange and abnormal condition in which this singular being, of whom we are speaking, passed the most of his time. It was a state of exaltation and trance, which yet appeared not at all to impede the exercise of his outward and physical faculties, but rather to give them a preternatural keenness and intensity, such as sometimes attends the more completely developed phenomena of somnambulism.

In regard to his physical system there was also much that was peculiar. Our readers may imagine a human body of the largest and keenest vitality to grow up so completely under the nursing influences of nature, that it may seem to be as perfectly *en rapport* with them as a tree; so that the rain, the wind, and the thunder, all those forces from which human beings generally seek shelter, seem to hold with it a kind of fellowship, and to be familiar companions of existence.

Such was the case with Dred. So completely had he come into sympathy and communion with nature, and with those forms of it which more particularly surrounded him in the swamps, that he moved about among them with as much ease as a lady treads her Turkey carpet. What would seem to us in recital to be incredible hardship was to him but an ordinary condition of existence. To walk knee-deep in the spongy soil of the swamp, to force his way through thickets, to lie all night sinking in the porous soil, or to crouch, like the alligator, among reeds and rushes, were to him situations of as much comfort as well-curtained beds and pillows are to us.

It is not to be denied, that there is in this savage perfection of the natural organs a keen and almost fierce delight, which must excel the softest seductions of luxury. Anybody who has ever watched the eager zest with which the hunting-dog plunges through the woods, darts through the thicket, or dives into water, in an ecstasy of enjoyment, sees something of what such vital force must be.

Dred was under the inspiring belief that he was the subject of visions and supernatural communications. The

African race are said by mesmerists to possess, in the fullest
degree, that peculiar temperament which fits them for the
evolution of mesmeric phenomena; and hence the existence
among them, to this day, of men and women who are supposed to have peculiar magical powers.   The grandfather
of Dred, on his mother's side, had been one of these
reputed African sorcerers, and he had early discovered in
the boy this peculiar species of temperament.   He had
taught him the secret of snake-charming, and had possessed
his mind from childhood with expectations of prophetic
and supernatural impulses.   That mysterious and singular
gift, whatever it may be, which Highland seers denomi-
nate second sight, is a very common tradition among the
negroes; and there are not wanting thousands of reputed
instances among them to confirm belief in it.   What this
faculty may be, we shall not pretend to say.   Whether
there be in the soul a yet undeveloped attribute, which is
to be to the future what memory is to the past, or whether
in some individuals an extremely high and perfect condition of the sensuous organization endows them with something of that certainty of instinctive discrimination which
belongs to animals, are things which we shall not venture
to decide upon.

It was, however, an absolute fact with regard to Dred,
that he had often escaped danger by means of a peculiarity
of this kind.   He had been warned from particular places
where the hunters had lain in wait for him; had foreseen
in times of want where game might be ensnared, and
received intimations where persons were to be found in
whom he might safely confide; and his predictions with
regard to persons and things had often chanced to be so
strikingly true, as to invest his sayings with a singular
awe and importance among his associates.

It was a remarkable fact, but one not peculiar to this
case alone, that the mysterious exaltation of mind in this

individual seemed to run parallel with the current of
shrewd, practical sense; and like a man who converses
alternately in two languages, he would speak now the
language of exaltation, and now that of common life, inter-
changeably. This peculiarity imparted a singular and
grotesque effect to his whole personality.

On the night of the camp-meeting, he was, as we have
already seen, in a state of the highest ecstasy. The wanton
murder of his associate seemed to flood his soul with an
awful tide of emotion, as a thundercloud is filled and
shaken by slow-gathering electricity. And although the
distance from his retreat to the camp-ground was nearly
fifteen miles, most of it through what seemed to be impassable swamps, yet he performed it with as little consciousness of fatigue as if he had been a spirit. Even had he
been perceived at that time, it is probable that he could
no more have been taken, or bound, than the demoniac of
Gadara.

After he parted from Harry he pursued his way to the
interior of the swamp, as was his usual habit, repeating to
himself, in a chanting voice, such words of prophetic writ
as were familiar to him.

The day had been sultry, and it was now an hour or two
past midnight, when a thunderstorm, which had long
been gathering and muttering in the distant sky, began to
develop its forces. A low, shivering sigh crept through
the woods, and swayed in weird whistlings the tops of the
pines; and sharp arrows of lightning came glittering down
among the darkness of the branches, as if sent from the
bow of some warlike angel. An army of heavy clouds
swept in a moment across the moon; then came a broad,
dazzling, blinding sheet of flame, concentrating itself on
the top of a tall pine near where Dred was standing, and
in a moment shivered all its branches to the ground, as a
child strips the leaves from a twig. Dred clapped his

hands with a fierce delight; and while the rain and wind were howling and hissing around him, he shouted aloud: —

"Wake, O arm of the Lord! Awake, put on thy strength! The voice of the Lord breaketh the cedars — yea, the cedars of Lebanon! The voice of the Lord divideth the flames of fire! The voice of the Lord shaketh the wilderness of Kadesh! Hailstones and coals of fire!"

The storm, which howled around him, bent the forest like a reed, and large trees, uprooted from the spongy and tremulous soil, fell crashing with a tremendous noise; but as if he had been a dark spirit of the tempest, he shouted and exulted.

The perception of such awful power seemed to animate him, and yet to excite in his soul an impatience that He whose power was so infinite did not awake to judgment.

"Rend the heavens," he cried, "and come down! Avenge the innocent blood! Cast forth thine arrows, and slay them! Shoot out thy lightnings, and destroy them!"

His soul seemed to kindle with almost a fierce impatience, at the toleration of that Almighty Being, who, having the power to blast and to burn, so silently endures. Could Dred have possessed himself of those lightnings, what would have stood before him? But his cry, like the cry of thousands, only went up to stand in waiting till an awful coming day!

Gradually the storm passed by; the big drops dashed less and less frequently; a softer breeze passed through the forest, with a patter like the clapping of a thousand little wings; and the moon occasionally looked over the silvery battlements of the great clouds.

As Dred was starting to go forward, one of these clear revealings showed him the cowering form of a man, crouched at the root of a tree, a few paces in front of him. He was evidently a fugitive, and, in fact, was the one of whose escape to the swamps the Georgia trader had complained of the day of the meeting.

"Who is here, at this time of night?" said Dred, coming up to him.

"I have lost my way," said the other. "I don't know where I am!"

"A runaway?" inquired Dred.

"Don't betray me!" said the other apprehensively.

"Betray you! Would *I* do that?" said Dred. "How did you get into the swamp?"

"I got away from a soul-driver's camp, that was taking us on through the states."

"Oh, oh!" said Dred. "Camp-meeting and driver's camp right alongside of each other! Shepherds that sell the flock, and pick the bones! Well, come, old man; I'll take you home with me."

"I'm pretty much beat out," said the man. "It's been up over my knees every step; and I didn't know but they'd set the dogs after me. If they do, I'll let 'em kill me, and done with it, for I'm 'bout ready to have it over with. I got free once, and got clear up to New York, and got me a little bit of a house, and a wife and two children, with a little money beforehand; and then they nabbed me, and sent me back again, and mas'r sold me to the drivers, — and I believe I's 'bout as good's die. There's no use in trying to live — everything going agin a body so!"

"Die! No, indeed, you won't," said Dred; "not if I've got hold of you! Take heart, man, take heart! Before morning I'll put you where the dogs can't find you, nor anything else. Come, up with you!"

The man rose up, and made an effort to follow; but wearied, and unused as he was to the choked and perplexed way, he stumbled and fell almost every minute.

"How now, brother?" said Dred. "This won't do!

I must put you over my shoulder as I have many a buck
before now!" And suiting the action to the word, he
put the man on his back, and bidding him hold fast to
him, went on, picking his way as if he scarcely perceived
his weight.

It was now between two and three o'clock, and the
clouds, gradually dispersing, allowed the full light of the
moon to slide down here and there through the wet and
shivering foliage. No sound was heard, save the humming of insects and the crackling plunges by which Dred
made his way forward.

"You must be pretty strong!" said his companion.
"Have you been in the swamps long?"

"Yes," said the other, "I have been a wild man —
every man's hand against me — a companion of the dragons
and the owls, this many a year. I have made my bed
with the leviathan, among the reeds and the rushes. I
have found the alligators and the snakes better neighbors
than Christians. They let those alone that let them alone;
but Christians will hunt for the precious life."

After about an hour of steady traveling, Dred arrived at
the outskirts of the island which we have described. For
about twenty paces before he reached it, he waded waist-
deep in water. Creeping out, at last, and telling the other
one to follow him, he began carefully coursing along on his
hands and knees, giving, at the same time, a long, shrill,
peculiar whistle. It was responded to by a similar sound,
which seemed to proceed through the bushes. After a
while, a crackling noise was heard, as of some animal,
which gradually seemed to come nearer and nearer to them,
till finally a large water-dog emerged from the underbrush,
and began testifying his joy at the arrival of the newcomer, by most extravagant gambols.

"So, ho! Buck! quiet, my boy!" said Dred. "Show
us the way in!"

The dog, as if understanding the words, immediately turned into the thicket, and Dred and his companion followed him, on their hands and knees. The path wound up and down the brushwood, through many sharp turnings, till at last it ceased altogether, at the roots of a tree; and while the dog disappeared among the brushwood, Dred climbed the tree, and directed his companion to follow him, and proceeding out on to one of the longest limbs, he sprang nimbly on to the ground in the cleared space which we have before described.

His wife was standing waiting for him, and threw herself upon him with a cry of joy. "Oh, you 've come back! I thought, sure enough, dey 'd got you dis time!"

"Not yet! I must continue till the opening of the seals — till the vision cometh! Have ye buried him?"

"No; there 's a grave dug down yonder, and he 's been carried there."

"Come, then!" said Dred.

At a distant part of the clearing was a blasted cedar-tree, all whose natural foliage had perished. But it was veiled from head to foot in long wreaths of the tillandsia, the parasitic moss of these regions, and in the dim light of the approaching dawn, might have formed no unapt resemblance to a gigantic spectre dressed in mourning weeds. Beneath this tree Dred had interred, from time to time, the bodies of fugitives which he had found dead in the swamps, attaching to this disposition of them some peculiar superstitious idea.

The widow of the dead, the wife of Dred, and the new-comer were now gathered around the shallow grave; for the soil was such as scarcely gave room to make a place deep enough for a grave without its becoming filled with water. The dawn was just commencing a dim foreshadowing in the sky. The moon and stars were still shining. Dred stood and looked up, and spoke in a solemn voice: —

"Seek him that maketh Arcturus and Orion — that turneth the shadow of death into morning! Behold those lights in the sky — the lights in his hands pierced for the sins of the world, and spread forth as on a cross! But the day shall come that he shall lay down the yoke, and he will bear the sin of the world no longer. Then shall come the great judgment. He will lay righteousness to the line and judgment to the plummet, and the hail shall sweep away the refuges of lies."

He stooped, and lifting the body, laid him in the grave, and at this moment the wife broke into a loud lament.

"Hush, woman!" said Dred, raising his hand. "Weep ye not for the dead, neither bewail him; but weep ye sore for the living! He must rest till the rest of his brethren be killed; for the vision is sealed up for an appointed time. If it tarry, wait for it. It shall surely come, and shall not tarry!"

CHAPTER XXV

MORE SUMMER TALK

A GLORIOUS morning, washed by the tears of last night's shower, rose like a bride upon Canema. The rain-drops sparkled and winked from leaf to leaf, or fell in showery diamonds in the breeze. The breath of number-less roses, now in full bloom, rose in clouds to the win-dows. The breakfast-table, with its clean damask, glitter-ing silver, and fragrant coffee, received the last evening's participants of the camp-meeting in fresh morning spirits, ready to discuss, as an every-day affair, what, the evening before, they had felt too deeply, perhaps, to discuss.

On the way home, they had spoken of the scenes of the day, and wondered and speculated on the singular incident which closed it. But of all the dark circle of woe and crime, — of all that valley of vision which was present to the mind of him who spoke, — they were as practically ignorant as the dwellers of the curtained boudoirs of New York are of the fearful mysteries of the Five Points.

The aristocratic nature of society at the South so com-pletely segregates people of a certain position in life from any acquaintance with the movements of human nature in circles below them, that the most fearful things may be transacting in their vicinity unknown or unnoticed. The horrors and sorrows of the slave-coffle were a sealed book to Nina and Anne Clayton. They had scarcely dreamed of them; and Uncle John, if he knew their existence, took very good care to keep out of their way, as he would turn from any other painful and disagreeable scene.

All of them had heard something of negro-hunters, and regarded them as low, vulgar people, but troubled their heads little further on the subject; so that they would have been quite at a loss for the discovery of any national sins that could have appropriately drawn down the denunciations of Heaven.

The serious thoughts and aspirations which might have risen in any of the company, the evening before, assumed, with everything else, quite another light under the rays of morning.

All of us must have had experience, in our own histories, of the great difference between the night and the morning view of the same subject. What we have thought and said in the august presence of witnessing stars, or beneath the holy shadows of moonlight, seems with the hot, dry light of next day's sun to take wings, and rise to heaven with the night's clear drops. If all the prayers and good resolutions which are laid down on sleeping pillows could be found there on awaking, the world would be better than it is.

Of this Uncle John Gordon had experience, as he sat himself down at the breakfast-table. The night before, he realized, in some dim wise, that he, Mr. John Gordon, was not merely a fat, elderly gentleman, in blue coat and white vest, whose great object in existence was to eat well, drink well, sleep well, wear clean linen, and keep out of the way of trouble. He had within him a tumult of yearnings and aspirings, — uprisings of that great, life-long sleeper, which we call *soul*, and which, when it wakes, is an awfully clamorous, craving, exacting, troublesome inmate, and which is therefore generally put asleep again in the shortest time, by whatever opiates may come to hand. Last night, urged on by this troublesome guest, stimulated by the vague power of such awful words as judgment and eternity, he had gone out and knelt down as a mourner for sin and a seeker for salvation, both words standing for very real and awful facts; and this morning, although it was probably a more sensible and appropriate thing than most of the things he was in the habit of doing, he was almost ashamed of it. The question arose, at table, whether another excursion should be made to the camp-ground.

"For my part," said Aunt Maria, "I hope you 'll not go again, Mr. Gordon. I think you had better keep out of the way of such things. I really was vexed to see you in that rabble of such very common people! "

"You 'll observe," said Uncle John, "that, when Mrs. G. goes to heaven, she 'll notify the Lord, forthwith, that she has only been accustomed to the most select circles, and requests to be admitted at the front door."

"It is n't because I object to being with common people," said Anne Clayton, "that I dislike this custom of going to the altar; but it seems to me an invasion of that privacy and reserve which belong to our most sacred feelings. Besides, there are in a crowd coarse, rude, disagreeable people, with whom it is n't pleasant to come in contact."

"For my part," said Mrs. John Gordon, "I don't believe in it at all! It 's a mere temporary excitement. People go and get wonderfully wrought up, come away, and are just what they were before."

"Well," said Clayton, "is n't it better to be wrought up once in a while, than never to have any religious feelings? Is n't it better to have a vivid impression of the vastness and worth of the soul, — of the power of an endless life, — for a few hours once a year, than never to feel it at all? The multitudes of those people, there, never hear or think a word of these things at any other time in their lives. For my part," he added, "I don't see why it 's a thing to be ashamed of, if Mr. Gordon or I should have knelt at the altar last night, even if we do not feel like it this morning. We are too often ashamed of our better moments; — I believe Protestant Christians are the only people on earth who are ashamed of the outward recognition of their religion. The Mahometan will prostrate himself in the street, or wherever he happens to be, when his hour for prayer comes. The Roman Catholic sailor or soldier kneels down at the sound of the vesper bell. But we rather take pride in having it understood that we take our religion moderately and coolly, and that we are not going to put ourselves much out about it."

"Well, but, brother," said Anne, "I will maintain, still, that there is a reserve about these things which belongs to the best Christians. And did not our Saviour tell us that our prayers and alms should be in secret?"

"I do not deny at all what you say, Anne," said Clayton; "but I think what I said is true, notwithstanding; and both being true, of course, in some way they must be consistent with each other."

"I think," said Nina, "the sound of the singing at these camp-meetings is really quite spirit-stirring and exciting."

"Yes," said Clayton, "these wild tunes, and the hymns with which they are associated, form a kind of forest liturgy, in which the feelings of thousands of hearts have been embodied. Some of the tunes seem to me to have been caught from the song of birds, or from the rushing of wind among the branches. They possess a peculiar rhythmical energy, well suited to express the vehement emotions of the masses. Did camp-meetings do no other good than to scatter among the people these hymns and tunes, I should consider them to be of inestimable value."

"I must say," said Anne, "I always had a prejudice against that class both of hymns and tunes."

"You misjudge them," said Clayton, "as you refined,

cultivated women always do, who are brought up in the kid-slipper and carpet view of human life. But just imagine only the old Greek or Roman peasantry elevated to the level of one of these hymns. Take, for example, a verse of one I heard them sing last night: —

> 'The earth shall be dissolved like snow,
> The sun shall cease to shine,
> But God, who called me here below,
> Shall be forever mine.'

What faith is there! What confidence in immortality! How could a man feel it, and not be ennobled? Then, what a rough hearty heroism was in that first hymn! It was right manly!"

"Ah, but," said Anne, "half the time they sing them without the slightest perception of their meaning, or the least idea of being influenced by them."

"And so do the worshipers in the sleepiest and most aristocratic churches," said Clayton. "That's nothing peculiar to the camp-ground. But if it is true what a certain statesman once said, 'Let me make the ballads of the people, and I care not who makes their laws,' it is certainly a great gain to have such noble sentiments as many of these hymns contain circulating freely among the people."

"What upon earth," said Uncle John, "do you suppose that last fellow was about, up in the clouds, there? Nobody seemed to know where he was, or who he was; and I thought his discourse seemed to be rather an unexpected addition. He put it into us pretty strong, I thought! Declare, such a bundle of woes and curses I never heard distributed! Seemed to have done up all the old prophets into one bundle, and tumbled it down upon our heads! Some of them were quite superstitious about it, and began talking about warnings, and all that."

"Pooh!" said Aunt Maria, "the likelihood is that some itinerant poor preacher has fallen upon this trick for pro-

ducing a sensation.   There is no end to the trickeries and
the got-up scenes in these camp-meetings, just to produce
effect.   If I had had a pistol, I should like to have fired
into the tree, and see whether I could n't have changed
his tune."

"It seemed to me," said Clayton, "from the little that
I did hear, that there was some method in his madness.
It was one of the most singular and impressive voices I
ever heard; and really, the enunciation of some of those
latter things was tremendous.   But then, in the universal
license and general confusion of the scene, the thing was
not so much to be wondered at.   It would be the most
natural thing in the world that some crazy fanatic should
be heated almost to the point of insanity by the scene, and
take this way of unburdening himself.   Such excitements
most generally assume the form of denunciation."

"Well, now," said Nina, "to tell the truth, I should
like to go out again to-day.   It 's a lovely ride, and I like
to be in the woods.   And then, I like to walk around
among the tents, and hear the people talk, and see all the
different specimens of human nature that are there.   I
never saw such a gathering together in my life."

"Agreed!" said Uncle John.   "I 'll go with you.
After all, Clayton, here, has got the right of it, when he
says a fellow ought n't to be ashamed of his religion, such
as it is."

"Such as it is, to be sure!" said Aunt Maria sarcastically.

"Yes, I say again, such as it is!" said Uncle John,
bracing himself.   "I don't pretend it 's much.   We 'll all
of us bear to be a good deal better, without danger of being
translated.   Now, as to this being converted, hang me if
I know how to get at it!   I suppose that it is something
like an electric shock — if a fellow is going to get it, he
must go up to the machine!"

"Well," said Nina, "you do hear some queer things there. Don't you remember that jolly, slashing-looking fellow, whom they called Bill Dakin, that came up there with his two dogs? In the afternoon, after the regular services, we went to one of the tents where there was a very noisy prayer-meeting going on, and there was Bill Dakin, on his knees, with his hands clasped, and the tears rolling down his cheeks; and Father Bonnie was praying over him with all his might. And what do you think he said? He said, 'O Lord, here's Bill Dakin; he is converted; now take him right to heaven, now he is ready, or he'll be drunk again in two weeks!'"

"Well," said Anne Clayton, tossing her head indignantly, "that's blasphemy, in my opinion."

"Oh, perhaps not," said Clayton, "any more than the clownish talk of any of our servants is intentional rudeness."

"Well," said Anne, "don't you think it shows a great want of perception?"

"Certainly, it does," said Clayton. "It shows great rudeness and coarseness of fibre, and is not at all to be commended. But still we are not to judge of it by the rules of cultivated society. In well-trained minds every faculty keeps its due boundaries; but in this kind of wild-forest growth, mirthfulness will sometimes overgrow reverence, just as the yellow jessamine will completely smother a tree. A great many of the ordinances of the old Mosaic dispensation were intended to counteract this very tendency."

"Well," said Nina, "did you notice poor old Tiff, so intent upon getting his children converted? He didn't seem to have the least thought or reference to getting into heaven himself. The only thing with him was to get those children in. Tiff seems to me just like those mistletoes that we see on the trees in the swamps. He don't seem to have any root of his own; he seems to grow out of something else."

"Those children are very pretty-looking, genteel children," said Anne; "and how well they were dressed!"

"My dear," said Nina, "Tiff prostrates himself at my shrine, every time he meets me, to implore my favorable supervision as to that point; and it really is diverting to hear him talk. The old Caliban has an eye for color, and a sense of what is suitable, equal to any French milliner. I assure you, my dear, I always was reputed for having a talent for dress; and Tiff *appreciates* me. Is n't it charming of him? I declare, when I see the old creature lugging about those children, I always think of an ugly old cactus with its blossoms. I believe he verily thinks they belong to him just as much. Their father is entirely dismissed from Tiff's calculations. Evidently all he wants of him is to keep out of the way, and let him work. The whole burden of their education lies on his shoulders."

"For my part," said Aunt Nesbit, "I'm glad you've faith to believe in those children. I have n't; they'll be sure to turn out badly — you see if they don't."

"And I think," said Aunt Maria, "we have enough to do with our own servants, without taking all these miserable whites on our hands, too."

"I'm not going to take all the whites," said Nina. "I'm going to take these children."

"I wish you joy!" said Aunt Maria.

"I wonder," said Aunt Nesbit, "if Harry is under concern of mind. He seems to be dreadfully down, this morning."

"Is he?" said Nina. "I had n't noticed it."

"Well," said Uncle John, "perhaps he'll get set up, to-day — who knows? In fact, I hope I shall myself. I tell you what it is, parson," said he, laying his hand on Clayton's shoulder, "you should take the gig, to-day, and drive this little sinner, and let me go with the ladies. Of course you know Mrs. G. engrosses my whole soul; but then, there 's a kind of insensible improvement that comes from such celestial bodies as Miss Anne, here, that ought n't to be denied to me. The clergy ought to enumerate female influence among the means of grace. I 'm sure there 's nothing builds me up like it."

Clayton, of course, assented very readily to this arrangement; and the party was adjusted on this basis.

"Look ye here, now, Clayton," said Uncle John, tipping him a sly wink, after he had handed Nina in, "you must confess that little penitent! She wants a spiritual director, my boy! I tell you what, Clayton, there is n't a girl like that in North Carolina. There 's blood, sir, there. You must humor her on the bit, and give her her head a while. Ah, but she 'll draw well at last! I always like a creature that kicks to pieces harness, wagon, and all, to begin with. They do the best when they are broken in." With which profound remarks Uncle John turned to hand Anne Clayton to the carriage.

Clayton understood too well what he was about to make any such use of the interview as Uncle John had suggested. He knew perfectly that his best chance, with a nature so restless as Nina's, was to keep up a sense of perfect freedom in all their intercourse; and, therefore, no grandfather could have been more collected and easy in a *tête-à-tête* drive than he. The last conversation at the camp-meeting he knew had brought them much nearer to each other than they had ever stood before, because both had spoken in deep earnestness of feeling of what lay deepest in their heart; and one such moment, he well knew, was of more binding force than a hundred nominal betrothals.

The morning was one of those perfect ones which succeed a thunder-shower in the night; when the air, cleared

of every gross vapor, and impregnated with moist exhala-
tions from the woods, is both balmy and stimulating.
The steaming air developed to the full the balsamic properties of the pine groves through which they rode; and
where the road skirted the swampy land, the light fell
slanting on the leaves of the deciduous trees, rustling and
dripping with the last night's shower. The heavens were
full of those brilliant, island-like clouds, which are said to
be a peculiarity of American skies, in their distinct relief
above the intense blue. At a long distance they caught
the sound of camp - meeting hymns. But before they
reached the ground, they saw, in more than one riotous
group, the result of too frequent an application to Abijah
Skinflint's department, and others of a similar character.
They visited the quarters of Old Tiff, whom they found
busy ironing some clothes for the baby, which he had
washed and hung out the night before. The preaching
had not yet commenced, and the party walked about among
the tents. Women were busy cooking and washing dishes
under the trees; and there was a great deal of good-natured
gossiping.

One of the most remarkable features of the day was a
sermon from Father Dickson, on the sins of the church.
It concluded with a most forcible and solemn appeal to all
on the subject of slavery. He reminded both the Methodists and Presbyterians that their books of discipline had
most pointedly and unequivocally condemned it; that John
Wesley had denounced it as the sum of all villainies, and
that the general assemblies of the Presbyterian Church
had condemned it as wholly inconsistent with the religion
of Christ, with the great law which requires us to love
others as ourselves. He related the scene which he had
lately witnessed in the slave-coffle. He spoke of the horrors of the interstate slave-trade, and drew a touching
picture of the separation of families, and the rending of

all domestic and social ties, which resulted from it, and alluding to the unknown speaker of the evening before, told his audience that he had discerned a deep significance in his words, and that he feared, if there was not immediate repentance and reformation, the land would yet be given up to the visitations of divine wrath. As he spoke with feeling, he awakened feeling in return. Many were affected even to tears; but when the sermon was over, it seemed to melt away, as a wave flows back again into the sea. It was far easier to join in a temporary whirlwind of excitement than to take into consideration troublesome, difficult, and expensive reforms.

Yet, still, it is due to the degenerate Christianity of the slave states to say, that, during the long period in which the church there has been corrupting itself, and lowering its standard of right to meet a depraved institution, there have not been wanting, from time to time, noble confessors, who have spoken for God and humanity. For many years they were listened to with that kind of pensive tolerance which men give when they acknowledge their fault without any intention of mending. Of late years, however, the lines have been drawn more sharply, and such witnesses have spoken in peril of their lives; so that now seldom a voice arises except in approbation of oppression.

The sermon was fruitful of much discussion in different parts of the camp-ground; and none, perhaps, was louder in the approbation of it than the Georgia trader, who, seated on Abijah Skinflint's counter, declared: "That was a *parson* as *was* a parson, and that he liked his *pluck;* and, for his part, when ministers and church-members would give over buying, he should take up some other trade."

"That was a very good sermon," said Nina, "and I believe every word of it. But then, what do you suppose *we* ought to do? "

"Why," said Clayton, "we ought to contemplate emancipation as a future certainty, and prepare our people in
the shortest possible time."

This conversation took place as the party were seated at
their nooning under the trees, around an unpacked hamper
of cold provisions, which they were leisurely discussing.

"Why, bless my soul, Clayton," said Uncle John, "I
don't see the sense of such an anathema maranatha as we
got to-day. Good Lord, what earthly harm are we doing?
As to our niggers, they are better off than we are! I say
it coolly — that is, as coolly as a man can say anything
between one and two o'clock in such weather as this.
Why, look at my niggers! Do *I* ever have any chickens,
or eggs, or cucumbers? No, to be sure. All *my* chickens
die, and the cut-worm plays the devil with *my* cucumbers;
but the niggers have enough. Theirs flourish like a green
bay-tree; and of course I have to buy of them. *They*
raise chickens. I buy 'em and cook 'em, and then they
eat 'em! That's the way it goes. As to the slave-coffles,
and slave-prisons, and the trade, why, that's abominable,
to be sure. But, Lord bless you, I don't want it done!
I'd kick a trader off my doorsteps forthwith, though I'm
all eaten up with woolly-heads, like locusts. I don't like
such sermons, for my part."

"Well," said Aunt Nesbit, "our Mr. Titmarsh preached
quite another way when I attended church in E——. He
proved that slavery was a Scriptural institution, and established by God."

"I should think anybody's common sense would show
that a thing which works so poorly for both sides couldn't
be from God," said Nina.

"Who is Mr. Titmarsh?" said Clayton to her, aside.

"Oh, one of Aunt Nesbit's favorites, and one of my
aversions! He isn't a man — he's nothing but a theological dictionary with a cravat on! I can't bear him!"

"Now, people may talk as much as they please of the educated democracy of the North," said Uncle John. "*I* don't like 'em. What do workingmen want of education? — Ruins 'em! I've heard of their learned blacksmiths bothering around, neglecting their work, to make speeches. I don't like such things. It raises them above their sphere. And there's nothing going on up in those northern states but a constant confusion and hubbub. All sorts of heresies come from the North, and infidelity, and the Lord knows what! We have peace, down here. To be sure, our poor whites are in a devil of a fix; but we have n't got 'em under yet. We shall get 'em in, one of these days, with our niggers, and then all will be contentment."

"Yes," said Nina, "there's Uncle John's view of the millennium!"

"To be sure," said Uncle John, "the lower classes want governing — they want care; that's what they want. And all they need to know is, what the Episcopal Church catechism says, 'to learn and labor truly to get their own living in the state wherein it has pleased God to call them.' That makes a well-behaved lower class, and a handsome, gentlemanly, orderly state of society. The upper classes ought to be instructed in their duties. They ought to be considerate and condescending, and all that. That's my view of society."

"Then you are no republican," said Clayton.

"Bless you, yes I am! I believe in the equality of gentlemen, and the equal rights of well-bred people. That's my idea of a republic."

Clayton, Nina, and Anne laughed.

"Now," said Nina, "to see uncle so jovial and free, and 'Hail fellow well met' with everybody, you'd think he was the greatest democrat that ever walked. But, you see, it's only because he's so immeasurably certain of his

superior position — that's all.   He isn't afraid to kneel
at the altar with Bill Dakin, or Jim Sykes, because he's
so sure that his position can't be compromised."

"Besides that, chick," said Uncle John, "I *have* the
sense to know that, in my Maker's presence, all human
differences are child's play."   And Uncle John spoke with
a momentary solemnity which was heartfelt.

It was agreed by the party that they would not stay to
attend the evening exercises.   The novelty of the effect
was over, and Aunt Nesbit spoke of the bad effects of falling dew and night air.   Accordingly, as soon as the air
was sufficiently cooled to make riding practicable, the party
were again on their way home.

The woodland path was streaked with green and golden
bands of light thrown between the tree-trunks across the
way, and the trees reverberated with the evening song of
birds.   Nina and Clayton naturally fell into a quiet and
subdued train of conversation.

"It is strange," said Nina, "these talkings and search-
ings about religion.   Now, there are people who have
something they call religion, which I don't think does
them any good.   It isn't of any use — it doesn't make
them better — and it makes them very disagreeable.   I
would rather be as I am than to have what they call religion.   But then, there are others that have something
which I know *is* religion; something that I know I have
not; something that I'd give all the world to have, and
don't know how to get.   Now, there was Livy Ray —
you ought to have seen Livy Ray — there was something
so superior about her; and what was extraordinary is,
that she was good without being stupid.   What do you
suppose the reason is that good people are generally so
stupid?"

"A great deal," said Clayton, "is called goodness
which is nothing but want of force.   A person is said to

have self-government simply because he has nothing to govern. They talk about self-denial, when their desires are so weak that one course is about as easy to them as another. Such people easily fall into a religious routine, get by heart a set of phrases, and make, as you say, very stupid, good people."

"Now, Livy," said Nina, "was remarkable. She had that kind of education that they give girls in New England, stronger and more like a man's than ours. She could read Greek and Latin as easily as she could French and Italian. She was keen, shrewd, and witty, and had a kind of wild grace about her, like these grapevines; yet she was so strong! Well, do you know, I almost worship Livy? And I think, the little while she was in our school, she did me more good than all the teachers and studying put together. Why, it does one good to know that such people are possible. Don't you think it does?"

"Yes," said Clayton; "all the good in the world is done by the personality of people. Now, in books, it is n't so much what you learn from them, as the contact it gives you with the personality of the writer, that improves you. A real book always makes you feel that there is more in the writer than anything that he has said."

"That," said Nina eagerly, "is just the way I feel toward Livy. She seems to me like a mine. When I was with her the longest, I always felt as if I had n't half seen her. She always made me hungry to know her more. I mean to read you some of her letters, some time. She writes beautiful letters; and I appreciate that very much because I can't do it. I can talk better than I can write. Somehow my ideas will not take a course down through my arms; they always will run up to my mouth. But you ought to see Livy; such people always make me very discontented with myself. I don't know what the reason is that I like to see superior people, and things, when they always make me realize what a poor concern I am. Now, the first time I heard Jenny Lind sing, it spoiled all my music and all my songs for me, — turned them all to trash at one stroke, — and yet I liked it. But I don't seem to have got any further in goodness than just dissatisfaction with myself."

"Well," said Clayton, "there's where the foundation-stone of all excellence is laid. The very first blessing that Christ pronounced was on those who were poor in spirit. The indispensable condition to all progress in art, science, or religion, is to feel that we have nothing."

"Do you know," said Nina, after something of a pause, "that I can't help wondering what you took up with me for? I have thought very often that you ought to have Livy Ray."

"Well, I'm much obliged to you," said Clayton, "for your consideration in providing for me. But supposing I should prefer my own choice, after all? We men are a little willful, sometimes, like you of the gentler sex."

"Well," said Nina, "if you will have the bad taste, then, to insist on liking me, let me warn you that you don't know what you are about. I'm a very unformed, unpractical person. I don't keep accounts. I'm nothing at all of a housekeeper. I shall leave open drawers, and scatter papers, and forget the day of the month, and tear the newspaper, and do everything else that is wicked; and then, one of these days, it will be, 'Nina, why haven't you done this? and why haven't you done that? and why don't you do the other? and why *do* you do something else?' Ah, I've heard you men talk before! And then, you see, I sha'n't like it, and I sha'n't behave well. Haven't the least hope of it; won't ever engage to! — So, now, won't you take warning?"

"No," said Clayton, looking at her with a curious kind of smile, "I don't think I shall."

"How dreadfully positive and self-willed men are!" said Nina, drawing a long breath, and pretending to laugh.

"There's so little of that in you ladies," said Clayton, "we have to do it for both."

"So, then," said Nina, looking round with a half-laugh and half-blush, "you will persist?"

"Yes, you wicked little witch!" said Clayton, "since you challenge me, I will." And as he spoke, he passed his arm round Nina firmly, and fixed his eyes on hers. "Come, now, my little Baltimore oriole, have I caught you?" And —

But we are making our chapter too long.

CHAPTER XXVI

THE visit of Clayton and his sister, like all other pleasant things, had its end. Clayton was called back to his law office and books, and Anne went to make some summer visits previous to her going to Clayton's plantation of Magnolia Grove, where she was to superintend his various schemes for the improvement of his negroes.

Although it was gravely insisted to the last that there was no engagement between Nina and Clayton, it became evident enough to all parties that only the name was wanting. The warmest possible friendship existed between Nina and Anne; and notwithstanding that Nina almost every day said something which crossed Anne's nicely adjusted views, and notwithstanding Anne had a gentle infusion of that disposition to sermonize which often exists in very excellent young ladies, still the two got on excellently well together.

It is to be confessed that, the week after they left, Nina was rather restless and lonesome, and troubled to pass her time. An incident, which we shall relate, however, gave her something to think of, and opens a new page in our story.

While sitting on the veranda, after breakfast, her attention was called by various exclamations from the negro department, on the right side of the mansion; and looking out, to her great surprise, she saw Milly standing amid a group, who were surrounding her with eager demonstrations. Immediately she ran down the steps to inquire

what it might mean. Approaching nearer, she was somewhat startled to see that her old friend had her head bound
up and her arm in a sling; and as she came towards her,
she observed that she seemed to walk with difficulty, with
a gait quite different from her usual firm, hilarious tread.

"Why, Milly!" she said, running towards her with
eagerness, "what is the matter?"

"Not much, chile, I reckon, now I's got home!" said
Milly.

"Well, but what's the matter with your arm?"

"No great! Dat ar man shot me; but, praise de Lord,
he did n't kill me! I don't owe him no grudge; but I
thought it was n't right and fit that I should be treated so;
and so I just *put!*"

"Why, come in the house this minute!" said Nina,
laying hold of her friend, and drawing her towards the
steps. "It's a shame! Come in, Milly, come in! That
man! I knew he was n't to be trusted. So, this is the
good place he found for you, is it?"

"Jes so," said Tomtit, who, at the head of a dark stream
of young juveniles, came after, with a towel hanging over
one arm, and a knife half cleaned in his hand, while Rose
and Old Hundred, and several others, followed to the
veranda.

"Laws-a-me!" said Aunt Rose, "just to think on 't!
Dat 's what 't is for old fam'lies to hire der niggers out to
common people!"

"Well," said Old Hundred, "Milly was allers too high
feelin'; held her head up too much. Ain't noways surprised at it!"

"Oh, go 'long, you old hominy-beetle!" said Aunt
Rose. "Don't know nobody dat holds up der head higher
nor you does!"

Nina, after having dismissed the special train of the
juveniles and servants, began to examine into the condition

of her friend.   The arm had evidently been grazed by a
bullet, producing somewhat of a deep flesh wound, which
had been aggravated by the heat of the weather and the
fatigue which she had undergone.   On removing the band-
age round her head, a number of deep and severe flesh
cuts were perceived.

"What's all this?" said Nina.

"It's whar he hit me over de head!   He was in drink,
chile; he didn't well know what he was 'bout!"

"What an abominable shame!" said Nina.   "Look
here," turning round to Aunt Nesbit, "see what comes of
hiring Milly out!"

"I am sure I don't know what's to be done!" said
Aunt Nesbit pitifully.

"Done! why, of course, these are to be bandaged and
put up, in the first place," said Nina, bustling about with
great promptness, tearing off bandages, and ringing for
warm water.   "Aunt Milly, I'll do them up for you
myself.   I'm a pretty good nurse, when I set about it."

"Bless you, chile, but it seems good to get home 'mong
friends!"

"Yes; and you won't go away again in a hurry!" said
Nina, as she proceeded rapidly with her undertaking, washing and bandaging the wound.   "There, now," she said,
"you look something like; and now you shall lie down in
my room, and take a little rest!"

"Thank ye, honey, chile, but I'll go to my own room;
'pears like it's more homelike," said Milly.   And Nina,
with her usual energy, waited on her there, closed the
blinds, and spread a shawl over her after she had lain
down, and after charging her two or three times to go to
sleep and be quiet, she left her.   She could hardly wait
to have her get through her nap, so full was she of the
matter, and so interested to learn the particulars of her
story.

"A pretty business, indeed!" she said to Aunt Nesbit. "We'll prosecute those people, and make them pay dear for it."

"That will be a great expense," said Aunt Nesbit apprehensively, "besides the loss of her time."

"Well," said Nina, "I shall write to Clayton about it directly. I know he'll feel just as I do. He understands the law, and all about those things, and he'll know how to manage it."

"Everything will make expense!" said Aunt Nesbit in a deplorable voice. "I'm sure misfortunes never come single! Now, if she don't go back, I shall lose her wages! And here's all the expenses of a lawsuit, besides! I think she ought to have been more careful."

"Why, aunt, for pity's sake, you don't pretend that you wish Milly to go back?"

"Oh no, of course I don't; but then, it's a pity. It will be a great loss, every way."

"Why, aunt, you really talk as if you didn't think of anything but your loss. You don't seem to think anything about what Milly has had to suffer!"

"Why, of course, I feel sorry for that," said Aunt Nesbit. "I wonder if she is going to be laid up long. I wish, on the whole, I had hired out one that wasn't quite so useful to me."

"Now, if that isn't just like her!" said Nina in an indignant tone, as she flung out of the room, and went to look softly in at Milly's door. "Never can see, hear, or think of anything but herself, no matter what happens! I wonder why Milly couldn't have belonged to me!"

After two or three hours' sleep, Milly came out of her room, seeming much better. A perfectly vigorous physical system, and vital powers all moving in the finest order, enabled her to endure much more than ordinary; and Nina soon became satisfied that no material injury had been sustained, and that in a few days she would be quite recovered.

"And now, Milly, do pray tell me where you have been," said Nina, "and what this is all about."

"Why, you see, honey, I was hired to Mr. Barker, and dey said 'he was a mighty nice man;' and so he was, honey, most times; but den, you see, honey, dere's some folks dere's two men in 'em, — one is a good one and t'oder is very bad. Well, dis yer was just dat sort. You see, honey, I wouldn't go for to say dat he got drunk; but he was dat sort dat if he took ever so little, it made him kind o' ugly and cross, and so dere wa'n't no suiting him. Well, his wife, she was pretty far; and so he was, too, 'cept in spots. He was one of dese yer streaked men, dat has drefful ugly streaks; and some of dem times de Lord only knows what he won't do! Well, you see, honey, I thought I was getting along right well, at first, and I was mighty pleased. But dere was one day he came home, and 'peared like dere couldn't nobody suit him. Well, you see, dey had a gal dere, and she had a chile, and dis yer chile was a little thing. It got playing with a little burnt stick, and it blacked one of his clean shirts, I had just hung up, — for I'd been ironing, you see. Just den he came along, and you never heerd a man go on so! I's heerd bad talk afore, but I never heerd no sich! He swore he'd kill de chile; and I thought my soul he would! De por little thing run behind me, and I just kep him off on it, 'cause I knowed he wa'n't fit to touch it; and den he turned on me, and he got a cowhide, and he beat me over de head. I thought my soul he'd kill me! But I got to de door, and shut de chile out, and Hannah, she took it and run with it. But, bless you, it 'peared like he was a tiger, — screeching, and foaming, and beating me! I broke away from him, and run. He just caught de rifle, — he always kep one loaded, — and shot at me, and de ball just struck my arm, and glanced off again. Bless de Lord, it did n't break it. Dat ar was a mighty close run, I can tell you! But I did run, 'cause, thinks I, dere ain't no safety for me in dat ar house; and, you see, I run till I got to de bush, and den I got to whar dere was some free colored folks, and dey did it up, and kep me a day or two. Den I started and came home, just as you told me to."

"Well," said Nina, "you did well to come home; and I tell you what, I 'm going to have that man prosecuted!"

"Oh, laws, no, Miss Nina! don't you goes doing nothing to him! His wife is a mighty nice woman, and 'peared like he did n't rightly know what he was 'bout."

"Yes, but, Milly, you ought to be willing, because it may make him more careful with other people."

"Laws, Miss Nina, why, dere is some sense in dat; but I would n't do it as bearing malice."

"Not at all," said Nina. "I shall write to Mr. Clayton, and take his advice about it."

"He 's a good man," said Milly. "He won't say nothing dat ain't right. I spect dat will do very well, dat ar way."

"Yes," said Nina, "such people must be taught that the law will take hold of them. That will bring them to their bearings!"

Nina went immediately to her room, and dispatched a long letter to Clayton, full of all the particulars, and begging his immediate assistance.

Our readers, those who have been in similar circumstances, will not wonder that Clayton saw in this letter an immediate call of duty to go to Canema. In fact, as soon as the letter could go to him, and he could perform a rapid horseback journey, he was once more a member of the domestic circle. He entered upon the case with great confidence and enthusiasm.

"It is a debt which we owe," he said, "to the character of our state, and to the purity of our institutions, to prove the efficiency of the law in behalf of that class of our population whose helplessness places them more particularly under our protection. They are to us in the condition of children under age; and any violation of their rights should be more particularly attended to."

He went immediately to the neighboring town, where Milly had been employed, and found, fortunately, that the principal facts had been subject to the inspection of white witnesses. A woman, who had been hired to do some sewing, had been in the next room during the whole time; and Milly's flight from the house, and the man's firing after her, had been observed by some workmen in the neighborhood. Everything, therefore, promised well, and the suit was entered forthwith.

CHAPTER XXVII

THE TRIAL

"WELL, now," said Frank Russel to one or two lawyers with whom he was sitting, in a side room of the court
house at E——, "look out for breakers! Clayton has
mounted his war-horse, and is coming upon us, now, like
leviathan from the rushes."

"Clayton is a good fellow," said one of them. "I like
him, though he does n't talk much."

"Good?" said Russel, taking his cigar from his mouth;
"why, as the backwoodsmen say, he ain't nothing else!
He is a great seventy-four pounder, charged to the muzzle
with goodness! But, if he should be once fired off, I 'm
afraid he 'll carry everything out of the world with him.
Because, you see, abstract goodness does n't suit our present
mortal condition. But it is a perfect godsend that he has
such a case as this to manage for his maiden plea, because
it just falls in with his heroic turn. Why, when I heard
of it, I assure you I bestirred myself. I went about, and
got Smithers and Jones and Peters to put off suits, so as
to give him fair field and full play. For, if he succeeds in
this, it may give him so good a conceit of the law, that
he will keep on with it."

"Why," said the other, "don't he like the law?
What 's the matter with the law?"

"Oh, nothing, only Clayton has got one of those ethereal
stomachs that rise against almost everything in this world.
Now, there is n't more than one case in a dozen that he 'll
undertake. He sticks and catches just like an old bureau

drawer. Some conscientious crick in his back is always taking him at a critical moment, and so he is knocked up for actual work. But this defending a slave-woman will suit him to a T."

"She is a nice creature, is n't she?" said one of them.

"And belongs to a good old family," said another.

"Yes," said the third, "and I understand his lady-love has something to do with the case."

"Yes," said Russel, "to be sure she has. The woman belongs to a family connection of hers, I'm told. Miss Gordon is a spicy little puss — one that would be apt to resent anything of that sort; and the Gordons are a very influential family. He is sure to get the case, though I'm not clear that the law is on his side, by any means."

"Not?" said the other barrister, who went by the name of Will Jones.

"No," said Russel. "In fact, I'm pretty clear it is n't. But that will make no odds. When Clayton is thoroughly waked up, he is a whole team, I can tell you. He'll take jury and judge along with him, fast enough."

"I wonder," said one, "that Barker did n't compound the matter."

"Oh, Barker is one of the stubbed sort. You know these middling kind of people always have a spite against old families. He makes fight because it is the Gordons, that's all. And there comes in his republicanism. He is n't going to be whipped in by the Gordons. Barker has got Scotch blood in him, and he'll hang on to the case like death."

"Clayton will make a good speech," said Jones.

"Speech? that he will!" said Russel. "Bless me, I could lay off a good speech on it, myself. Because, you see, it really was quite an outrage; and the woman is a presentable creature. And then, there's the humane dodge; that can be taken, beside all the chivalry part of

defending the helpless, and all that sort of thing. I
would n't ask for a better thing to work up into a speech.
But Clayton will do it better yet, because he is actually
sincere in it. And after all 's said and done, there 's a
good deal in that. When a fellow speaks in solemn earnest, he gives a kind of weight that you can't easily get
at any other way."

"Well, but," said one, "I don't understand you, Russel, why you think the law is n't on Clayton's side. I 'm
sure it 's a very clear case of terrible abuse."

"Oh, certainly it is," said Russel, "and the man is a
dolt, and a brute beast, and ought to be shot, and so forth;
but then, he has n't really exceeded his legal limits, because, you see, the law gives to the hirer all the rights of
the master. There 's no getting away from that, in my
opinion. Now, any master might have done all that, and
nobody could have done anything about it. They do do
it, for that matter, if they 're bad enough, and nobody
thinks of touching them."

"Well, I say," said Jones, "Russel, don't you think
that 's too bad?"

"Laws, yes, man; but the world is full of things that
are too bad. It 's a bad kind of a place," said Russel, as
he lit another cigar.

"Well, how do you think Clayton is going to succeed,"
said Jones, "if the law is so clearly against him?"

"Oh, bless you, you don't know Clayton. He is a
glorious mystifier. In the first place, he mystifies himself.
And now, you mark me. When a powerful fellow mystifies himself, so that he really gets himself thoroughly on
to his own side, there 's nobody he can't mystify. I speak
it in sober sadness, Jones, that the want of this faculty is
a great hindrance to me in a certain class of cases. You
see I can put on the pathetic and heroic, after a sort; but
I don't take myself along with me — I don't really believe

myself. There's the trouble. It's this power of self-mystification that makes what you call earnest men. If men saw the real bread and butter and green cheese of life, as I see it, — the hard, dry, primitive facts, — they could n't raise such commotions as they do."

"Russel, it always makes me uncomfortable to hear you talk. It seems as if you did n't believe in anything!"

"Oh yes, I do," said Russel; "I believe in the multiplication table, and several other things of that nature at the beginning of the arithmetic; and also, that the wicked will do wickedly. But as to Clayton's splendid abstractions, I only wish him joy of them. But then, I shall believe him while I hear him talk; so will you; so will all the rest of us. That's the fun of it. But the thing will be just where it was before, and I shall find it so when I wake up to-morrow morning. It's a pity such fellows as Clayton could n't be used as we use big guns. He is death on anything he fires at; and if he only would let me load and point him, he and I together would make a firm that would sweep the land. But here he comes, upon my word.

"Hallo, Clayton, all ready?"

"Yes," said Clayton, "I believe so. When will the case be called?"

"To-day, I'm pretty sure," said Russel.

Clayton was destined to have something of an audience in his first plea; for the Gordons being an influential and a largely connected family, there was quite an interest excited among them in the affair. Clayton also had many warm personal friends, and his father, mother, and sister were to be present; for though residing in a different part of the state, they were at this time on a visit in the vicinity of the town of E——.

There is something in the first essay of a young man, in any profession, like the first launching of a ship, which has a never-ceasing hold on human sympathies. Clayton's father, mother, and sister, with Nina, at the time of the dialogue we have given, were sitting together in the parlor of a friend's house in E——, discussing the same event.

"I am sure that he will get the case," said Anne Clayton, with the confidence of a generous woman and warm-hearted sister. "He has been showing me the course of his argument, and it is perfectly irresistible. Has he said anything to you about it, father?"

Judge Clayton had been walking up and down the room, with his hands behind him, with his usual air of considerate gravity. Stopping short at Anne's question, he said, "Edward's mind and mine work so differently, that I have not thought best to embarrass him by any conference on the subject. I consider the case an unfortunate one, and would rather he could have had some other."

"Why," said Anne eagerly, "don't you think he'll gain it?"

"Not if the case goes according to law," said Judge Clayton. "But then, Edward has a great deal of power of eloquence, and a good deal of skill in making a diversion from the main point; so that, perhaps, he may get the case."

"Why," said Nina, "I thought cases were always decided according to law! What else do they make laws for?"

"You are very innocent, my child," said Judge Clayton.

"But, father, the proof of the outrage is most abundant. Nobody could pretend to justify it."

"Nobody will, child. But that's nothing to the case. The simple point is, did the man exceed his legal power? It's my impression he did not."

"Father, what a horrible doctrine!" said Anne.

"I simply speak of what is," said Judge Clayton. "I don't pretend to justify it. But Edward has great power of exciting the feelings, and under the influence of his eloquence the case may go the other way, and humanity triumph at the expense of law."

Clayton's plea came on in the afternoon, and justified the expectations of his friends. His personal presence was good, his voice melodious, and his elocution fine. But what impressed his auditors, perhaps, more than these, was a certain elevation and clearness in the moral atmosphere around him, — a gravity and earnestness of conviction which gave a secret power to all he said. He took up the doctrine of the dependent relations of life, and of those rules by which they should be guided and restrained; and showed that while absolute power seems to be a necessary condition of many relations of life, both reason and common sense dictate certain limits to it. "The law guarantees to the parent, the guardian, and the master, the right of enforcing obedience by chastisement; and the reason for it is, that the subject being supposed to be imperfectly developed, his good will, on the whole, be better consulted by allowing to his lawful guardian this power.

"The good of the subject," he said, "is understood to be the foundation of the right; but when chastisement is inflicted without just cause, and in a manner so inconsiderate and brutal as to endanger the safety and well-being of the subject, the great foundation principle of the law is violated. The act becomes perfectly lawless, and as incapable of legal defense as it is abhorrent to every sentiment of humanity and justice.

"He should endeavor to show," he said, "by full testimony, that the case in question was one of this sort."

In examining witnesses Clayton showed great dignity and acuteness, and as the feeling of the court was already prepossessed in his favor, the cause evidently gathered strength as it went on. The testimony showed, in the most conclusive manner, the general excellence of Milly's character, and the utter brutality of the outrage which had been committed upon her. In his concluding remarks, Clayton addressed the jury in a tone of great elevation and solemnity, on the duty of those to whom is intrusted the guardianship of the helpless.

"No obligation," he said, "can be stronger to an honorable mind than the obligation of entire dependence. The fact that a human being has no refuge from our power, no appeal from our decisions, so far from leading to careless security, is one of the strongest possible motives to caution and to most exact care. The African race," he said, "had been bitter sufferers. Their history had been one of wrong and cruelty, painful to every honorable mind. We of the present day, who sustain the relation of slave-holder," he said, "receive from the hands of our fathers an awful trust. Irresponsible power is the greatest trial of humanity, and if we do not strictly guard our own moral purity in the use of it, we shall degenerate into despots and tyrants. No consideration can justify us in holding this people in slavery an hour, unless we make this slavery a guardian relation, in which our superior strength and intelligence are made the protector and educator of their simplicity and weakness.

"The eyes of the world are fastened upon us," he said. "Our continuing in this position at all is, in many quarters, matter of severe animadversion. Let us therefore show, by the spirit in which we administer our laws, by the impartiality with which we protect their rights, that the master of the helpless African is his best and truest friend."

It was evident, as Clayton spoke, that he carried the whole of his audience with him. The counsel on the other side felt himself much straitened. There is very little possibility of eloquence in defending a manifest act of tyranny and cruelty; and a man speaks, also, at great disadvantage, who not only is faint-hearted in his own cause, but feels the force of the whole surrounding atmosphere against him.

In fact, the result was, that the judge charged the jury, if they found the chastisement to have been disproportionate and cruel, to give verdict for the plaintiff. The jury, with little discussion, gave it unanimously, accordingly, and so Clayton's first cause was won.

If ever a woman feels proud of her lover, it is when she sees him as a successful public speaker; and Nina, when the case was over, stood half-laughing, half-blushing, in a circle of ladies, who alternately congratulated and rallied her on Clayton's triumph.

"Ah," said Frank Russel, "we understand the magic. The knight always fights well when his lady-love looks down! Miss Gordon must have the credit of this. She took all the strength out of the other side, — like the mountain of loadstone, that used to draw all the nails out of the ship."

"I am glad," said Judge Clayton, as he walked home with his wife, "I am very glad that Edward has met with such success. His nature is so fastidious that I have had my fears that he would not adhere to the law. There are many things in it, I grant, which would naturally offend a fastidious mind, and one which, like his, is always idealizing life."

"He has established a noble principle," said Mrs. Clayton.

"I wish he had," said the judge. "It would be a very ungrateful task, but I could have shattered his argument all to pieces."

"Don't tell him so!" said Mrs. Clayton apprehensively; "let him have the comfort of it."

"Certainly I shall. Edward is a good fellow, and I hope, after a while, he'll draw well in the harness."

Meanwhile, Frank Russel and Will Jones were walking along in another direction.

"Did n't I tell you so?" said Russel. "You see, Clayton run Bedford down, horse and foot, and made us all as solemn as a preparatory lecture."

"But he had a good argument," said Jones.

"To be sure he had — I never knew him to want that. He builds up splendid arguments, always, and the only thing to be said of him, after it 's all over, is, it is n't so; it 's no such thing. Barker is terrible wroth, I can assure you. He swears he 'll appeal the case. But that 's no matter. Clayton has had his day all the same. He is evidently waked up. Oh, he has no more objection to a little popularity than you and I have, now; and if we could humor him along, as we would a trout, we should have him a firstrate lawyer, one of these days. Did you see Miss Gordon while he was pleading? By George! she looked so handsome I was sorry I had n't taken her myself!"

"Is she that dashing little flirting Miss Gordon that I heard of in New York?"

"The very same."

"How came she to take a fancy to him?"

"She? How do I know? She 's as full of streaks as a tulip; and her liking for him is one of them. Did you notice her, Will? — scarf flying one way, and little curls and pennants and streamers and veil the other! And then, those eyes! She 's alive, every inch of her! She puts me in mind of a sweet-brier bush, winking and blinking full of dewdrops, full of roses, and brisk little thorns, beside! Ah, she 'll keep him awake!"

CHAPTER XXVIII

JUDGE CLAYTON was not mistaken in supposing that his son would contemplate the issue of the case he had defended with satisfaction. As we have already intimated, Clayton was somewhat averse to the practice of the law. Regard for the feelings of his father had led him to resolve that he would at least give it a fair trial. His own turn of mind would have led him to some work of more immediate and practical philanthropy. He would have much preferred to retire to his own estate, and devote himself, with his sister, to the education of his servants. But he felt that he could not, with due regard to his father's feelings, do this until he had given professional life a fair trial.

After the scene of the trial which we have described, he returned to his business, and Anne solicited Nina to accompany her for a few weeks to their plantation at Magnolia Grove, whither, as in duty bound, we may follow her.

Our readers will therefore be pleased to find themselves transported to the shady side of a veranda belonging to Clayton's establishment at Magnolia Grove. The place derived its name from a group of these beautiful trees, in the centre of which the house was situated. It was a long, low cottage, surrounded by deep verandas, festooned with an exuberance of those climbing plants which are so splendid in the southern latitude. The range of apartments which opened on the veranda where Anne and Nina were sitting was darkened to exclude the flies; but the doors, standing open, gave picture-like gleams of the interior. The white, matted floors, light bamboo furniture, couches covered with glazed white linen, and the large vases of roses disposed here and there, where the light would fall upon them, presented a background of inviting coolness.

It was early in the morning, and the two ladies were enjoying the luxury of a *tête-à-tête* breakfast before the sun had yet dried the heavy dews which give such freshness to the morning air. A small table which stood between them was spread with choice fruits, arranged on dishes in green leaves; a pitcher of iced milk, and a delicate little *tête-à-tête* coffee-service, dispensing the perfume of the most fragrant coffee. Nor were they wanting those small delicate biscuits, and some of those curious forms of corn-bread, of the manufacture of which every southern cook is so justly proud. Nor should we omit the central vase of monthly roses, of every shade of color, the daily arrangement of which was the special delight of Anne's brown little waiting-maid Lettice.

Anne Clayton, in a fresh white morning-wrapper, with her pure, healthy complexion, fine teeth, and frank, beaming smile, looked like a queenly damask rose. A queen she really was on her own plantation, reigning by the strongest of all powers, that of love. The African race have large ideality and veneration; and in no drawing-room could Anne's beauty and grace, her fine manners and carriage, secure a more appreciating and unlimited admiration and devotion. The negro race, with many of the faults of children, unite many of their most amiable qualities, in the simplicity and confidingness with which they yield themselves up in admiration of a superior friend.

Nina had been there but a day, yet could not fail to read in the eyes of all how absolute was the reign which Anne held over their affections.

"How delightful the smell of this magnolia blossom!" said Nina. "Oh, I 'm glad that you waked me so early, Anne!"

"Yes," said Anne, "in this climate early rising becomes a necessary of life to those who mean to have any real, positive pleasure in it, and I 'm one of the sort that must have *positive* pleasures. Merely negative rest, lassitude, and dreaming are not enough for me. I want to feel that I 'm alive, and that I accomplish something."

"Yes, I see," said Nina, "you are not nominally like me, but really housekeeper. What wonderful skill you seem to have! Is it possible that you keep nothing locked up here?"

"No," said Anne, "nothing. I am released from the power of the keys, thank fortune! When I first came here, everybody told me it was sheer madness to try such a thing. But I told them that I was determined to do it, and Edward upheld me in it: and you can see how well I 've succeeded."

"Indeed," said Nina, "you must have magic power, for I never saw a household move on so harmoniously. All your servants seem to think and contrive and take an interest in what they are doing. How did you begin? What did you do?"

"Well," said Anne, "I 'll tell you the history of the plantation. In the first place, it belonged to mamma's uncle; and not to spoil a story for a relation's sake, I must say he was a dissipated, unprincipled man. He lived a perfectly heathen life here, in the most shocking way you can imagine; and so the poor creatures who were under him were worse heathen than he. He lived with a quadroon woman, who was violent tempered, and when angry ferociously cruel; and so the servants were constantly passing from the extreme of indulgence to the extreme of cruelty. You can scarce have an idea of the

state we found them in. My heart almost failed me; but
Edward said, 'Don't give it up, Anne; try the good that
is in them.' Well, I confess, it seemed very much as it
seemed to me when I was once at a water-cure establishment, — patients would be brought in languid, pale, cold,
half dead, and it appeared as if it would kill them to apply
cold water; but, somehow or other, there was vital power
in them that reacted under it. Well, just so it was with
my servants. I called them all together, and I said to
them, 'Now, people have always said that you are the
greatest thieves in the world; that there is no managing
you except by locking up everything from you. But I
think differently. I have an idea that you can be trusted.
I have been telling people that they don't know how much
good there is in you; and now, just to show them what
you can do, I'm going to begin and leave the closets and
doors, and everything, unlocked, and I shall not watch
you. You can take my things, if you choose; and if,
after a time, I find that you can't be trusted, I shall go
back to the old way.' Well, my dear, I would n't have
believed myself that the thing would have answered so
well. In the first place, approbativeness is a stronger
principle with the African race than almost any other;
they like to be thought well of. Immediately there was
the greatest spirit in the house, for the poor creatures,
having suddenly made the discovery that somebody thought
they were to be trusted, were very anxious to keep up the
reputation. The elder ones watched the younger; and,
in fact, my dear, I had very little trouble. The children
at first troubled me going into my store-closet and getting
the cake, notwithstanding very spirited government on the
part of the mammies. So I called my family in session
again, and said that their conduct had confirmed my good
opinion; that I always knew they could be 'trusted, and
that my friends were astonished to hear how well they

did; but that I had observed that some of the children probably had taken my cake. 'Now, you know,' said I, 'that I have no objection to your having some. If any of you would enjoy a piece of cake, I shall be happy to give it to them, but it is not agreeable to have things in my closet fingered over — I shall therefore set a plate of cake out every day, and anybody that wishes to take some I hope will take that.' Well, my dear, my plate of cake stood there and dried. You won't believe me, but in fact it was n't touched."

"Well," said Nina, "I should n't think you could have had our Tomtit here! Why, really this goes beyond the virtue of white children."

"My dear, it is n't such a luxury to white children to be thought well of, and have a character. You must take that into account. It was a taste of a new kind of pleasure, made attractive by its novelty."

"Yes," said Nina, "I have something in me which makes me feel this would be the right way. I know it would be with me. There's nothing like confidence. If a person trusts me, I'm bound."

"Yet," said Anne, "I can't get the ladies of my acquaintance to believe in it. They see how I get along, but they insist upon it that it's some secret magic, or art, of mine."

"Well, it is so," said Nina. "Such things are just like the divining rod; they won't work in every hand; it takes a real, generous, warm-hearted woman, like you, Anne. But, could you carry your system through your plantation, as well as your house?"

"The field-hands were more difficult to manage, on some accounts," said Anne, "but the same principle prevailed with them. Edward tried all he could to awaken self-respect. Now, I counseled that we should endeavor to form some decent habits before we built the cabins over.

I told him they could not appreciate cleanliness and order.
' Very likely they cannot,' he said, ' but we are not to suppose it;' and he gave orders immediately for that pretty
row of cottages you saw down at the quarters. He put
up a large bathing-establishment. Yet he did not enforce
at first personal cleanliness by strict rules. Those who
began to improve first were encouraged and noticed; and
as they found this a passport to favor, the thing took rapidly. It required a great while to teach them how to be
consistently orderly and cleanly even after the first desire
had been awakened, because it is n't every one that likes
neatness and order who has the forethought and skill
to secure it. But there has been a steady progress in
these respects. One curious peculiarity of Edward's management gives rise to a good many droll scenes. He has
instituted a sort of jury trial among them. There are
certain rules for the order and well-being of the plantation, which all agree to abide by; and in all offenses the
man is tried by a jury of his peers. Mr. Smith, our agent,
says that these scenes are sometimes very diverting, but
on the whole there 's a good deal of shrewdness and sense
manifested; but he says that, in general, they incline much
more to severity than he would. You see, the poor creatures have been so barbarized by the way they have been
treated in past times, that it has made them hard and
harsh. I assure you, Nina, I never appreciated the wisdom of God, in the laws which he made for the Jews in
the wilderness, as I have since I 've tried the experiment
myself of trying to bring a set of slaves out of barbarism.
Now, this that I 'm telling you is the fairest side of the
story. I can't begin to tell you the thousand difficulties
and trials which we have encountered in it. Sometimes
I 've been almost worn out and discouraged. But then,
I think, if there is a missionary work in this world, it is
this."

"And what do your neighbors think about it?" said Nina.

"Well," said Anne, "they are all very polite, well-bred people, the families with whom we associate; and such people, of course, would never think of interfering, or expressing a difference of opinion, in any very open way; but I have the impression that they regard it with suspicion. They sometimes let fall words which make me think they do. It's a way of proceeding which very few would adopt, because it is not a money-making operation, by any means. The plantation barely pays for itself, because Edward makes that quite a secondary consideration. The thing which excites the most murmuring is our teaching them to read. I teach the children myself two hours every day, because I think this would be less likely to be an offense than if I should hire a teacher. Mr. Smith teaches any of the grown men who are willing to take the trouble to learn. Any man who performs a certain amount of labor can secure to himself two or three hours a day to spend as he chooses; and many do choose to learn. Some of the men and the women have become quite good readers, and Clayton is constantly sending books for them. This, I'm afraid, gives great offense. It is against the law to do it; but as unjust laws are sometimes lived down, we thought we would test the practicability of doing this. There was some complaint made of our servants, because they have not the servile, subdued air which commonly marks the slave, but look, speak, and act, as if they respected themselves. I'm sometimes afraid that we shall have trouble; but then, I hope for the best."

"What does Mr. Clayton expect to be the end of all this?" said Nina.

"Why," said Anne, "I think Edward has an idea that one of these days they may be emancipated on the soil, just as the serfs were in England. It looks to me rather hopeless, I must say; but he says the best way is for some one to begin and set an example of what ought to be done, and he hopes that in time it will be generally followed. It would, if all men were like him; but there lies my doubt. The number of those who would pursue such a disinterested course is very small. But who comes there? Upon my word, if there is n't my particular admirer, Mr. Bradshaw!"

As Anne said this, a very gentlemanly middle-aged man came up on horseback, on the carriage-drive which passed in front of the veranda. He bore in his hand a large bunch of different-colored roses; and alighting, and delivering his horse to his servant, came up the steps and presented it to Anne.

"There," said he, "are the firstfruits of my roses, in the garden that I started in Rosedale."

"Beautiful," said Anne, taking them. "Allow me to present to you Miss Gordon."

"Miss Gordon, your most obedient," said Mr. Bradshaw, bowing obsequiously.

"You are just in season, Mr. Bradshaw," said Anne, "for I 'm sure you could n't have had your breakfast before you started; so sit down and help us with ours."

"Thank you, Miss Anne," said Mr. Bradshaw, "the offer is too tempting to be refused." And he soon established himself as a third at the little table, and made himself very sociable.

"Well, Miss Anne, how do all your plans proceed — all your benevolences and cares? I hope your angel ministrations don't exhaust you."

"Not at all, Mr. Bradshaw; do I look like it?"

"No, indeed! but such energy is perfectly astonishing to us all."

Nina's practiced eye observed that Mr. Bradshaw had that particular nervous, restless air which belongs to a man who is charged with a particular message, and finds himself unexpectedly blockaded by the presence of a third person. So, after breakfast, exclaiming that she had left her crochet-needle in her apartment, and resisting Anne's offer to send a servant for it, by declaring that nobody could find it but herself, she left the veranda. Mr. Bradshaw had been an old family friend for many years, and stood with Anne almost on the easy footing of a relation, which gave him the liberty of speaking with freedom. The moment the door of the parlor was closed after Nina, he drew a chair near to Anne, and sat down, with the unmistakable air of a man who is going into a confidential communication.

"The fact is, my dear Miss Clayton," he said, "I have something on my mind that I want to tell you; and I hope you will think my long friendship for the family a sufficient warrant for my speaking on matters which really belong chiefly to yourself. The fact is, my dear Miss Clayton, I was at a small dinner-party of gentlemen, the other day, at Colonel Grandon's. There was a little select set there, you know, — the Howards, and the Elliotts, and the Howlands, and so on, — and the conversation happened to turn upon your brother. Now, there was the very greatest respect for him; they seemed to have the highest possible regard for his motives; but still they felt that he was going on a very dangerous course."

"Dangerous?" said Anne a little startled.

"Yes, really dangerous; and I think so myself, though I, perhaps, don't feel as strongly as some do."

"Really," said Anne, "I'm quite at a loss!"

"My dear Miss Anne, it's these improvements, you know, which you are making. Don't misapprehend me! Admirable, very admirable, in themselves, — done from the most charming of motives, Miss Anne, — but dangerous, dangerous!"

The solemn, mysterious manner in which these last words were pronounced made Anne laugh; but when she saw the expression of real concern on the face of her good friend, she checked herself, and said, —

"Pray, explain yourself. I don't understand you."

"Why, Miss Anne, it's just here. We appreciate your humanity, and your self-denial, and your indulgence to your servants. Everybody is of opinion that it's admirable. You are really quite a model for us all. But when it comes to teaching them to read and write, Miss Anne," he said, lowering his voice, "I think you don't consider what a dangerous weapon you are putting into their hands. The knowledge will spread on to the other plantations; bright niggers will pick it up; for the very fellows who are most dangerous are the very ones who will be sure to learn."

"What if they should?" said Anne.

"Why, my dear Miss Anne," said he, lowering his voice, "the facilities that it will afford them for combinations, for insurrections! You see, Miss Anne, I read a story once of a man who made a cork leg with such wonderful accuracy that it would walk of itself, and when he got it on he couldn't stop its walking — it walked him to death — actually did! Walked him up hill and down dale, till the poor man fell down exhausted; and then it ran off with his body. And it's running with its skeleton to this day, I believe."

And good-natured Mr. Bradshaw conceived such a ridiculous idea, at this stage of his narrative, that he leaned back in his chair and laughed heartily, wiping his perspiring face with a cambric pocket-handkerchief.

"Really, Mr. Bradshaw, it's a very amusing idea, but I don't see the analogy," said Anne.

"Why, don't you see? You begin teaching niggers, and having reading and writing, and all these things, going on, and they begin to open their eyes, and look round and think; and they are having opinions of their own, they won't take yours; and they want to rise directly. And if they can't rise, why, they are all discontented; and there's the what's-his-name to pay with them! Then come conspiracies and insurrections, no matter how well you treat them; and now, we South Carolinians have had experience in this matter. You must excuse us, but it is a terrible subject with us. Why, the leaders of that conspiracy, all of them, were fellows who could read and write, and who had nothing in the world to wish for, in the way of comfort, treated with every consideration by their masters. It is a most melancholy chapter in human nature. It shows that there is no trust to be placed in them. And now, the best way to get along with negroes, in my opinion, is to make them happy; give them plenty to eat and drink and wear, and keep them amused and excited, and don't work them too hard. I think it's a great deal better than this kind of exciting instruction. Mind," he said, seeing that Anne was going to interrupt him, "mind, now, I'd have religious instruction, of course. Now, this system of oral instruction, teaching them hymns and passages of Scripture suited to their peculiar condition, it's just the thing; it isn't so liable to these dangers. I hope you'll excuse me, Miss Anne, but the gentlemen really feel very serious about these things; they find it's affecting their own negroes. You know, somehow everything goes round from one plantation to another; and one of them said that he had a very smart man who is married to one of your women, and he actually found him with a spelling-book, sitting out under a tree. He said if the man had had a rifle he couldn't have been more alarmed; because the man was just one of those sharp, resolute fellows, that, if he knew how to read and write, there's no knowing what he would do. Well, now, you see how it is. He takes the spelling-book away, and he tells him he will give him

nine-and-thirty if he ever finds him with it again. What's
the consequence? Why, the consequence is, the man
sulks and gets ugly, and he has to sell him. That's the
way it's operating."

"Well, then," said Anne, looking somewhat puzzled,
"I will strictly forbid our people to allow spelling-books
to go out of their hands, or to communicate any of these
things off of the plantation."

"Oh, I tell you, Miss Anne, you can't do it. You
don't know the passion in human nature for anything that
is forbidden. Now, I believe it's more that than love of
reading. You can't shut up such an experiment as you
are making here. It's just like a fire. It will blaze; it
will catch on all the plantations round; and I assure you
it's matter of life and death with us. You smile, Miss
Anne, but it's so."

"Really, my dear Mr. Bradshaw, you could not have
addressed me on a more unpleasant subject. I am sorry
to excite the apprehension of our neighbors; but " —

"Give me leave to remind you, also, Miss Anne, that
the teaching of slaves to read and write is an offense to
which a severe penalty is attached by the laws."

"I thought," said Anne, "that such barbarous laws were
a dead letter in a Christian community, and that the best
tribute I could pay to its Christianity was practically to
disregard them."

"By no means, Miss Anne, by no means! Why, look
at us here in South Carolina. The negroes are three to
one over the whites now. Will it do to give them the
further advantages of education and facilities of communication? You see, at once, it will not. Now, well-bred
people, of course, are extremely averse to mingling in the
affairs of other families; and had you merely taught a few
favorites, in a private way, as I believe people now and
then do, it wouldn't have seemed so bad; but to have

regular provision for teaching school, and school hours —
I think, Miss Anne, you'll find it will result in unpleasant
consequences."

"Yes, I fancy," said Anne, raising herself up, and
slightly coloring, "that I see myself in the penitentiary
for the sin and crime of teaching children to read! I
think, Mr. Bradshaw, it is time such laws were disregarded. Is not that the only way in which many laws are
repealed? Society outgrows them, people disregard them,
and so they fall away, like the calyx from some of my
flowers. Come, now, Mr. Bradshaw, come with me to
my school. I'm going to call it together," said Anne,
rising, and beginning to go down the veranda steps.
"Certainly, my dear friend, you ought not to judge without seeing. Wait a moment, till I call Miss Gordon."

And Anne stepped across the shady parlor, and in a few
moments reappeared with Nina, both arrayed in white
cape-bonnets. They crossed to the right of the house, to
a small cluster of neat cottages, each one of which had its
little vegetable garden, and its plot in front, carefully
tended, with flowers. They passed onward into a grove
of magnolias which skirted the back of the house, till they
came to a little building, with the external appearance of
a small Grecian temple, the pillars of which were festooned
with jessamine.

"Pray what pretty little place is this?" said Mr. Bradshaw.

"This is my schoolroom," said Anne.

Mr. Bradshaw repressed a whistle of astonishment; but
the emotion was plainly legible in his face, and Anne said,
laughing, —

"A lady's schoolroom, you know, should be lady-like.
Besides, I wish to inspire ideas of taste, refinement, and
self-respect in these children. I wish learning to be associated with the idea of elegance and beauty."

They ascended the steps, and entered a large room, surrounded on three sides by blackboards. The floor was covered with white matting, and the walls hung with very pretty pictures of French lithographs, tastefully colored. In some places cards were hung up, bearing quotations of Scripture. There were rows of neat desks, before each of which there was a little chair.

Anne stepped to the door and rang a bell, and in about ten minutes the patter of innumerable little feet was heard ascending the steps, and presently they came streaming in — all ages, from four or five to fifteen and from the ebony complexion of the negro, with its closely curling wool, to the rich brown cheek of the quadroon, with melancholy, lustrous eyes and waving hair. All were dressed alike, in a neat uniform of some kind of blue stuff, with white capes and aprons.

They filed in to the tune of one of those marked rhythmical melodies which characterize the negro music, and moving in exact time to the singing, assumed their seats, which were arranged with regard to their age and size. As soon as they were seated, Anne, after a moment's pause, clapped her hands, and the whole school commenced a morning hymn, in four parts, which was sung so beautifully that Mr. Bradshaw, quite overpowered, stood with tears in his eyes. Anne nodded at Nina, and cast on him a satisfied glance.

After that there was a rapid review of the classes. There was reading, spelling, writing on the blackboard, and the smaller ones were formed in groups in two adjoining apartments, under the care of some of the older girls. Anne walked about superintending the whole; and Nina, who saw the scene for the first time, could not repress her exclamation of delight. The scholars were evidently animated by the presence of company, and anxious to do credit to the school and teacher, and the two hours passed

rapidly away. Anne exhibited to Mr. Bradshaw specimens of the proficiency of her scholars in handwriting,
and the drawing of maps, and even the copying of small
lithograph cards, which contained a series of simple draw-
ing-patterns. Mr. Bradshaw seemed filled with astonishment.

"'Pon my word," said he, "these are surprising! Miss
Anne, you are a veritable magician — a worker of miracles!
You must have found Aaron's rod, again! My dear
madam, you run the risk of being burned for a witch!"

"Very few, Mr. Bradshaw, know how much of beauty
lies sealed up in this neglected race," said Anne, with
enthusiasm.

As they were walking back to the house, Mr. Bradshaw
fell a little behind, and his face wore a thoughtful and
almost sad expression.

"Well," said Anne, looking round, "a penny for your
thoughts!"

"Oh, I see, Miss Anne, you are for pursuing your
advantage. I see triumph in your eyes. But yet," he
added, "after all this display, the capability of your children makes me feel sad. To what end is it? What purpose will it serve, except to unfit them for their inevitable
condition — to make them discontented and unhappy?"

"Well," replied Anne, "there ought to be no inevitable
condition that makes it necessary to dwarf a human mind.
Any condition which makes a full development of the
powers that God has given us a misfortune cannot, certainly, be a healthy one — cannot be right. If a mind
will grow and rise, make way and let it. Make room for
it, and cut down everything that stands in the way!"

"That's terribly leveling doctrine, Miss Anne."

"Let it level, then!" said Anne. "I don't care! I
come from the old Virginia Cavalier blood, and am not
afraid of anything."

"But, Miss Anne, how do you account for it that the best-educated and best-treated slaves — in fact, as you say, the most perfectly developed human beings — were those who got up the insurrection in Charleston?"

"How do you account for it," said Anne, "that the best-developed and finest specimens of men have been those that have got up insurrections in Italy, Austria, and Hungary?"

"Well, you admit, then," said Mr. Bradshaw, "that if you say A in this matter, you 've got to say B?"

"Certainly," said Anne, "and when the time comes to say B I 'm ready to say it. I admit, Mr. Bradshaw, it 's a very dangerous thing to get up steam, if you don't intend to let the boat go. But when the steam is high enough, let her go, say I."

"Yes, but, Miss Anne, other people don't want to say so. The fact is, we are not all of us ready to let the boat go. It 's got all our property in it — all we have to live on. If you are willing yourself, so far as your people are concerned, they 'll inevitably want liberty, and you say you 'll be ready to give it to them; but your fires will raise a steam on our plantations, and we must shut down these escape-valves. Don't you see? Now, for my part, I 've been perfectly charmed with this school of yours; but, after all, I can't help inquiring whereto it will grow."

"Well, Mr. Bradshaw," said Anne, "I 'm obliged to you for the frankness of this conversation. It 's very friendly and sincere. I think, however, I shall continue to compliment the good sense and gallantry of this state, by ignoring its unworthy and unchristian laws. I will endeavor, nevertheless, to be more careful and guarded as to the manner of what I do; but if I should be put into the penitentiary, Mr. Bradshaw, I hope you 'll call on me."

"Miss Anne, I beg ten thousand pardons for that unfortunate allusion."

"I think," said Anne, "I shall impose it as a penance

upon you to stay and spend the day with us, and then I 'll
show you my rose-garden. I have great counsel to hold
with you on the training of a certain pillar-rose. You see,
my design is to get you involved in my treason. You 've
already come into complicity with it, by visiting my school."

"Thank you, Miss Anne; I should be only too much
honored to be your abettor in any treason you might medi-
tate. But, really, I 'm a most unlucky dog! Think of
my having four bachelor friends engaged to dine with me,
and so being obliged to decline your tempting offer! In fact,
I must take horse before the sun gets any hotter."

"There he goes, for a good-hearted creature as he is!"
said Anne.

"Do you know," said Nina, laughing, "that I thought
that he was some poor desperate mortal who was on the
verge of a proposal, this morning, and I ran away like a
good girl to give him a fair field?"

"Child," said Anne, "you are altogether too late in the
day. Mr. Bradshaw and I walked that little figure some
time ago, and now he is one of the most convenient and
agreeable of friends."

"Anne, why in the world don't you get in love with
somebody?" said Nina.

"My dear, I think there was something or other left out
when I was made up," said Anne, laughing, "but I never
had much of a fancy for the lords of creation. They do
tolerably well till they come to be lovers; but then they
are perfectly unbearable. Lions in love, my dear, don't
appear to advantage, you know. I can't marry papa or
Edward, and they have spoiled me for everybody else.
Besides, I 'm happy, and what do I want of any of
them? Can't there be now and then a woman sufficient
to herself? But, Nina, dear, I 'm sorry that our affairs
here are giving offense and making uneasiness."

"For my part," said Nina, "I should go right on. I

have noticed that people try all they can to stop a person who is taking an unusual course; and when they are perfectly certain that they can't stop him, then they turn round and fall in with him; and I think that will be the case with you."

"They certainly will have an opportunity of trying," said Anne. "But there is Dulcimer coming up the avenue with the letter-bag. Now, child, I don't believe you appreciate half my excellence, when you consider that I used to have all these letters that fall to you every mail."

At this moment Dulcimer rode up to the veranda steps, and deposited the letter-bag in Anne's hands.

"What an odd name you have given him!" said Nina, "and what a comical-looking fellow he is! He has a sort of waggish air that reminds me of a crow."

"Oh, Dulcimer don't belong to our régime," said Anne. "He was the prime minister and favorite under the former reign, — a sort of licensed court jester, — and to this day he hardly knows how to do anything but sing and dance; and so brother, who is for allowing the largest liberty to everybody, imposes on him only such general and light tasks as suit his roving nature. But there!" she said throwing a letter on Nina's lap, and at the same time breaking the seal of one directed to herself. "Ah, I thought so! You see, puss, Edward has some law business that takes him to this part of the state forthwith. Was ever such convenient law business? We may look for him to-night. Now there will be rejoicings! How now, Dulcimer? I thought you had gone," she said, looking up, and observing that personage still lingering in the shade of a tulip-tree near the veranda.

"Please, Miss Anne, is Master Clayton coming home to-night?"

"Yes, Dulcimer; so now go and spread the news; for that's what you want, I know."

And Dulcimer, needing no second suggestion, was out of sight in the shrubbery in a few moments.

"Now, I'll wager," said Anne, "that creature will get up something or other extraordinary for this evening."

"Such as what?" said Nina.

"Well, he is something of a troubadour, and I should n't wonder if he should be cudgeling his brain at this moment for a song. We shall have some kind of operatic performance, you may be sure."

CHAPTER XXIX

THE TROUBADOUR

ABOUT five o'clock in the evening Nina and Anne amused themselves with setting a fancy tea-table on the veranda. Nina had gathered a quantity of the leaves of the live-oak which she possessed a particular faculty of plaiting in long, flat wreaths, and with these she garlanded the social round table, after it had been draped in its snowy damask, while Anne was busy arranging fruit in dishes with vine leaves.

"Lettice will be in despair to-night," said Anne, looking up and smiling at a neatly dressed brown mulatto girl, who stood looking on with large lustrous eyes; "her occupation 's gone!"

"Oh, Lettice must allow me to show my accomplishments," said Nina. "There are some household arts that I have quite a talent for. If I had lived in what's-its-name there, that they used to tell about in old times — Arcadia — I should have made a good housekeeper; for nothing suits me better than making wreaths, and arranging bouquets. My nature is dressy. I want to dress everything. I want to dress tables and dress vases, and adorn dishes, and dress handsome women, Anne! So look out for yourself, for when I have done crowning the table, I shall crown you!"

As Nina talked, she was flitting hither and thither, taking up and laying down flowers and leaves, shaking out long sprays, and fluttering from place to place, like a bird.

"It's a pity," said Anne, "that life can't be all Arcadia!"

"Oh yes!" said Nina. "When I was a child, I remember there was an old torn translation of a book called Gesner's Idyls, that used to lie about the house; and I used to read in it most charming little stories about handsome shepherds, dressed in white, playing on silver and ivory flutes; and shepherdesses, with azure mantles and floating hair; and people living on such delightful things as cool curds and milk and grapes and strawberries and peaches; and there was no labor, and no trouble, and no dirt, and no care. Everybody lived like the flowers and the birds, — growing and singing and being beautiful. Ah, dear, I have never got over wanting it since! Why couldn't it be so?"

"It's a thousand pities!" said Anne. "But what constant fight we have to maintain for order and beauty!"

"Yes," said Nina; "and, what seems worse, beauty itself becomes dirt in a day. Now, these roses that we are arranging, to-morrow or next day we shall call them litter, and wish somebody would sweep them out of the way. But I never want to be the one to do that. I want some one to carry away the withered flowers and wash the soiled vases; but I want to be the one to cut the fresh roses every day. If I were in an association, I should take that for my part. I'd arrange all their flowers through the establishment, but I should stipulate expressly that I should do no clearing up."

"Well," said Anne, "it's really a mystery to me what a constant downward tendency there is to everything — how everything is gravitating back as you may say into disorder. Now, I think a cleanly, sweet, tasteful house, and, above all, table, are among the highest works of art. And yet, how everything attacks you when you set out to attain it — flies, cockroaches, ants, mosquitoes! And then, it seems to be the fate of all human beings, that they are constantly wearing out and disarranging and destroying all that is about them."

"Yes," said Nina, "I could n't help thinking of that when we were at the camp-meeting. The first day I was perfectly charmed. Everything was so fresh, so cool, so dewy and sweet; but by the end of the second day they had thrown egg-shells and pea-pods and melon-rinds and all sorts of abominations around among the tents, and it was really shocking to contemplate."

"How disgusting!" said Anne.

"Now, I'm one of that sort," said Nina, "that love order dearly, but don't want the trouble of it myself. My prime minister, Aunt Katy, thanks to mamma, is an excellent hand to keep it, and I encourage her in it with all my heart; so that any part of the house where *I* don't go much is in beautiful order. But, bless me, I should have to be made over again before I could do like Aunt Nesbit! Did you ever see her take a pair of gloves or a collar out of a drawer? She gets up, and walks *so* moderately across the room, takes the key from under the napkin on the right-hand side of the bureau, and unlocks the drawer as gravely as though she was going to offer a sacrifice. Then, if her gloves are at the back side, underneath something else, she takes out one thing after another so moderately; and then, when the gloves or collar are found, lays everything back exactly where it was before, locks the drawer, and puts the key back under the towel. And all this she'd do if anybody was dying, and she had to go for the doctor! The consequence is, that her room, her drawers, and everything are a standing sermon to me. But I think I've got to be a much calmer person than I am before this will come to pass in my case. I'm always in such a breeze and flutter! I fly to my drawer and scatter things into little whirlwinds; ribbons, scarf, flowers —

everything flies out in a perfect rainbow. It seems as if
I should die if I did n't get the thing I wanted that minute; and after two or three such attacks on a drawer, then
comes repentance, and a long time of rolling up and arranging, and talking to little naughty Nina, who always promises herself to keep better order in future. But, my dear,
she does n't do it, I 'm sorry to say, as yet, though perhaps
there are hopes of her in future. Tell me, Anne, — you are
not stiff and *poky*, and yet you seem to be endowed with
the gift of order. How did it come about ? "

"It was not natural to me, I assure you," said Anne.
"It was a second nature, drilled into me by mamma."

"Mamma! ah, indeed!" said Nina, giving a sigh.
"Then you are very happy! But, come now, Lettice,
I 've done with all these; take them away. My tea-table
has risen out of them like the world out of chaos," she
said, as she swept together a heap of rejected vines, leaves,
and flowers. "Ah! I always have a repenting turn, when
I 've done arranging vases, to think I 've picked so many
more than were necessary! The poor flowers droop their
leaves and look at me reproachfully, as if they said, ' You
did n't want us — why could n't you have left us alone ? ' "

"Oh," said Anne, "Lettice will relieve you of that.
She has great talents in the floral line, and out of these she
will arrange quantities of bouquets," she said, as Lettice,
blushing perceptibly through her brown skin, stooped and
swept up the rejected flowers into her apron.

"What have we here ? " said Anne, as Dulcimer, attired
with most unusual care, came bowing up the steps, presenting a note on a waiter. "Dear me, how stylish! gilt-edged
paper smelling of myrrh and ambergris!" she continued, as
she broke the seal. "What 's this?

"' The Magnolia Grove troubadours request the presence
of Mr. and Miss Clayton and Miss Gordon at an operatic

performance, which will be given this evening at eight o'clock, in the grove.'

"Very well done! I fancy some of my scholars have been busy with the writing. Dulcimer, we shall be happy to come."

"Where upon earth did he pick up those phrases?" said Nina, when he had departed.

"Oh," said Anne, "I told you that he was prime favorite of the former proprietor, who used to take him with him wherever he traveled, as people sometimes will a pet monkey; and, I dare say, he has lounged round the lobbies of many an opera house. I told you that he was going to get up something."

"What a delightful creature he must be!" said Nina.

"Perhaps so, to you," said Anne; "but he is a troublesome person to manage. He is as wholly destitute of any moral organs as a jackdaw. One sometimes questions whether these creatures have any more than a reflected mimicry of a human soul — such as the German stories imagine in kobolds and water-spirits. All I can see in Dulcimer is a kind of fun-loving animal. He don't seem to have any moral nature."

"Perhaps," said Nina, "his moral nature is something like the cypress-vine seeds which I planted three months ago, and which have just come up."

"Well, I believe Edward expects to see it along, one of these days," said Anne. "His faith in human nature is unbounded. I think it one of his foibles, for my part; but yet I try to have hopes of Dulcimer, that some day or other he will have some glimmering perceptions of the difference between a lie and the truth, and between his own things and other people's. At present, he is the most lawless marauder on the place. He has been so used to having his wit to cover a multitude of sins, that it's difficult for a scolding to make any impression on him. But, hark! is n't that a horse? Somebody is coming up the avenue."

Both listened.

"There are two," said Nina.

Just at this instant Clayton emerged to view accompanied by another rider, who, on nearer view, turned out to be Frank Russel. At the same instant, the sound of violins and banjos was heard, and, to Anne's surprise, a gayly dressed procession of servants and children began to file out from the grove, headed by Dulcimer and several of his associates, playing and singing.

"There," said Anne, "did n't I tell you so. There's the beginning of Dulcimer's operations."

The air was one of those inexpressibly odd ones whose sharp, metallic accuracy of rhythm seems to mark the delight which the negro race feel in that particular element of music. The words, as usual, amounted to very little. Nina and Anne could hear, —

> " Oh, I see de mas'r a-comin' up de track,
> His horse's heels do clatter, with a clack, clack, clack!"

The idea conveyed in these lines being still further carried out by the regular clapping of hands at every accented note, while every voice joined in the chorus: —

> " Sing, boys, sing; de mas'r is come!
> Give three cheers for de good man at home!
> Ho! he! ho! Hurra! hurra!"

Clayton acknowledged the compliment as he came up, by bowing from his horse; and the procession arranged itself in a kind of lane, through which he and his companion rode up to the veranda.

" 'Pon my word," said Frank Russel, "I was n't prepared for such a demonstration. Quite a presidential reception!"

When Clayton came to the steps and dismounted, a dozen

sprang eagerly forward to take his horse, and in the crowding round for a word of recognition the order of the procession was entirely broken. After many kind words, and inquiries in every direction for a few moments, the people quietly retired, leaving their master to his own enjoyments.

"You really have made quite a triumphal entry," said Nina.

"Dulcimer always exhausts himself on all such occasions," said Anne, "so that he is n't capable of any further virtue for two or three weeks."

"Well, take him while he is in flower, then!" said Russel. "But how perfectly cool and inviting you look. Really, quite idyllic! We must certainly have got into a fairy queen's castle!"

"But you must show us somewhere to shake the dust off of our feet," said Clayton.

"Yes," said Anne, "there's Aunt Praw waiting to show you your room. Go and make yourselves as fascinating as you can."

In a little while the gentlemen returned, in fresh white linen suits, and the business of the tea-table proceeded with alacrity.

"Well, now," said Anne, after tea, looking at her watch, "I must inform the company that we are all engaged to the opera this evening."

"Yes," said Nina, "the Magnolia Grove Opera House is to be opened, and the Magnolia Troubadour Troupe to appear for the first time."

At this moment they were surprised by the appearance, below the veranda, of Dulcimer, with three of his colored associates, all wearing white ribbons in their buttonholes, and carrying white wands tied with satin ribbon, and gravely arranging themselves two and two on each side of the steps.

"Why, Dulcimer, what's this?" said Clayton.

Dulcimer bowed with the gravity of a raven, and announced that the committee had come to wait on the gentlemen and ladies to their seats.

"Oh," said Anne, "we were not prepared for our part of the play!"

"What a pity I did n't bring my opera-hat!" said Nina. "Never mind," she said, snatching a spray of multiflora rose, "this will do." And she gave it one twist round her head, and her toilet was complete.

"'Pon my word, that's soon done!" said Frank Russel, as he watched the coronet of half-opened buds and roses.

"Yes," said Nina. "Sit down, Anne; I forgot your crown. There, wait a moment; let me turn this leaf a little, and weave these buds in here — so. Now you are a Baltimore belle, to be sure! Now for the procession."

The opera house for the evening was an open space in the grove behind the house. Lamps had been hung up in the trees, twinkling on the glossy foliage. A sort of booth or arbor was built of flowers and leaves at one end, to which the party were marshaled in great state. Between two magnolia-trees a white curtain was hung up; and the moment the family party made their appearance, a chorus of voices from behind the scenes began an animated song of welcome.

As soon as the party was seated the curtain rose, and the chorus, consisting of about thirty of the best singers, males and females, came forward, dressed in their best holiday costume, singing, and keeping step as they sung, and bearing in their hands bouquets, which, as they marched round the circle, they threw at the feet of the company. A wreath of orange-blossoms was significantly directed at Nina, and fell right into her lap.

"These people seem to have had their eyes open. Coming events cast their shadows before!" said Russel.

After walking around, the chorus seated themselves at the

side of the area, and the space behind was filled up with a
dense sea of heads — all the servants and plantation hands.

"I declare," said Russel, looking round on the crowd
of dark faces, "this sable cloud is turning a silver lining
with a witness! How neat and pretty that row of children
looks!" And as they spoke, a procession of the children
of Anne's school came filing round in the same manner that
the other had done, singing their school songs, and casting
flowers before the company. After this, they seated
themselves on low seats in front of all the others.

Dulcimer and four of his companions now came into the
centre.

"There," said Anne, "Dulcimer is going to be the
centre-piece. He is the troubadour."

Dulcimer, in fact, commenced a kind of recitative, to
the tune "Mas'r 's in the cold, cold ground." After singing a few lines, the quartette took up the chorus, and their
voices were really magnificent.

"Why," said Nina, "it seems to me they are beginning
in a very doleful way."

"Oh," said Anne, "wait a minute. This is the old
mas'r, I fancy. We shall soon hear the tune changed."

And accordingly, Dulcimer, striking into a new tune,
began to rehearse the coming in of a new master.

"There," said Anne, "now for a catalogue of Edward's
virtues! They must all be got in, rhyme or no rhyme."

Dulcimer kept on rehearsing. Every four lines the quartette struck in with the chorus, which was then repeated
by the whole company, clapping their hands and stamping
their feet to the time, with great vivacity.

"Now, Anne, is coming your turn," said Nina, as Dulcimer launched out, in most high-flown strains, on the
beauty of Miss Anne.

"Yes," said Clayton, "the catalogue of your virtues will
be something extensive."

"I shall escape, at any rate," said Nina.

"Don't you be too sure," said Anne. "Dulcimer has had his eye on you ever since you 've been here."

And true enough, after the next stanza, Dulcimer assumed a peculiarly meaning expression.

"There," said Anne, "do see the wretch flirting himself out like a saucy crow! It 's coming! Now look out, Nina!"

With a waggish expression from the corner of his downcast eyes, he sung: —

> " Oh, mas'r is often absent — do you know where he goes ?
> He goes to North Carolina, for de North Carolina rose."

"There you are!" said Frank Russel. "Do you see the grin going round? What a lot of ivory! They are coming in this chorus, strong!"

And the whole assembly, with great animation, poured out on the chorus: —

> " Oh, de North Carolina rose!
> Oh, de North Carolina rose!
> We wish good luck to mas'r,
> With de North Carolina rose!"

This chorus was repeated with enthusiasm, clapping of hands, and laughing.

"I think the North Carolina rose ought to rise!" said Russel.

"Oh, hush!" said Anne; "Dulcimer has n't done yet."

Assuming an attitude, Dulcimer turned and sang to one of his associates in the quartette: —

> " Oh, I see two stars arising,
> Up in de shady skies!"

To which the other responded, with animation: —

> " No, boy, you are mistaken;
> 'T is de light of her fair eyes!"

"That 's *thorough*, at any rate!" said Russel.

While Dulcimer went on: —

> " Oh, I see two roses blowing,
> Togeder on one bed!"

And the other responded: —

> "No, boy, you are mistaken;
> Dem are her cheeks so red!"

"And they are getting redder!" said Anne, tapping Nina with her fan. "Dulcimer is evidently laying out his strength upon you, Nina!"

Dulcimer went on singing: —

> "Oh, I see a grapevine running,
> With its curly rings, up dere!"

And the response: —

> "No, boy, you are mistaken;
> 'T is her rings of curly hair!"

And the quartette here struck up: —

> "Oh, she walks on de veranda,
> And she laughs out of de door,
> And she dances like de sunshine
> Across de parlor floor.
> Her little feet, dey patter,
> Like de rain upon de flowers;
> And her laugh is like sweet waters,
> Through all de summer hours!"

"Dulcimer has had help from some of the muses along there!" said Clayton, looking at Anne.

"Hush!" said Anne; "hear the chorus."

> "Oh, de North Carolina rose!
> Oh, de North Carolina rose!
> Oh, plant by our veranda
> De North Carolina rose!"

This chorus was repeated with three times three, and the whole assembly broke into a general laugh, when the performers bowed and retired, and the white sheet, which was fastened by a pulley to the limb of a tree, was let down again.

"Come, now, Anne, confess that was n't all Dulcimer's work!" said Clayton.

"Well, to tell the truth," said Anne, "'t was got up between him and Lettice, who has a natural turn for versifying, quite extraordinary. If I chose to encourage and push her on, she might turn out a second Phillis Wheatley."

Dulcimer and his coadjutors now came round, bearing trays with lemonade, cake, sliced pineapples, and some other fruits.

"Well, on my word," said Russel, "this is quite prettily got up!"

"Oh, I think," said Clayton, "the African race evidently are made to excel in that department which lies between the sensuous and the intellectual — what we call the elegant arts. These require rich and abundant animal nature, such as they possess; and if ever they become highly civilized, they will excel in music, dancing, and elocution."

"I have often noticed," said Anne, "in my scholars, how readily they seize upon anything which pertains to the department of music and language. The negroes are sometimes laughed at for mispronouncing words, which they will do in a very droll manner; but it's only because they are so taken with the sounds of words that they will try to pronounce beyond the sphere of their understanding, like bright children."

"Some of these voices here are perfectly splendid," said Russel.

"Yes," said Anne, "we have one or two girls on the place who have that rich contralto voice which, I think, is oftener to be found among them than among whites."

"The Ethiopian race is a slow-growing plant, like the aloe," said Clayton; "but I hope, some of these days, they'll come into flower; and I think, if they ever do, the blossoming will be gorgeous."

"That will do for a poet's expectation," said Russel.

The performance now gave place to a regular dancing-party, which went on with great animation, yet decorum.

"Religious people," said Clayton, "who have instructed the negroes, I think have wasted a great deal of their energy in persuading them to give up dancing and singing songs. I try to regulate the propensity. There is no use in trying to make the negroes into Anglo-Saxons any more than making a grapevine into a pear-tree. I train the grapevine."

"Behold," said Russel, "the successful champion of negro rights!"

"Not so very successful," said Clayton. "I suppose you've heard my case has been appealed; so that my victory isn't so certain, after all."

"Oh," said Nina, "yes, it must be! I'm sure no person of common sense would decide any other way; and your own father is one of the judges, too."

"That will only make him the more careful not to be influenced in my favor," said Clayton.

The dancing now broke up, and the servants dispersed in an orderly manner, and the company returned to the veranda, which lay pleasantly checkered with the light of the moon falling through trailing vines. The air was full of those occasional pulsations of fragrance which rise in the evening from flowers.

"Oh, how delightful," said Nina, "this fragrance of the honeysuckles! I have a perfect passion for perfumes! They seem to me like spirits in the air."

"Yes," said Clayton, "Lord Bacon says, 'that the breath of flowers comes and goes in the air, like the warbling of music.'"

"Did Lord Bacon say that?" said Nina in a tone of surprise.

"Yes; why not?" said Clayton.

"Oh, I thought he was one of those musty old philosophers who never thought of anything pretty!"

"Well," said Clayton, "then to-morrow let me read you

his essay on gardens, and you 'll find musty old philosophers often do think of pretty things."

"It was Lord Bacon," said Anne, "who always wanted musicians playing in the next room while he was composing."

"He did?" said Nina. "Why, how delightful of him! I think I should like to hear some of his essays."

"There are some minds," said Clayton, "large enough to take in everything. Such men can talk as prettily of a ring on a lady's finger as they can wisely on the courses of the planets. Nothing escapes them."

"That's the kind of man you ought to have for a lover, Anne," said Nina, laughing; "you have weight enough to risk it. I 'm such a little whisk of thistledown that it would annihilate me. Such a ponderous weight of wisdom attached to me would drag me under water, and drown me. I should let go my line, I think, if I felt such a fish bite."

"You are tolerably safe in our times," said Clayton. "Nature only sends such men once in a century or two. They are the road-makers for the rest of the world. They are quarry-masters, that quarry out marble enough for a generation to work up."

"Well," said Nina, "I should n't want to be a quarry-master's wife. I should be afraid that some of his blocks would fall on me."

"Why, would n't you like it, if he were wholly your slave?" said Frank Russel. "It would be like having the genius of the lamp at your feet."

"Ah," said Nina, "if I could keep him my slave; but I 'm afraid he 'd outwit me at last. Such a man would soon put *me* up on a shelf for a book read through. I 've seen some great men, — I mean great for our times, — and they did n't seem to care half as much for their wives as they did for a newspaper."

"Oh," said Anne, "that 's past praying for, with any

husband. The newspaper is the standing rival of the American lady. It must be a warm lover that can be attracted from *that*, even before he is secure of his prize."

"You are severe, Miss Anne," said Russel.

"She only speaks the truth. You men are a bad set," said Nina. "You are a kind of necessary evil, half civilized at best. But if ever I set up an establishment, I shall insist upon taking precedence of the newspaper."

CHAPTER XXX

WOULD the limits of our story admit of it, we should gladly linger many days in the shady precincts of Magnolia Grove, where Clayton and Nina remained some days longer, and where the hours flew by on flowery feet; but the inevitable time and tide, which wait for no man, wait not for the narrator. We must therefore say, in brief, that when the visit was concluded Clayton accompanied Nina once more to Canema, and returned to the circle of his own duties.

Nina returned to her own estate, with views somewhat chastened and modified by her acquaintance with Anne. As Clayton supposed, the influence of a real noble purpose in life had proved of more weight than exhortations, and she began to feel within herself positive aspirations for some more noble and worthy life than she had heretofore led. That great, absorbing feeling which determines the whole destiny of woman's existence is in its own nature an elevating and purifying one. It is such even when placed on an unworthy object, and much more so when the object is a worthy one. Since the first of their friendship, Clayton had never officiously sought to interfere with the growth and development of Nina's moral nature. He had sufficient sagacity to perceive that, unconsciously to herself, a deeper power of feeling, and a wider range of thought, was opening within her; and he left the development of it to the same quiet forces which swell the rosebud and guide the climbing path of the vine. Simply and

absolutely he lived his own life before her, and let hers
alone; and the power of his life therefore became absolute.

A few mornings after her return, she thought that she
would go out and inquire after the welfare of our old friend
Tiff.   It was a hazy, warm, bright summer morning, and
all things lay in that dreamy stillness, that trance of volup-
tuous rest, which precedes the approach of the fiercer heats
of the day.   Since her absence there had been evident
improvement in Tiff's affairs.   The baby, a hearty, handsome little fellow, by dint of good nursing, pork-sucking,
and lying outdoors in the tending of breezes and zephyrs,
had grown to be a creeping creature, and followed Tiff
around, in his garden ministrations, with unintelligible
chatterings of delight.

At the moment when Nina rode up Tiff was busy with
his morning work in the garden.   His appearance, it is to
be confessed, was somewhat peculiar.   He usually wore,
in compliment to his nursing duties, an apron in front;
but as his various avocations pressed hard upon his time,
and as his own personal outfit was ever the last to be
attended to, Tiff's nether garments had shown traces of
that frailty which is incident to all human things.

"Bress me," he said to himself, that morning, as he
with difficulty engineered his way into them, "holes here,
and holes dar!   Don't want but two holes in my breeches,
and I's got two dozen!   Got my foot through de wrong
place!   Por old Tiff!   Laws-a-massy! wish I could get
hold of some of dem dar clothes dey were telling 'bout at
de camp-meeting, dey wore forty years in de wilderness!
'Mazing handy dem ar times was!   Well, anyhow, I'll
tie an apron behind, and another in front.   Bress de
Lord, I's got aprons, anyhow!   I must make up a par of
breeches, some of dese yer days, when de baby's teeth is
all through, and Teddy's clothes don't want no mending,
and de washing is done, and dese yer weeds stops a-grow-

ing in de garden. Bress if I know what de Lord want of so many weeds 'Pears like dey comes just to plague us; but den, we does n't know. Maybe dere 's some good in 'em. We does n't know but a leetle, noway."

Tiff was sitting on the ground weeding one of his garden-beds, when he was surprised by the apparition of Nina on horseback coming up to the gate. Here was a dilemma, to be sure! No cavalier had a more absolute conception of the nature of politeness, and the claims of beauty, rank, and fashion, than Tiff. Then, to be caught sitting on the ground, with a blue apron on in front and a red one on behind, was an appalling dilemma! However, as our readers may have discovered, Tiff had that essential requisite of good breeding, the moral courage to face an exigency; and wisely considering that a want of cordiality is a greater deficiency than the want of costume, he rose up, without delay, and hastened to the gate to acknowledge the honor.

"Lord bress yer sweet face, Miss Nina!" he said, while the breezes flapped and fluttered his red and blue sails, "Old Tiff 's 'mazin' happy to see you. Miss Fanny 's well, thank ye; and Mas'r Teddy and the baby all doing nicely. Bress de Lord, Miss Nina, be so good as to get down and come in. I 's got some nice berries dat I picked in de swamp, and Miss Fanny 'll be proud to have you take some. You see," he said, laughing heartily, and regarding his peculiar costume, "I was n't looking for any quality long dis yer time o' day, so I just got on my old clothes."

"Why, Uncle Tiff, I think they become you immensely!" said Nina. "Your outfit is really original and picturesque. You 're not one of the people that are ashamed of their work, are you, Uncle Tiff? So if you just lead my horse to that stump, I 'll get down."

"Laws, no, Miss Nina!" said Tiff, as with alacrity he obeyed her orders. "Spects, if Old Tiff was 'shamed of work, he'd have a heap to be 'shamed of; 'cause it's pretty much all work with him. 'T is so!"

"Tomtit pretended to come with me," said Nina, as she looked round; "but he lagged behind by the brook to get some of those green grapes, and I suspect it's the last I shall see of him. So, Tiff, if you please to tie Sylphine in the shade, I'll go in to see Miss Fanny."

And Nina tripped lightly up the walk, now bordered on either side by china asters and marigolds, to where Fanny was standing bashfully in the door waiting for her. In her own native woods this child was one of the boldest, freest, and happiest of romps. There was scarce an eligible tree which she could not climb, or a thicket she had not explored. She was familiar with every flower, every bird, every butterfly, of the vicinity. She knew precisely when every kind of fruit would ripen, and flower would blossom; and was so *au fait* in the language of birds and squirrels, that she might almost have been considered one of the fraternity. Her only companion and attendant, Old Tiff, had that quaint, fanciful, grotesque nature which is the furthest possible removed from vulgarity; and his frequent lectures on proprieties and conventionalities, his long and prolix narrations of her ancestral glories and distinctions, had succeeded in infusing into her a sort of childish consciousness of dignity, while at the same time it inspired her with a bashful awe of those whom she saw surrounded with the actual insignia and circumstances of position and fortune. After all, Tiff's method of education, instinctive as it was, was highly philosophical, since a certain degree of self-respect is the nurse of many virtues, and a shield from many temptations. There is also something, perhaps, in the influence of descent. Fanny certainly inherited from her mother a more delicate organization than generally attends her apparent station in life. She had, also, what perhaps belongs to the sex, a capability of receiving the

mysteries and proprieties of dress; and Nina, as she stood
on the threshold of the single low room, could not but be
struck with the general air of refinement which characterized both it and its little mistress.   There were flowers
from the swamps and hedges arranged with care and taste;
feathers of birds, strings of eggs of different colors, dried
grasses, and various little woodland curiosities, which
showed a taste refined by daily intercourse with nature.
Fanny herself was arrayed in a very pretty print dress,
which her father had brought home in a recent visit, with
a cape of white muslin.   Her brown hair was brushed
smoothly from her forehead, and her clear blue eyes, and
fair, rosy complexion, gave her a pleasing air of intelligence and refinement.

"Thank you," said Nina, as Fanny offered her the only
chair the establishment afforded; "but I'm going with Tiff
out in the garden.   I never can bear to be in the house
such days as this.   You didn't expect me over so early,
Uncle Tiff; but I took a notable turn, this morning, and
routed them up to an early breakfast, on purpose that I
might have time to get over here before the heat came on.
It's pleasant out here, now the shadow of the woods falls
across the garden so.   How beautifully those trees wave!
Tiff, go on with your work — never mind me."

"Yes, Miss Nina, it's mighty pleasant.   Why, I was
out in dis yer garden at four o'clock dis morning, and
'peared like dese yer trees was waving like a psalm, so sort
o' still, you know!   Kind o' spreading out der hands like
dey'd have prayers; and dere was a mighty handsome star
a-looking down.   I spects dat ar star is one of de very
oldest families up dar."

"Most likely," said Nina cheerily.   "They call it Venus,
the star of love, Uncle Tiff; and I believe that is a very
old family."

"Love is a mighty good ting, anyhow," said Tiff.

"Lord bress you, Miss Nina, it makes everyting go kind o' easy. Sometimes, when I'm studding upon dese yer tings, I says to myself, 'pears like de trees in de wood, dey loves each oder. Dey stands kind o' locking arms so, and dey kind o' nod der heads, and whispers so! 'Pears like de grapevines, and de birds, and all dem ar tings, dey lives comfortable togeder, like dey was peaceable, and liked each oder. Now, folks is apt to get a-stewin' and a-frettin' round, and turning up der noses at dis yer ting, and dat ar; but 'pears like de Lord's works takes everyting mighty easy. Dey just kind o' lives along peaceable. I tink it's mighty 'structive!"

"Certainly it is," said Nina. "Old Mother Nature is an excellent manager, and always goes on making the best of everything."

"Dere's heaps done dat ar way, and no noise," said Tiff. "Why, Miss Nina, I studies upon dat ar out here in my garden. Why, look at dat ar corn, way up over your head, now! All dat ar growed dis yer summer. No noise 'bout it — 'pears like nobody could n't see when 't was done. Dey were telling us in camp-meeting how de Lord created de heaven and de earth. Now, Miss Nina, Tiff has his own thoughts, you know; and Tiff says 'pears like de Lord is creating de heaven and de earth all de time. 'Pears like you can see Him a-doing of it right afore your face; and dem growing tings are so curus! Miss Nina, 'pears for all de world like as if dey was critters! 'Pears like each of 'em has der own way, and won't go no oder! Dese yer beans, dey will come up so curus right top o' de stalks; dey will turn round de pole one way, and if you was to tie 'em, you could n't make 'em go round t'oder! Dey's set in der own way — dey is, for all dey's so still 'bout it! Laws, Miss Nina, dese yer tings makes Tiff laugh — does so!" he said, sitting down, and indulging in one of his fits of merriment.

"You are quite a philosopher, Tiff," said Nina.

"Laws, Miss Nina, I hopes not!" said Tiff solemnly; "'cause one of de preachers at de camp-meeting used up dem folk terrible, I tell you! Dat ar pretty much all I could make out of de sermon, dat people must n't be 'loso-phers! Laws, Miss Nina, I hope I ain't no sich!"

"Oh, I mean the good kind, Uncle Tiff. But how were you pleased, upon the whole, at the camp-meeting?" said Nina.

"Well," said Tiff, "Miss Nina, I hope I got something — I don't know fa'rly how much 't is. But, Miss Nina, it 'pears like as if you had come out here to instruct us 'bout dese yer tings. Miss Fanny, she don't read very well yet, and 'pears like if you could read us some out of de Bible, and teach us how to be Christians" —

"Why, Tiff, I scarcely know how myself!" said Nina. "I'll send Milly to talk to you. She is a real good Chris-tian."

"Milly is a very nice woman," said Tiff, somewhat doubtfully; "but, Miss Nina, 'pears like I would rather have white teaching; 'pears like I would rather have you, if it would n't be too much trouble."

"Oh no, Uncle Tiff! If you want to hear me read, I'll read to you now," said Nina. "Have you got a Bible, here? Stay; I'll sit down. I'll take the chair and sit down in the shade, and then you need n't stop your work."

Tiff hurried into the house to call Fanny; produced a copy of a Testament, which, with much coaxing, he had persuaded Cripps to bring on his last visit; and while Fanny sat at her feet making larkspur rings, Nina turned over the pages, to think what to read. When she saw Tiff's earnest and eager attention, her heart smote her to think that the book so valuable in his eyes was to her almost an unread volume.

"What shall I read to you, Tiff? What do you want to hear?"

"Well, I wants to find out de shortest way I ken, how dese yer chil'en 's to be got to heaven!" said Tiff. "Dis yer world is mighty well long as it holds out; but den, yer see, it don't last forever! Tings is passing away!"

Nina thought a moment. The great question of questions, so earnestly proposed to her! The simple, childlike old soul hanging confidingly on her answer! At last she said, with a seriousness quite unusual with her: —

"Tiff, I think the best thing I can do is to read to you about our Saviour. He came down into this world to show us the way to heaven. And I'll read you, when I come here days, all that there is about Him — all He said and did; and then, perhaps, you'll see the way yourself. Perhaps," she added, with a sigh, "I shall, too!"

As she spoke, a sudden breeze of air shook the clusters of a prairie rose, which was climbing into the tree under which she was sitting, and a shower of rose leaves fell around her.

"Yes," she said to herself, as the rose leaves fell on her book, "it's quite true, what he says. Everything is passing!"

And now, amid the murmur of the pine-trees, and the rustling of the garden vines, came on the ear of the listeners the first words of that sweet and ancient story: —

"Now, when Jesus was born in Bethlehem of Judea, in the days of Herod the King, behold there came wise men from the East, saying, ' Where is *He* that is born King of the Jews? For we have seen his star in the East, and are come to worship Him.' "

Probably more cultivated minds would have checked the progress of the legend by a thousand questions, statistical and geographical, as to where Jerusalem was, and who the wise men were, and how far the East was from Jerusalem, and whether it was probable they would travel so far. But Nina was reading to children, and to an old child-man, in whose grotesque and fanciful nature there was yet treasured a believing sweetness, like the amulets supposed to belong to the good genii of the fairy tales. The quick fancy of her auditors made reality of the story as it went along. A cloudy Jerusalem built itself up immediately in their souls, and became as well known to them as the neighboring town of E——. Herod, the king, became a real walking personage in their minds, with a crown on his head. And Tiff immediately discerned a resemblance between him and a certain domineering old General Eaton, who used greatly to withstand the cause of virtue, and the Peytons, in the neighborhood where he was brought up. Tiff's indignation, when the slaughter of the innocents was narrated, was perfectly outrageous. He declared he wouldn't have believed that of King Herod, bad as he was! and good hearted and inoffensive as Tiff was in general, it really seemed to afford him comfort "dat de debil had got dat ar man 'fore now."

"Sarves him right, too!" said Tiff, striking fiercely at a weed with his hoe. "Killing all dem por little chil'en! Why, what harm had dey done him, anyway? Wonder what he thought of hisself!"

Nina found it necessary to tranquillize the good creature, to get a hearing for the rest of the story. She went on reading of the wild night-journey of the wise men, and how the star went before them till it stood over the place where the child was. How they went in, and saw the young child, and Mary his mother, and fell down before him, offering gifts of gold, frankincense, and myrrh.

"Lord bless you! I wish I'd 'a' been dar!" said Tiff. "And dat ar chile was de Lord of glory, sure 'nough, Miss Nina! I hearn 'em sing dis yer hymn at de camp-meeting — you know, 'bout cold on his cradle. You know it goes dis yer way." And Tiff sung, to a kind of rocking lullaby, words whose poetic imagery had hit his fancy before he knew their meaning.

> "Cold on his cradle the dewdrops are shining,
> Low lies his head with the beasts of the stall;
> Angels adore, in slumber reclining,
> Maker, and Saviour, and Monarch of all."

Nina had never realized, till she felt it in the undoubting faith of her listeners, the wild, exquisite poetry of that legend, which, like an immortal lily, blooms in the heart of Christianity as spotless and as tender now as eighteen hundred years ago. That child of Bethlehem, when afterwards he taught in Galilee, spoke of seed which fell into a good and honest heart; and words could not have been more descriptive of the nature which was now receiving this seed of paradise.

When Nina had finished her reading, she found her own heart touched by the effect which she had produced. The nursing, child-loving Old Tiff was ready, in a moment, to bow before his Redeemer, enshrined in the form of an infant; and it seemed as if the air around him had been made sacred by the sweetness of the story.

As Nina was mounting her horse to return, Tiff brought out a little basket full of wild raspberries.

"Tiff wants to give you something," he said.

"Thank you, Uncle Tiff. How delightful! Now, if you 'll only give me a cluster of your Michigan rose!"

Proud and happy was Tiff, and pulling down the very topmost cluster of his rose, he presented it to her. Alas! before Nina reached home, it hung drooping from the heat.

"The grass withereth, and the flower fadeth; but the word of our God shall stand forever."

CHAPTER XXXI

In life organized as it is at the South there are two currents: one, the current of the master's fortunes, feelings, and hopes; the other, that of the slave's. It is a melancholy fact in the history of the human race, as yet, that there have been multitudes who follow the triumphal march of life only as captives, to whom the voice of the trumpet, the waving of the banners, the shouts of the people, only add to the bitterness of inthrallment.

While life to Nina was daily unfolding in brighter colors, the slave-brother at her side was destined to feel an additional burden on his already unhappy lot.

It was toward evening, after having completed his daily cares, that he went to the post-office for the family letters. Among these, one was directed to himself, and he slowly perused it as he rode home through the woods. It was as follows: —

My dear Brother, — I told you how comfortably we were living on our place — I and my children. Since then, everything has been changed. Mr. Tom Gordon came here and put in a suit for the estate, and attached me and my children as slaves. He is a dreadful man. The case has been tried and gone against us. The judge said that both deeds of emancipation — both the one executed in Ohio and the one here — were of no effect; that my boy was a slave, and could no more hold property than a mule before a plough. I had some good friends here, and people pitied me very much; but nobody could help me. Tom Gordon is a bad man — a *very* bad man. I cannot tell you all that he said to me. I only tell you that I will kill myself and my children before we will be his slaves. Harry, I have been free, and I know what liberty is. My children have been brought up free, and if I can help it they never shall know what slavery is. I have got away, and am hiding with a colored family here in Natchez. I hope to get to Cincinnati, where I have friends.

My dear brother, I did hope to do something for you. Now I cannot. Nor can you do anything for me. The law is on the side of our oppressors; but I hope God will help us. Farewell! Your affectionate

SISTER.

It is difficult to fathom the feelings of a person brought up in a position so wholly unnatural as that of Harry. The feelings which had been cultivated in him by education, and the indulgence of his nominal possessors, were those of an honorable and gentlemanly man. His position was absolutely that of the common slave, without one legal claim to anything on earth, one legal right of protection in any relation of life. What any man of strong nature would feel on hearing such tidings from a sister, Harry felt.

In a moment there rose up before his mind the picture of Nina in all her happiness and buoyancy — in all the fortunate accessories in her lot. Had the vague thoughts which crowded on his mind been expressed in words, they might have been something like these: —

"I have two sisters, daughters of one father, both beautiful, both amiable and good; but one has rank, and position, and wealth, and ease, and pleasure; the other is an outcast, unprotected, given up to the brutal violence of a vile and wicked man. She has been a good wife, and a

good mother.   Her husband has done all he could to save
her; but the cruel hand of the law grasps her and her
children, and hurls them back into the abyss from which
it was his life-study to raise them.   And I can do nothing!
I am not even a man!   And this curse is on me, and on
my wife, and on my children and children's children, forever!   Yes, what does the judge say in this letter?   ' He
can no more own anything than the mule before his
plough!'   That's to be the fate of every child of mine!
And yet people say, ' You have all you want; why are
you not happy?'   I wish they could try it!   Do they
think broadcloth coats and gold watches can comfort a man
for all this?"

Harry rode along, with his hands clenched upon the
letter, the reins drooping from the horse's neck, in the
same unfrequented path where he had twice before met
Dred.   Looking up, he saw him the third time, standing
silently, as if he had risen from the ground.

"Where did you come from?" said he.   "Seems to me
you are always at hand when anything is going against
me!"

"Went not my spirit with thee?" said Dred.   "Have
I not seen it all?   It is because we *will* bear this that we
have it to bear, Harry."

"But," said Harry, "what can we do?"

"Do?   What does the wild horse do?   Launch out our
hoofs! rear up, and come down on them!   What does the
rattlesnake do?   Lie in their path, and bite!   Why did
they make slaves of us?   They tried the wild Indians first.
Why did n't they keep to them?   They would n't be
slaves, and we will!   They that will bear the yoke may
bear it!"

"But," said Harry, "Dred, this is all utterly hopeless.
Without any means, or combination, or leaders, we should
only rush on to our own destruction."

"Let us die, then!" said Dred. "What if we do die? What great matter is that? If they bruise our head, we can sting their heels! Nat Turner — they killed him; but the fear of him almost drove them to set free their slaves! Yes, it was argued among them. They came within two or three votes of it in their assembly. A little more fear, and they would have done it. If my father had succeeded, the slaves in Carolina would be free to-day. Die? — Why not die? Christ was crucified! Has everything dropped out of you, that you can't die — that you 'll crawl like worms, for the sake of living?"

"I 'm not afraid of death myself," said Harry. "God knows I would n't care if I did die; but" —

"Yes, I know," said Dred. "She that letteth will let, till she be taken out of the way. I tell you, Harry, there 's a seal been loosed — there 's a vial poured out on the air; and the destroying angel standeth over Jerusalem, with his sword drawn!"

"What do you mean by that?" said Harry.

Dred stood silent for a moment; his frame assumed the rigid tension of a cataleptic state, and his voice sounded like that of a person speaking from a distance, yet there was a strange distinctness in it.

"The words of the prophet, and the vision that he hath from the Lord, when he saw the vision, falling into a trance, and having his eyes open, and behold he saw a roll flying through the heavens, and it was written, within and without, with mourning and lamentation and woe! Behold, it cometh! Behold, the slain of the Lord shall be many! They shall fall in the house and by the way! The bride shall fall in her chamber, and the child shall die in its cradle! There shall be a cry in the land of Egypt, for there shall not be a house where there is not one dead!"

"Dred! Dred! Dred!" said Harry, pushing him by the

shoulder; "come out of this—come out! It's frightful!"

Dred stood looking before him, with his head inclined
forward, his hand upraised, and his eyes strained, with the
air of one who is trying to make out something through
a thick fog. "I see her!" he said. "Who is that by
her? His back is turned. Ah! I see—it is he! And
there's Harry and Milly! Try hard—try! You won't
do it. No, no use sending for the doctor. There's not
one to be had. They are all too busy. Rub her hands!
Yes. But—it's no good. 'Whom the Lord loveth he
taketh away from the evil to come.' Lay her down. Yes,
it is Death! Death! Death!"

Harry had often seen the strange moods of Dred, and he
shuddered now, because he partook somewhat in the common superstitions, which prevailed among the slaves, of
his prophetic power. He shook and called him; but he
turned slowly away, and with eyes that seemed to see
nothing, yet guiding himself with his usual dextrous agility, he plunged again into the thickness of the swamp, and
was soon lost to view.

After his return home it was with the sensation of chill
at his heart that he heard Aunt Nesbit reading to Nina
portions of a letter, describing the march through some
northern cities of the cholera, which was then making fearful havoc on our American shore. "Nobody seems to
know how to manage it," the letter said; "physicians are
all at a loss. It seems to spurn all laws. It bursts upon
cities like a thunderbolt, scatters desolation and death, and
is gone with equal rapidity. People rise in the morning
well, and are buried before evening. In one day houses
are swept of a whole family."

"Ah," said Harry to himself, "I see the meaning now,
but what does it portend to us?"

How the strange foreshadowing had risen to the mind

of Dred we shall not say. Whether there be mysterious electric sympathies which, floating through the air, bear dim presentiments on their wings, or whether some stray piece of intelligence had dropped on his ear, and been interpreted by the burning fervor of his soul, we know not. The news, however, left very little immediate impression on the daily circle at Canema. It was a dread reality in the far distance. Harry only pondered it with anxious fear.

CHAPTER XXXII

THE MORNING STAR

NINA continued her visits to Tiff's garden on almost every pleasant morning or evening. Tiff had always some little offering, either berries or flowers, to present, or a nice little luncheon of fish or birds, cooked in some mode of peculiar delicacy; and which, served up in sylvan style, seemed to have something of the wild relish of the woods. In return, she continued to read the story so interesting to him; and it was astonishing how little explanation it needed — how plain honesty of heart, and lovingness of nature, interpreted passages over which theologians have wrangled in vain. It was not long before Tiff had impersonated to himself each of the disciples, particularly Peter; so that, when anything was said by him, Tiff would nod his head significantly, and say, "Ah, ah! dat ar's just like him! He's allers a-puttin' in; but he's a good man, arter all!"

What impression was made on the sensitive young nature, through whom, as a medium, Tiff received this fresh revelation, we may, perhaps, imagine. There are times in life when the soul, like a half-grown climbing vine, hangs wavering tremulously, stretching out its tendrils for something to ascend by. Such are generally the great transition periods of life, when we are passing from the ideas and conditions of one stage of existence to those of another. Such times are most favorable for the presentation of the higher truths of religion. In the hazy, slumberous stillness of that midsummer atmosphere, in the

long, silent rides through the pines, Nina half awakened
from the thoughtless dreams of childhood, yearning for
something nobler than she yet had lived for, thought over,
and revolved in her mind, this beautiful and spotless image
of God, revealed in man, which her daily readings presented; and the world that he created seemed to whisper
to her in every pulsation of its air, in every breath of its
flowers, in the fanning of its winds, "He still liveth, and
he loveth thee." The voice of the Good Shepherd fell on
the ear of the wandering lamb, calling her to his arms;
and Nina found herself one day unconsciously repeating,
as she returned through the woods, words which she had
often heard read at church: —

"When thou saidst unto me, Seek ye my face, my heart
said unto thee, Thy face, Lord, will I seek."

Nina had often dreaded the idea of becoming a Christian, as one shrinks from the idea of a cold, dreary passage
which must be passed to gain a quiet home. But suddenly, as if by some gentle invisible hand, the veil seemed
to be drawn which hid the face of Almighty Love from
her view. She beheld the earth and the heavens transfig-
ured in the light of his smile. A strange and unspeakable
joy arose within her, as if some loving presence were
always near her. It was with her when she lay down at
night, and when she awoke in the morning the strange
happiness had not departed. Her feelings may be best
expressed by an extract from a letter which she wrote at
this time to Clayton: —

It seems to me that I have felt a greater change in me
within the last two months than in my whole life before.
When I look back at what I was in New York, three
months ago, actually I hardly know myself. It seems to
me in those old days that life was only a frolic to me, as
it is to the kitten. I don't really think that there was

much harm in me, only the want of good. In those days, sometimes I used to have a sort of dim longing to be better, particularly when Livy Ray was at school. It seemed as if she woke up something that had been asleep in me; but she went away, and I fell asleep again, and life went on like a dream. Then I became acquainted with you, and you began to rouse me again, and for some time I thought I did n't like to wake; it was just as it is when one lies asleep in the morning — it 's so pleasant to sleep and dream, that one resists any one who tries to bring him back to life. I used to feel quite pettish when I first knew you, and sometimes wished you 'd let me alone, because I saw that you belonged to a different kind of sphere from what I 'd been living in. And I had a presentiment that, if I let you go on, life would have to be something more than a joke with me. But *you would*, like a very indiscreet man as you are, you would insist on being in sober earnest.

I used to think that I had no heart; I begin to think I have a good deal now. Every day it seems as if I could love more and more; and a great many things are growing clear to me that I did n't use to understand, and I 'm growing happier every day.

You know my queer old protégé, Uncle Tiff, who lives in the woods here. For some time past I have been to his house every day, reading to him in the Testament, and it has had a very great effect on me. It affected me very much, in the first place, that he seemed so very earnest about religion, when I, who ought to know so much more, was so indifferent to it; and when the old creature, with tears in his eyes, actually insisted upon it that I should show his children the road to heaven, then I began to read to him the Testament, the life of Jesus. I did n't know myself how beautiful it was — how suited to all our wants. It seemed to me I never saw so much beauty in anything before; and it seems as if it had waked a new life in me. Everything is changed; and it is the beauty of Christ that has changed it. You know I always loved beauty above all things, in music, in nature, and in flowers; but it seems to me that I see something now in Jesus more beautiful than all. It seems as if all these had been shadows of beauty, but He is the substance. It is strange, but I have a sense of him, his living and presence, that sometimes almost overpowers me. It seems as if he had been following me always, but I had not seen him. He has been a good shepherd, seeking the thoughtless lamb. He has, all my life, been calling me child; but till lately my heart has never answered, Father! Is this religion? Is this what people mean by conversion? I tried to tell Aunt Nesbit how I felt, because now I feel kinder to everybody; and really my heart smote me to think how much fun I had made of her, and now I begin to love her very much. She was so anxious I should talk with Mr. Titmarsh, because he is a minister. Well, you know I did n't want to do it, but I thought I ought to, because poor aunty really seemed to feel anxious I should. I suppose, if I were as perfect as I ought to be, a good man's stiff ways would n't trouble me so. But stiff people, you know, are my particular temptation.

He came and made a pastoral call, the other day, and talked to me. I don't think he understood me very well, and I 'm sure I did n't understand him. He told me how many kinds of faith there were, and how many kinds of love. I believe there were three kinds of faith, and two kinds of love; and he thought it was important to know whether I had got the right kind. He said we ought not to love God because he loves us, but because he is holy. He wanted to know whether I had any just views of sin, as an infinite evil; and I told him I had n't the least idea of what infinite was; and that I had n't any views of anything, but the beauty of Christ; that I did n't understand anything about the different sorts of faith, but that I felt perfectly sure that Jesus is so good that he would make me feel right, and give me right views, and do everything for me that I need.

He wanted to know if I loved him because he magnified the law, and made it honorable; and I told him I did n't understand what that meant.

I don't think, on the whole, that the talk did me much good. It only confused me, and made me very uncomfortable. But I went out to Old Tiff's in the evening, and read how Jesus received the little children. You never saw anybody so delighted as Old Tiff was. He got me to read it to him three or four times over; and now he gets me to read it every time I go there, and he says he likes it better than any other part of the Testament. Tiff and I get along very well together. He does n't know any more about faith than I do, and has n't any better views than I have. Aunt Nesbit is troubled about me, because I 'm so happy. She says she 's afraid I have n't any sense of sin. Don't you remember my telling you how happy I felt the first time I heard *real* music? I thought, before that, that I could sing pretty well; but in one hour all my music became trash in my eyes. And yet, I would not have missed it for the world. So it is now. That beautiful life of Jesus — so sweet, so calm, so pure, so unselfish, so perfectly natural, and yet so far beyond nature — has shown me what a poor, sinful, low creature I am; and yet I rejoice. I feel, sometimes, as I did when I first heard a full orchestra play some of Mozart's divine harmonies. I forgot that I was alive; I lost all thought of myself entirely; and I was perfectly happy. So it is now. This loveliness and beauty that I see makes me happy without any thought of myself. It seems to me, sometimes, that while I see it I never can suffer.

There is another thing that is strange to me; and that is, that the Bible has grown so beautiful to me. It seems to me that it has been all my life like the transparent picture, without any light behind it; and now it is all illuminated, and its words are full of meaning to me. I am light hearted and happy — happier than ever I was. Do you remember, the first day you came to Canema, that I told you it seemed so sad that we must die? That feeling is all gone, now. I feel that Jesus is everywhere, and that there is no such thing as dying; it is only going out of one room into another.

Everybody wonders to see how light hearted I am; and poor aunty says, "she trembles for me." I could n't help thinking of that, the other morning I was reading to Tiff, — what Jesus said when they asked him why his disciples did not fast: "Can the children of the bride-chamber mourn while the bridegroom is with them?"

Now, my dear friend, you must tell me what you think of all this, because, you know, I always tell you everything. I have written to Livy about it, because I know it will make her so happy. Milly seems to understand it all, and what she says to me really helps me very much. I always used to think that Milly had some strange, beautiful kind of inward life, that I knew nothing of, because she would speak with so much certainty of God's love, and *act* as if it was so real to her; and she would tell me so earnestly, "Chile, he loves you!" Now I see into it — that mystery of his love to us, and how he overcomes and subdues all things by love; and I understand how "perfect love casteth out fear."

To this letter Nina soon received an answer, from which also we give an extract: —

If I was so happy, my dearest one, as to be able to

awaken that deeper and higher nature which I always knew was in you, I thank God. But if I ever was in any respect your teacher, you have passed beyond my teachings now. Your childlike simplicity of nature makes you a better scholar than I in that school where the first step is to forget all our worldly wisdom and become a little child. We men have much more to contend with, in the pride of our nature, in our habits of worldly reasoning. It takes us long to learn the lesson that faith is the highest wisdom. Don't trouble your head, dear Nina, with Aunt Nesbit or Mr. Titmarsh. What you feel is faith. They define it, and you feel it. And there's all the difference between the definition and the feeling that there is between the husk and the corn.

As for me, I am less happy than you. Religion seems to me to have two parts to it. One part is the aspiration of man's nature, and the other is God's answer to those aspirations. I have, as yet, only the first; perhaps, because I am less simple and less true; perhaps, because I am not yet become a little child. So you must be my guide, instead of I yours; for I believe it is written of the faithful, that a little child shall lead them.

I am a good deal tried now, my dear, because I am coming to a crisis in my life. I am going to take a step that will deprive me of many friends, of popularity, and that will, perhaps, alter all my course for the future. But if I should lose friends and popularity, *you* would love me still, would you not? It is wronging you to ask such a question; but yet I should like to have you answer it. It will make me stronger for what I have to do. On Thursday of this week my case will come on again. I am very busy just now; but the thought of you mingles with every thought.

CHAPTER XXXIII

THE time for the session of the Supreme Court had now arrived, and Clayton's cause was to be reconsidered. Judge Clayton felt exceedingly chagrined as the time drew near. Being himself the leading judge of the Supreme Court, the declaration of the bench would necessarily be made known through him.

"It is extremely painful to me," he said to Mrs. Clayton, "to have this case referred to me; for I shall be obliged to reverse the decision."

"Well," said Mrs. Clayton, "Edward must have fortitude to encounter the usual reverses of his profession. He made a gallant defense, and received a great deal of admiration, which will not be at all lessened by this."

"You do not understand me," said Judge Clayton. "It is not the coming out in opposition to Edward which principally annoys me. It is the nature of the decision that I am obliged to make — the doctrine that I feel myself forced to announce."

"And must you, then?" said Mrs. Clayton.

"Yes, I must," said Judge Clayton. "A judge can only perceive and declare. What I see, I must speak, though it go against all my feelings and all my sense of right."

"I don't see, for my part," said Mrs. Clayton, "how that decision can possibly be reversed, without allowing the most monstrous injustice."

"Such is the case," said Judge Clayton; "but I sit in

my seat, not to make laws, nor to alter them, but simply
to declare what they are. However bad the principle
declared, it is not so bad as the proclamation of a falsehood
would be. I have sworn truly to declare the laws, and I
must keep my oath."

"And have you talked with Edward about it?"

"Not particularly. He understands, in general, the
manner in which the thing lies in my mind."

This conversation took place just before it was time for
Judge Clayton to go to his official duties.

The court - room, on this occasion, was somewhat
crowded. Barker, being an active, resolute, and popular
man, with a certain class, had talked up a considerable
excitement with regard to his case. Clayton's friends
were interested in it on his account; lawyers were, for
the sake of the principle; so that, upon the whole, there
was a good deal of attention drawn towards this decision.

Among the spectators, on the morning of the court, Clayton remarked Harry. For reasons which our readers may
appreciate, Harry's presence there was a matter of interest
to Clayton. He made his way towards him.

"Harry," he said, "how came you here?"

"The ladies," said Harry, "thought they would like to
know how the thing went, and so I got on to my horse
and came over."

As he spoke he placed in Clayton's hand a note, and
as the paper touched his hand, a close spectator might
have seen the color rise in his cheek. He made his way
back to his place, and opened a law-book, which he held
up before his face. Inside the law-book, however, was
a little sheet of gilt-edged paper, on which were written
a few words in pencil, more interesting than all the law
in the world. Shall we commit the treason of reading
over his shoulder? It was as follows: —

You say you may to-day be called to do something which you think right, but which will lose you many friends; which will destroy your popularity, which may alter all your prospects in life; and you ask if I can love you yet. I say, in answer, that it was not your friends that I loved, nor your popularity, nor your prospects, but you. I can love and honor a man who is not afraid nor ashamed to do what he thinks to be right; and therefore I hope ever to remain yours, NINA.

P. S. I only got your letter this morning, and have but just time to scribble this and send by Harry. We are all well, and shall be glad to see you as soon as the case is over.

"Clayton, my boy, you are very busy with your authorities," said Frank Russel, behind him. Clayton hastily hid the paper in his hand.

"It's charming!" said Russel, "to have little manuscript annotations on law. It lights it up, like the illuminations in old missals. But say, Clayton, you live at the fountain-head: how is the case going?"

"Against me!" said Clayton.

"Well, it's no great odds, after all. You have had your triumph. These after-thoughts cannot take away that. . . . But hush! There's your father going to speak!"

Every eye in the court-room was turned upon Judge Clayton, who was standing with his usual self-poised composure of manner. In a clear, deliberate voice, he spoke as follows: —

"A judge cannot but lament when such cases as the present are brought into judgment. It is impossible that the reasons on which they go can be appreciated but where institutions similar to our own exist and are thoroughly understood. The struggle, too, in the judge's own breast, between the feelings of the man and the duty of the magistrate, is a severe one, presenting strong temptation to put aside such questions, if it be possible. It is useless, however, to complain of things inherent in our political state. And it is criminal in a court to avoid any responsibility which the laws impose. With whatever reluctance, therefore, it is done, the court is compelled to express an opinion upon the extent of the dominion of the master over the slave in North Carolina. The indictment charges a battery on Milly, a slave of Louisa Nesbit. . . .

"The inquiry here is, whether a cruel and unreasonable battery on a slave by the hirer is indictable. The judge below instructed the jury that it is. He seems to have put it on the ground, that the defendant had but a special property. Our laws uniformly treat the master, or other person having the possession and command of the slave, as entitled to the same extent of authority. The object is the same, the service of the slave; and the same powers must be confided. In a criminal proceeding, and, indeed, in reference to all other persons but the general owner, the hirer and possessor of the slave, in relation to both rights and duties, is, for the time being, the owner. . . . But upon the general question, whether the owner is answerable, *criminaliter*, for a battery upon his own slave, or other exercise of authority or force, not forbidden by statute, the court entertains but little doubt. That he is so liable has never been decided, nor, as far as is known, been hitherto contended. There has been no prosecution of the sort. The established habits and uniform practice of the country, in this respect, is the best evidence of the portion of power deemed by the whole community requisite to the preservation of the master's dominion. If we thought differently, we could not set our notions in array against the judgment of everybody else, and say that this or that authority may be safely lopped off.

"This has indeed been assimilated at the bar to the other domestic relations: and arguments drawn from the well-established principles, which confer and restrain the authority of the parent over the child, the tutor over the pupil, the master over the apprentice, have been pressed on us.

"The court does not recognize their application. There is no likeness between the cases. They are in opposition to each other, and there is an impassable gulf between them. The difference is that which exists between freedom and slavery; and a greater cannot be imagined. In the one, the end in view is the happiness of the youth born to equal rights with that governor on whom the duty devolves of training the young to usefulness, in a station which he is afterwards to assume among free men. To such an end, and with such a subject, moral and intellectual instruction seem the natural means; and, for the most part, they are found to suffice. Moderate force is superadded only to make the others effectual. If that fail, it is better to leave the party to his own headstrong passions, and the ultimate correction of the law, than to allow it to be immoderately inflicted by a private person. With slavery it is far otherwise. The end is the profit of the master, his security, and the public safety; the subject, one doomed, in his own person and his posterity, to live without knowledge, and without the capacity to make anything his own, and to toil that another may reap the fruits. What moral considerations shall be addressed to such a being, to convince him what it is impossible but that the most stupid must feel and know can never be true, — that he is thus to labor upon a principle of natural duty, or for the sake of his own personal happiness? Such services can only be expected from one who has no will of his own; who surrenders his will in implicit obedience to that of another. Such obedience is the consequence only of uncontrolled authority over the body. There is nothing else which can operate to produce the effect. The power of the master must be absolute, to render the submission of the slave perfect. I most freely confess my sense of the harshness of this proposition. I feel it as deeply as any man can. And as a principle of moral right, every person in his retirement must repudiate it. But, in the actual condition of things, it must be so. There is no remedy. This discipline belongs to the state of slavery. They cannot be disunited without abrogating at once the rights of the master, and absolving the slave from his subjection. It constitutes the curse of slavery to both the bond and the free portions of our population. But it is inherent in the relation of master and slave. That there may be particular instances of cruelty and deliberate barbarity, where in conscience the law might properly interfere, is most probable. The difficulty is to determine where a *court* may properly begin. Merely in the abstract, it may well be asked which power of the master accords with right. The answer will probably sweep away all of them. But we cannot look at the matter in that light. The truth is that we are forbidden to enter upon a train of general reasoning on the subject. We cannot allow the right of the master to be brought into discussion in the courts of justice. The slave, to remain a slave, must be made sensible that there is no appeal from his master; that his power is, in no instance, usurped, but is conferred by the laws of man, at least, if not by the law of God. The danger would be great, indeed, if the tribunals of justice should be called on to graduate the punishment appropriate to every temper and every dereliction of menial duty.

"No man can anticipate the many and aggravated provocations of the master which the slave would be constantly stimulated by his own passions, or the instigation of others, to give; or the consequent wrath of the master, prompt-

ing him to bloody vengeance upon the turbulent traitor;
a vengeance generally practiced with impunity, by reason
of its privacy. The court, therefore, disclaims the power
of changing the relation in which these parts of our people
stand to each other.

.   .   .   .

"I repeat, that I would gladly have avoided this ungrateful question. But being brought to it, the court is
compelled to declare that while slavery exists amongst us
in its present state, or until it shall seem fit to the legislature to interpose express enactments to the contrary, it
will be the imperative duty of the judges to recognize the
full dominion of the owner over the slave, except where
the exercise of it is forbidden by statute.

"And this we do upon the ground that this dominion is
essential to the value of slaves as property, to the security
of the master and the public tranquillity, greatly dependent
upon their subordination; and, in fine, as most effectually
securing the general protection and comfort of the slaves
themselves. Judgment below reversed; and judgment
entered for the defendant."

During the delivery of the decision Clayton's eyes, by
accident, became fixed upon Harry, who was standing
opposite to him, and who listened through the whole with
breathless attention. He observed, as it went on, that
Harry's face became pale, his brow clouded, and that a fierce
and peculiar expression flashed from his dark blue eye.
Never had Clayton so forcibly realized the horrors of slavery as when he heard them thus so calmly defined in the
presence of one into whose soul the iron had entered. The
tones of Judge Clayton's voice, so passionless, clear, and
deliberate; the solemn, calm, unflinching earnestness of
his words were more than a thousand passionate appeals.
In the dead silence that followed Clayton rose, and requested permission of the court to be allowed to say a few

words in view of the decision. His father looked slightly surprised, and there was a little movement among the judges. But curiosity, perhaps, among other reasons, led the court to give consent. Clayton spoke: —

"I hope it will not be considered a disrespect or impertinence for me to say that the law of slavery and the nature of that institution have for the first time been made known to me to-day in their true character. I had before flattered myself with the hope that it might be considered a guardian institution, by which a stronger race might assume the care and instruction of the weaker one; and I had hoped that its laws were capable of being so administered as to protect the defenseless. This illusion is destroyed. I see but too clearly now the purpose and object of the law. I cannot, therefore, as a Christian man, remain in the practice of law in a slave state. I therefore relinquish the profession into which I have just been inducted, and retire forever from the bar of my native state."

"There! — there! — there he goes!" said Frank Russel. "The sticking-point has come at last. His conscience is up, and start him now who can!"

There was a slight motion of surprise in the court and audience. But Judge Clayton sat with unmoved serenity. The words had struck to the depth of his soul. They had struck at the root of one of his strongest hopes in life. But he had listened to them with the same calm and punctilious attention which it was his habit to give to every speaker; and with unaltered composure, he proceeded to the next business of the court.

A step so unusual occasioned no little excitement. But Clayton was not one of the class of people to whom his associates generally felt at liberty to express their opinions of his conduct. The quiet reserve of his manners discouraged any such freedom. As usual, in cases where a person takes an uncommon course from conscientious motives, Clayton was severely criticised. The more trifling among the audience contented themselves with using the good set phrases, quixotic, absurd, ridiculous. The elder lawyers, and those friendly to Clayton, shook their heads, and said, rash, precipitate, unadvised. "There's a want of ballast about him, somewhere!" said one. "He is unsound!" said another. "Radical and impracticable!" added a third.

"Yes," said Frank Russel, who had just come up, "Clayton is as radical and impracticable as the Sermon on the Mount, and that's the most impracticable thing I know of in literature. We all *can* serve God and Mammon. We have discovered that happy medium in our day. Clayton is behind the times. He is Jewish in his notions. Don't you think so, Mr. Titmarsh?" addressing the Rev. Mr. Titmarsh.

"It strikes me that our young friend is extremely *ultra*," said Mr. Titmarsh. "I might feel disposed to sympathize with him in the feelings he expressed, to some extent; but it having pleased the Divine Providence to establish the institution of slavery, I humbly presume it is not competent for human reason to judge of it."

"And if it had pleased the Divine Providence to have established the institution of piracy, you'd say the same thing, I suppose!" said Frank Russel.

"Certainly, my young friend," said Mr. Titmarsh. "Whatever is divinely ordered becomes right by that fact."

"I should think," said Frank Russel, "that things were divinely ordered because they were right."

"No, my friend," replied Mr. Titmarsh moderately; "they are right because they are ordered, however contrary they may appear to any of our poor notions of justice and humanity." And Mr. Titmarsh walked off.

"Did you hear that?" said Russel. "And they expect

really to come it over us with stuff like that! Now, if a
fellow don't go to church Sundays, there's a dreadful out-
cry against him for not being religious! And if they get
us there, that's the kind of thing they put down our
throats! As if they were going to make practical men
give in to such humbugs!"

And the Rev. Mr. Titmarsh went off in another direction, lamenting to a friend as follows: —

"How mournfully infidelity is increasing among the
young men of our day! They quote Scripture with the
same freedom that they would a book of plays, and seem
to treat it with no more reverence! I believe it's the
want of catechetical instruction while they are children.
There's been a great falling back in the teaching of the
Assembly's Catechism to children when they are young!
I shall get that point up at the General Assembly. If
that were thoroughly committed when they are children,
I think they would never doubt afterwards."

Clayton went home and told his mother what he had
done, and why. His father had not spoken to him on
this subject; and there was that about Judge Clayton
which made it difficult to introduce a topic unless he sig-
nified an inclination to enter upon it. He was, as usual,
calm, grave, and considerate, attending to every duty with
unwearying regularity.

At the end of the second day, in the evening, Judge
Clayton requested his son to walk in to his study. The
interview was painful on both sides.

"You are aware, my son," he said, "that the step you
have taken is a very painful one to me. I hope that it
was not taken precipitately, from any sudden impulse."

"You may rest assured it was not," said Clayton. "I
followed the deepest and most deliberate convictions of my
conscience."

"In that case, you could not do otherwise," replied

Judge Clayton. "I have no criticisms to make. But will your conscience allow you to retain the position of a slave-holder?"

"I have already relinquished it," replied Clayton, "so far as my own intentions are concerned. I retain the legal relation of owner simply as a means of protecting my servants from the cruelties of the law, and of securing the opportunity to educate and elevate them."

"And suppose this course brings you into conflict with the law of the state?" said Judge Clayton.

"If there is any reasonable prospect of having the law altered, I must endeavor to do that," said Clayton.

"But," said Judge Clayton, "suppose the law is so rooted in the nature of the institution that it cannot be repealed without uprooting the institution? What then?"

"I say repeal the law if it do uproot the institution," said Clayton. "'Fiat justitia, ruat cœlum.'"

"I supposed that would be your answer," said Judge Clayton patiently. "That is undoubtedly the logical line of life. But you are aware that communities do not follow such lines; your course, therefore, will place you in opposition to the community in which you live. Your conscientious convictions will cross self-interest, and the community will not allow you to carry them out."

"Then," said Clayton, "I must, with myself and my servants, remove to some region where I can do this."

"That I supposed would be the result," said Judge Clayton. "And have you looked at the thing in all its relations and consequences?"

"I have," said Clayton.

"You are about to form a connection with Miss Gordon," said Judge Clayton. "Have you considered how this will affect her?"

"Yes," said Clayton. "Miss Gordon fully sustains me in the course I have taken."

"I have no more to say," said Judge Clayton. "Every man must act up to his sense of duty."

There was a pause of a few moments, and Judge Clayton added: —

"You, perhaps, have seen the implication which your course throws upon us who still continue to practice the system and uphold the institution which you repudiate."

"I meant no implications," said Clayton.

"I presume not. But they result, logically, from your course," said his father. "I assure you, I have often myself pondered the question with reference to my own duties. My course is a sufficient evidence that I have not come to the same result. Human law is, at best, but an approximation, a reflection of many of the ills of our nature. Imperfect as it is, it is, on the whole, a blessing. The worst system is better than anarchy."

"But, my father, why could you not have been a reformer of the system?"

"My son, no reform is possible, unless we are prepared to give up the institution of slavery. That will be the immediate result; and this is so realized by the instinct of self-preservation, which is unfailing in its accuracy, that every such proposition will be ignored, till there is a settled conviction in the community that the institution itself is a moral evil, and a sincere determination felt to be free from it. I see no tendency of things in that direction. That body of religious men of different denominations, called, *par excellence*, the church, exhibit a degree of moral apathy on this subject which is to me very surprising. It is with them that the training of the community, on which any such reform could be built, must commence; and I see no symptoms of their undertaking it. The decisions and testimonies of the great religious assemblies in the land, in my youth, were frequent. They have grown every year less and less decided; and now the morality of

the thing is openly defended in our pulpits, to my great
disgust. I see no way but that the institution will be
left to work itself out to its final result, which will, in
the end, be ruinous to our country. I am not myself gifted
with the talents of a reformer. My turn of mind fits me
for the situation I hold. I cannot hope that I have done
no harm in it; but the good, I hope, will outweigh the
evil. If you feel a call to enter on this course, fully understanding the difficulties and sacrifices it would probably involve, I would be the last one to throw the influence
of my private wishes and feelings into the scale. We live
here but a few years. It is of more consequence that we
should do right than that we should enjoy ourselves."

Judge Clayton spoke this with more emotion than he
usually exhibited, and Clayton was much touched.

"My dear father," he said, putting Nina's note into his
hand, "you made allusion to Miss Gordon. This note,
which I received from her on the morning of your decision,
will show you what her spirit is."

Judge Clayton put on his spectacles, and read over the
note deliberately, twice. He then handed it formally to
his son, and remarked, with his usual brevity, —

"She will do!"

CHAPTER XXXIV

THE CLOUD BURSTS

THE shadow of that awful cloud which had desolated other places now began to darken the boundaries of the plantation of Canema. No disease has ever more fully filled out the meaning of those awful words of Scripture, "The pestilence that walketh in darkness." None has been more irregular, and apparently more perfectly capricious, in its movements. During the successive seasons that it has been epidemic in this country, it has seemed to have set at defiance the skill of the physicians. The system of medical tactics which has been wrought out by the painful experience of one season seems to be laughed to scorn by the varying type of the disease in the next. Certain sanitary laws and conditions would seem to be indispensable; yet those who are familiar with it have had fearful experience how like a wolf it will sometimes leap the boundaries of the best and most carefully guarded fold, and, spite of every caution and protection, sweep all before it.

Its course through towns and villages has been equally singular. Sometimes descending like a cloud on a neighborhood, it will leave a single village or town untouched amidst the surrounding desolations, and long after, when health is restored to the whole neighborhood, come down suddenly on the omitted towns, as a ravaging army sends back a party for prey to some place which has been overlooked or forgotten. Sometimes, entering a house, in twenty-four hours it will take all who are in it. Sometimes it will ravage all the city except some one street or locality, and then come upon that, while all else is spared. Its course, upon southern plantations, was marked by similar capriciousness, and was made still more fatal by that peculiar nature of plantation life which withdraws the inmates so far from medical aid.

When the first letters were received describing the progress of it in northern cities, Aunt Nesbit felt much uneasiness and alarm. It is remarkable with what tenacity people often will cling to life, whose enjoyments in it are so dull and low that a bystander would scarcely think them worth the struggle of preservation. When at length the dreaded news began to be heard from one point and another in their vicinity, Aunt Nesbit said, one day, to Nina, —

"Your cousins, the Gordons, in E——, have written to us to leave the plantation, and come and spend some time with them till the danger is over."

"Why," said Nina, "do they think the cholera can't come there?"

"Well," said Aunt Nesbit, "they have their family under most excellent regulations; and living in a town so, they are within call of a doctor, if anything happens."

"Aunt," said Nina, "perhaps you had better go; but I will stay with my people."

"Why, don't you feel afraid, Nina?"

"No, aunt, I don't. Besides, I think it would be very selfish for me to live on the services of my people all my life, and then run away and leave them alone when a time of danger comes. The least I can do is to stay and take care of them."

This conversation was overheard by Harry, who was standing with his back to them, on the veranda, near the parlor door where they were sitting.

"Child," said Aunt Nesbit, "what do you suppose you

can do? You have n't any experience. Harry and Milly can do a great deal better than you can. I'll leave Milly here. It's our first duty to take care of our health."

"No, aunt, I think there are some duties before that," said Nina. "It's true I have n't a great deal of strength, but I have courage; and I know my going away would discourage our people, and fill them with fear; and that, they say, predisposes to the disease. I shall get the carriage up, and go directly over to see the doctor, and get directions and medicines. I shall talk to our people, and teach them what to do, and see that it is done. And when they see that I am calm, and not afraid, they will have courage. But, aunt, if you are afraid, I think you had better go. You are feeble; you can't make much exertion; and if you feel any safer or more comfortable, I think it would be best. I should like to have Milly stay, and she, Harry, and I, will be a board of health to the plantation.

"Harry," she said, "if you'll get up the carriage, we'll go immediately."

Again Harry felt the bitterness of his soul sweetened and tranquillized by the noble nature of her to whose hands the law had given the chain which bound him. Galling and intolerable as it would have been otherwise, he felt, when with her, that her service was perfect freedom. He had not said anything to Nina about the contents of the letter which he had received from his sister. He saw that it was an evil which she had no power over, and he shrank from annoying her with it. Nina supposed that his clouded and troubled aspect was caused wholly by the solicitude of responsibility.

In the same carriage which conveyed her to the town sat Aunt Nesbit also, and her cap-boxes, whose importance even the fear of the cholera could not lessen in her eyes. Nina found the physician quite *au fait* on the subject.

He had been reading about miasma and animalculæ, and he entertained Nina nearly half an hour with different theories as to the cause of the disease, and with the experiments which had been made in foreign hospitals.

Among the various theories there was one which appeared to be his particular pet; and Nina could n't help thinking, as he stepped about so alertly, that he almost enjoyed the prospect of putting his discoveries to the test. By dint, however, of very practical and positive questions, Nina drew from him all the valuable information which he had to give her; and he wrote her a very full system of directions, and put up a case of medicines for her, assuring her that he should be happy to attend in person if he had time.

On the way home Nina stopped at Uncle John Gordon's plantation, and there had the first experience of the difference between written directions for a supposed case and the actual, awful realities of the disease. Her Uncle John had been seized only half an hour before, in the most awful manner. The household was all in terror and confusion, and the shrieks and groans of agony which proceeded from his room were appalling. His wife, busy with the sufferer, did not perceive that the messengers who had been sent in haste for the doctor were wringing their hands in fruitless terror, running up and down the veranda, and doing nothing.

"Harry," said Nina, "take out one of the carriage-horses, and ride quick for your life, and bring the doctor over here in a minute!"

In a few moments the thing was done, and Harry was out of sight. She then walked up to the distracted servants, and commanded them, in a tone of authority, to cease their lamentations. Her resolute manner, and the quiet tone of voice which she preserved, acted as a sedative on their excited nerves. She banished all but two or

three of the most reasonable from the house, and then
went to the assistance of her aunt.

Before long the doctor arrived. When he had been in
the sick room a few moments, he came out to make some
inquiries of Nina, and she could not help contrasting the
appalled and confounded expression of his countenance
with the dapper, consequential air, with which, only two
hours before he had been holding forth to her on animalculæ and miasma.

"The disease," he said, "presented itself in an entirely
different aspect from what he had expected. The remedies," he said, "did not work as he anticipated; the case
was a peculiar one."

Alas! before the three months were over, poor doctor,
you found many peculiar cases!

"Do you think you can save his life?" said Nina.

"Child, only God can save him!" said the physician;
"nothing works right."

But why prolong the torture of that scene, or rehearse
the struggles, groans, and convulsions? Nina, poor flowery child of seventeen summers, stood with the rest in
mute despair. All was tried that could be done or
thought of; but the disease, like some blind, deaf destroyer, marched on, turning neither to right nor left, till
the cries and groans grew fainter, the convulsed muscles
relaxed, and the strong, florid man lay in the last stages
of that fearful collapse which in one hour shrivels the most
healthy countenance and the firmest muscles to the shrunken
and withered image of decrepit old age. When the breath
had passed, and all was over, Nina could scarcely believe
that that altered face and form, so withered and so worn,
could have been her healthy and joyous uncle, and who
never had appeared healthier and more joyous than on that
morning. But as a person passing under the foam and
spray of Niagara clings with blind confidence to a guide

whom he feels, but cannot see, Nina, in this awful hour, felt that she was not alone. The Redeemer, all-powerful over death and the grave, of whom she had been thinking so much of late, seemed to her sensibly near. And it seemed to her as if a voice said to her continually, "Fear not, for I am with thee. Be not dismayed, for I am thy God."

"How calm you are, my child!" said Aunt Maria to her. "I would n't have thought it was in you. I don't know what we should do without you."

But now a frightful wail was heard.

"Oh, we are all dying! we are all going! Oh, missis, come quick! Peter has got it! Oh, daddy has got it! Oh, my child! my child!"

And the doctor, exhausted as he was by the surprise and excitement of this case, began flying from one to another of the cabins, in the greatest haste. Two or three of the house servants also seemed to be struck in the same moment, and only the calmness and courage which Nina and her aunt maintained prevented a general abandonment to panic. Nina possessed that fine, elastic temperament which, with the appearance of extreme delicacy, possesses great powers of endurance. The perfect calmness which she felt enabled her to bring all her faculties to bear on the emergency.

"My good aunty, you must n't be afraid! Bring out your religion; trust in God," she said to the cook, who was wringing her hands in terror. "Remember your religion; sing some of your hymns, and do your duty to the sick."

There is a magic power in the cheerful tone of courage, and Nina succeeded in rallying the well ones to take care of the sick; but now came a messenger, in hot haste, to say that the cholera had broken out on the plantation at home.

"Well, Harry," said Nina, with a face pale, yet unmoved, "our duty calls us away."

And accompanied by the weary physician, they prepared
to go back to Canema. Before they had proceeded far, a
man met them on horseback.

"Is Dr. Butler with you?"

"Yes," said Nina, putting her head out of the carriage.

"Oh, Doctor, I 've been riding all over the country after
you. You must come back to town this minute! Judge
Peters is dying! I 'm afraid he is dead before this time,
and there 's a dozen more cases right in that street. Here,
get on to my horse, and ride for your life."

The doctor hastily sprang from the carriage, and mounted
the horse; then stopping a moment, he cast a look of
good-natured pity on the sweet, pale face that was leaning out of the carriage window.

"My poor child," he said, "I can't bear to leave you.
Who will help you?"

"God," said Nina; "I am not afraid!"

"Come, come," said the man, "do hurry!" And with
one hasty glance more he was gone.

"Now, Harry," said Nina, "everything depends upon
our keeping up our courage and our strength. We shall
have no physician. We must just do the best we can.
After all, it is our Lord Jesus that has the keys of death,
and *he* loved us and died for us. He will certainly be
with us."

"Oh, Miss Nina, you are an angel!" said Harry, who
felt at that moment as if he could have worshiped her.

Arrived at home, Nina found a scene of terror and confusion similar to that she had already witnessed. Old
Hundred lay dead in his cabin, and the lamenting crowd,
gathering round, were yielding to the full tide of fear and
excitement, which predisposed them to the same fate.

Nina rode up immediately to the group. She spoke to them calmly; she silenced their outcries, and bade them obey her.

"If you wish, all of you, to die," she said, "this is the way towards it; but if you'll keep quiet and calm, and do what ought to be done, your lives may be saved. Harry and I have got medicines — we understand what to do. You must follow our directions exactly."

Nina immediately went to the house, and instructed Milly, Aunt Rose, and two or three of the elderly women in the duties to be done. Milly rose up, in this hour of terror, with all the fortitude inspired by her strong nature.

"Bress de Lord," she said, "for his grace to you, chile! De Lord is a shield. He's been wid us in six troubles, and he'll be wid us in seven. We can sing in de swellings of Jordan."

Harry, meanwhile, was associating to himself a band of the most reliable men on the place, and endeavoring in the same manner to organize them for action. A messenger was dispatched immediately to the neighboring town for unlimited quantities of the most necessary medicines and stimulants. The plantation was districted off, and placed under the care of leaders, who held communication with Harry. In the course of two or three hours, the appalling scene of distress and confusion was reduced to the resolute and orderly condition of a well-managed hospital.

Milly walked the rounds in every direction, appealing to the religious sensibilities of the people, and singing hymns of trust and confidence. She possessed a peculiar voice, suited to her large development of physical frame, almost as deep as a man's bass, with the rich softness of a feminine tone; and Nina could now and then distinguish, as she was moving about the house or grounds, that triumphant tone, singing: —

"God is my sun,
  And he my shade,
  To guard my head,
By night or noon.
Hast thou not given thy word
  To save my soul from death ?
And I can trust my Lord,
  To keep my mortal breath,
I 'll go and come,
  Nor fear to die,
  Till from on high
Thou call me home."

The house that night presented the aspect of a belea-
guered garrison. Nina and Milly had thrown open all the
chambers; and such as were peculiarly exposed to the
disease, by delicacy of organization or tremulousness of
nervous system, were allowed to take shelter there.

"Now, chile," said Milly, when all the arrangements
had been made, "you jes lie down and go to sleep in yer
own room. I see how 't is with you; de spirit is willing,
but de flesh is weak. Chile, dere is n't much of you, but
dere won't nothing go widout you. So, you take care of
yerself first. Never you be 'fraid! De people's quiet
now, and de sick ones is ben took care of, and de folks is
all doing de best dey can. So, now, you try and get some
sleep; 'cause if you goes we shall all go."

Accordingly Nina retired to her room, but before she
lay down she wrote to Clayton: —

We are all in affliction here, my dear friend. Poor
Uncle John died this morning of the cholera. I had been
to E—— to see a doctor and provide medicines. When
I came back I thought I would call a few moments at the
house, and I found a perfect scene of horror. Poor uncle
died, and there are a great many sick on the place now;
and while I was thinking that I would stay and help aunt,
a messenger came in all haste, saying that the disease had
broken out on our place at home.

We were bringing the doctor with us in our carriage, when we met a man riding full speed from E——, who told us that Judge Peters was dying, and a great many others were sick on the same street. When we came home we found the poor old coachman dead, and the people in the greatest consternation. It took us some time to tranquillize them and to produce order, but that is now done. Our house is full of the sick and the fearful ones. Milly and Harry are firm and active, and inspire the rest with courage. About twenty are taken with the disease, but not as yet in a violent way. In this awful hour I feel a strange peace, which the Bible truly says "passeth all understanding." I see, now, that though the world and all that is in it should perish, "Christ can give us a beautiful immortal life." I write to you because, perhaps, this may be the only opportunity. If I die, do not mourn for me, but thank God, who giveth us the victory through our Lord Jesus Christ. But then, I trust, I shall not die. I hope to live in this world, which is more than ever beautiful to me. Life has never been so valuable and dear as since I have known you. Yet I have such trust in the love of my Redeemer, that, if *he* were to ask me to lay it down, I could do it almost without a sigh. I would follow the Lamb whithersoever he goeth. Perhaps the same dreadful evil is around you, — perhaps at Magnolia Grove. I will not be selfish in calling you here, if Anne needs you more. Perhaps she has not such reliable help as Harry and Milly are to me. So do not fear, and do not leave any duty for me. Our Father loves us, and will do nothing amiss. Milly walks about the entries singing. I love to hear her sing, she sings in such a grand triumphant tone. Hark, I hear her now!

> "I'll go and come,
> Nor fear to die,
> Till from on high
> Thou call me home."

I shall write you every mail, now, till we are better.
Living or dying, ever your own

NINA.

After writing this, Nina lay down and slept — slept all
night as quietly as if death and disease were not hanging
over her head.   In the morning she rose and dressed herself, and Milly, with anxious care, brought to her room
some warm coffee and crackers, which she insisted on her
taking before she left her apartment.

"How are they all, Milly?" said Nina.

"Well, chile," said Milly, "de midnight cry has been
heard among us.   Aunt Rose is gone; and Big Sam, and
Jack, and Sally, dey's all gone; but de people is all more
quiet, love, and dey's determined to stand it out!"

"How is Harry?" said Nina in a tremulous voice.

"He isn't sick; he has been up all night working over
de sick, but he keeps up good heart.   De older ones is
going to have a little prayer-meeting after breakfast, as a
sort of funeral to dem dat's dead; and, perhaps, Miss
Nina, you'd read us a chapter."

"Certainly I will," said Nina.

It was yet an early hour, when a large circle of family
and plantation hands gathered together in the pleasant,
open saloon, which we have so often described.   The day
was a beautiful one; the leaves and shrubbery round the
veranda moist and tremulous with the glittering freshness
of morning dew.   There was a murmur of tenderness and
admiration as Nina, in a white morning-wrapper, and a
cheek as white, came into the room.

"Sit down, all my friends," she said, "sit down," looking at some of the plantation men, who seemed to be diffi-
dent about taking the sofa, which was behind them; "it's
no time for ceremony now.   We are standing on the brink
of the grave, where all are equal.   I'm glad to see you so

calm and so brave. I hope your trust is in the Saviour, who gives us the victory over death. Sing," she said. Milly began the well-known hymn: —

> " And must this feeble body fail,
> And must it faint and die ?
> My soul shall quit this gloomy vale,
> And soar to realms on high;

> "Shall join the disembodied saints,
> And find its long-sought rest;
> That only rest for which it pants,
> On the Redeemer's breast."

Every voice joined, and the words rose triumphant from the very gates of the grave. When the singing was over, Nina, in a tremulous voice, which grew clearer as she went on, read the undaunted words of the ancient psalm: —

" ' He that dwelleth in the secret place of the most High shall abide under the shadow of the Almighty. I will say of the Lord, He is my refuge and my fortress. My God, in him will I trust. Surely he shall deliver thee from the snare of the fowler, and from the noisome pestilence. He shall cover thee with his feathers. Under his wings shalt thou trust. Thou shalt not be afraid for the terror by night, nor for the arrow that flieth by day, nor for the pestilence that walketh in darkness, nor for the destruction that wasteth at noonday. A thousand shall fall by thy side, and ten thousand at thy right hand; but it shall not come nigh thee. He shall give his angels charge over thee to keep thee in all thy ways. '

"It is possible," said Nina, "that we may, some of us, be called away. But to those that love Christ, there is no fear in death. It is only going home to our Father. Keep up courage, then!"

In all cases like this, the first shock brings with it more terror than any which succeeds. The mind can become familiar with anything, even with the prospect of danger and death, so that it can appear to be an ordinary condition of existence. Everything proceeded calmly on the plantation; and all, stimulated by the example of their young mistress, seemed determined to meet the exigency firmly and faithfully. In the afternoon of the second day, as Nina was sitting in the door, she observed the wagon of Uncle Tiff making its way up the avenue; and with her usual impulsiveness, ran down to meet her humble friend.

"Oh, Tiff, how do you do, in these dreadful times!"

"Oh, Miss Nina," said the faithful creature, removing his hat, with habitual politeness, "ef yer please, I's brought de baby here, 'cause it's drefful sick, and I's been doing all I could for him, and he don't get no better. And I's brought Miss Fanny and Teddy, 'cause I's 'fraid to leave 'em, 'cause I see a man yesterday, and he tell me dey was dying eberywhar on all de places round."

"Well," said Nina, "you have come to a sorrowful place, for they are dying here, too! But if you feel any safer here, you and the children may stay, and we'll do for you just as we do for each other. Give me the baby while you get out. It's asleep, is n't it?"

"Yes, Miss Nina, it's 'sleep pretty much all de time, now."

Nina carried it up the steps, and put it into the arms of Milly.

"It's sleeping nicely," she said.

"Ah, honey!" said Milly, "it'll neber wake up out of dat ar! Dat ar sleep ain't de good kind!"

"Well," said Nina, "we'll help him take care of it, and we'll make room for him and the children, Milly; because we have medicines and directions, and they have nothing out there."

So Tiff and his family took shelter in the general fortress. Towards evening the baby died. Tiff held it in his arms to the very last; and it was with difficulty that

Nina and Milly could persuade him that the little flicker-ing breath was gone forever. When forced to admit it, he seemed for a few moments perfectly inconsolable. Nina quietly opened her Testament, and read to him: —

"And they brought little children unto him, that he should touch them; and his disciples rebuked those that brought them. But Jesus said, Suffer little children to come unto me, and forbid them not, for of such is the kingdom of heaven."

"Bressed Lord!" said Tiff, "I 'll gib him up, I will! I won't hold out no longer! I won't forbid him to go, if it does break my old heart! Laws, we 's drefful selfish! But de por little ting, he was getting so pretty!"

CHAPTER XXXV

THE VOICE IN THE WILDERNESS

CLAYTON was quietly sitting in his law office, looking over and arranging some papers necessary to closing his business. A colored boy brought in letters from the mail. He looked them over rapidly; and selecting one, read it with great agitation and impatience. Immediately he started, with the open letter crushed in his hand, seized his hat, and rushed to the nearest livery stable.

"Give me the fastest horse you have — one that can travel night and day!" he said. "I must ride for life or death!"

And half an hour more saw Clayton in full speed on the road. By the slow, uncertain, and ill-managed mail route, it would have taken three days to reach Canema. Clayton hoped, by straining every nerve, to reach there in twenty-four hours. He pushed forward, keeping the animal at the top of his speed; and at the first stage-stand, changed him for a fresh one. And thus proceeding along, he found himself, at three o'clock of the next morning, in the woods about fifteen miles from Canema. The strong tension of the nervous system, which had upheld him insensible to fatigue until this point, was beginning slightly to subside. All night he had ridden through the loneliness of pine forests, with no eye looking down on him save the twinkling mysterious stars. At the last place where he had sought to obtain horses everything had been horror and confusion. Three were lying dead in the house, and another was dying.

All along upon the route, at every stopping-place, the air had seemed to be filled with flying rumors and exaggerated reports of fear and death. As soon as he began to perceive that he was approaching the plantation he became sensible of that shuddering dread, which all of us may remember to have had, in slight degrees, in returning home after a long absence, under a vague expectation of misfortune, to which the mind can set no definite limits. When it was yet scarcely light enough to see, he passed by the cottage of Old Tiff. A strange impulse prompted him to stop and make some inquiries there before he pushed on to the plantation. But as he rode up, he saw the gate standing ajar, the door of the house left open; and after repeated callings, receiving no answer, he alighted, and leading his horse behind him, looked into the door. The gloaming starlight was just sufficient to show him that all was desolate. Somehow this seemed to him like an evil omen. As he was mounting his horse, preparing to ride away, a grand and powerful voice rose from the obscurity of the woods before him, singing in a majestic, minor-keyed tune, these words: —

> " Throned on a cloud our God shall come,
>   Bright flames prepare his way ;
>   Thunder and darkness, fire and storm,
>   Lead on the dreadful day ! "

Wearied with his night ride, his nervous system strained to the last point of tension by the fearful images which filled his mind, it is not surprising that these sounds should have thrilled through the hearer with even a superstitious power. And Clayton felt a singular excitement, as, under the dim arcade of the pine-trees, he saw a dark figure approaching. He seemed to be marching with a regular tread, keeping time to the mournful music which he sung.

"Who are you?" called Clayton, making an effort to recall his manhood.

"I?" replied the figure, "I am the voice of one crying in the wilderness! I am a sign unto this people of the judgment of the Lord!"

Our readers must remember the strange dimness of the hour, the wildness of the place and circumstances, and the singular quality of the tone in which the figure spoke. Clayton hesitated a moment, and the speaker went on: "I saw the Lord coming with ten thousand of his saints! Before him went the pestilence, and burning coals went forth at his feet! Thy bow is made quite naked, O God, according to the oaths of the tribes! I saw the tents of Cushan in affliction, and the curtains of the land of Midian did tremble!"

Pondering in his mind what this wild style of address might mean, Clayton rode slowly onward. And the man, for such he appeared to be, came out of the shadows of the wood and stood directly in his path, raising his hand with a commanding gesture.

"I know whom you seek," he said; "but it shall not be given you; for the star, which is called wormwood, hath fallen, and the time of the dead is come, that they shall be judged! Behold, there sitteth on the white cloud *one* like the Son of Man, having on his head a golden crown, and in his hand a sharp sickle!"

Then waving his hand above his head, with a gesture of wild excitement, he shouted: "Thrust in thy sharp sickle, and gather the clusters of the vine of the earth, for her grapes are fully ripe! Behold, the winepress shall be trodden without the city, and there shall be blood even to the horses' bridles! Woe, woe, woe to the inhabitants of the earth, because of the trumpets of the other angels, which are yet to sound!"

The fearful words pealed through the dim aisles of the forest like the curse of some destroying angel. After a pause, the speaker resumed, in a lower and more plaintive tone: "Weep ye not for the dead! neither bewail her! Behold, the Lamb standeth on Mount Zion, and with him a hundred and forty and four thousand, having his Father's name written on their foreheads. These are they which follow the Lamb whithersoever he goeth; and in their mouth is found no guile, for they are without fault before the throne of God. Behold the angel having the seal of God is gone forth, and she shall be sealed in her forehead unto the Lamb."

The figure turned away slowly, singing, as he made his way through the forest, in the same weird and funereal accents; but this time the song was a wild, plaintive sound, like the tolling of a heavy bell: —

> "Ding dong ! dead and gone!
> Farewell, father !
> Bury me in Egypt's land,
> By my dear mother !
> Ding, dong ! ding, dong !
> Dead and gone ! "

Clayton, as he slowly wound his way along the unfrequented path, felt a dim, brooding sense of mystery and terror creeping over him. The tones of the voice, and the wild style of the speaker, recalled the strange incident of the camp-meeting; and though he endeavored strenuously to reason with himself that probably some wild and excited fanatic, made still more frantic by the presence of death and destruction all around, was the author of these fearful denunciations, still he could not help a certain weight of fearful foreboding.

This life may be truly called a haunted house, built as it is on the very confines of the land of darkness and the shadow of death. A thousand living fibres connect us with the unknown and unseen state; and the strongest hearts, which never stand still for any mortal terror, have sometimes hushed their very beating at a breath of a whisper from within the veil. Perhaps the most resolute

unbeliever in spiritual things has hours of which he would
be ashamed to tell, when he, too, yields to the powers of
those awful affinities which bind us to that unknown
realm.

It is not surprising that Clayton, in spite of himself,
should have felt like one mysteriously warned. It was
a relief to him when the dusky dimness of the solemn
dawn was pierced by long shafts of light from the rising sun, and the day broke gladsome and jubilant, as if
sorrow, sighing, and death were a dream of the night.
During the whole prevalence of this fearful curse, it was
strange to witness the unaltered regularity, splendor, and
beauty with which the movements of the natural world
went on. Amid fears, and dying groans, and wailings,
and sobs, and broken hearts, the sun rose and set in splendor, the dews twinkled, and twilight folded her purple
veil heavy with stars; birds sang, waters danced and
warbled, flowers bloomed, and everything in nature was
abundant, and festive, and joyous.

When Clayton entered the boundaries of the plantation,
he inquired eagerly of the first person he met for the
health of its mistress. "Thank God, she is yet alive!"
said he. "It was but a dream, after all!"

CHAPTER XXXVI

THE mails in the State of North Carolina, like the prudential arrangements of the slave states generally, were very little to be depended upon; and therefore a week had elapsed after the mailing of Nina's first letter, describing the danger of her condition, before it was received by Clayton. During that time the fury of the shock which had struck the plantation appeared to have abated; and while on some estates in the vicinity it was yet on the increase, the inhabitants of Canema began to hope that the awful cloud was departing from them. It was true that many were still ailing; but there were no new cases, and the disease in the case of those who were ill appeared to be yielding to nursing and remedies.

Nina had risen in the morning early, as her custom had been since the sickness, and gone the rounds, to inquire for the health of her people. Returned, a little fatigued, she was sitting in the veranda, under the shadow of one of the pillar-roses, enjoying the cool freshness of the morning. Suddenly the tramp of horse's feet was heard, and looking, she saw Clayton coming up the avenue. There seemed but a dizzy, confused moment before his horse's bridle was thrown to the winds, and he was up the steps, holding her in his arms.

"Oh, you are here yet, my rose, my bride, my lamb! God is merciful! This is too much! Oh, I thought you were gone!"

"No, dear, not yet," said Nina. "God has been with

us. We have lost a great many; but God has spared me to you."

"Are you really well?" said Clayton, holding her off, and looking at her. "You look pale, my little rose!"

"That's not wonderful," said Nina; "I've had a great deal to make me look pale; but I am very well. I have been well through it all — never in better health — and it seems strange to say it, but never happier. I have felt so peaceful, so sure of God's love!"

"Do you know," said Clayton, "that that peace alarms me — that strange, unearthly happiness? It seems so like what is given to dying people."

"No," said Nina, "I think that when we have no one but our Father to lean on, he comes nearer than he does any other time; and that is the secret of this happiness. But come, — you look woefully tired; have you been riding all night?"

"Yes, ever since yesterday morning at nine o'clock. I have ridden down four horses to get to you. Only think, I didn't get your letter till a week after it was dated!"

"Well, perhaps that was the best," said Nina; "because I have heard them say that anybody coming suddenly and unprepared in the epidemic, when it is in full force, is almost sure to be taken by it immediately. But you must let me take care of you. Don't you know that I'm mistress of the fortress here — commander-in-chief and head physician? I shall order you to your room immediately, and Milly shall bring you up some coffee, and then you must have some sleep. You can see with your eyes, now, that we are all safe, and there's nothing to hinder your resting. Come, let me lead you off, like a captive."

Released from the pressure of overwhelming fear, Clayton began now to feel the reaction of the bodily and mental straining which he had been enduring for the last twenty-four hours, and therefore he willingly yielded himself to the directions of his little sovereign. Retired to his room, after taking his coffee, which was served by Milly, he fell into a deep and tranquil sleep, which lasted till some time in the afternoon. At first, overcome by fatigue, he slept without dreaming; but when the first weariness was past, the excitement of the nervous system, under which he had been laboring, began to color his dreams with vague and tumultuous images. He thought that he was again with Nina at Magnolia Grove, and that the servants were passing around in procession, throwing flowers at their feet; but the wreath of orange-blossoms which fell in Nina's lap was tied with black crape. But she took it up, laughing, threw the crape away, and put the wreath on her head, and he heard the chorus singing: —

> "Oh, de North Carolina rose !
> Oh, de North Carolina rose !"

And then the sound seemed to change to one of lamentation, and the floral procession seemed to be a funeral, and a deep, melancholy voice, like the one he had heard in the woods in the morning, sang: —

> "Weep, for the rose is withered!
> The North Carolina rose !"

He struggled heavily in his sleep, and at last waking, sat up and looked about him. The rays of the evening sun were shining on the treetops of the distant avenue, and Nina was singing on the veranda below. He listened, and the sound floated up like a rose leaf carried on a breeze: —

> "The summer hath its heavy cloud,
>   The rose leaf must fall;
> But in our land joy wears no shroud,
>   Never doth it pall!
> Each new morning ray
> Leaves no sigh for yesterday —
> No smile passed away
>   Would we recall !"

The tune was a favorite melody, which has found much

favor with the popular ear, and bore the title of "The
Hindoo Dancing-Girl's Song;" and is, perhaps, a fragment of one of those mystical songs in which Oriental literature abounds, in which the joy and reunion of earthly
love are told in shadowy, symbolic resemblance to the
everlasting union of the blessed above. It had a wild,
dreamy, soothing power, as verse after verse came floating
in, like white doves from paradise, as if they had borne
healing on their wings: —

> "Then haste to the happy land,
>   Where sorrow is unknown;
> But first in a joyous band,
>   I 'll make thee my own.
> Haste, haste, fly with me
> Where love's banquet waits for thee ;
> Thine all its sweets shall be, —
>   Thine, thine, alone !"

A low tap at his door at last aroused him. The door
was partly opened, and a little hand threw in a half-
opened spray of monthly rosebuds.

"There 's something to remind you that you are yet in
the body!" said a voice in the entry. "If you are rested,
I 'll let you come down, now." And Clayton heard the
light footsteps tripping down the stairs. He roused himself, and after some little attention to his toilet, appeared
on the veranda.

"Tea has been waiting for some time," said Nina. "I
thought I 'd give you a hint."

"I was lying very happy, hearing you sing," said Clayton. "You may sing me that song again."

"Was I singing?" said Nina; "why I did n't know it!
I believe that 's my way of thinking, sometimes. I 'll
sing to you again, after tea. I like to sing."

After tea they were sitting again in the veranda, and
the whole heavens were one rosy flush of filmy clouds.

"How beautiful!" said Nina. "It seems to me I 've

enjoyed these things, this summer, as I never have before. It seemed as if I felt an influence from them going through me, and filling me, as the light does those clouds."

And as she stood looking up into the sky, she began singing again the words that Clayton had heard before: —

> "I am come from the happy land,
>   Where sorrow is unknown;
> I have parted a joyous band,
>   To make thee mine own!
> Haste, haste, fly with me,
>   Where love's banquet waits for thee;
> Thine all its sweets shall be, —
>   Thine, thine, alone!

> " The summer hath its heavy cloud,
>   The rose leaf must fall " —

She stopped her singing suddenly, left the veranda, and went into the house.

"Do you want anything?" said Clayton.

"Nothing," said she hurriedly. "I 'll be back in a moment."

Clayton watched, and saw her go to a closet in which the medicines and cordials were kept, and take something from a glass. He gave a start of alarm.

"You are not ill, are you?" he said fearfully, as she returned.

"Oh no; only a little faint. We have become so prudent, you know, that if we feel the least beginning of any disagreeable sensation we take something at once. I have felt this faintness quite often. It is n't much."

Clayton put his arm around her, and looked at her with a vague yearning of fear and admiration.

"You look so like a spirit," he said, "that I must hold you."

"Do you think I 've got a pair of hidden wings?" she said, smiling, and looking gayly in his face.

"I am afraid so!" he said. "Do you feel quite well, now?"

"Yes, I believe so. Only, perhaps, we had better sit down. I think, perhaps, it is the reaction of so much excitement makes me feel rather tired."

Clayton seated her on the settee by the door, still keeping his arm anxiously around her. In a few moments she drooped her head wearily on his shoulder.

"You are ill!" he said in tones of alarm.

"No, no! I feel very well — only a little faint and tired. It seems to me it is getting a little cold here, is n't it?" she said, with a slight shiver.

Clayton took her up in his arms, without speaking, carried her in and laid her on the sofa, then rang for Harry and Milly.

"Get a horse, instantly," he said to Harry, as soon as he appeared, "and go for a doctor!"

"There 's no use in sending," said Nina; "he is driven to death, and can't come. Besides, there 's nothing the matter with me, only I am a little tired and cold. Shut the doors and windows, and cover me up. No, no, don't take me upstairs! I like to lie here; just put a shawl over me, that 's all. I am thirsty, — give me some water!"

The fearful and mysterious disease, which was then in the ascendant, has many forms of approach and development. One, and the most deadly, is that which takes place when a person has so long and gradually imbibed the fatal poison of an infected atmosphere that the resisting powers of nature have been insidiously and quietly subdued, so that the subject sinks under it, without any violent outward symptom, by a quiet and certain yielding of the vital powers, such as has been likened to the bleeding to death by an internal wound. In this case, before an hour had passed, though none of the violent and distressing symptoms of the disease appeared, it became evident that the seal of death was set on that fair young brow. A messenger had been dispatched, riding with the desperate speed which love and fear can give, but Harry remained in attendance.

"Nothing is the matter with me — nothing is the matter," she said, "except fatigue, and this change in the weather. If I only had more over me! and, perhaps, you had better give me a little brandy, or some such thing. This is water, is n't it, that you have been giving me?"

Alas! it was the strongest brandy; but there was no taste, and the hartshorn that they were holding had no smell. And there was no change in the weather; it was only the creeping deadness, affecting the whole outer and inner membrane of the system. Yet still her voice remained clear, though her mind occasionally wandered.

There is a strange impulse, which sometimes comes in the restlessness and distress of dissolving nature, to sing; and as she lay with her eyes closed, apparently in a sort of trance, she would sing, over and over again, the verse of the song which she was singing when the blow of the unseen destroyer first struck her: —

> " The summer hath its heavy cloud,
> The rose leaf must fall ;
> But in our land joy wears no shroud,
> Never doth it pall."

At last she opened her eyes, and seeing the agony of all around, the truth seemed to come to her. "I think I 'm called!" she said. "Oh, I 'm so sorry for you all! Don't grieve so; my Father loves me so well, — he cannot spare me any longer. He wants me to come to him. That 's all — don't grieve so. It 's *home* I 'm going to — *home!* 'T will be only a little while, and you 'll come too, all of you. You are satisfied, are you not, Edward?"

And again she relapsed into the dreamy trance, and sang, in that strange, sweet voice, so low, so weak: —

> " In our land joy wears no shroud,
> Never doth it pall."

Clayton, — what did he? What could he do? What have any of us done, who have sat holding in our arms a dear form, from which the soul was passing — the soul for which gladly we would have given our own in exchange! When we have felt it going with inconceivable rapidity from us; and we, ignorant and blind, vainly striving, with this and that, to arrest the inevitable doom, feeling every moment that some *other* thing might be done to save, which is not done, and that that which we are doing may be only hastening the course of the destroyer! Oh, those awful, agonized moments, when we watch the clock and no physician comes, and every stroke of the pendulum is like the approaching step of death! Oh, is there anything in heaven or earth for the despair of such hours?

Not a moment was lost by the three around that dying bed, chafing those cold limbs, administering the stimulants which the dead, exhausted system no longer felt.

"She doesn't suffer! Thank God, at any rate, for that!" said Clayton, as he knelt over her in anguish.

A beautiful smile passed over her face as she opened her eyes and looked on them all, and said: —

"No, my poor friends, I don't suffer. I'm come to the land where they never suffer. I'm only *so* sorry for you! Edward," she said to him, "do you remember what you said to me once? — It has come now. You must bear it like a man. God calls you to some work — don't shrink from it. You are baptized with fire. It all lasts only a little while. It will be over soon, very soon! Edward, take care of my poor people. Tell Tom to be kind to them. My poor, faithful, good Harry! Oh! I'm going so fast!"

The voice sank into a whispering sigh. Life now seemed to have retreated to the citadel of the brain. She lay apparently in the last sleep, when the footsteps of the doctor were heard on the veranda. There was a general spring to the door, and Dr. Butler entered, pale, haggard, and worn from constant exertion and loss of rest. He did not say in words that there was no hope, but his first dejected look said it but too plainly.

She moved her head a little, like one who is asleep uneasily upon her pillow, opened her eyes once more, and said, — "Good-by! I will arise and go to my Father!"

The gentle breath gradually became fainter and fainter, — all hope was over! The night walked on with silent and solemn footsteps — soft showers fell without, murmuring upon the leaves — within, all was still as death!

> "They watched her breathing through the night,
>   Her breathing soft and low,
>   As in her breast the wave of life
>   Kept heaving to and fro.
>
> "So silently they seemed to speak,
>   So slowly moved about,
>   As they had lent her half their powers
>   To eke her living out.
>
> "Their very hopes belied their fears,
>   Their fears their hopes belied —
>   They thought her dying when she slept,
>   And sleeping when she died.
>
> "For when the morn came dim and sad,
>   And chill with early showers,
>   Her quiet eyelids closed — she had
>   Another morn than ours."